Praise for the Works of Tiffany Reisz

"Daring, sophisticated, and literary.... Exactly what good erotica should be." — **Kitty Thomas on *The Siren***

"Kinky, well-written, hot as hell." — **Little Red Reading Hood on *The Red: An Erotic Fantasy***

"Impossible to stop reading." — **Heroes & Heartbreakers on *The Bourbon Thief***

"Stunning.... Transcends genres and will leave readers absolutely breathless." — ***RT Book Reviews* on the Original Sinners series**

"I worship at the altar of Tiffany Reisz!" — ***New York Times* bestselling author Lorelei James**

More Original Sinners

Novels

THE SIREN (Book #1)

THE ANGEL (Book #2)

THE PRINCE (Book #3)

THE MISTRESS (Book #4)

THE SAINT (Book #5)

THE KING (Book #6)

THE VIRGIN (Book #7)

THE QUEEN (Book #8)

THE PRIEST (Book #9)

THE CHATEAU (Standalone)

PICTURE PERFECT COWBOY (Standalone)

Novellas and Collections

THE CONFESSIONS

THE GIFT (previously published as SEVEN DAY LOAN)

IMMERSED IN PLEASURE

THE LAST GOOD KNIGHT (PARTS I—V)

LITTLE RED RIDING CROP

MICHAEL'S WINGS

MISCHIEF • THE MISTRESS FILES

SOMETHING NICE

SUBMIT TO DESIRE

WINTER TALES

TIFFANY REISZ

THE PRIEST

8TH CIRCLE PRESS
LOUISVILLE, KY

THE PRIEST

Trade Paperback ISBN: 978-1-949769-13-5

eBook available from 8th Circle Press

Audiobook available from Tantor Audio

Cover design by BookCoverZone and Andrew Shaffer

Front cover image used under license from DepositPhotos. Interior title
page image used under license from Shutterstock.

www.8thcirclepress.com

FIRST EDITION

Author's Note

The Priest is the ninth full-length title in the ongoing Original Sinners series. For those reading chronologically, this story takes place in New Orleans four months after the end of *The Queen*.

For new readers, welcome! The series follows the adventures of Nora Sutherlin, an erotic-romance writer who moonlights as a dominatrix, and the many men (and women) in her life.

While events in previous books in the series are alluded to, *The Priest* can be read as a standalone—no prior reading necessary. If you enjoy it, I invite you to read the rest of the series, beginning with *The Siren*.

A full listing of Original Sinners titles can be found in the front of this book, as well as at www.tiffanyreisz.com.

Dedicated to the ghosts of New Orleans.

Here is the world. Beautiful and terrible things will happen. Don't be afraid.

— **FREDERICK BUECHNER**

One cannot live the afternoon of life according to the program of life's morning; for what was great in the morning will be of little importance in the evening, and what in the morning was true will at evening become a lie.

— **CARL JUNG**

Chapter One

A priest was dead. That's all Cyrus Tremont had been told in the thirty-second phone call that had summoned him to a house on the corner of Rose and Annunciation Street.

When he arrived at the yellow house, he was let in by a uniformed police officer guarding a body lying face down on a small red rug. On second look, Cyrus saw it wasn't a rug.

"Jesus, God." He slapped a hand over his mouth and took a step back. One of these days he would learn not to answer his phone when the police called him.

Cyrus stared at the dead man, what was left of him. White male, tall, thin, but not unhealthy. Couldn't see the face, so he looked at the hands. Put the man's age between fifty and sixty. He wore a bright red Casio watch on his left wrist. He'd seen that watch before.

"Christ, that's Father Ike."

The cop nodded. "Killed himself. You know him?"

"A little bit. He and my fiancée used to work together," Cyrus said. He stared down at the body again, the blood turning from red to brown as it oxidized. Blood was alive even when the body was dead, but the blood turned brown as the oxygen fled the cells. It had outlived its host. It wasn't drying so much as dying.

"What did he use?" Cyrus didn't see a gun anywhere.

"A .243 Winchester hunting rifle. It's being processed," the officer said, his voice cracking a little. Cyrus glanced at him. Kid didn't look more than twenty-two, twenty-three. This might be his first suicide.

"Makes sense," Cyrus said. "He liked to deer hunt."

He heard a car pull in the gravel drive. The uniform skirted the edge of the floor and went out the front, trading places with the new arrival, Detective Katherine Naylor. About time, too. She was the one who'd dragged him into this nightmare.

"Katherine," he said, nodding. She wore a trim gray suit, white blouse, an expression that was all business.

"Cyrus. I hear congratulations are in order. Paulina's finally making an honest man out of you."

She probably expected a joke, but he did not joke about Paulina. Keeping his face and tone neutral, he tersely replied, "Thank you."

"Sorry to get you out of bed so early."

"I was already up," he said. She raised an eyebrow. "Working a case."

"Something you can drop?"

"You serious? You know this is not my area." Cyrus wasn't a police detective anymore, but a private detective. He helped women with cheating husbands and children with deadbeat dads. Women and children first. Women and children *only*. That was his motto. He'd seen enough death in his days on the force to last him a dozen lifetimes.

"Didn't you know him?"

"Yeah, but I don't work suicides. Wait, this *is* a suicide, right?"

"It's definitely a suicide," Katherine said. "Approximate time of death was 11:30 last night. House was locked from the inside. No signs of forced entry. No signs of a struggle. No drugs or alcohol in the place except for a few bottles of wine under the sink—all unopened. Rifle recently fired. Plus, he left a voicemail message with a Sister Margaret last night at 11:25, which is why I'm guessing TOD was 11:30. That might change, though."

"What did he say in the message?"

"I haven't heard it, but according to the sister, he said..." Katherine pulled a small notebook out of her jacket pocket and flipped to a page. "'I'm sorry for what I'm about to do, but I'd be sorrier if I didn't do it. I can't do this anymore. Forgive me. Pray for me, Margaret.' She missed the call, didn't hear the message until five a.m., and panicked when she didn't find him in his apartment at the parish house. She knew he came here a lot, so she asked the police to check the house. An officer performed a wellness check, saw the body through the window at 6 a.m."

"What is this place?"

"Belongs to St. Valentine's parish. It's a guest house for visiting priests or sisters, sometimes an emergency shelter. Sister Margaret says Father Murran came here all the time for peace and quiet when it was unoccupied. He liked the neighborhood, she said."

"I'm still waiting on why you called me." God, how was he going to break this to Paulina? They'd eaten barbeque with the man at their engagement party not four months ago.

Katherine peeked through the blinds. "Coroner's here. Let's go out back."

The backyard wasn't much more than a postage stamp surrounded by a wooden fence that needed repainting. An elderly couple sat in rockers on their porch across the street, watching with interest. A pretty brown girl of about eleven or twelve walked slowly past the yard, clearly trying not to linger but also curious about the fuss. A pair of fairy wings on her back glittered in the early morning light.

He and Katherine waited in silence for the girl to pass. This was no place for children to be playing. Not now, maybe not ever. Once she turned the corner, Cyrus spoke.

"Talk."

Katherine took a deep breath and leaned back against the fence. He stood opposite her, a small fire pit full of ashes between their feet.

"Thanks for taking my call," she said.

"Call, yeah. Case? Not yet."

"Look, I get it. You don't want to work with us, and I don't blame you. But hear me out. Please."

No, Cyrus did not want to work with the police. Two years ago, he'd been shot on the job by a fellow officer who had a file overflowing with excessive force complaints. Luckily, Cyrus had a good lawyer who'd wrangled a very nice settlement from the city. Nice enough, he didn't have to take any case he didn't want to take.

"I'm not comfortable with this," he said. "Working with you? For you? Investigating someone I knew personally? Ike and Paulina used to work together at Blessed Sacrament. You ever hear the phrase 'conflict of interest'?"

He so did not want to take this case. Katherine had a way of getting on his nerves—she was white, and acted like that made her something special down here.

She was also the last woman he'd slept with before meeting Paulina.

His life was B.P. and A.P.—Before Paulina and After Paulina. All that was B.P. meant as much to him as the ashes in the fire pit at his feet. But he tried not to hold that against Katherine. Not her fault they met on the wrong side of his salvation.

"Do you know how hard it was for me to ask you for help? You were a real ass to me, and you know it," she said. Cyrus turned away, didn't admit it, but he didn't deny it either. "Doesn't that tell you how serious I am? Something is wrong here. You're the only PI in this town I even halfway trust."

"Thank you very much."

"You're good and we both know it. There. Happy?"

"Thrilled. Now please tell me what the hell is going on here. Even if I don't take the case, whatever you've found, you know I'm not going to tell anyone."

She gave a dry laugh. "It's not even seven yet, and Archbishop Dunn's already making phone calls. He says everyone knew Isaac Murran suffered from depression. That's all. Open and shut and lock it up. We are not allowed to investigate this, I've been told. And when someone tells me not to investigate..."

"Catholic Church trying to cover up something embarrassing? This is my shocked face."

"Right," she said. "That's why I called you. I need you to dig."

"Dig for what? What aren't you telling me?"

"First of all, Sister Margaret swears up and down that Isaac Murran was not depressed. Not now, not ever, from what she could tell. She's got a degree in counseling, and she's been pouring his tea for fifteen years. She knows the symptoms of depression, and she knows him. *Knew* him."

Cyrus stuck his hands in his suit pockets. He was tired.

He'd been on a stakeout all last night watching the comings and goings of a man who was going places he shouldn't be going and coming with people he didn't need to be coming with.

"Look, I'm sorry," Katherine said. "I wish I knew someone else to call. I was here for ten minutes before Captain Latour was telling me to drop it. I shouldn't even be back here now. I'm going to get hell for it."

Katherine had been in a turf war with the Catholic Church for years. She'd been sent to investigate a robbery at a church, and the priest had demanded a male officer instead. He'd said police work was too dangerous for women, especially for a woman who dressed so "provocatively."

"Sometimes people kill themselves and we never figure out why," Cyrus said.

"I might know why."

He raised an eyebrow. Now she'd gotten him curious.

Katherine reached into her blouse and pulled something out of her bra. She held it out to him, and he reluctantly took it. A business card in a plastic evidence bag.

"You didn't get this from me," Katherine said. "You didn't get it from anyone. That card doesn't exist. Unless I decide it needs to exist."

"Where'd you get it from?"

"Our victim's pocket."

"You're contaminating a crime scene and interfering with a police investigation, Katherine."

"Not if there's no investigation to interfere with. Look at it."

He exhaled heavily before looking at the card.

"Red business card, black ink," Cyrus said, flipping it

over. "Only a phone number. No name. That's unusual. A 212 area code. New York City?"

"Manhattan," she said. "The number's a Chinese place now, but it used to be registered to a woman named Eleanor Schreiber. She writes dirty books under the name Nora Sutherlin."

"You're worried Father Ike liked dirty books? He's a sixty-year-old celibate priest. Give the man a break."

"If that were all, I wouldn't be here and neither would you. I saw his phone. He called that number last night before he shot himself. He called Sister Margaret, then he called that number. We know why he called Sister Margaret. We need to know why he called Nora Sutherlin."

"Maybe he just likes her books? Maybe he thought it was a suicide hotline?"

"Maybe he was following orders?"

"Orders? What the hell does that mean?"

"I mean Nora Sutherlin moonlights. I'll give you one guess."

He sighed heavily. "Just so you know, next time you call me with a case," he said, "I am *not* answering."

Chapter Two

Cyrus meant to be at Paulina's at eight, but he squeaked in the driveway at 8:10. While he knew she'd forgive him for being late, he still jogged from his car to the house to shave those last few seconds off his time. He found her in the bright white-tile kitchen pouring coffee into two yellow mugs.

"About time," she said, playing grumpy. He came up behind her, putting his hands on her hips and kissing her cheek. She stirred the cream into her coffee, and left his black.

"Long night. Bad morning. I'm sorry," he said.

"It's all right. Sit. Tell me about it."

Cyrus took his seat and watched Paulina finish breakfast. Seeing her bustling around the kitchen in her red summer dress and sandals with the straps around her pretty ankles was a balm to his soul. She worked at a local Catholic middle school as a guidance counselor. Monday through Friday, she wore neck-high blouses and ankle-length skirts or suit pants. She saved her pretty dresses for weekends, for him.

"You're beautiful," he said.

"You're stalling. Is it bad?"

"Baby, come here. Please."

She knew him too well to fall for that. She turned to face him, hip against the counter, arms crossed over her chest. "What happened?"

"I got some bad news. Father Ike's dead."

Paulina gasped. "What?"

"That's why I'm late. A detective called and asked me to come by the scene. I needed a shower after."

"The scene? A crime scene? Was he murdered? Jesus." Paulina crossed herself before clasping her hands as if to pray.

He shook his head. "Suicide."

"No," Paulina put her hand over her heart. "Father Ike? Why?"

"That's what they want me to find out."

"Was there a note?"

"No note," Cyrus said. "But he called a friend of his, a sister, and left her a voicemail message that made it very clear he was planning to kill himself."

"Do you think he was sick? Cancer or something?"

"They want me to look into that." He rubbed his temples with his fingertips.

"Cyrus? What is it? What aren't you telling me about this?"

He didn't want to tell Paulina. Normally, he wouldn't. He made it a rule to never drag her into his cases, for her sake and the sake of the women he helped. But she and Ike had been friends. This was different.

"They found a business card in his pocket."

"Do I want to know?"

"It was for a sex worker." He didn't mention she was a

dominatrix. He hadn't quite wrapped his head around that part yet.

Paulina turned away, placed her hands on the counter. She lowered her head, closed her eyes. Praying, knowing her. Her long dark eyelashes fluttered on her cheeks, and he felt a wave of tenderness toward her. Most days, she wore her curly brown hair down around her face, a look she jokingly called Shirley Temple Black. Today, it was pulled back in a red ribbon to match her dress.

"You think you know someone." She raised her head and stared out the back window.

"You know we can't know anybody. Not really. If we did, I'd be out of a job."

"It shouldn't be a betrayal, but it is," Paulina said. "You know what I mean? It shouldn't be our business but it still matters. It's like having married friends, and you think their marriage is strong, and you admire them because their marriage is strong, and you want something strong like that. Then you find out he hits her or she cheats. You know their marriage is private, but it hurts something in you to know you've been watching nothing but a show all that time. Father Ike was married to God."

"I don't know if anybody gets married or becomes a priest planning to break their vows."

"No, I know. Still."

"We could be jumping to conclusions," Cyrus said softly. "He might have been counseling her, trying to help her get out of that life."

"You think that?" she asked. He could hear the hope in her voice.

"It's possible." True, it was possible. But not very probable.

"Is this going to get out?"

"We're going to try to keep it quiet," Cyrus said. "Until we know something, I guess."

"He's an adult man, and I'm gonna assume she was an adult woman if she's handing out business cards. This shouldn't be something for the press. This is between that man and God, and he's in God's hands now."

"I wish it worked like that. Look, if you don't want me digging, I won't take the case. But if you think I should—"

Paulina faced him. "If he was seeing somebody like that and somebody knew and told him they knew..."

"Blackmail, you mean?" Cyrus asked.

She shrugged. "Maybe. Maybe not. But if there's any chance something else was going on, somebody making him do it, I'd hope *somebody* was investigating, that's all." Paulina checked the oven, all business. He knew the tears were coming, but not yet. She was still in shock.

"How long until breakfast is ready?" he asked.

"About ten minutes? Biscuits need to cool."

"You mind if I go out back for a minute?"

"Gotta think your thinks?"

"Gotta think my thinks."

She smiled sadly at him, and he kissed her forehead. She closed her eyes and leaned against him. He wrapped his arms around her and let her lean. He'd let her lean forever if she wanted to.

"Ten minutes," she said softly. Cyrus kissed her again and started to leave. He watched from the backdoor as she packed her grief away, her sense of betrayal, saving it up for later when she could be alone to talk it out with God.

He went out into the backyard and took a seat on the wooden bench between Paulina's bright orange zinnias and pink and yellow begonia bushes.

Cyrus always found it easier to meditate when he was

outside and alone, close to trees, close to water. The morning sunlight trickled through the trees and over the grass like ripples on the surface of a living river.

He closed his eyes and went to his river.

In the beginning, when he first learned how to meditate, Cyrus would have to wait nearly an hour to get even a distant glimpse of that cosmic river in the deepest, oldest, wisest part of his mind. Now he could find it in seconds. He'd close his eyes and open his inner eyes and there was the pine forest and there was the winding dirt path, and just over the hill flowed the river.

He heard the water rising.

Cyrus focused on the coolness of the soft dirt under his feet as he walked and nothing but the cool soft dirt. The path was short and the river came into view quickly. Today it flowed slowly and the sun on it was gentle. On the opposite bank, a man stood, waiting. If they were to meet, they would meet in the river.

And if they were to meet in the river, Cyrus had to wade in first.

He reached the muddy bank and didn't stop to roll up his pants. No need. This river was a river of truth and dreams and meaning. It ran only through his mind. Without fear—that had taken months to learn as well— Cyrus stepped into the water and found it warm and welcoming. The bottom was sandy but sturdy and shallow, though there were parts of this river that went over his head. Sometimes truth was like that.

The man on the opposite bank saw him and smiled. He, too, entered the river. And at the mid-point, halfway from bank to bank, they met.

Father Ike Murran.

He wasn't wearing his usual clerical garb. He had on a

light gray suit—a bit loose like he'd lost weight he didn't need to lose—and a white shirt. No tie. His brown-gray hair was neatly combed. Cyrus could see the ghost of the handsome man Father Ike had been twenty years, thirty years ago. Even at sixty, he was a dignified-looking man.

Never too dignified for a smile, though.

"Cyrus Tremont," Father Ike said with a wide grin. "You broke my heart."

Cyrus laughed, couldn't help it. Father Ike was the tenth man to say that to him today.

Today? What was today?

"I'm not gonna say I'm sorry," Cyrus said.

"When's the wedding again?" Father Ike asked.

"Not soon enough."

"The way you keep looking at her, I'd say yesterday wouldn't be soon enough."

"That's the damn truth," Cyrus said. Father Ike held a beer bottle in his hand, a Miller Lite. They had it at the engagement party back in June. That was it...that's where they were. The river had brought them to Cyrus and Paulina's engagement party, held in her backyard.

The last time Cyrus had seen Father Ike alive.

"I know you heard it from everyone in this city," Father Ike continued, "but you are one lucky man. She's one of the great ones."

"Truer words, man. Look, feel free to say 'no,'" Cyrus said, "but we're doing the full wedding Mass. Would you be willing to help out? Paulina loves you, you know."

Nothing unusual about having more than one priest at a wedding Mass.

"It's November seventh," Cyrus pressed on.

Ike winced and the crow's feet around his eyes went deep. "I don't think I'll be around then," he said. "I think

I'm getting transferred. New school. Not in Nola. I'd hate to say 'yes,' then have to back out. But if I'm around, I'll be there as a guest."

"It's fine," Cyrus said, because it was.

"But I will pray for you and Paulina. Every day."

"I appreciate that, Father."

"And you'll pray for me, too?" Ike asked, smile gone.

Cyrus didn't do much praying. That was Paulina's thing, not his. But he was too polite to say that to a priest.

"Yeah, definitely. I better get back to my lady."

"Give her a kiss for me. Or two." Ike winked at him. Cyrus patted Father Ike on the shoulder and waded back to the riverbank, leaving the memory behind.

When he turned around, Father Ike was in the middle of the river. He wasn't holding a beer in his hand anymore, but a rifle.

"Ike!"

Cyrus sat up with a start, eyes open to the real world. He drank it all in—the begonias, the neatly-mown grass, the picnic table on the patio. He texted Katherine.

Father Ike told me he was getting transferred. Ask the archbishop's secretary what that was about, Cyrus wrote. *Don't ask Archbishop Dunn—ask the secretary. Call her at home, right now before Dunn gets to her.*

Cyrus didn't know much about Archbishop Thomas Dunn, but he knew bishops liked keeping things quiet.

Katherine wrote back almost immediately. *Got it. You on the case?*

I don't know yet.

Know soon, Katherine wrote back. Cyrus rolled his eyes and stuffed his phone back into his jacket pocket. He got up and went back into the house, back into the kitchen.

Paulina smiled at him as she brought two plates over to the table. "Ready to eat?"

"Yes, ma'am." He sat down at his plate. Today's feast was scrambled eggs, bacon, biscuits, and yogurt with an assortment of toppings (raspberries, walnuts, chocolate chips). The woman was a health nut every day but Saturday morning, God bless her.

"Grace," she said.

He began, "Bless us, O Lord, and these your gifts which we are about to receive from your bounty. Through Christ Our Lord. Amen."

"Amen," Paulina said, crossing herself as he did.

He reached for his fork but felt his phone vibrating in his pocket. He grabbed it to silence it.

He groaned at the sight of the number. Katherine again.

"You can answer it," Paulina said.

"It can wait." Everything could wait when he was with her.

"A priest is dead, a priest I cared about. Table manners can take the day off."

"I love you."

She winked at him as he rose from the table. He went outside to the sidewalk, where he called Katherine back. He wasn't about to talk to a woman he'd slept with while standing in his own fiancée's house.

"Secretary swears up and down Father Murran never put in for a transfer anywhere," Katherine said without preamble.

"And she would know," he said.

"She handles all the paperwork. Did you hear different?"

"He came to our engagement party in June," he told

her. "When I asked him if he'd help perform our wedding Mass, he said he wouldn't be around for the wedding because he was being transferred."

"He wasn't."

"Yeah."

"He lied to you."

"He did."

"Maybe he was already planning on killing himself?"

"Maybe," Cyrus said. "He also asked me to pray for him."

"Did he say why?"

"No."

"Did you pray for him?"

"Kind of forgot to," he confessed.

"Take the case, Tremont," Katherine said. "Please? You already have a lead."

Cyrus remembered the river, the gut-churning feeling of seeing Ike with the rifle in his hand. He would have tried to stop it if he'd been there. He wasn't there then, but he was here now.

"I'll look into it. Just in case there's more going on here."

Katherine exhaled so hard the phone rattled in Cyrus's ear. "Thank you," she said with obvious relief. "I'll sleep better tonight knowing somebody's looking into this. The Church has way too much power in this town."

Cyrus agreed, but he didn't say that aloud. Not with his Catholic saint of a fiancée inside the house waiting on him to come finish breakfast.

"What about those digits on the red card?" Cyrus asked. He dug his reporter's notebook out of his pocket.

"The previous address associated with the number is

just a P.O. box, no longer Sutherlin's. But our dominatrix friend has a file. A big one."

"Criminal record?"

"Nothing in Nola. All in New York, mostly Manhattan. Plus a sealed juvenile record."

"What's in the file?" Cyrus asked, scribbling everything down she told him.

"Arrests. Lots of arrests. Now, the last arrest was years ago, but there was a period from about 2004 to 2008 she was arrested over ten times."

"Prostitution?"

"Two arrests, yes. But mostly assault," Katherine said. "But hey, that's kind of what dominatrixes do, right? How's a cop to know you're slapping Joe Blow around by request?"

Cyrus could picture that scene playing out, a nosy neighbor calling the cops on suspicious noises from next door. He'd seen stranger things back in his days on the force.

"Jail time?"

"The woman is Teflon. I'll email you the basics, but no convictions. Nothing went to court. Not even a plea. Everything dropped every single time."

"What about blackmail? Any arrests?" Cyrus could easily imagine a sex worker blackmailing a priest-client. He knew quite a few priests with money tooling around town in big black Caddies, rushing to get morning Mass over with so they could make their ten o'clock tee-times at the golf course.

"No, but she does have a known associate who was investigated for blackmail. And he's local, too. I couldn't find an address for her, but I found one for him."

"Name?"

"Kingsley Boissonneault."

"Never heard of him."

"AKA Kingsley Edge. Owns The Marquis Club. Jazz club, supposedly."

Cyrus winced. "Him I've heard of." A husband he was tailing last year had spent a lot of money at The Marquis Club, a lot of money that should have been going to his ex-wife and kid.

"What's Edge's address?"

Katherine gave him an address in the Garden District. "You think Sutherlin's there?" he asked.

"They'll know where she is if she isn't. Better hurry. She might skip town when she finds out Murran's dead. Plus, you know you want to meet this lady."

"Believe it or not, I'm not looking forward to getting slapped around by a big lady with a whip today. That is not my type."

Katherine laughed. "You're forgetting I know you, Cyrus. Every woman is your type."

He looked back at the house, the little brick cottage painted white. His heart was in that house.

"Not anymore."

Chapter Three

✦✦✦

Nora Sutherlin set her paintbrush down onto the tray and stepped back. She stood in the center of the nursery, which had been emptied of all furnishings. Everything was in storage, waiting for the mother-to-be to pick a paint color and for the aunt-to-be to do the painting.

"Okay, take your time. But not too much time. You're about to pop," Nora said. "The green one is Sounds of Nature. The pink one is Cotton Candy. The yellow one is Enchanted. Which one do you like best?"

Juliette Toussaint, thirty-five weeks pregnant with the child of the notorious Kingsley Edge, narrowed her eyes at the wall where Nora had painted three large sections in baby-friendly hues. With her right hand on her protruding pregnant belly and her left hand toying at a string of pearls around her long graceful neck, Juliette gave each swatch a long look before finally turning to Nora.

"No blues?" Juliette asked.

Nora dropped her chin to her chest and counted to three.

"You told me no blues," Nora said.

"No, *he* told you no blues," Juliette reminded her.

"He's buying. Therefore, no blues."

Juliette only sighed.

"If there is any white woman on the planet who shouldn't have a Pinterest account, it's me," Nora said. "But I opened a Pinterest account in my quest to get you the perfect nursery wall color, because your baby deserves the best. These three are the best. These are the colors Martha Stewart dreams in. If the Virgin Mary had a ten-thousand-dollar nursery budget, baby Jesus would have had one of these colors painted on His walls. Any one of these colors in a nursery will give the most diehard childless free spirit—me, for example—aching ovaries because she wants to have a baby for the sole reason she can have a room one of these colors in her house."

"I like blue," Juliette said.

"What are ovaries?" Céleste asked.

Nora looked over her shoulder at Juliette and Kingsley's three-year-old daughter Céleste, who was currently applying gold star stickers to the back of a large black German Shepherd.

"Nothing but trouble, kid. Nothing but trouble."

Juliette looked at her. Nora laughed.

"You want blue, you can have blue," Nora said. "I'll do stripes, squares, polka dots of blue. But...you have to promise Kingsley won't kill me. I have just gotten off his shit list. Please don't put me back on it."

"You said a bad word, *Tata Elle*."

"I say a lot of them," Nora said. "Especially where your Papa is concerned. And what are you doing to my dog?"

"Making him pretty."

"Gmork, are you getting a makeover?" Nora asked her dog. Gmork made a happy rumbling sound and licked Céleste's face before settling down again.

"I think I want blue," Juliette said. "He'll have to live with it."

"What does he have against blue anyway?" Nora said.

"He doesn't want a boy."

"That die's been cast. And I think that's the first time I've ever compared sperm to dice."

"What's sperm?" Céleste asked.

Nora rolled her eyes. "Kid's got ears like a bat, I swear. Why did we teach her English?"

"I'll explain later, princess," Juliette told her daughter. Céleste seemed satisfied with that, although knowing Juliette, "later" meant "in ten to twenty years."

"What's wrong with boys? Other than the whole pissing-in-the-face thing they do."

"He says we should have just cloned her." Juliette nodded at Céleste. Nora couldn't blame Kingsley there. Céleste was about as easy and endearing a child anyone could ask for, even if she was in that incessant question-asking phase.

"You think it's a boy, don't you?" Nora asked.

"That one," she said, pointing at Céleste, "was a lamb. This one." She patted her stomach. "This one's a lion. She felt like part of me. This one feels like someone's in there planning a prison break. She's me. This one is all him."

"What do you think it is, baby?" Nora asked Céleste. "A boy or a girl."

"I don't care," Céleste said. "I want a kitten."

"Talk to your *Oncle* Søren about that," Nora said. "He's the cat person in the family."

"Speaking of," Juliette said and lowered her voice. "Any news?"

Nora raised her hands, both empty. "I got a postcard from Idaho last week," she said. *"Idaho."*

"Any idea when he'll come home?" Juliette said, her voice hopeful.

Nora's stomach clenched. Her heart, too. She shook her head. "He just took off," she said, mostly to herself. "Without a word. I still can't believe he did that."

"You can't complain," Juliette said in her most motherly chiding tone. "You run away all the time without telling us where you are. You didn't even send a postcard a few of those times."

"I wasn't complaining. I'm just worried about him. Don't tell him I said that."

She knew she shouldn't worry. Søren was an adult. He had a big cushion of family money and brains to spare. There was absolutely no reason for her to worry. But she did anyway.

"'He whom one waits is, because he is expected, already present, already master,'" Juliette said, quoting a famous line from Kingsley's favorite novel, *Histoire d'O*.

"Fine. He can be the master. As long as he gets his ass home and fucks me. I haven't gotten laid in a month. My pussy has cobwebs."

Juliette started to laugh but then stopped and pulled a white lace handkerchief out of her blouse, pressing it over her mouth and nose.

"Paint fumes?" Nora asked. Juliette nodded behind her handkerchief. "Go outside and get some fresh air. I'll figure out the paint."

Juliette waved her hand dismissively. She hated being fussed over just because she was pregnant. Since Kingsley couldn't stop fussing over her, he'd been banished from the house between the hours of ten a.m. and five p.m. Juliette said the banishment had saved both their minds and, quite possibly, his life.

"I'll open a window." Juliette walked to the large street-facing window in the nursery and parted the curtains. "Oh, *bonjour, monsieur.*"

"What is it?" Nora asked, walking over to her.

"We have company. Very handsome company."

"I'll be the judge of that. You're so hopped on up hormones you flirted with the UPS driver yesterday. That's my job."

Nora peered out the window and saw a man on the sidewalk staring at his phone in the shade of a magnolia tree—a trim black man with a tight fade. He wore a tailored brown suit and aviator sunglasses. Nora put him at about thirty, thirty-five years old. He took off his sunglasses, and she had to admit he wasn't bad at all. Tall but not too tall. Strong build like a former high school quarterback who'd stayed in fighting shape. Something about his strict posture, his confident bearing, put her in mind of the sort of man she'd had dealings with before.

"Handsome, yes. Bad news, definitely."

Juliette looked at her from the side of her eyes.

"Police?" Juliette said under her breath so as not to scare Céleste. No woman lived with Kingsley Edge for ten years without learning how to pick out a plainclothes detective in a crowd.

"I definitely get that vibe from him," Nora muttered in reply. "Don't see a badge on him, though." The man had put his hand in his pocket, which revealed nothing—no badge, no gun. "I better talk to him. He's either here for King or he's here for me."

"Why would he be here for you?"

"Why wouldn't he be?" Nora replied.

"Ah, true," Juliette said, patting Nora on the back. "You're so good to us, sometimes I forget how bad you are."

Chapter Four

Cyrus tried to never go into a new situation blind, a habit that had saved his ass more than once. In the shade under the magnolia tree, he took a moment to search for this Nora Sutherlin. Supposedly she was a professional dominatrix, according to Katherine, but the only hits were for her dirty books.

He clicked on the one with the most reviews on Amazon. *The Red: An Erotic Fantasy.* There was a half-naked lady on the cover, which he did not object to in the least. He bought it with one click, smiling at the idea of it sharing space on his digital bookshelf with Carl Jung and Walter Mosley. He doubted either gentleman would mind.

He found the ABOUT THE AUTHOR section in the table of contents. *Nora Sutherlin lives in New England. Find her online at www.norasutherlin.com.*

That was it? Just one line? Okay. He went to her website. Not much more there. Her bio had been updated to read, *Nora Sutherlin lives in New Orleans.*

Great. So the lady liked her privacy a little. He could respect that. How many cheating husbands had he caught because they were sloppy online with their social media pages, leaving geo-markers on, claiming to be on a work trip while their phone tattled on them? Just out of curiosity, he went back to her book, picked a chapter at random and started to read.

"Put your arms behind your head," he said. "Clasp your fingers and keep your elbows open. Like a butterfly's wings."

She did as she was told. The move made her arch her back, thrust her breasts forward. He stood before her, inspecting her.

"Legs wider," he said. He touched the floor with the tip of the riding crop in two places—here and there, showing her where to place her feet. She moved her feet wider apart, a foot and a half, and stood quivering in place.

"Very nice." He raised the crop and tapped her left nipple with it. Then her right. He caressed the underside of each breast with the triangle of leather on the crop's end. He ran the shaft of the crop down the sides of her body from each elbow to each ankle and back up again. It tickled and made her shiver. She would have given anything to feel his body against her right now. She craved it and with every passing second she craved it more. No doubt this was the intention.

He stepped close again. It was torture to be so close without touching. He brought the crop up between them and pressed the flat side of the tip to his lips. Then he pressed the opposite side to her lips.

"Think of it as a kiss," he said when the leather lay against her mouth. "That's all it is. Just a kiss from me to you."

"Most kisses don't leave welts," she said. "I prefer French kissing."

"Well, I'm English. This is English kissing."

"Holy shit," Cyrus breathed to himself. He glanced over his shoulder just to make sure nobody had heard him, or worse, seen what was on his phone. He scrolled a few pages ahead.

"Open your eyes," he said, and when she did it was to find him holding the dripping tip at her chin. He didn't have to tell her to take it into her mouth. He placed his hand under the back of her head and lifted it with all the gentleness of a nurse raising the head of a sick patient to drink some water. She did it willingly, wrapping the tip with her lips and sucking. A small burst of semen shot into her mouth and she swallowed it eagerly. It was merely a taste of what was to come...

"Jesus H." Cyrus decided he better shut that right down before he had to take a personal break. They let people put stuff like that on Amazon?

Cyrus was about to search for a photo of the crazy lady who'd dreamt this stuff up—he'd finish the book later, then go to confession after—when he saw the front door of the big white house opening. A woman half-walked, half-skipped down the stone stairway to the walkway that led to the main gate. She didn't look like the sort of woman to emerge from such a grand door in such a grand house. She was white, pale, and not very tall. Her black hair was pulled back in a messy ponytail. Her cut-off denim shorts were ratty, her black t-shirt rattier. Tiny paint splotches dotted her from head to toe.

She came to the gate but didn't open it. She left it closed and smiled at him through a six-inch space between the bars.

"Can I help you, sir?" she asked.

"I'm looking for a woman named Nora Sutherlin. I'm told she knows the owners of this house."

"Are you a police officer?"

When he'd watched her nearly skipping down the steps, he'd guessed her age at about twenty-four, twenty-five. When she pushed her sunglasses up to her head to reveal a pair of cunning green eyes regarding him ironically, he revised his estimate up a little. Thirties, definitely. Too confident for her twenties. Too cynical, too suspicious.

"Private detective. Cyrus Tremont." He handed her his business card and showed her his identification.

"That was my next guess. Who are you working for?"

"Don't we all ultimately work for ourselves? I take cases that talk to me."

"Give me a second, will you?"

"For what?"

She didn't answer. She took an iPhone out of her back pocket, typed something in. He waited as she scrolled. Finally, she nodded in approval.

"You have very good Yelp reviews, Mr. Tremont. 'Betty P' says, 'He caught the bastard in the act in twenty-four hours. Never getting married again but if I do, I'm putting Cyrus Tremont on the job. Five stars.' Well done."

He smiled. "You Googled me."

"ID's can be faked."

"So can reviews."

"*Touché*," she said, continuing to look at her phone. "Says here on your website you only take the cases of women and children. Why is that?"

"They need the help. Grown men don't."

"So, a knight-errant."

"You could say that."

"Well, since you are who you say you are, what can I do for you?"

"You can tell me where to find Miss Nora Sutherlin. I'll take an address, a phone number..."

"I'm Nora Sutherlin. Pleased to meet you." She extended her hand through the bars for him to shake. It was covered in pastel paint the color of cotton candy. Whoever this woman was, she did not intimidate him. He was fairly certain a dominatrix would intimidate him, or at least try to.

"Yeah, no, I don't think so. But nice try," he said, ignoring the hand. This little lady did not write about ladies getting their pussies slapped around with riding crops. She definitely didn't do the slapping in her free time, either.

"I swear, I'm her," the woman said, smiling.

If there hadn't been a gate between them, he might have laughed in her face. "Ma'am, Nora Sutherlin is a dominatrix," he said. "And a porno writer."

"I know. I'm her, remember? Although technically it's erotica, not porn. Not that there's anything wrong with porn."

"Right. Fine. I'll leave you my card. If you see her, you can have her call me."

"I can call you right now, but we're already talking. Just picture me in a corset. And not splattered with paint."

To humor the woman, he started to fish his phone out of his jacket when a little black girl wearing a pink ballet tutu came running out the front door, a large dog at her heels, and pink pigtail ribbons flying.

"*Tata*, I taught Gmork a new trick!" the girl yelled. She ran over to the paint-splattered woman.

"Show me, baby," the woman said.

The girl faced the enormous black dog and pointed her finger at it. "*Couche!*"

The dog lay on the ground.

The woman applauded. "Very good," she said. "But he already knows how to lay down."

"I know," the girl said. "But now he knows how to do it in French."

"You're teaching my *German* Shepherd French? You're going to give him an identity crisis."

Cyrus watched the whole show with a smile on his face. In three or four years, he and Paulina might have a little girl of their own running around in a pink tutu, a little girl who looked just like this one. And surely this lady was not a dominatrix. She was a nanny or an auntie.

"Princess?" A woman's voice called to the girl. "You know you're not supposed to interrupt grown-ups talking. Come back in the house."

"Sorry, *Maman*." The little girl ran to the woman standing at the top of the steps and wrapped her arms around the woman's leg.

If he'd been wearing a hat, he would have taken it off out of sheer respect for the woman's otherworldly beauty. Her elegant dark skin shimmered in the morning sun, and her black hair was braided into a crown—a fitting style for a woman so statuesque and regal. Her white dress stretched across a very pregnant stomach. She glowed like she'd swallowed the moon and carried it inside her.

The pregnant goddess said something to the woman he'd been talking to, the woman who Cyrus had briefly forgotten existed. She replied in French. This elicited a smirk from the goddess, who took her little girl back into the house.

"Mr. Tremont?" the woman who was not Nora Sutherlin said. "You dropped something."

"I did?"

"Yes. Your jaw."

He looked at her with pursed lips.

"Don't sweat it," the woman said. "Juliette's the reason the phrase 'jaw-dropping' was coined."

"That's Edge's missus?"

The woman nodded.

"My respect for the man has gone up a notch or two."

"Don't worry. It'll go down again any minute."

"You don't like Mr. Edge?"

"Love him. But I also know him. You want to come in and continue our conversation? It's hot out."

"That dog don't look too friendly." The dog in question stood looking right at him, the lines of his body tense as a soldier at attention.

"He doesn't like men very much, but he's well-trained," the woman said. "Watch. Gmork." She snapped her fingers and the dog snapped to attention. "*Gib laut.*"

The dog barked once.

"Gmork. *Sitz.*"

The dog sat.

"Gmork, *verehre mich.*"

The dog dropped his head and licked the woman's toes.

"What command is that?" Cyrus asked.

The woman smiled. For a second—only a second—something about that smile made him think he might be in the presence of another goddess. But not the sort of goddess one put on a pedestal and admired. No, she was the sort of goddess one sacrificed doves and cattle and virgins to, in the vain hope of not inciting her wrath.

"Worship me," she said.

"Excuse me?"

"The command I gave my dog was 'worship me.' This is called foot worship." She snapped her fingers and the dog stopped his licking. He lay at her feet, gazing up at her with adoring dark doggy eyes.

"Okay. So maybe you are Nora Sutherlin."

Chapter Five

Kingsley Edge might yet live up to his reputation —mercenary, perverted, and dangerous—but Cyrus couldn't fault him his taste in women or his taste in home decor. If Juliette was a goddess, her home was a worthy temple.

Nora Sutherlin—if this really was Nora Sutherlin—led him up the steps to the large arched front door, her giant dog following at her heels. Cold air blasted him right in the face, and he basked in it. Although only ten in the morning, the city was already starting to steam.

"Very nice," Cyrus said. "Mr. Edge has a beautiful home."

She took him down a hallway to a parlor room filled with furniture the likes he'd never seen outside a Chartres Street antique store.

"A king needs his castle. Do you mind very much if I change clothes before we talk?" she asked. "I shouldn't get paint on anything. King would tan my hide."

"Literally?"

She smiled. "So you have heard of him."

"His reputation precedes him."

Her smiled widened. "Make yourself at home. Wet bar's there if you're thirsty. I'll be right back."

She disappeared with her dog, and Cyrus helped himself to a bottle of water from the mini-fridge. He wandered the room, taking it all in. Fancy sofas—tufted velvet, exposed wood arms, carved wooden legs. Versailles-type stuff, very old world. The parlor was wallpapered with some kind of old-fashioned Victorian-looking stuff—red with an ivory floral pattern. Paulina would have liked it. A little too ostentatious for his taste. Then again, this was the Garden District. "Ostentatious" was standard proce-dure in most of these houses.

The only personal touches in the room were the framed photographs on the top of the marble fireplace mantel.

The same man appeared in each one of them. Kingsley Edge. Cyrus wasn't the best judge of whether a man was good-looking or not, but even his eyes told him Edge was a head-turner. Of course, with a woman like Juliette in his house and bed, he'd have to be.

Mr. Edge had wavy dark hair that needed cutting. Dark eyes that were cutting. If hadn't already known otherwise, Cyrus might have assumed Edge was of Louisiana Creole ancestry like Paulina—a little Spanish, a little French, a little Afro-Caribbean, a little who knows what...

According to his record, Edge was fifty. In the photos —which appeared recent, based on the age of his daughter in one—he didn't look a day older than forty. Money, Juli-ette, and looks. Lucky bastard.

The picture of Edge and his girl had been taken in winter. His daughter was wearing a white coat and pink mittens, while Edge was sporting a tuxedo. Both of them had on wide smiles for the camera, and the little girl had her arms around her father's neck.

In another photo, Edge and Juliette were slow dancing, looking at each other like nobody else existed in the world. Edge had on the same tuxedo jacket, and a patterned kilt. Scottish wedding?

The last photograph on the mantle had been taken at the same wedding. Edge and a pale, blond man were arm-wrestling at a table covered in wine bottles. Their eyes were locked on each other in a death stare, although it was clear both men were trying hard not to laugh. The blond was almost as much of a head-turner as Edge. Possibly. Men were not his specialty.

Cyrus glanced over the pictures again. These were the photographs of a man who loved his family. He might not have believed it without seeing it, knowing what he knew about Edge. But it was better this way, wasn't it? Better to have a bad reputation that hid a secret good side, than to have a good reputation with a secret bad side?

In his career, Father Ike worked tirelessly as a church pastor, a school chaplain and a prison chaplain. Paulina had said students adored Father Ike. She certainly had liked and trusted the man. And all that time that good man had a secret dark side.

Or maybe not. Maybe it was all just a misunderstanding.

Right. And Cyrus was the next Miss America, too.

"Sorry to keep you waiting."

He turned and saw Nora Sutherlin standing in the doorway to the room, her dog beside her like a shadow. She'd changed out of her shorts and paint-splattered shirt into a black halter top dress with a high thigh slit and red high heels that gave her the illusion of height. She'd taken her hair out of the ponytail and now it fell around her shoulders in lively black waves. That was more like it. Now he believed this was a woman men paid money to spend time with.

"You were gone three minutes. I expected thirty," he said.

"I'm not very high maintenance on Saturdays," she said. "Here, proof I am who I say I am."

She passed him a business card—solid black with silver lettering, the words MISTRESS NORA and a phone number. He dialed the number.

Her phone rang. She held it up, showing him he was calling her.

"All right. I buy it now." He ended the call.

"Thank you. Would you like to have a seat?"

"I'll stand."

"So will I then. What can I do for you?"

"You live here?" he asked.

"I have my own place, but I'm here a lot. I'm on the day shift."

"Day shift?"

She walked to the mini-bar and poured herself a glass of ice water.

"Juliette's at thirty-five weeks. She could go into labor any time now. Papa is with her at night. She needs someone with her during the day. At least Papa thinks so," she said and smiled. "Papa Kingsley."

"How do you happen to know Mr. Edge?"

"We're...family. In a way. I live just one street over."

"Related?"

"Sort of," she said, wagging her head from side to side. "Céleste calls me Aunt Elle. And Kingsley's like a brother to me. Same father, in a way."

"Foster father?"

She seemed to think good and hard about that.

"More like a godfather." She smiled behind her glass.

"I see." Cyrus wrote all that down. He saw her rub a spot of paint off her arm with her thumb. "You're repainting the house?"

"Just the nursery," she said.

"No offense, and I'm sure you're a fine housepainter, but I'd think a man with Mr. Edge's money could hire a whole team of professional housepainters."

"He could. But he's feeling extra protective of Juliette lately. He's not comfortable with strange men in the house, even to paint. I offered to do it."

"Wouldn't I count as a strange man in the house?" Cyrus asked. He watched her over the water bottle as he took a sip.

"I don't know," she said, shrugging. "Are you strange?"

"Stranger than I look. I might not be the best judge of that, though."

"Strange but not dangerous. You're not even carrying a gun."

"People might think threat of force is a good way to get to the truth," he said. "But it's not. People lie more when they're scared, not less."

"I'm not scared," she said. "I'll be honest with you if you're honest with me."

"That's a good deal," he said. "Should I start?"

"Please. I'm sure you didn't come here to hire me for my painting skills."

"I'm here about a dead priest."

Her reaction wasn't what he expected. She set her glass down with a thud that sent water spilling over the lip.

Then she sat—almost falling—onto the sofa, her lips parted in a gasp, her eyes wide with shock and horror.

"What?" she breathed.

"Father Isaac Murran. Do you know that name?"

She took a shuddering breath and leaned over, head on her knees.

"Ma'am? Ms. Sutherlin?"

"I'm fine," she said. She held up a hand. "Give me a minute."

"Of course. Take all the time you need."

The dog trotted over to his mistress and rested his head on her knee. She sat up and exhaled through her lips.

"I'm all right, boy," she said to the dog.

"I assume you know Father Ike then?" Cyrus asked.

The woman shook her head. "Never heard of him."

"That was a strong reaction over the death of a total stranger."

"I know a few priests. I thought...I thought maybe it was one of them."

"How do you know priests?"

"I'm Catholic."

Cyrus snorted a laugh.

"What?" she asked, anger flaring into her eyes. They looked black now in the low light, not green.

"You're Catholic?"

"Of course I'm Catholic. This is New Orleans, right? Everybody's Catholic here." She leaned back on the sofa and stuck one leg out, sprawling for a moment like a woman who'd been expecting a death sentence from her doctor and instead heard the word "benign." She laughed a little drunkenly.

"Don't scare me like that, Mr. Tremont."

"Sorry about that." He sat down on the opposite end of

the sofa from her, watched as she rubbed her forehead between her eyes. He saw she wore a silver saint's medal, which rested between her ample breasts. He had to wonder if this particular saint had ever imagined his reward for a life of godliness would be an eternity pillowed in beautiful cleavage.

"It's not your fault. You're doing your job," she said.

"What saint do you wear?" Cyrus said as she sat up and adjusted her necklace.

"Saint Ignatius."

"Interesting choice for a saints medal," he said. "Patron of soldiers and the Jesuits. You have someone in the service? Or the Jesuits?"

"You know your saints," she said, which didn't answer his question. He waited. "This medal belongs to my lover. He's on a long trip right now. I wanted something of his close to my heart."

"Your lover? That's what you call him?"

"I'd call him my 'owner,' but that would make probably make you uncomfortable."

"A little, yeah. Something wrong with calling him your 'boyfriend'?"

"He's fifty-one. There's no boy in that man. Although I am seeing a twenty-seven-year-old as well."

"And he's your boyfriend?"

"No. He's my *other* lover."

"You're playing with me."

"I always play with handsome men. It's my job."

She patted her dog on the head and stood up, went straight to the wet bar, and poured herself a drink. Not water this time, but whiskey from the looks of it. She downed the shot in one take.

"Now I believe you're Catholic," he said.

"By the way, I don't usually drink bourbon before brunch. You gave me a shock."

"Sometimes you have to shock someone to get their attention."

She seemed to be considering taking another shot of her whiskey. Instead, she screwed the lid back on the bottle and took a seat opposite him on the smaller sofa.

"Why me?" she asked. "Why are you asking me about this dead priest? I'm guessing he was killed?"

"Suicide," Cyrus said.

"How am I involved in a priest's suicide? Was my name in his note or something?"

"This was in his pocket when he died." Cyrus pulled out the little red business card. "That's yours, yes?"

She reached out and took the card from him, nodded, handed it back to him.

"Mine. Old card, though. That's not even my number anymore. Hasn't been since we moved down here."

"When was that?"

"Let's see," she said, counting backward. "Two years, eight months ago."

Cyrus jotted all that down. "And the name Isaac Murran means nothing to you? Everyone called him Father Ike."

"Nothing."

"What about him? Ever seen him before?" Cyrus handed her a photograph of Murran he'd gotten from Paulina.

"Never seen him before," she said.

"You're certain?"

"I have never seen that man in my life. He might have known me, but I don't know him."

"You're going to have to forgive me for being skeptical.

Most of the time, I tail husbands cheating on their wives or blowing money that should go to their kids. One guy blew a lot of his kid's college fund at your friend Edge's club."

"How is that Kingsley's fault? He runs a club for adults, not a daycare center."

"Just saying, the work I do...it makes you a little skeptical of everyone."

"Most of the time, I flog husbands who are afraid to tell their wives they're masochists or submissives. There's a lack of trust on both sides."

"You don't care those men are cheating?"

She shrugged again. "That's between them and their significant others. I'm just the hired help."

"You're a little more than a housekeeper."

"Not much more. No kissing. No sex. Only pain and dominance."

He raised an eyebrow at her. "You were arrested for prostitution twice in New York. In 2006 and 2007."

"I wasn't convicted. Charges were dropped."

"Charges get dropped for lots of reasons."

"I won't lie and say I've never had sex with a client. But I will say I've never exchanged sex for money—not that, as the kids say, there's anything wrong with that. One detective tried to get me to give him private information about a client. When I didn't, he arrested me for prostitution in retaliation. Another arrest was a case of mistaken identity. A wife thought her husband was seeing a prostitute behind her back. He wasn't. He was seeing me."

"You've never blackmailed a client?" he asked.

"I wouldn't have too many clients if I did."

"So that's a no?"

She took a deep breath. He was annoying her. Good. The feeling was mutual.

"Do you have any clients who are in the clergy?" he asked.

"Back in New York, one of my clients was a rabbi. There was also a Baptist youth pastor, but don't tell his momma."

"So you're saying you've never been in a sexual relationship with a Catholic priest?"

"I'm saying I've never seen, met, or had any kind of relationship—sexual or otherwise—with this priest." She returned the photograph to Cyrus.

"But he had your card."

"A lot of people have my card. You have my card."

"True. But I didn't call your number right before I killed myself."

He'd shocked her again.

"You didn't tell me that part." She spoke softly, breathlessly. He'd upset her.

"He made two calls in the five minutes before his suicide. The first to a friend to say he was sorry for what he was about to do. The last call he made was to you. You want to tell me why he was calling you?"

"I'd tell you if I knew."

"You would?"

"Maybe," she said. "Maybe not. But I really don't know."

"How about this? How about you tell me how he might have gotten your card?"

She took a long breath, puffing her cheeks out as she exhaled. "Well...that's my old New York number. Maybe he went there on a trip looking for kink."

"Did Mr. Edge ever give out your cards?"

"Yes."

"I'll need to speak to him then."

"Good luck."

He ignored that. "You say Father Ike might have gone to New York looking for kink. I'm not very familiar with what dominatrixes do. Can you walk me through it?"

"You really think he wanted to do kink right before he died?"

"I don't know what he wanted right before he died. But I do need to find out."

She looked away, crossed her legs, nodded. "What do you want to know?"

"Father Isaac Murran was sixty years old. Do you have a lot of clients in their sixties?"

"A few."

"Really?"

"Many sixty-year-old men still have strong libidos and sexual longings. The man I love will be sixty in nine years, and I fully intend to have good sex with him nine years from now. I mean, before then too but also nine years from now."

She was playing with him again.

"Can you tell me what goes on between you and your clients? The basics?"

She sat forward and gave him her full attention. "A basic session begins like this. A client comes to my dungeon—"

"And where is your dungeon?"

"Do you really need to know that?"

"I really need to know that. I'm not the cops, okay?"

"Fine—828 Piety Street. Old brick factory."

"You have a dungeon on *Piety* Street?"

"It's not my fault half the streets in this town have religious names."

"Okay," Cyrus said. "Go on. Who are your clients, mostly?"

"We'll go with the usual demographics. Most of my clients are straight white men between the ages of twenty-five and seventy-five who are middle class or above. Professional men—white-collar types. A few military guys but mostly doctors, lawyers, bankers, that sort. The bulk of my clients are in their forties and fifties, midlife crisis age. The 'it's now or never' stage."

"A client arrives at your dungeon and then what?"

"I greet them at the door and they come in. Then I make them take off all their clothes."

"But not for sex?"

"For protection. I need to see they aren't hiding any weapons."

"Got it. Go on."

"We'll talk a few minutes about what he wants. Most of the time, it's some pain and dominance, like I said. Maybe some foot worship. Maybe he wants to be called a specific name like 'slut' or 'bitch' or 'baby boy.' Something that's part of his fantasies. I'll leave him alone a minute or two to get into the right headspace. He'll probably kneel on the floor and close his eyes. I'll come back in and the scene will start."

"The scene?"

"That's what we call it. A scene. Scening. A roleplay scene. A Mommy scene. A humiliation scene. Whatever he's paid for. Anyway, let's say it's a pain scene. I'll put him on the St. Andrew's cross and hurt him with various instruments of kink-play—floggers, whips, paddles, canes. I see a lot of masochists in my dungeon. Most of them can orgasm from pain or can orgasm very easily after a beating."

"The men do that?" Cyrus cleared his throat.

"They're allowed to touch themselves. I don't jack them off or anything."

"Isn't that...unsanitary?"

"Germaphobes don't usually become dominatrixes. I make them clean up after themselves."

"What do they use? To clean it up, I mean? Lysol?"

"Something like that. Or their own tongues if I'm feeling particularly sadistic. And then Lysol after. And bleach. I keep a very clean dungeon."

Cyrus stared at her, stared a long time.

"Yes?" she said with a smile.

"Sorry. Head swam there a second," he said.

"Kink isn't for everybody."

Cyrus wiped a drop of sweat off his forehead. The cold house was suddenly not so cool anymore.

"All right. The scene ends with him coming and cleaning it up. Then he pays you?"

"Oh, forgot that part. I get paid upfront."

"How much, can I ask?"

"Really depends on what he wants. A basic two-hour pain session is going to be about five hundred dollars, and I usually get tipped another hundred. That's here in Nola. I charged a lot more in New York."

"Nola gets a discount?"

"Nola's got a much lower cost of living than Manhattan."

Cyrus chuckled. "I believe that."

"For more serious scenes—blood-play, fire-play, all-nighters—it can run into the thousands of dollars."

"That's a lot of money. You must be rich."

"I do okay. I mostly see clients now for fun. Old regulars from New York fly down. And I have a few new locals I adore. I might only see five to ten clients a week."

"So a regular two-hour scene, just the basics, would cost a man six hundred dollars minimum?"

"Right."

"That's a lot of money."

"I'm worth it."

Cyrus nodded, leaned back on the sofa, and exhaled.

"Another question...you do anything they pay you to do?"

"Within reason," she said. "We all have our limits. But if it's something I'm not into, I can refer the client to someone who will do it. I know a specialist for almost every fantasy, every fetish."

"What won't you do?" he asked and didn't know why he was asking. Just nosy, if he was being honest.

"You'd be surprised by the guys who want me to dress up like a 'sexy Nazi' and order them around in German. That's a hard 'no' for me," she said. "Nazis aren't sexy."

"That's one hell of a fantasy."

"Many of the men I know with those sorts of fetishes are as horrified by them as you are. The brain is weird. If a man gets the standard set of wiring, he'll find a woman sexy, or another man, or both. Nothing fancy. If you get a slightly different set of wiring, you're turned on by popping balloons, dressing like a baby, getting beat up by Nazis, and you have very little say in the matter."

"Wait. Balloons? You serious?"

"They're called looners," she said. Cyrus boggled at her. "Don't judge. They can't help it. Even vanilla people have unwanted fantasies—rape, violence, incest. Just because someone calls their lover 'Daddy' during sex doesn't mean they want to fuck their own father."

Cyrus looked up at her in surprise.

"Yes?" she asked.

"Nothing."

"Your eyes got very wide when I said the word 'Daddy.' Did it get to you?" Her tone of voice wasn't flirtatious, but curious. She sounded like a therapist trying to diagnose a patient. He better get out of here fast or she'd be interviewing him instead of the other way around.

"I didn't know it was considered a kink, that's all," Cyrus said. "Girls say it all the time as a joke."

She bowed her head. He could see she was trying not to smile, trying not to smirk.

"You like being a sex worker?"

"I wouldn't do it if I didn't find it satisfying on more than one level. There are, I promise, easier ways to make money."

"Then why do it?" he asked.

"I'm a sadist."

Cyrus laughed.

"You don't believe me?"

"Of all the crazy shit you just told me, that's the craziest. You're a sadist?"

"I'm a sadist."

"I used to be a cop. I met sadists. You are *not* a sadist."

"You're confusing sadists with psychopaths. Maybe this answer will make more sense to you," she continued. "I like having power over people."

"Power?"

"Power. Have you ever felt it? Power over someone?"

Hard question. Easy answer. "Yeah."

"Did you like it?"

He answered it honestly before he could stop himself. "Too much."

"There's your answer."

"You like having power enough to order someone to kill himself?" he asked, casually as he could.

Either she was the best actress in the world or his question had caught her completely off-guard.

"I would never do that," she said, almost breathless. "Never."

He believed her. Maybe he shouldn't but he did. "Had to ask."

"Right. Of course." She stood up. "Now if we're done here, there's a little girl and a very pregnant woman upstairs who are expecting me to take them to get chocolate chip waffles at eleven, and I would hate to disappoint them. And me. Since we're being honest with each other, the waffles are mostly for me."

Cyrus stood up. He knew when he was being dismissed. He followed her from the room to the front door of the house and down to the gate. Her fingers flew over the keypad too fast for him to see the code. The gate yawned open.

"I'm sorry I couldn't help you more, Mr. Tremont. Truly. I don't like knowing a priest called me before he shot himself. Maybe if he got me on the phone, I could have helped him."

Cyrus stepped onto the sidewalk and turned back to face her.

"Could you answer one more question for me?"

"Of course."

"This is all speculation, but can you imagine any scenario where a man would call you right before he killed himself? Anything? Anything at all?"

She exhaled through her nose. Her brow furrowed.

"I had a client once who called me after he committed a crime. Hit and run. He'd been drinking. He thought he'd killed the other driver."

"What did you tell him?"

"I told him to tell me where he was. That way if he hung up, I could call 911 and tell them where to look for him. After that I tried talking him into turning himself in to the police immediately, that a couple years in jail was better than eternity in a grave. Thank God he listened."

"Can you think of any other reason Father Murran might have called you?"

"Maybe," she said.

"What?"

"I can't say."

"Can you give me a hint?"

"No."

She hit a button on the keypad. The iron gate started to close.

She turned and walked back toward the house.

"Ms. Sutherlin? Nora? Nora?"

"I told you I was a sadist, Mr. Tremont. Do you believe me now?" she called to him without looking back. Then she was in the house with the door closed behind her. The queen was back in her castle, the knight-errant on the wrong side of the drawbridge.

He believed her.

Chapter Six

N ora kept a mental list of men who somehow managed to get even more handsome after turning fifty than they were before. George Clooney was on that list. Christopher Plummer, of course, her personal favorite. Two of the men on her list she'd had the pleasure of sleeping with. Alas, Captain von Trapp wasn't one of the two.

Standing in the doorway of Céleste's pretty pink ballet-themed bedroom, Nora watched as one of those men on her list read a bedtime story to his three-year-old daughter. A scene from a fairy tale: the handsome papa with the rakish dark hair only beginning to show the gray, and the little girl enraptured with the story or, far more likely, with her father and his tender voice.

The girl was small, and so was her room. But it was a work of art in miniature—pink-and-white striped wallpaper, white wainscoting, white princess bed, a barre and mirror on one wall because Papa could not tell his baby ballerina "no." On the nightstand, a milk glass lamp with a lace lampshade was on, bathing the room in the softest gentlest light, and next to it sat a framed photograph of famed ballerina Misty Copland leaping like a gazelle in a white tutu, grace and power incarnate. Céleste's idol right after her Papa.

"Maître Corbeau, sur un arbre perché, Tenait en son bec un fromage..." Kingsley read aloud.

The Fox and The Crow. An ancient story warning of the dangers of believing your own reviews. The consequences could be dire. One might lose one's cheese, and Nora had enough German ancestry in her to consider this not a fable, but a horror story.

Anything but the cheese.

It would have been sublime—the handsome papa, the adoring little girl, the picture-perfect bedroom—except for one thing. Nora was in trouble. Again.

Papa closed his storybook. Nora went into the room and stood at his side over his shoulder.

"King?" she said softly.

"Céleste," Kingsley said, "would you tell your *Tata Elle* I'm not speaking to her?"

"Papa's not speaking to you, *Tata Elle*."

Nora grimaced but tried to make it look like a grin. "Yes, I've noticed, baby. Can you tell your Papa he's being childish?"

"Papa, really. You kind of are." Céleste, almost four, had already mastered the art of the French shrug, the ever more French eyes-to-heaven look.

"I know," he said, grinning. "I'm enjoying it."

"Céleste," Nora said. "You know I love your Papa, right?"

"I know."

"You know I'd never *really* hurt him, right?" Nora asked.

"Right."

"Good. Now kiss him goodnight before I drag him out of your room by his hair."

Céleste rolled up, grabbed her Papa Kingsley by the face and kissed him on both cheeks, twice.

"Goodnight, Papa. I love you."

"I love you too, my angel princess darling cabbagehead."

"Very sweet. Now excuse us, Céleste. Goodnight."

Nora grabbed Kingsley by the back of his hair and yanked him out of his little chair.

"Ow," he said.

"Come on, Big Papa. We need to talk."

"Help me, *petite*," he said to Céleste who only shook her head.

"You're on your own, Papa," she said, before dramatically throwing the covers over her head.

"On my own? You've been spending too much time with your auntie," Kingsley said to her as Nora dragged him into the hallway.

"There is no such thing as 'too much time' with me." Nora released his hair once they were outside Céleste's room.

"I beg to differ."

"You'll beg to breathe if you don't behave. Come with me." She slapped her thigh the way she did when signaling Gmork to follow her. Luckily this maneuver also worked on Frenchmen.

She went into the guest room she usually commandeered when she spent the night at the house—a red and gilt room that looked like the sort of place where French

Bourbon kings sodomized their courtesans. This was Kingsley's typical aesthetic.

"Sit," she said, pointing at a Rococo chair with gilt scrollwork arms. "Speak."

Out in the hallway, Gmork barked.

"Not you, Gmork."

"That is the stupidest name I've ever heard for a dog," Kingsley said, disgusted.

"It's from *The Neverending Story*, which is a classic of German children's literature. Show some respect."

"*Le bête noire*," he muttered. *The black beast*, a fancy French way of saying Gmork was the bane of Kingsley's existence.

"My dog is not a *bête noire*."

He pointed a finger at her. "I meant you."

"What did I do this time?" she demanded.

He sat back in the chair, stretched out his legs and crossed his feet at the ankles. She straddled his calves and stood arms akimbo. If he tried to escape, he'd have to go through her first.

"Did you or did you not let a strange man into this house today?" he asked, dark eyes narrowed.

"He wasn't all that strange. Certainly less strange than the man who lives in the house."

"Juliette is thirty-five weeks pregnant. We don't let strange men near her. I'd ban strange women as well, but we need you to babysit."

"Juliette told me I should invite him in."

"You shouldn't have listened to her."

"Is this the key to happiness in your relationship? She says something calm and rational and not paranoid and you ignore it?" Nora asked.

"So far so good," he said.

"I swear to God I would slap you if I didn't know for a fact you'd like it."

"You could have called me. I would have come right home."

"Cyrus Tremont is a P.I. who helps women catch cheating husbands and parents find missing kids. And he has very good Yelp reviews. He's not a serial killer. I Googled him."

"We do not vet visitors to this house with Google."

"I do."

"And we do not help P.I.s destroy the lives of our clients."

"They're my clients now, not yours," she reminded him. "I don't work for you anymore. And he wasn't even asking me about a client."

"Then why the hell was he here?"

"Because some priest killed himself last night."

Kingsley's head snapped up and he started to stand. Nora put her hand out, pressing him back down into the chair.

"Not *him*," Nora said, rolling her eyes. As if she'd still be vertical and breathing if anything happened to *him*. "A priest named Isaac Murran. Apparently he tried to call my old number a few minutes before he shot himself. My business card was in his pocket. Tremont wanted to know why. The end."

"What did you tell him?"

"The truth—that I have no idea who Isaac Murran is, that we've never met, that he's certainly not a client of mine."

"Did you tell him—"

"I know what I'm doing, King. And you can't guard Juliette all the time. She's a grown woman."

"She's vulnerable right now."

"Obviously, she is not the only one."

Without warning, Kingsley rolled forward in his chair and rested the top of his head on her stomach. "Help me."

Sighing, she put her hands on the back of his head and stroked his hair.

"Do the thing," he said.

"The thing? Oh, right, the thing." Nora brushed his soft wavy hair off the back of his neck and found the two pressure points at the base of his skull that when massaged just right, helped relax Kingsley more than a bottle of wine.

These two spots, known in the acupressure world as "the heavenly pillars" were about an inch below the hairline and an inch apart. For some reason, no one but Nora could ever find them on Kingsley. Juliette had tried, plus two doctors, a massage therapist...even Søren. Only she could "do the thing," and since the thing needed done, she did it.

As she rubbed his heavenly pillars, she felt the tension in his neck and back and then slowly felt it leaving. Not all the way, but a little bit—enough for his broad shoulders to slump slightly, enough for him to exhale.

"*Merci,*" he whispered. "But don't stop."

"King, talk to me. What's wrong?"

His back moved with his long deep breath. Nora reached under his neck and unbuttoned his shirt to the center of his chest. He didn't try to stop her as she pushed it down his arms to bare his shoulders and back. She massaged his arms, his shoulder blades, ran her fingernails up and down his spine the way she knew relaxed him best. It was easy to be with him like this. They had been passionate lovers long ago. And they'd hated each other, long ago. Both passions had burned themselves out. Only the softer feelings survived the flames—affection, friendship, tenderness.

"I slept in a chair last night. Everything hurts," he said.

"There are six bedrooms in this house. Why would you sleep in a chair?"

"There's only one bed in the master bedroom. Juliette was sleeping in it."

"That bed is huge. There's room for her, the baby, and you and half the National Guard."

He shook his head. "I had a nightmare last night. I woke up tangled in the covers. Woke Juliette up, too."

"Ah..." She stroked his hair gently. "Are they back? The bad dreams?"

"For a month now, they've been back."

"What do you dream?"

"They're awful."

"I can handle awful."

Kingsley shuddered. "I dream Céleste is lost in the house, and I can hear her crying for me but...no matter where I look, I can't find her. I dream men with guns come for Juliette and take her from me while she screams my name. I dream someone is trying to shoot at Nico, and I see you running to stop the bullet. Sometimes you take it. Sometimes it hits Nico and I see him fall...and you hold him while he bleeds."

Nico. King's son. Nora's *other* lover.

Her hands went to her heart. "Oh, God, Kingsley."

"Last night was the worst one yet."

"What happened?"

Kingsley didn't answer at first. Nora braced herself and when Kingsley finally did speak, it was in a whisper, as if he were afraid to hear his own words.

"Juliette lost the baby."

Nora blinked tears from her eyes. She dipped her head and kissed the back of his neck.

"Just bad dreams," she said. "You're about to have your third child. It's a lot to handle. Of course you're having anxiety dreams. That's all it is."

He looked up at her. His eyes were bright, almost feverish. Something in his eyes scared her. Something in his eyes she didn't want to see.

"You know your past. I know mine. Do we have any right to be as happy as we are?"

"I don't know if we have a right," she said. "I don't know if anyone has a right to be as happy as we are."

"You never worry it'll catch up with us?"

"What?" she asked, her brow furrowed.

"Our sins? Søren's finally caught up with him. We're next, aren't we?"

She wanted to laugh, to laugh away his fears. This was irrational. Superstitious nonsense. She knew it. And yet, his words chilled her.

"You sound very Catholic right now," she said.

"Tell me it's sleep deprivation."

"It's just sleep deprivation," she said and prayed that was all. "You did sleep in a chair last night."

"I slept in the chair because I couldn't bear to leave Juliette alone and unprotected in the room, but I was afraid to sleep next to her in case I had the dream again and started thrashing around. What if I hurt her in my sleep? I would never forgive myself if I hurt her or the baby."

"You want me to sleep with her tonight in your bed? She won't be alone, and you can sleep in another room?" Nora asked.

"I can't ask you to do that. You've given us too much of your time already. You have your own life."

"One night won't kill me. It's worth it if you can get some sleep."

"Would you?"

"If Juliette agrees. You know I love sleeping with beautiful women."

Kingsley sat up but Nora didn't stop rubbing. She pulled his earlobes gently and he exhaled with relief.

"It's the great bait and switch," he said. "You want something your entire life and you know that you won't be truly happy until you have it. And then you have it and you can't be truly happy because you're now terrified of losing it. It's enough to drive a man mad. I can't lose Juliette. I can't. I can't lose my children. I can't lose you or Nico or—"

"Søren?"

Kingsley glanced up at her before lowering his head again. Ah. So that was the problem. With Søren gone on his impromptu road trip, Kingsley was quickly losing his mind.

Nora ran her fingers through his hair again, soothing him with her touch as best she could. Times like this she felt woefully inadequate. She might have the magic fingers but she didn't have any magic words.

"He just needed some time to himself, I'm sure. He'll be back."

"Unless he gets hit by a truck and is dying in a ditch right now."

"Kingsley. Now you're just being pathetic."

"What if he joined the Hells Angels?" Kingsley asked. "They're not nice people."

"Our pacifist pretentious priest did *not* join the Hells Angels," Nora said. "He rides a Ducati, not a Harley."

"They could force him to trade it in. He could come home covered in tattoos and dying of hepatitis."

"That's it. I'm leaving." Nora tried to pull away. Kingsley grabbed her by the arm to stop her.

"Don't go," Kingsley said. "Do the thing again."

He rolled forward and put his head on her stomach again. Nora did the thing.

When Kingsley finally calmed down, Nora went to Juliette and told her about Kingsley's nightmares. Juliette politely declined Nora's offer to sleep with her—if she couldn't sleep with Kingsley she would sleep alone—but she graciously agreed to sleep with the baby monitor in the room so Kingsley could hear her right next door. Kingsley agreed to the compromise. Nora kissed them both goodnight and started to head out. He stopped her at the front door.

"He won't hurt himself, will he?" Kingsley asked. She was glad he kept his head down when he asked that question so he wouldn't see the look of horror that crossed Nora's face.

"No," she said. "He's too in love with himself for that."

"I'm not kidding," Kingsley said. "I'm worried about him. I'm not used to being worried about him. He worries about us. That's how it works."

"He's still a priest," Nora said. "Just a suspended priest. When the one year's suspension is over, he'll go back to the Jesuits, and everything will go back to normal. Our version of 'normal' anyway."

"Do you want things to go back to normal? I don't," he said.

"Doesn't matter what I want. If he wants to go back, he'll go back."

"What do you want?"

"I just want him to come home."

He nodded. "*Moi, aussi.*"

"Goodnight, King. I'm going to bed. You should, too."

"Not yet." He raised a finger, pointed it at her face. "This detective of yours."

"He's not *my* detective. He's just *a* detective. And what about him?" she asked.

"Is he done with us?"

Nora shook her head. "He's going to come see you. He wants to find out how this dead priest had my business card."

"I don't know how."

"Then tell him that. It's no big deal."

Kingsley raised his eyebrow. She pushed it back down.

"Goodnight," she said again.

She started to walk away. Kingsley called out after her, and Nora went back to him.

"If you hear from him," Kingsley said softly, "tell him I bought him a present. He needs to come home so I can give it to him."

"You bought Søren a present?" she repeated.

"A little one," Kingsley said. "A trifle."

"A trifle?"

"Barely a trinket."

Nora raised her eyebrow now. Kingsley pushed it back down.

"Just tell him," Kingsley said.

"I'll tell him."

"And remember," Kingsley continued, "no strange men

in the house. We keep the barbarians at the gate. That's why I have the fucking gate." He pointed at the iron fence that encircled the house.

"You're forgetting something, King." She patted his cheek. "We are the barbarians."

Chapter Seven

Nora whistled for Gmork, who followed her from the house, neatly avoiding Kingsley's outstretched hand on their way out the back door. Poor King. The man loved dogs, and yet Gmork had never warmed up to him or Søren or any man he'd ever met.

Nora left Kingsley's house and walked in the direction of her home.

But she wasn't going home. She was going to church.

Søren had been given a key to St. Mary's, a few blocks from her house, as he occasionally celebrated Mass there when one of their usual priests was sick or out of town. She took Søren's key with her to St. Mary's, unlocked the side door, and slipped inside the darkened sanctuary.

Tonight the city cooled off quickly after dark. When she arrived at St. Mary's around eleven, she could smell the slightest trace of autumn in the air. That was all Nora missed from living in New England—autumn, and nothing else. Not the traffic. Not the toll roads. Not the hectic pace of life.

Only autumn, which did come to New Orleans, but slowly and late, late in the season. No winter either, unless she counted Søren who carried winter with him, wherever he went. Winter in the scent of his skin, like frost on sleeping tree branches and the hard freeze of new snow under star-wild skies. Winter in his eyes when he glared, a look that could bring the temperature of any room down if you happened to be on the wrong side of that icy gray stare. Winter in his touch...when she burned for him, only his touch would cool the fires. But only after fanning the flames.

God, she missed him.

Nora sat in the third pew from the front. Gmork curled up on the floor at her feet. The arched windows cast long shadows in the chapel dark. From her purse, she took out a velvet bag that contained a set of tarnished silver rosary beads that had belonged to her late mother.

She didn't pray the rosary. Nora couldn't even remember the last time she prayed the rosary. But Søren prayed it often, his fingers flicking through the beads like gears turning on a bicycle.

Once Nora had asked Søren, "Does it mean anything to you? The rosary? Or are you just doing it because you're a priest and they expect you to do it?"

His answer surprised her.

"All over the world, thousands of Catholics are praying the rosary right this very moment. I like thinking about them, about all of us reaching out to God together. If enough people all over the world were singing the same song at the same time, the whole world could hear it. I like singing in God's choir."

"You're a good priest," she said to that and kissed him. But he wasn't a priest anymore.

No. Not true. Søren was still a priest. It was a sacrament, after all, the priesthood. Once a priest, always a priest, they said. Even if a priest were to leave the priesthood, even leave the Church altogether, he would still bear on his soul a brand that said PRIEST in ornate all-capital letters.

What he wasn't anymore—technically—was a Jesuit. Six weeks ago, after the very last day of the summer course he'd been teaching at Loyola, he'd gone to his Jesuit superiors with a photograph. He showed it to them, a picture of a blond three-year-old boy in a suit jacket and short pants. "This is Fionn," he said. "This is my son."

The silence that followed, Søren told her, had sucked the sound from the entire city.

But thanks to a severe shortage of priests in the Church, he'd been spared the worst-case scenarios—he hadn't been laicized or excommunicated. The punishment handed down was still severe: he was to be suspended from the Jesuits for the period of no less than one year for the crime of fathering a child with a married woman.

Alone in the dark, stuffy chapel, she cried. She cried because Søren had disappeared without a word to her or Kingsley, which meant he was in such deep pain he wanted to protect them from the sight of it.

She cried because she was afraid for him out there alone with only his thoughts to keep him company. And though she didn't know his thoughts, she knew they were dangerous company.

"Keep him safe, God," she prayed aloud. "Don't let him forget how loved he is. I love him and Kingsley loves him. Protect him and bring him home."

These were simple prayers, children's prayers, but they were all Nora had.

Usually, she prayed and went home again. But tonight her prayers felt insufficient. She needed something more. Not for God's sake, really, but her own peace of mind. She left Gmork lightly snoozing on the floor by her pew and walked through the nave to the narthex, where she found a bank of votive candles and matches on an iron stand.

She stuffed a twenty into the offering box. A dollar for the candle. Nineteen dollars as a guilt-offering for all the dog hairs Gmork left behind.

With a practiced flick of the match, Nora lit a votive candle and whispered her brief prayer as she touched the tip of the flame to the wick.

"God, bring Søren home to us."

Nora left her little prayer burning and slipped out the side door, Gmork at her heels. She saw almost no one out and about as she walked back to her house, Gmork at her side, keeping her safe from all the ghosts and goblins and dangerous drunks of New Orleans. Where Kingsley lived in a six-thousand square-foot Italianate mansion, she lived in a much smaller house, painted red and nearly hidden by a wrought iron fence and an enormous oak tree. The fence and tree were both festooned with Mardi Gras beads.

The beads were there when she bought the place, and she'd left them there since they were colorful and pretty. She assumed they'd wear out and drop off at some point, but mysteriously they'd multiplied. She never saw anyone adding to the beads, but there were undeniably more beads now than when she'd moved in. Reds and blues and purples and gold and black and white. But mostly silver.

One of these days, she was going to catch someone in the act of beading her house and she'd ask them why her and no one else on the street.

And why silver?

So far, no luck. But she could live with a little mystery in her life. Kept things from getting boring. Søren had taken a few strands of beads off her tree once and tied her up with them. It had been Mardi Gras in her bed that night.

"Søren," Nora said to herself as she unlocked her back-door. "Hurry up and get home, please. I miss you. My pussy misses you..."

That was not a prayer.

It was a cry for help.

Nora entered through the back door into her kitchen and flipped on the lights. She had mail—a handful of junk mail flyers. An electricity bill for her dungeon. A vet appointment reminder. The book she'd ordered (*The Power and the Glory*)...and a check from her publisher. A large check. After paying her bills with it, she'd have enough left over to buy that Harley-Davidson SuperLow in Iced Pearl she'd been eying. One step closer to being a Hells Angel than Søren.

A postcard slipped out from between the junk mail as she was tossing it into recycling. She bent to pick it up off the floor.

For weeks now, she'd been receiving postcards from her lover. It was the only communication either she or Kingsley had received from him on his trip. No calls, no texts, no emails, no letters. Nora had simply woken up one morning a month ago to find her bed empty. Two days later, she received a postcard from Texas with nothing written on the back but her name and address in Søren's handwriting.

Nora had no idea what specifically set Søren off on a cross-country road trip without so much as a goodbye kiss, but she planned on asking him—loudly. After he fucked her, of course.

Why couldn't Søren have a normal midlife crisis like every other man she knew? She'd much prefer he buy a sports car and get a twenty-two-year-old girlfriend than simply disappear on them. He could have at least written something on the postcards. Something like, *I love you. I miss you. I wish your vagina was here.*

For a month, she'd been sneaking to St. Mary's at night to pray for Søren's return. And for a month, Søren was getting further away from her, not closer. She had over a dozen postcards now—Houston, Austin, Oklahoma City, Phoenix, Denver, Wyoming, South Dakota, Montana, Salt Lake City. The last one was a photo of Hells Canyon in Idaho. A week ago. She assumed the next postcard would come from Oregon or Washington, maybe even Canada.

Instead, the postcard was from, of all places, a French Quarter hotel right here in New Orleans.

When she flipped it over, she found a message this time.

Suite 301. Key at the desk under your name.

Søren's handwriting. No stamp or postmark.

Nora took a deep breath. Her head fell back and she closed her eyes.

"About God damn time."

Then she sent Kingsley a quick text message.

Søren's back.

Kingsley replied in typical Kingsley fashion.

Thank fuck, he wrote, which was the closest Kingsley Edge ever got to saying a prayer.

Chapter Eight

Priority number two was figuring out why Father Ike killed himself. Priority one was getting Paulina's mind off Father Ike until Cyrus could. And he knew just what to do. He ordered take-out—Honduran food from Los Catrachos—poured cocktails, hit PLAY on his favorite jazz album, and put Paulina on the love seat. Although not a cure for sadness, Christian Scott's trumpet was a highly effective treatment. And if that didn't work, a kiss or two or ten thousand. As many as Cyrus could get away with.

He slid his hand across Paulina's stomach, soft and trembling under the lightweight linen of her blouse and held her by the hip. She turned her face to meet his eyes. There was no woman in the world who had eyes like Paulina. They reminded him of sepia photos, pale brown, and out of another time and place with lashes almost long enough to tickle his cheeks. But even more, they were honest eyes that hid nothing, nothing at all from him and asked him to hide nothing, nothing at all from her. So he didn't hide a thing from her. He let her see how much he loved her, adored her, treasured her, wanted her, and then he kissed her on her soft full lips to make sure she got the message.

The kiss she gave him in return was the kiss he wanted —nervous at first, slowly growing bolder, and by the time one song switched to another, they were both breathing each other's breaths. He pushed her gently down onto her back on the plush sofa and guided her legs around his waist. He didn't ask for much in this world...but if he didn't feel her heels on his lower back right this second, his heart would break right in two. When he told Paulina that, she laughed and he felt her breasts moving against his chest.

"Well, I'd hate to break your heart," she said. "Especially when it's so easy to keep it in one piece." She let her heels come to rest on his back. It was enough to make a grown man cry. "Better?"

"So much better."

Her tongue tasted sweet like the blueberry wine she'd had after dinner. Sweet and spiked and he couldn't get enough of it. He knew marriage wouldn't be like this all the time. He'd be a fool to think it was all low lights, jazz, and making out like teenagers on the sofa. But still, he would have married her in that room that second if he could have talked her into it. Especially since he knew any minute now...any second...she would say...

"All right, behave, Cyrus." She said this right when he slipped his hand under her shirt and started inching up and up.

"I am behaving," he said.

"Behaving bad."

"Behaving bad is still behaving." He bit her earlobe. She laughed, but she placed her hands on his chest.

"That's enough," Paulina said. Cyrus groaned and sat up.

"Already?"

"Already." Paulina slowly pulled herself back up and righted her clothes and her hair. He was pleased to see she was at least breathing hard. Maybe he could flatter himself that she stopped because she was about to lose control, not him.

"Will you marry me?" he asked.

"I will. I said 'yes' six months ago. I'll say 'yes' again tonight."

"No, I meant right now. Right damn now."

He picked up his bourbon sour and drank the rest of it down to the rocks. He was half-tempted to take the ice in his hand and put it all down his pants.

"I will marry you on November seventh like we planned and not a day sooner."

"I could be dead by November seventh."

"Then I will throw you the finest funeral this town has ever seen."

"Second line?"

"Second line, Trombone Shorty leading the way."

"Not fair I have to miss my own funeral."

"Better not die then," she said.

"Better not."

She started to stand, but he grabbed her around the waist and pulled her into his lap. She was heaven in his arms, all curves and warm skin and wildflower perfume.

"You're ornery tonight," she said, pinching his nose. "What's gotten into you?"

He leaned back on the couch, resting his head on the back.

"It was a strange day."

"I know it was. You got to talk to that lady?"

"Lady? Yeah, I talked to the lady."

"What was she like?"

"Different," he said. "Not what I expected. I guess someone with her job isn't on duty 24/7. Even dominatrixes take Saturdays off apparently."

"Did she help you?"

"She swears up and down she doesn't know Father Ike. But I don't know. I just don't know..."

"You think she's lying?" Paulina asked.

"Not about that. But she's hiding something. She even told me she was hiding something before she shut the door in my face."

"That's brass, right there."

"Tell me about it."

"Was she pretty?" Paulina asked. He knew she was asking out of curiosity, not jealousy. Paulina had too much self-respect for something like that.

"She's not my type but she wasn't bad. I can see the appeal. Her appeal, not the appeal of what she does. I've been beat up. It's not fun. But she can make a couple thousand dollars a day just beating men up. And they're the ones paying for it. Crazy."

"Sounds like a good racket to me. Hat's off to her," Paulina said, tipping an imaginary hat.

"Now who's being ornery?"

"Hey, whoa," she said, reaching for the remote on the coffee table. "Archbishop Dunn's on the news."

She unmuted the television. Archbishop Thomas Dunn was on the screen. He was a tall white man in his late sixties, with a broad smiling, ruddy face and thick white hair with a widow's peak.

Paulina leaned forward, elbows on her knees. Cyrus sat back, waiting to be unimpressed.

A young pretty reporter had caught the man outside St. Louis Cathedral.

"Your Excellency, can you confirm that a priest has been found dead on a church property?"

"Unfortunately, I can confirm that. Out of respect for the family, we are not commenting further, though we are asking the faithful of New Orleans for their prayers during this difficult hour. And please, pray for your pastors. Even called by God, this can be a stressful, thankless vocation. Depression, burnout, they can take their toll on all of us."

"The exact cause of death has not been disclosed by police, but a firearm was found at the scene. Could you—"

"Thank you, that will be all." The archbishop was already walking away, back into the cathedral.

"Useless," Cyrus said. He took the remote from her and turned the TV off. He pulled her close. "How you feeling, baby?"

She rested her head on his chest. "I just keep trying to focus on all the good Father Ike did. There's nothing else I can do except pray for him. And pray for you."

His phone buzzed on the table. He ignored the first ring, but knew he couldn't ignore the second. Paulina knew, too. She passed him his phone.

A 504 number. He answered. "Tremont."

"Mr. Tremont, this is Sister Margaret at St. Valentine's."

He sat up. "Thanks for calling me back, Sister. I guess Detective Naylor told you I'd be calling about Father Ike."

"She did, yes, sir."

"I'm very sorry about Father Ike. I know you were old friends."

"Thirty years," she said, a crack in her gentle voice. "I was hoping you would come by tonight."

"Tonight?" It was past ten o'clock. Paulina was clearing their glasses from the table.

"Yes, I did something I wasn't supposed to do," Sister Margaret said. "I went into Ike's apartment here at the clergy house. He has a sister in DC, and I wanted to talk to her. I met her once years ago and thought...well, I'm sure you understand."

"Did you see something in his apartment?" Cyrus's heart was racing now, hard as it had when Paulina's heels had been on his back.

"I did, Mr. Tremont. I don't know what it is but I think you should come take a look at it."

"I can do that, Sister. I'll be right there."

Cyrus kissed Paulina goodnight and it did his heart good that as he pulled away from her house, she was still standing on the stoop, watching him go and waving. The only other woman who'd ever watched his car drive away was his mother. He took it as a good sign he'd found a woman who could love him that hard and wasn't afraid to show it.

He held onto that vision of her in the porch light, her arms wrapped around herself until she raised one hand to her lips to blow him a kiss goodbye. He held onto it all the way to St. Valentine's.

The church itself was a nice one—a beautiful brick structure about two hundred years old—but the clergy house wasn't much to look at. Built in the late '60s or '70s, he'd guess. Square and squat. Not much to distinguish it, except for the two front windows on either side of the porch. They were stained-glass, but the colors were faded and hazy.

Cyrus knocked softly on the front door. He waited, ready to knock again, louder, when he heard the rattle of keys and locks, and the door opened to reveal a small round woman in a gray habit and a tired smile on her face.

"Mr. Tremont, thank you for coming," she said. When he gave her his hand to shake, she took it in both her hands and held it a moment. She seemed to be on the verge of a breakdown.

"Of course, Sister," Cyrus said as she ushered him into the house. The staircase in the foyer was carpeted red, with a dark wooden bannister. "You and Father Ike were good friends?"

"I run the house here," she said. "He's been living here ever since he came to the city, almost fifteen years. He was very kind to me. Never took me for granted." She lowered her voice. "I can't say the same about some of the others who've graced these halls with their holy and anointed selves." A sarcastic sister. He liked that.

"Was he close with any of the other priests in the house?"

"No. There are only two other men living here now, both new arrivals. Father Adamu arrived from Kenya only three weeks ago. The other, Danilo Lucas, is a twenty-one-year-old seminarian from Brazil. He's in his first semester at Notre Dame, at school from dawn 'til dusk. I don't believe he's even met Isaac yet."

"Did Father Ike have any close friends?"

She looked up, almost an eye roll. "The Archbishop."

"Shit. Sorry." So much for that line of questioning. No way was he going to the Archbishop. Katherine would lose her job in a minute.

"I understand." She smiled kindly. "They're old friends from seminary. They went hunting together every

November. Frankly, I don't know anyone who knew him better than I did."

"I believe that."

"You saw him on television tonight?" she asked. Cyrus nodded. "He wants everyone to think Isaac was depressed. Isaac was not depressed. He loved his work, his life. At least I thought he did."

"You said you found something?" he gently prompted.

"Yes. This way."

Cyrus followed her up the steps. She had a nun's way of walking—head bowed low, clinging to the side-wall so people could pass her coming down the stairs with ease. A humble walk for a humble servant.

As they neared a door at the end of the hallway, Sister Margaret pulled her keys from a pocket in her voluminous skirt he hadn't noticed until her hand was deep inside it. That took him back to Catholic school—the sisters with their habits and all their hidden treasures. Hidden rosary beads, hidden keys. Hidden candy for students who impressed them. Hidden apples and packages of crackers for students who'd come to school hungry.

"This is his apartment?"

"It is. *Was*," she said, correcting herself. She paused outside the door and briefly rested her forehead against the frame in a moment of quiet grief.

She stood up again and opened the door. Inside Cyrus found a neat little living room, not much bigger than the sort he'd seen in your average three-star hotel suite. Green love seat, green and brown rug, coffee table, side table, a few books on a wooden bookcase with a bottle of Scotch and a shot glass on top. Either a brand-new bottle or Father Ike wasn't much of a drinker.

"The bedroom's through this door."

She led him to another room with little in it but a full-size bed covered in a red and white quilt, a closet, a floor lamp, a cross hanging on the wall and a nightstand.

"I found it in the nightstand when I went to look for an address book, phone numbers. I suppose no one has those anymore."

"You never know," Cyrus said. He pulled a pair of latex gloves from his pocket and snapped them on. Sister Margaret went into the living room and closed the door. He had no idea what he was looking for, no idea what he would find, but whatever it was, Sister Margaret clearly didn't want to see it again.

Bracing himself, Cyrus eased the top drawer of the nightstand open and saw something that would have jarred anyone, religious or not. It was metal with a round section connected to a curved tube of sorts only a couple inches long with a little padlock holding it together. Gingerly, Cyrus removed it from inside the drawer and found it surprisingly heavy. He turned it this way and that, examining it in the lamp light. If he'd been forced to guess, he'd say it was possibly some sort of metal codpiece, but who the hell wore codpieces in this century? And even if someone did wear a codpiece, it probably wouldn't have little metal spikes on the inside.

Metal spikes. Cyrus shuddered looking at the thing. Surely there was more to this thing than he understood. He looked around, saw an empty waste basket with a fresh plastic bag inside. He took the bag out, and carefully wrapped the metal object in it.

When he returned to the sitting room, he found Sister Margaret on the sofa, her head bowed in prayer.

"Well?" she asked when she finally looked up at him.

"I don't know what it is, either. I don't think I want to guess."

"Whatever it is, I think it's...well, it's not good."

"I'd guess you're right. I'll take this and ask someone who might know what it is."

"Who?"

He looked at the sister in her habit, her veil, with her rosary beads clutched in her small pale hand.

"Trust me," he said. "Nobody you know."

Chapter Nine

❦

Nora took Gmork back to Kingsley's, where she put him in his outdoor doghouse with food and water. She petted his head and told him she'd see him tomorrow. He started to whine as she walked away. "Sorry, buddy," she whispered. "Mamma needs get to laid."

Before Nora left the house, she ran upstairs to her bedroom, threw open the closet door, and pulled down a rosewood box on the top shelf. From it, she took out her white leather collar, wrapped in velvet, and slipped it in her bag.

She drove to the French Quarter and parked on a side street near the Hotel Richelieu. Of course Søren would get them a room at a hotel named for the most infamous cardinal in all of Catholic history.

Søren had left her a key at the front desk. As she made her way to the room, her excitement built to a fever pitch. Once, she'd seen a cat on a windowsill vibrating with excitement over the sight of a fluttering moth on the other side of the glass. That was her.

Her hand shook so hard she could barely get the key into the lock. But then it was in, and the knob was turning and she was inside the darkened room.

She locked the door behind her, dropped the key on the floor. She'd find it later when keys mattered again. Maybe tomorrow morning. Maybe never.

Her eyes adjusted quickly. The room wasn't completely pitch black—this was the French Quarter. The lights outside never went out. She slipped out of her red heels and stepped deeper into the room. No sign of Søren.

She walked barefoot to the dormer window that over-looked Chartres Street. Pedestrians passed by, some sober, some not. Some laughing, some not. Two lovers kissed in the glow of a streetlamp before stumbling off to darker corners for deeper kisses.

The floor creaked under the carpet behind her. Nora smiled.

Although she desperately wanted to turn to him, look at him, drink him in, she kept her eyes forward and down. She removed her collar from her bag, and dropped the bag onto the floor. She held her collar up in the palm of her hand.

He took it from her without a word and locked it around her neck.

When he lifted her hair and kissed her neck, Nora tensed. Instinct told her to panic, to pull the curtains closed and to step back into the dark where no one could see them together. Habits die hard, especially the habit of hiding that she was the mistress of a Catholic priest.

But now...Nora let go.

Søren brought his hands to her head and tied a sash around her eyes. Two cool fingers slipped under the straps of her black dress. He slowly brought the straps down her arms, down her body, down her legs, down to the floor. Black panties came next. In seconds, she was naked but for the blindfold. She felt the scrape of soft fabric on her bare back. He was still dressed.

She felt a hand between their bodies—her lower back and his waist—and the brief touch of cold metal. A belt buckle. Then the rush of sliding leather on bare skin as he pulled his belt out of the loops. It grazed her skin as he brought it around her.

She didn't need to see to know that he held the ends of the leather belt in both hands in front of her. First, he pulled it taut against her hips, forcing her back against him so that she couldn't run or flee if she wanted to, and no, no, no she did not want to, especially not when he kissed her naked shoulder. The kiss felt different. Off, somehow...like it wasn't him. She stiffened in fear and confusion. Had someone tricked her into coming here?

"Shh..." he whispered into her ear as he caressed the side of her face with two fingers. She turned her head toward him, into his hand, into his palm and it was like breathing in a gust of winter wind. Oh yes, this was him.

She relaxed and started to say something like, "You scared me, you monster," when he brushed his fingers over her lips, silencing her. She didn't need his words to tell her none were allowed. Not until he gave her permission to speak.

He kissed her shoulder again. A chill as delicious as a cool breeze on a steaming New Orleans night passed through her, down to her toes. Twenty-three years together, and he could still make her toes curl and give her goosebumps and scare her down to the bone. Especially when he lifted the belt to her neck and pulled her back against him again. The pressure on her throat wasn't painful—the collar protected her vocal cords—but it did change her breathing. Her breathing and his.

Søren held the belt steady, keeping the pressure constant, and she felt his chest panting and heard his breaths coming as quick as her own. It was a sacred thing to be loved by a sadist like Søren. Sacred like a sacrifice, like a vestal virgin offered to a god. What was a god, anyway, but one who held the power of life and death in his hands? By that measure, surely Søren qualified, if only when they made love.

A long minute—maybe two or three—passed before he lowered the belt from her throat. Nothing would happen quickly tonight. She understood this, and accepted it. Other men who'd gone a month without sex would rush to the deed quickly, no delay. Other men would have had her in bed already. Ah, but Søren wasn't other men. He wasn't other men and that's why after, twenty-three years, she was as alive to his touch as she'd been at seventeen. She tried to touch him with her hands and he caught her wrists in his iron grasp. She gasped, the sound loud enough to echo off the ceiling and drop to the floor.

"Shh..." he said again, not to silence but to soothe her. He brought her arms down to her sides and then pulled them behind her back, the fearsome grip unrelenting as he held her still in that spot, her back arching. They still stood by the window. Although she was blindfolded, there was a chance anyone passing by could see them. He knew this as well as she did. There was only one explanation for why he hadn't moved her from the window—Søren wanted them to be seen.

He pulled harder on her wrists and her back arched even more. He pressed his body to hers but didn't kiss her. Ten minutes or more had passed since she'd stepped foot into the room...yet he hadn't once kissed her on the mouth.

The cruelest thing he could deny her was himself.

In the blackness behind her blindfold, she'd lost track of what he'd done with his belt. But now she felt it as he pushed even closer to her. He'd slung it over his shoulder, and the cold metal buckle tickled her back. That he still had it with him, hadn't dropped on the floor meant he wasn't done with it yet.

Søren released her wrists, but only long enough to wrap the belt around them. Using the belt as a leash, he pulled her backward into the room, taking her slowly, very slowly, a step at a time to where-she-didn't-know. Likely the bed. She wondered if anyone out on the street had seen the sight of the naked, blindfolded woman and the statuesque blond man behind her? Let the whole world watch if it wanted. What did they have to be ashamed of, now?

He brought her to the bed. The heavy fabric of the duvet brushed the back of her thighs. He took the belt off her wrists, and blood rushed back into her grateful fingers. When he took her wrist in hand again, it was gently this time, though his purposes were no less nefarious than before. He brought her hand to his crotch and pressed her palm into his erection. She felt the hardness, the thickness, the long length of it even though the thick denim of the jeans he almost always wore when riding his Ducati.

With her palm still against him, he opened his pants and she took him in hand, nearly moaning from the sheer pleasure of his skin on her skin. He pushed his hips into her grasp and she stroked him from base to tip, tip to base, back again and again. A month apart, choking her with the belt...it was a miracle he wasn't inside her already, a miracle she hadn't begged for it either.

His hands came to her shoulders, and he pressed her down to the rug on the floor. She knelt there, trapped between him and the bed. When he nudged her mouth with the tip of his cock, she opened wide to take it into her throat. In the small space between his hips and the bed, she could barely move her head an inch. No matter. She didn't have to. He slipped his hands into her hair and held her while he moved in and out of her mouth.

Nora moaned in pleasure. She had missed this...the taste of him, the scent of him, the sheer force of him. While sucking him, she slid her hands up his thighs and to his stomach where she caressed him under his shirt. Caressed and then scratched him with her fingernails, digging in, not afraid to hurt him. Taking such a liberty was a risk and one sure to be punished. But the punishment was even sweeter than the crime. He grabbed her wrists once more and held them locked together behind her head. This was brutal mouth fucking. He even lifted his knee and rested it on the mattress by her head, imprisoning her in that tiny space between him and the bed.

Søren was a man of uncommon desires. Nothing aroused him more than inflicting pain on a willing victim. The chronology was usually linear—pain first, arousal after, sex as the finale. But in his more sadistic moods he managed to combine the three into one. If the sex was rough enough to cause her pain, it would fuel his arousal. She might be trapped while he fucked her mouth all night.

Nora heard him inhale sharply and while it was a small sound, to her it was more erotic than another man's loud moaning, and she would have smiled if her mouth weren't otherwise occupied. There was nothing like the triumph of making a man like Søren lose control, if only for the space of one gasp, one groan.

He pulled out of her mouth so quickly she nearly fell forward on the floor. She caught herself with her hands and sat there, waiting and obedient, her hair falling into her face. He stood at her side and twined one hand into her hair again, lifting her gently by the long locks and bringing her to rest her cheek against his thigh.

This was bliss. She was his again, his slave and his servant and his slut. Her lips were already swollen, her throat raw, her knees aching.

His grip on her hair tightened. He pulled—not hard but firmly—and she knew he wanted her to stand. She moved into a kneeling position again, tucking her toes under and rising straight up off the floor, a skill she'd learned at his knee when she was young and had never forgotten.

When she came to her feet, he turned her toward the bed. With the tips of his fingers alone, he pushed her forward until her face rested against the duvet. She placed her hands on the bed by her head as he used his bare feet to spread her legs apart.

A snap. She flinched. He hadn't struck with the belt. Not yet. For now, he was merely using it to get her attention.

He had it.

"Thirty-four," he said, and that was all he said. Thirty-four...that was how many nights he'd been gone. It was also how many times he would belt her. She'd belted enough of her clients to know he would double it in his hand to shorten the length and make it easier to control. And with the first strike right on her upper right thigh, she knew she was right. When it came to a sustained beating, precision was far more important than power.

The second strike was far harder than the first, and she

buried her mouth against the bed to silence her cries of pain. They were in the middle of a bustling neighborhood in a hotel with dozens of guests in the rooms around and under them. Screaming was discouraged...but not forbidden. This was the French Quarter. These things happened.

The blows built and built upon her ass and thighs. She breathed harder, moaned softer. She'd lost count at twenty. The impact barely registered anymore, only the fire, only the burning. Leather on flesh creates friction. Friction creates heat. The room was cold when she'd arrived. Now it felt like a hundred degrees.

Nora flinched as something landed next to her on the bed. She waited, but nothing happened. It was over. The beating done and the belt discarded. With her eyes hidden behind the sash, her sense of hearing heightened. She heard the sounds she wanted to hear—the rustle of fabric as Søren took off his clothes. When he came back to her, she felt his bare thighs against hers. He touched the welts he'd left on her body, probing them lightly with his fingers, tracing the raised edges, feeling the heat of them against his palm. Admiring his work, of course.

Nora let herself go limp as Søren pulled and turned her this way and that, until she lay on the bed on her back, hips at the edge of the mattress. He spread her thighs wide as he moved between them and pushed his fingers into her. He stroked upward, rubbing the front wall where she was so wet and tender and aching. He wetted his fingers inside her and massaged the wetness over her throbbing clitoris. Nora's shoulders nearly came off the bed as he touched every part of her that needed touching.

She heard his low mocking laugh and fought off the urge to "accidentally" kick him. It was his fault she was this desperate. A whole month? Was the man trying to kill her? He pressed the tip of his cock at the entrance of her body, and pushed in slow, deep, and hard and she groaned in relief.

She arched as he filled her, stretching her out and open. A month without him inside her and he was big enough to hurt, but it didn't hurt because she wanted him so much. She'd been wet and ready for him from the second he shoved his cock into her throat, and she was even wetter now as he moved on top of her. He took her wrists in his hands and held them hard into the bed. It hurt, and she groaned in her pleasure at the pain.

Søren still hadn't kissed her on the mouth. She would have begged for it if she'd been allowed to speak. He hadn't given her permission, so she suffered in silence as he pounded into her. Absolute torture that she couldn't tell him how good his big thick cock felt in her pussy, how much she'd missed him, how she'd fantasized about this moment when they were together again.

Since she couldn't speak with words, she let her body tell him everything he needed to know. Nora lifted her hips, pushing them into him, taking every inch of him until she couldn't take anymore. It was all she could do, lying helpless on the bed, held down by his impossibly strong hands on her wrists. But she wasn't completely helpless...

She contracted her vagina around his cock as hard as she could. He gasped, and she grinned, triumphant. A short-lived triumph. He released her wrists, dug his hands into her hair and held her immobile underneath. His thrusts were vicious, stabbing, and split her wide open. She felt his hot breath on her shoulder.

"I missed your cunt," he breathed into her ear. Nora

gasped again. A month without a word from him, and that was the first thing he said to her?

Terrible man. She adored every inch of his wicked body.

He held her down and fucked her. Maybe they'd make love later. Maybe it would be tender and sweet—as tender and sweet as any sadist could make love—but she needed fucked first, and he needed to fuck her. Nora lifted her hips faster, pumping them with her heels dug into the bed until she was almost out of her mind with need. Søren reached between their bodies, found her clitoris, and stroked it with wet fingers. She stiffened, back arched, breasts pressed to his chest, and came with a near-silent grunt in the back of her throat.

She came around him in a thousand sharp contractions. Lost in her own pleasure, she barely noticed when he dug his fingers into the back of her neck, held her head to his chest, and came inside her. Only when he lowered her gently back down and pulled out of her did she feel the rush of hot semen on her thighs pouring onto the bed.

Søren lay with her, leg over her hip, every inch of his long body pressed close to her.

"I'll take your blindfold off now," he said, "but you have to promise not to laugh."

"Laugh at what?" she asked, and he answered by taking off her blindfold.

She raised a hand to Søren's face and stroked his brand-new blond and gray beard. She didn't laugh, but she did smile.

"I like it."

Chapter Ten

For the second time that day, Nora found herself giving a beautiful man a neck massage. She straddled Søren's lower back and dug her hands deep into the muscles of his neck and shoulders. He released a small groan of pleasure.

"You missed more than my cunt, I guess," she said.

He grinned, laughed softly. "I did," he said. "But especially that."

"Do I want to know what you've been doing for the past month?" She ran her fingers through his hair. It needed cutting, but wasn't quite out of control yet. She decided he looked like a well-groomed Viking with the beard and the longer hair.

"Riding. Thinking. Trying not to think."

"Did you play with anyone?"

"That is between me and Vegas."

He laughed and rolled over. She let him. Instead of straddling his back, she straddled his stomach. The bright streetlights of the French Quarter shone into the room.

She could see his face, his eyes, his smile. She bent and kissed him, then rubbed her cheek against his cheek.

"Mmm...abrasion play," she said. "I could get used to this."

He wrapped his arms around her and dragged her down to his chest. She was content to just lay there a good long while...until she remembered how mad she was at him.

Nora sat up again on his stomach and pointed her finger down at her face.

"Why did you leave us?" she demanded. "Kingsley's been a wreck. I've been a wreck. Even Juliette's been worried."

"I sent postcards."

"Yes. Blank ones."

"I didn't know what to write." He sounded almost sorry. Almost. "Just know every card meant 'I love you, I miss you, this is where you can find me.'"

"Find you? From a postcard? You didn't even take your phone with you. What if you'd gotten in an accident? What if the Hells Angels decided to beat you up and forced you to get tattoos and hepatitis?"

His brow furrowed. "Eleanor, what are you talking about?"

"Kingsley was worried the Hells Angels would force you to join their motorcycle club and commit crimes with them. And then he said something about tattoos and hepatitis. He's having a minor mental breakdown. Again."

"I didn't join the Hells Angels. But might have gotten a tattoo."

"You did not."

"I did." He smiled at her.

"I have begged to get a tattoo of the Jabberwocky on

my back for a decade, and you've told me 'no' every time. Why can you get a tattoo and I can't?"

"First of all—mine is very small. Second, you can't see your own back. I can. I don't want to be forced to make awkward eye contact with a creature from a demented children's book while I'm attempting to sodomize you."

Nora thought about that.

"All right, fair," she said. "Now show me your ink. What did you get? Virgin Mary surfing on your bicep? Flag of Denmark on your ass?"

He turned his arms, and she saw he had no ink on his biceps.

"Legs?" she asked. "Girly little ankle tattoo of my name surrounded by hearts and stars? Wait, tramp stamp?"

"A name, yes, but not yours," he said. He held out his left arm, wrist up. Nora took his hand in hers and moved his wrist into the light. In small but feminine script, one word was inked onto his wrist right under this thumb.

"'Fionn,'" Nora read aloud and smiled. She should have known. "You got your son's name tattooed on your wrist."

"I did."

"Why your wrist?" she asked.

"Touch it," he said. She raised her eyebrow but did what he said.

She placed one finger over the tattoo and immediately felt the throbbing of Søren's pulse under his skin.

His son. His heartbeat. His son and his heartbeat, combined and entwined.

Nora blinked. Two hot tears rolled down her face. She raised his wrist to her lips and kissed the name that was the name of his heart.

"It's your handwriting," Søren said.

"I thought that looked familiar. It's beautiful."

"You and Kingsley know I love you. You see me all the time. You have me in your lives. Fionn lives across the ocean. He doesn't know I exist. If the time comes and we meet again and I need to explain myself to him..." Søren took a breath. "I want him to know I always loved him, that's all."

"He'll know," she said, barely able to speak. Her words came out in a breath.

"I wanted it for me, too," he said. He laid his wrist against his chest, over his heart, his beautiful heart.

"I love you," Nora said.

"Still?" he asked.

She nodded. "Still." She took his hands in hers and held them to her heart, kissed them and let them go. She rested her palms on his chest to steady herself as she stared down at his face.

"Why *did* you leave?" she asked, not joking anymore. "It was so sudden. I woke up and you were just...gone."

He glanced away, his eyes staring out the window by the bed.

"Søren?"

"I don't know about you," he said, "but I could use a drink."

"A drink?" Nora said. "Where on earth would we get an alcoholic beverage at one in the morning in the French Quarter of New Orleans? Hmm..."

"I have a wild idea," Søren said.

They both tapped the sides of their noses, pointed at each other and said in unison, "Bourbon Street."

Ten minutes later they were dressed and walking the street of the French Quarter. They found a bar—couldn't miss one if they tried—and Nora ordered Jack and Coke for herself, a Tröegs' Double Bock for Søren. She made sure the bartender knew she was not a tourist. No watering down her cocktail.

When they had their drinks, they left and strolled down Bourbon toward Toulouse. Nora caught herself unable to stop glancing around to see if anyone was watching them.

"This is weird, walking with you at night in public."

He put his arm around her waist and even patted her twice on her hip, possessively. She liked it and it terrified her. Liked it, because this might have been the first time she and Søren had ever walked around like a normal couple in their own town. Before they'd had to run away to foreign countries to play man and wife. Terrified her, because she liked it so much and knew she shouldn't.

"You know you're still a priest, right? Even if they are making you take a leave of absence, you still have to behave."

"Why start now?" He pulled her a little closer and kissed her. A guy dressed as the pirate Jean Lafitte hooted his approval. Søren lifted his drink back in a salute.

Nora kept glancing at him out of the corner of her eye. This was a Søren she didn't know. And it wasn't just the beard. Although the beard was definitely intriguing.

"What do you think?" He raised his chin, and she patted his cheek.

"Very sexy. Very distinguished. Midlife crisis looks good on you."

"Crisis," he said. "From the Greek '*krisis*' and '*krinein*,' meaning 'decision' or 'to decide.'"

"So a midlife crisis is a midlife decision-making time?"

"Precisely," he said.

"You have a big decision to make."

"Several, actually."

"What does that mean?"

"I'll show you."

He took her hand and led her off Bourbon and up Saint Peter Street.

"Where are we going?" she asked.

"You'll see."

They walked about two blocks until Søren stopped suddenly in front of a house, an exquisite pale blue camelback with white plantation shutters on the four front windows.

From the front door hung a realtor's lockbox.

Nora nodded slowly as she put two and two together. She put her hand to her forehead.

"Kingsley..." she said with a growl.

"My sentiments exactly."

"He said he bought you a 'little' present, a trinket. That is not a trinket. That is a house."

"Shall we go in?" he asked.

"Lead the way," she said.

Søren punched in a code on the lockbox, which released the door key.

"He doesn't know you know about this, does he?" Nora asked. "He told me to tell you he had a present for you."

"He doesn't know I know," Søren said.

"How did you find out?"

"Two days before I left, I was with him. He was sleeping when his phone buzzed. I was worried it might be Juliette, so I glanced at it. A message from a realtor giving him the lockbox code. It included the MLS number and a very nice message from the agent saying, 'I think your retired priest friend will love it. And if he doesn't, I'll take it.'"

"Retired priest friend?"

"Yes, apparently I'm retired now. At fifty-one. Either Kingsley was lying to her or engaging in some very wishful thinking."

Wishful thinking. Nora had no doubt.

Søren put the key in the lock and opened the door. He went inside first and turned on the lights for her. Nora followed.

"Wow," she said as she stepped into the entry hall. On each side of the hall was an arched doorway. To her left was an empty sitting room, empty but for an elegant love seat and an antique wooden music stand.

"Music room?" she asked.

"I believe it's where my piano is supposed to go," he said.

To the right was a larger sitting room, a parlor decorated in pale blue paint set off by bright white crown molding and a white fireplace. Gilt-framed winter landscapes hung on the walls. Chestnut leather chaise lounge. A round table with an elaborately carved pedestal and matching chairs. A crystal chandelier.

"He never does anything by halves, does he?" Søren asked.

"If this room were a man, I'd ride its cock until it snapped off."

Søren raised his chin and looked down at her.

"I'm just saying it's really nice," she said. "I like it."

"Oh, but there's more..." Søren led her down the central hallway. "Guest bedroom."

She loved the guest room immediately. A queen canopy bed with diaphanous white curtains hung from the iron frame. A white fireplace, the mantel covered in unlit candles. A leather armchair by the fireplace. A steamer trunk full of secrets at the foot of the bed.

"Simple. Elegant. Great bed for bondage," she said. "I'll take it."

They passed to the next door.

"Formal dining room," Søren said and flipped on the switch to display the dining table for six—Søren, Kingsley, Juliette, Céleste, and her, plus one guest. Cream damask wallpaper in a fleur-de-lis pattern. An antique China cabinet large enough that the top of it nearly scraped the eight-foot ceiling.

"This is getting ridiculous," Nora said.

"We're not even done yet," Søren said. Down the hall again, next door. "Breakfast room."

"You have your own room just for eating breakfast?"

"Apparently the kitchen is not good enough for coffee and toast anymore."

Nora peeked into the room. A smaller version of the dining room with a table only for two. Silver-gray wallpaper and a small sideboard.

"Who's gonna cook? You or Kingsley?" she asked.

"He does make good crêpes." Søren led her to the gleaming bright white kitchen. White cabinets. White tile floors. Stainless steel appliances.

"Not bad," Nora said. "Still doesn't make me want to learn how to cook though. What's the backyard like?"

She pointed at the French doors leading out of the kitchen to the backyard.

"Enclosed courtyard," he said and took her to the door. He hit a lightswitch, and Nora saw a small in-ground swimming pool appear in the dark before Søren flipped the light off again.

"Damn. I'm kind of afraid to ask about the bathroom. I assume there's an enormous claw-foot bathtub in there, gilt mirrors, and a year's supply of lube?"

"Not in the hall bathroom, but in the master bath, yes. Let me show you the master bedroom. It's ludicrous."

"Kingsley put the 'master' in master bedroom?"

"I have no idea where you buy St. Andrew's Crosses in New Orleans but he must have found a supplier. Oh, and the handcuffs are engraved."

"With what?"

"The phrase '*la douleur exquise.*'"

La douleur exquise meant literally "the exquisite pain," a French phrase with a rather nebulous meaning. Kingsley had told her it could mean the pain of loving someone you can never truly have or the pain of being hurt by the one you love. A good motto for anyone in love with a Catholic priest who also happened to be a sadist.

Søren started to open the door opposite the dining room, and Nora stopped him with a hand over his.

"You don't want to see it?" he asked. "It's a sight to behold."

"I'm sure it is," she said. "But that's your room with King. He'd probably prefer I stay out of it."

Søren took his hand off the doorknob. He leaned back against the closed door and Nora leaned back against the opposite wall. The house was old and the hallway narrow. Her toes touched Søren's.

"You approve?" Søren asked.

How could she not? Pale blue walls with white trim, snowy landscapes, crystal chandeliers... In this sultry southern city where it was never not summer, Kingsley had created for Søren an oasis of winter.

"It's perfect," Nora said. "King can remodel my house next. He obviously loves you a lot more than I do."

Søren laughed ruefully, looking up at the ceiling, eyes

on a brass lantern light fixture probably original to the house.

"You're not going to tell him 'no,' are you?" Nora asked, more than slightly horrified. "He'll be devastated if you don't take the house. And it's not that big of a house. Probably cost under a million."

"Under a million." His tone was dry as fine-grit sandpaper.

"Is that the problem? Too extravagant?"

He didn't answer at first. Nora searched his face for any hint of what he was thinking, feeling, but his eyes were stormy gray, and the clouds were hiding his thoughts from her.

"I have two Ph.Ds. I speak seventeen languages. I have over thirty years of work experience—teaching, pastoring, and leading a church congregation," Søren said. "I don't need taken care of. Just because I'm on a forced leave of absence for a year doesn't mean I need Kingsley to support me emotionally, spiritually, or financially."

"Ah," Nora said. "So this is your male pride talking. You don't want Kingsley playing Sugar Daddy while you're out of a job."

"I'm suspended. One year only. I can go back in ten months and two weeks."

"And what are you going to do for the next ten months and two weeks? Live with me? We tried that, remember? You moved out of the Jesuit house and in with me, and it was one week before you disappeared. Do I snore? Is that it?"

"Eleanor."

"What are you going to do? Seriously? Have you thought about it?"

These were important questions, and she'd much rather be having sex with him than asking them.

"I can get a job. I can teach piano lessons. I can work as a translator. Hospitals are desperate for trained translators. I can—"

"You can take the gift Kingsley is giving you and actually enjoy a year off? Spend time with me, him, Juliette and Céleste, and the new baby. Catch up on your sleeping, your reading. Take a Pilates class."

He narrowed his eyes at her.

"Okay, skip Pilates," she said. "I do. You know, I think you're forgetting something very important here."

"Do tell," he said.

"You inherited a massive trust fund when you were eighteen and you gave every cent of it to Kingsley. You can't let him do one nice extravagant thing for you in return?"

"He set up a trust fund for Fionn. That's more than enough."

"God, you're stubborn," she said.

He glanced away again and Nora saw a flash of something in his eyes, an expression she rarely if ever saw on his face.

"What are you afraid of?" she asked him.

"I want it."

"You want the house?"

He nodded.

"It's okay to want things," she said. "I've made a career of it."

"Vow of poverty since I was eighteen. And if you think a vow of chastity is hard to keep..." He paused, looked away, then asked, "What if I can't go back? What if I'm too happy here?"

"Too happy would be a good problem to have."

"I'm not sure I should get to be that happy."

"You fathered a child with a married woman, who you had permission to be with from both me and her husband. She wanted a kid. You gave her one. You didn't rape anyone, murder anyone. You'd didn't even steal. And you're only suspended for one year. Even the Jesuits don't think it's that big of a deal."

"There's more to my punishment than I told you."

"Ah, let me guess. Therapy."

"Yes."

God help that poor therapist.

"Spiritual counseling?" she asked.

"Yes."

"Forty lashes?"

"You wish," he said. "I have to attend Mass every day when possible."

"That's all?"

It wasn't all. Søren went silent for a moment, and Nora braced herself.

"I also have to present a notarized letter from Grace and Zachary stating that they want me to have no formal or informal relationship with Fionn."

Nora stared at him, wide-eyed. "Are you serious?"

"In the old days, it was normal for the Church to keep a priest's child a secret, to cover the whole affair up. Things are changing, as they should. If a Catholic priest fathers a child, he's expected to leave the priesthood to be a part of his child's life. If I'm going to be allowed back in the Jesuits, Grace and Zachary have to make it clear—and legally binding—that they don't want or need me in Fionn's life."

"They'll write the letter if you want them to," she said.

"It's just words on a piece of paper. They would never stop you from checking on him, you know."

"I know," he said. "I think. But the time may come when he knows. How will he feel when he finds out I picked the Church over him? That I asked to be exiled from his life?"

"It's only a piece of paper," she said. "If you go back to the Jesuits, they'll do what they have to even if they don't mean it."

"*If*," he said. "Even you're not sure I'll go back."

She tapped the toe of his shoe with the toe of hers.

"How are we?" he asked, meeting her eyes again.

A serious question, so she took a second before answering. It deserved serious thought and a serious answer.

"We're good," she said.

"Solid?"

"Rock solid."

"You're certain?"

Nora smiled. "You don't think we are?"

"I keep waiting," he said, "for you to finally get angry at me."

"I get angry at you all the time. I was highly perturbed at you earlier today when I was horny, and you were not there to do anything about it."

"Angry about Fionn."

She knew that's what he'd meant.

"We've talked about it a hundred times. Hard talks. Serious talks."

"Talked about it, yes. Never fought about it."

"I love Fionn as much as you do. If you're waiting for me to be angry that you wanted a kid and I didn't, so you found a way to have a kid without trying to make me into something I'm not? You'll have to wait a long time."

"Still," he said, "something tells me it's coming. Storm clouds gathering. I can see them. Can't you?"

"Stop being so paranoid. You're as bad as Kingsley."

She tapped his toe again with hers.

"The next ten months will be hard," he said. "If I'm going to make it through this, I'll need you."

"You have me," she said. "And Kingsley. Unless you tell him you can't accept the house. Then he'll kill you, and I'll help him bury the body."

"How can I accept a gift this extravagant? I'd be in his debt."

"Allow me to explain the submissive mindset to you, Master Søren, because you clearly know nothing about it."

"Enlighten me, Mistress Nora." He waved his hand, indicating she had the floor.

"I know you think Kingsley gave you this house because he's trying to coddle you or something while you're going through a rough time. You're worried accepting the house will throw off the balance of power. But that's not how it works. I've had male clients give me tens of thousands of dollars in jewelry, vacations, cars...an Aston Martin..." She crossed herself as she spoke that hallowed name. "That's what submissives do. They shower their masters and mistresses with tribute—gifts of worship, adoration, and gratitude—as they should."

"Is that so?"

"It's so. This house is not the gift of a man who sees a crying child and buys him an ice cream to cheer the kid up. This is the gift of a devoted submissive trying to show —in any way he can—that he worships the very ground you walk on. You turn down the gift of this house, you will be throwing Kingsley's love and devotion and submission to you in his face."

Søren said nothing. Then he smiled.

"Well, when you put it that way."

"The way you handle it is this—he gives you the house, you look at it, nod, and say 'I suppose it'll do.' Then you pat him on the head, fuck him blind, and never mention that he gave you the house again. He'll secretly hope for a feast of gratitude. Meanwhile, you'll dole out mere crumbs. And he will eat those crumbs off your fingertips."

Søren reached out and patted her on the top of the head.

Nora laughed, a laugh that bounced down the hall. She grabbed his hand and held it tight.

"Now I just have to figure out a housewarming gift for you," she said.

They locked the house up and walked back to the hotel. As they laid down in bed together, Søren wrapped her in his arms and pulled her to his chest.

"I'm still your priest, aren't I, Little One?" he asked.

She kissed his chest over his heart. She knew if she could cut his chest open and look at his heart, she'd see her name tattooed across it, right next to Kingsley's and Fionn's and God's. "You'll always be my priest."

Chapter Eleven

Sunday morning, when all God's children ought to be in church, Cyrus was trying to hunt down a dominatrix.

He'd stopped by Edge's Garden District house/palace again, and while Nora Sutherlin's black German Shepherd came to the gate and glared at him, his owner didn't come with him. When he buzzed the intercom, no one answered.

Cyrus considered any time after 8:30 in the morning safe for making phone calls. At 8:31, he'd called Nora's cell phone number that had been on the card she'd given him. The call went straight to voicemail. He'd asked her to call him back, but after waiting over two hours, he decided to try again.

She picked up this time. It was 10:30.

"Ah, Ms. Sutherlin," he began. "This is Cyrus Tremont."

"Good morning," she said. "Isn't it? I think it's good." Then she laughed.

"It is for somebody," he said.

"How can I help you?" she asked.

"I have kind of a weird favor to ask."

"That sounds interesting. Ask it."

"If I bring you something, can you tell me what it is?"

"What is it?"

"If I knew what it was, I wouldn't have to bring it to you, would I?"

"True. But can you give me a hint? Animal? Vegetable? Criminal?"

"No, ma'am."

"Send me a pic?" she said.

"I'd rather not have a record of this."

"Come over then. I'm in the French Quarter. Le Richelieu Hotel. Suite 301."

"I'll be right over."

"If a well-groomed Viking opens the door, don't worry. He's with me."

She hung up before Cyrus could ask about the Viking. He had a feeling she was trying to freak him out.

It was working.

Turned out she hadn't been kidding about the Viking. When Cyrus knocked at the door to room 301, a tall, broad-shouldered blond man with a neatly-trimmed beard answered the door. He looked like he'd pillaged his share of villages.

"Mr. Tremont, I presume?"

"The Viking, I presume?"

The Viking smiled and Cyrus knew he'd seen this man somewhere before... It came to him—this was the guy arm-wrestling Kingsley Edge in the photograph on Edge's mantel. Didn't have the beard in the picture, though.

The blond held out his hand to shake. Cyrus took it, a little apprehensively, worried this was the sort of big guy who had to prove how tough he was by crushing fingers.

But no. While firm and confident, the handshake didn't hurt.

Cyrus stepped into the room. He figured the Viking explained Nora's good mood. He saw an unmade bed in the other room, clothes on the floor, his and hers. Cyrus felt a pang of jealousy. Two more months, he told himself. He just had to make it two more months until the wedding.

"Is that Cyrus?" Nora's voice came from behind a half-closed bathroom door.

"I assume so," the Viking said, raising his voice so she could hear him through the door.

"Nora?" Cyrus called to her. "I just need to show you this thing really quick. Then I'll leave you two alone."

"Show the Viking. If he doesn't know what it is, neither will I."

Cyrus heard water sloshing in the bathtub. Reluctantly, he pulled the Nike duffel bag off his shoulder and unzipped the it.

"Well?" Nora called again from the bathroom. "What is it?"

"A male chastity device," the Viking said loud enough for Nora to hear in the bathroom.

"There's your answer, Cyrus. You're welcome."

Cyrus cleared his throat. "You can't just tell me it's a...*that*...and then expect me not to have follow-up questions."

"What kind of chastity device is it?" Nora called out from the bathroom. "A PA-5000? A CB-6000? Custom?"

"That I don't know," the Viking said. "That's your area of expertise, not mine. And I'd rather not touch it."

"Can you bring it in here, Cyrus?" Nora asked.

"Are you dressed?"

"No, but it's a bubble bath. You can't see anything."

Cyrus looked at the bathroom door and back at the Viking, at the door, at the Viking. The Viking only gestured with his coffee cup toward the door as if it were the most natural thing in the world for a man to let another man hang out in the bathroom with his girlfriend.

Cyrus generally tried to avoid making big sweeping generalizations about groups of people, but he was starting to get the feeling kinky people were a little on the eccentric side.

"So I should just go in?" Cyrus said to the Viking.

"You were invited," the Viking said.

"All right. Going in. I'll just take this bag of Satan's toys with me."

The Viking grinned behind his cup of coffee. Cyrus went to the bathroom door and leaned in a little while rapping one knuckle lightly on the frame.

"Nora?"

"Come on in. Show me what you've got."

She hadn't been kidding. The bathtub was full of bubbles that covered her all the way to her neck.

"Sorry to bother you at...bath time?"

"No bother," she said. "Søren and I just finished breakfast. We weren't doing anything that couldn't be interrupted."

"Wait. What's his name? 'Sir'?"

"Close enough," she said, grinning. "Søren. A Danish name. *S*, slashed *O, R, E, N*. Looks like 'SORE-in,' but Danes say 'SIR-in.' Almost rhymes with 'stern.'" She giggled for some reason. "You can put that in your notes. Don't forget the slash. He hates when people forget the slash."

"Got it," he said, fumbling with whatever the hell a

"slashed *O*" was supposed to look like. "He's not really a Viking, is he?"

"Nah." She stuck her foot out of the water and rested it on the bathtub ledge. "I'm only teasing him because he grew a beard while he was gone for a month on a cross-country road trip. I've never seen him with a beard before. I kind of like it. The Scandinavians were some of the first lumberjacks in America. We can thank them for deforesting most of the Pacific Northwest. Thanks, assholes!" She'd raised her voice for that last part.

"Judge not lest ye be judged, *Kraut*," the Viking called back.

"Ohh...that hurt," she said, wincing. "He always goes straight for Hitler. So unfair. Hitler was Austrian."

"You two married?" Cyrus asked. The question made her laugh.

"No, why do you ask?"

"No reason. Look, I won't take up any more of your time," Cyrus said. "If you just take a look at this."

Nora rose up out of the water to look inside Cyrus's duffle bag, giving him a good peek at her wet bare back.

"Interesting," she said. "Can you hand me a washcloth?"

Cyrus glanced around, found a stack of white washcloths and passed one to her. She wrapped it around her fingers and lifted the whatever from the bag.

"Have you seen one of those before?" Cyrus asked.

"Not this one exactly," Nora asked, examining it. "Close, but this looks custom-made. Do you know anything about male chastity?"

"Only that it's not all it's cracked up to be."

She glanced up at him and smiled. Her make-up had been washed off. Her naked face looked young and vulnerable. But her eyes were something else entirely. This lady had seen things.

"Some dominants enjoy controlling a male sub's access to his own body. Punishing unauthorized erections and that sort of thing," she said. "It's not necessarily long-term chastity that's the goal. Maybe only a few hours or a night. Anyway, this is a nice cage. Very good work."

She sunk back into the bath, and the water sloshed and parted just enough that Cyrus could see the tops of her very full breasts.

"I'm going to go out there and take my chances with the Viking," he said.

She only smiled at him. "Have some coffee. I'll be right out."

Cyrus retreated to the suite. He saw the unmade, very well-used bed, but no Viking. He poured himself a coffee. When he was sipping it, he noticed the door to the terrace. The Viking was seated outdoors at a black iron table reading the Sunday paper.

Nora stepped out of the bathroom wearing the hotel's white bathrobe, LE RICHELIEU embroidered in gold thread over the breast pocket.

"Let's go outside," she said, picking up a chair to take onto the terrace. "Can you grab the door?"

Cyrus stopped her. "Let me carry that."

"Oh my," she said. "Aren't you chivalrous?"

"Just polite," Cyrus said.

"That was the beginning, you know," Nora said, holding the glass door open for Cyrus. He watched as Søren, the Viking, put his paper down on the table and folded it neatly. One of those types. A little anal. A bit too proper. Secret wild side. Cyrus knew the type. Used to be the type.

"The beginning of what?" he asked Nora.

"Chivalry. The subculture of male submission," Nora said as she sat in the open chair, coffee cup cradled in both hands. Cyrus set his chair down and sat.

Nora continued, "It began in the courts of medieval Europe. Supposedly. Knights would choose a lady—almost always married because that was more proper—and he would devote himself to serving her chastely. Poems, heroic deeds, gifts... It was the start of the idea of Woman Superior and Man Inferior—not a common concept you find in most cultures outside a handful of matriarchal societies."

"So you're saying kink comes from King Arthur," Cyrus said. "Crazy."

"I still have male subs who bring me gifts, write me poems, offer to do all sorts of things for me. One offered to have him killed." She nodded at the Viking.

"You never told me that," the Viking said, giving her a look. Same look Cyrus might have given Paulina if she said one of her exes had offered to kill him.

"I wanted to keep my options open," she said, winking at Cyrus.

The Viking picked up his coffee cup and drank from it, keeping an eye steady on her the whole time.

"I didn't expect to be having these conversations when I agreed to find out the cause of Father Ike's suicide," Cyrus said.

"Any new news there?" Søren the Viking asked.

"He called Nora before he shot himself, and he had that thing in his bedside table," Cyrus said. "That's all I got right now."

"Did you decide what it was precisely?" the Viking asked Nora.

"Some custom piece," she said. "Stainless steel cock blocker. With that thing on, no way would he be able to get an erection without agony. Like putting your dick in a spiked vice. I need one."

The Viking's brow furrowed. Cyrus crossed his legs.

"And kinky men really get into that?"

"Oh yeah," she said. Her green eyes went bright and wide. "I could tell you stories, Cyrus Tremont."

"Don't tell me any stories," Cyrus said. "No stories at all." The Viking chuckled.

"Wish I could help you more," Nora said.

"You could help me find Mr. Edge. I better ask him if he remembers giving your card to anyone down here."

"You can ask him," Nora said, "but I asked him yesterday and he says he didn't."

"I'd like to see him anyway," Cyrus said. "The right question can jog the memory. I was hoping you'd be willing to come by Ike's apartment with me. In case there's more kinky stuff there, and I don't know what it is."

Nora glanced at the Viking, as if asking him permission.

"May I ask a few questions first?" Søren said.

Cyrus tensed. "Yeah, of course."

"Eleanor said—"

"That's me, by the way," Nora said.

"I figured. Go on." Cyrus nodded at the Viking.

"Eleanor said you wouldn't tell her who hired you to look into Father Murran's suicide. You seem like a very decent man," Søren said. "But I need to know that before I let her get more involved. I'm sure you understand."

Cyrus did. He respected the man for wanting to protect his girlfriend.

"No one actually hired me," Cyrus said. "I'm doing this

as a favor for a friend of mine on the police force. She was told to drop any investigation into his death, just rule it a suicide, clean up and move on. And with no evidence of foul play, she can't really justify putting any man hours on the job. She asked me to dig a little, make sure there's nothing more at play."

"This is quite a favor she asked of you," Søren said.

"Father Ike and my fiancée were friends. They worked together at St. Agnes Middle School a couple years ago. For her sake, and a little curiosity on my part, I'll do some digging."

Nora looked to her lover, waiting for his verdict.

"I'll allow Eleanor to go with you today," the Viking said, finally rendering his verdict. "If you promise to keep her out of harm's way."

"I can promise you that," Cyrus said.

Nora leaned over and kissed her Viking's bearded cheek. "I want you home by five at the latest," he said. "We're going to Mass with Juliette and Céleste."

"So you're Catholic, too," Cyrus said.

"This is New Orleans," the Viking said, smirking. "Isn't everyone?"

Chapter Twelve

❧

Cyrus sat on a red sofa in the lobby and called Paulina. She answered on the third ring.

"Hey, baby," he said. "How's your morning?"

"Good Mass," she said. "Missed you there."

"Working. I'll try to hit evening Mass tonight."

"I'll go with you, if you want. When nobody's looking, I'll let you put your hand on my knee."

"You know I can't turn that down."

"You coming over now? I can fix lunch."

Lunch with Paulina sounded almost as good as his hand on her knee.

"I gotta check a couple things out," he said. "I just wanted you to know I'll be with a lady today."

"Is that so?" Paulina sounded amused. Better amused than angry.

Cyrus lowered his voice. "I told you about the woman who Father Ike tried to call before...she's going to be helping me a little today."

"This sex worker lady?"

"I just had coffee with her and her boyfriend. Judging by him, I'm not her type."

"What's her type?"

"She called him a 'well-groomed Viking.' It fit."

"Oh my...I might like to see a well-groomed Viking."

"Hey," Cyrus said.

Paulina laughed her sweetest laugh.

"You know I love you and trust you. If you need this woman's help, that's fine. Finding out what happened to Father Ike is top priority."

"You're right," Cyrus said. "You're always right."

"You know it," she said. A long pause. Cyrus tensed. "You worried about something?"

"When am I not?"

"This lady?"

"She's not bad," Cyrus said. "But she's no *you.*"

Paulina had insisted on counseling once they'd officially decided to be "a thing." The first thing the counselor told Cyrus was, *Tell her everything, even the stuff you don't want to tell her. Especially the stuff you don't want to tell her.*

"Cyrus, one of these days you're gonna have to get used to being around women again," she said. "Women who aren't me. Dr. Rourke said you should even try to make friends with a woman."

"You want me to be friends with a dominatrix?"

"You never know who God's gonna send into your life. The Creator can get real creative sometimes."

"That's for sure."

"Think on it," she said. "Maybe talk to that lady about it."

Cyrus looked up as Nora entered the lobby wearing the same black dress and red strappy heels as yesterday. Was she a fine-looking lady? Definitely. But what he felt for her wasn't attraction really, more like curiosity. He'd never met a woman quite that...what was the word he was looking for? *Weird?*

"We'll see," Cyrus said. "Gotta go, baby. Love you."

"Love you, too, Daddy. See you tonight."

Cyrus ended the call and stood up.

"'Baby,'" Nora said, grinning the way women did when they caught a man in the act of doing something they approved of. "That's cute."

He ignored that. "You want to ride with me or me with you?"

She raised an eyebrow. "What's your ride?"

"Black Honda CR-V. Yours?"

"Red Mustang convertible."

Cyrus thought about that.

"You drive."

Cyrus rode shotgun and didn't mind at all when Nora put the top down. It wasn't quite eighty yet, but it would hit it any hour now so they might as well enjoy the morning.

She slipped on a pair of black cat-eye sunglasses and headed out of the French Quarter.

"Kingsley first, I guess?" she asked.

"Might as well get it over with," Cyrus said.

"Don't worry about King. He's fine. He's just tense lately with Juliette about to have the baby."

"It's all right. I'm sure I'll be the same way when it's me and Paulina's turn."

"Paulina, pretty name. You two been together long?"

"Met two years ago, been dating about a year and a half. Engaged since May," he said. "How about you and your Viking? Søren or whatever his name is?"

"Been together off and on since I was twenty," she said.

"And you're not married?"

She grinned as she made a left turn at a stop sign.

"We aren't the marrying kind."

"How about Edge and his Missus?"

"I think King would marry Juliette if only to make things easier on their kids. But Juliette's dead set against it. Bad past experience."

"Ah, I get that," Cyrus said. "I'm about the only guy in town who handles domestics. Stuff I'd seen, damn. Marriage can get ugly fast."

"Domestics?"

They'd picked up speed, so Nora had to raise her voice. The wind whipped her black hair around her face, but it didn't seem to bother her. She looked good, a little wild like that.

"Yeah, that's what we call it in the business. Domestic cases—those are cheating husbands, gambling husbands, deadbeat dads who buy brand-new Ford F-150s while their kids are wearing clothes from St. Vincent's."

"How'd you get into that line of work?" she asked.

"Mmm..." Cyrus considered telling her the whole story but stopped himself. No need to be getting personal. "I was a cop for ten years. Got shot on the job and decided not to go back. I feel like I can help more people this way. Women and children, I mean. That's all I ever work for. Husbands don't hire me. Just wives or girl-friends."

"So you really are a knight-errant then?" she asked, glancing at him to smile.

"Been called worse."

She pulled up to the drive of Edge's 6th Street palace, and punched in the security code for the iron gates. When they parked inside, her dog ran to her, panting and wagging his tail. She pushed her sunglasses up on her head and reached for her dog.

"Sorry I abandoned you last night, boy," she said, going down on her knees to scratch the Shepherd's enormous black ears. "Mama had a date."

"He's a good-looking boy," Cyrus said. "Too bad he eats men."

Nora stood and tucked her fingers into her dog's collar and held him against her thigh.

"Hasn't eaten a man yet," she said. "But every time Søren walks by, he does start to drool. Then again, so do I." Nora winked at him.

Cyrus heard laughter and voices as they walked around the house. In the backyard, they found Edge standing in the shallow end of a swimming pool waiting to catch his daughter, who was perched on the edge of the pool in a pink swimsuit, pink arm floaties, and a pink swim cap over her curls.

Edge said something in French and the little girl laughed and then launched herself into her father's arms.

"You speak French?" Nora asked Cyrus.

"Three years of French in Action in high school. Don't remember a damn word."

"He said, 'Don't jump on me. You'll mess up my hair,'" Nora translated. "So of course she jumped on him."

"Kids," Cyrus said.

With his daughter in his arms, her skinny stick legs around his waist, Edge waded over to the side of the pool. He had on black sunglasses that he pushed up to his forehead.

"Hi, *Tata Elle*," the little girl said, waving.

"Hello, my fishy," Nora said. "You playing with Papa in the pool today?"

"Mama's taking nap number one," the little girl said. Edge laughed.

"Céleste, you remember Mr. Tremont, right?" Nora asked her.

"Hello, Miss Céleste," Cyrus said.

"*Bonjour, Monsieur* Tremont," she said. Even Edge grinned at that and kissed his daughter on her forehead.

"Can you do me a favor, sweetheart?" Nora asked. "Can you run into the house with Gmork and change his black collar to his pink collar? He told me he wants to wear pink like you today."

"Can we dry off first?" Edge said to his daughter. "*S'il ti plait?*"

"I'll help." Nora held out her hands, and Edge passed his daughter to her. With a big pink towel, Nora dried off the girl and sent her scurrying into the house with a playful swat on her tiny pink-clad bottom, the big dog right behind her.

Edge put his hands on the side of the pool and rose up and out of the water. Cyrus breathed a sigh of relief. He'd thought all Europeans wore Speedos, but Edge had on a pair of black swim shorts.

"Mr. Edge—" Cyrus began, but Edge held up a hand. He said something in French to Nora. Nora replied, also in French. Edge nodded. Nora said something else, smiled, then laughed. Edge replied in what Cyrus assumed was a universal language, that of the middle finger. Nora didn't seem shocked or insulted.

"Sorry," Nora said to Cyrus. "King, Cyrus Tremont. Cyrus, Kingsley Edge." Nora waved her hand between them. "Cyrus has a couple quick questions, then we're leaving. I promise."

"Get it over with," Edge said, still dripping wet. He

grabbed a towel off the stack and ran it over his wet hair. First, Nora in the bathtub. Now, Edge in the pool. Were these people ever dry?

"I know Nora told you about Father Isaac Murran's death," Cyrus began. "And that he called her minutes before his suicide. She doesn't remember giving anyone in New Orleans her business card. Did you happen to give one of her red cards to anyone down here at any point?"

"What was the number?" Edge asked.

"My 3969 number," Nora said.

"That was after you quit working for me," Edge said.

"Right," Nora said, nodding. "I had a different number when I was an Edge Enterprises employee." Cyrus jotted that down his black reporter notebook. "But I quit working for him and went solo—stopped seeing almost all my clients but for a handful of favorites. That lasted about two years, then we moved down here."

"When was that exactly?" Cyrus asked, though he already knew the answer from Nora. Just wanted to make sure...

"We bought this house..." Edge said, pausing to think. "...November, three years ago. Elle bought hers in December, same year. Yes?"

"Right," Nora said.

"I'd guess you came down here to house hunt before buying the place," Cyrus said.

"Of course," Edge said.

"Any chance you gave someone down here Nora's card during those trips?"

"I don't know why I would. Trust me, this city has plenty of sin without needing me to import it," Edge said.

"But you did, right?"

Edge shrugged. "I left most of my sin in New York. But I couldn't bear to leave it all back there."

"What about you?" Cyrus turned to Nora. "You remember giving your card to anyone when you came down here to house hunt?"

She exhaled heavily. "That was a quick trip three years ago. I was here less than a week." She rubbed her forehead as if trying to jostle a memory loose. "It's possible, I admit. But I wasn't looking for clients. I'm trying to think if I met anyone kinky and exchanged information."

"You didn't go to any clubs or anything?" Edge asked.

"No," Nora said. "Not that I remember. Although it is New Orleans. I might have had too much to drink one night and given out my number to everyone on Bourbon Street. I didn't. I think."

"Did you do any drinking while you were in town?" Cyrus asked her. She looked at him, lips pursed.

"What do you think?"

"Maybe you got drunk and gave everyone on Bourbon Street your card. Narrows it down."

"Nobody called me after my trip down here," she said. "That I do know. And if I give someone my card...they call me."

"A dead priest did," Cyrus said.

"A dead priest I never met in my life," Nora said.

"So...either you got drunk—" he said, pointing at Nora with his pencil, "—and maybe gave your card to everyone on Bourbon. Or Father Ike went to New York, and he could have gotten your card from..."

"Literally any kinky person in the city," Nora said.

"Great. Fantastic," Cyrus said dryly. "I'll ask Sister Margaret if he took any trips to New York. You ready?"

Céleste came running out of the house then with

Nora's big dog now wearing a hot pink collar around his neck.

"Much better," Nora said.

"Come swim with me," she said to the dog, pulling him by the collar to the pool.

"No dogs in the pool," Edge said two seconds before Céleste and the dog waded into the shallow end via the pool steps.

"Out, Gmork," Nora said. Her dog obeyed, climbed out of the pool, and promptly shook himself dry all over Edge, who took it with impressive stoicism.

"I never knew I could hate a dog," Edge said. "But I can."

"Bye, King," Nora said. "Bye, princess!"

Céleste waved goodbye to them.

"Thank you, Mr. Edge." Cyrus held out his hand, and Edge only hesitated a second before shaking it. As Cyrus and Nora were leaving the backyard, he saw Edge jump back into the water, swoop Céleste into his arms, and toss her squealing and laughing into the air.

"I'm gonna say something," Cyrus said to Nora. "And you're gonna forget I said it after I said it."

"Say it."

"That is one good-looking man."

"Rich, too."

"Do I want to know where the money comes from?"

"He had a trust fund," she said. "Sort of. He used it to buy buildings in Manhattan in the '90s. Sold them twenty years later for ten times what he paid for them. Oh, he's hung like a horse, too."

"We're one-hundred percent done talking about this."

"Talking about what?" Nora said.

"Thank you."

Nora sent Gmork back to his doghouse, which was only slightly smaller than Cyrus's first adult apartment.

"So, we go to Father Ike's place now?" Nora asked.

Cyrus paused. "Once you tell me what you all were saying about me in French."

"Believe it or not," she said, "we weren't talking about you at all. Kingsley asked how our Viking was. I said he was okay. Then I asked King how well he slept last night. Kingsley said he slept very well. I said I didn't sleep much. He flipped me off."

"That part I got. He mad you got some and he didn't?"

"I don't blame him," she said. "And trust me, if King has something to say about you, he'll say it in English."

They returned to her car. "Where to?" she asked.

"St. Valentine's," Cyrus said, and gave her directions.

"You know, we might never figure out how he got my card. We had hundreds printed."

"*We?*" Cyrus said. "You investigating this case now?"

"Wouldn't you be a little curious if someone you didn't know called you two minutes before shooting themselves in the head?"

"Probably. But this is my job. It's not yours."

"If Father Ike was kinky, he was one of us," she said, pointing at herself. "Somehow we failed him if he thought the only way out was suicide."

"Don't blame yourself," Cyrus said. "People make their own choices."

"True. But I want to help if I can."

"You're kind of friendly for a dominatrix," Cyrus said. "Where's the whip and chains?"

"You wanna see 'em?" She glanced at him over the top of her sunglasses.

He pointed at her. "You're trouble."

"Yeah, sorry." She pushed her sunglasses back on and faced forward, eyes on the road. "Old habits die hard."

"I hear that," he said, wincing.

"Oh...there's a story there." She laughed. "Spill it."

"Not telling it."

"I'll tell you mine if you tell me yours."

"You already told me yours," he said.

"Not all of it."

Cyrus laughed. He liked her. That was a fact. Whether he *should* like her...well, that he didn't know.

"I'll tell you something," Cyrus said. "Doctor's orders."

"Now I'm intrigued," she said. "Tell me anything you want."

"I've had...ah...issues in the past. With women."

"Issues?"

"Honesty issues," he said. "I'm seeing someone for all that. And it's helping. One of the things I'm supposed to work on is being truthful with the women in my life. No false pretenses, no lies. Not even white lies. So, you know, don't ask me something if you don't want an honest answer."

"Are you lying to me about something?"

"No, no, not that. Just...I'm supposed to have a female friend. A woman in my life who I'm not related to who I can confide in and be friendly with. Paulina said today you might be a good candidate for the job."

"Me? Why me?"

"Throw me in the deep end, I guess."

"And I'm the deep end?"

"You are definitely not the kiddie pool, lady."

They'd turned into construction traffic and slowed to a crawl. The sun was high and hot, so Nora hit the button to raise the convertible top. Once latched into place, she turned the A/C on. Suddenly it was cooler, darker, and much more intimate in the car.

"This is coming from a therapist, right?" Nora asked. "Sounds like it. What do they call it? Exposure therapy. Spiders freak you out, so they have you make friends with a spider. Women freak you out, so they have you make friends with a woman?"

"Something like that," he said. "Therapy was Paulina's idea. And when I say 'idea,' I mean 'order.'"

Nora grinned again. "So you used to play around a lot, then you met your dream girl, and now you're behaving yourself?"

"I did not play around," he said. "There was no playing. I made girls my second full-time job."

"Nice work if you can get it. I guess you got it."

"I got it," he said. Cyrus didn't say anything and neither did Nora. She seemed to be waiting for him to go on. "I was not a great guy back then."

"No judgment here. I've been the bad guy, too," she said. "And trust me, you've got nothing on King. Even after he met Juliette, it took him a long time to settle down. Céleste finally did the trick. That man is lucky to be alive. In his heyday, it was a different girl—or guy—every day almost." She didn't sound like she was joking.

"That's almost better than what I was doing," Cyrus said. "A new girl every day and nobody really gets hurt because nobody expects anything. Me? I'd play the girls, play with their minds, their hearts, make them crazy about me, make them think we had something real. Then I'd get bored, pick a new girl, start all over. Run down my list..." he said, miming an imaginary list of women's names. "Get to the bottom. Start at the top again. Apologize. Flowers. Beg for forgiveness. Win them over."

"Power trip."

"You got it. Therapist thinks—I do, too—that it's because my father died of a heart attack when I was fifteen. Tough time to lose your dad. I started looking for any way to feel better, to feel in control. I found girls."

"What changed? You don't seem like much of a player anymore."

"I got shot," Cyrus said. "I was off-duty, rolled up on a bunch of squad cars outside a gas station. Owner got shot during a robbery. They had it under control so I went home. Drove past this alley, saw a kid running—matched the description down to his yellow Adidas tennis shoes. I knew it had to be our guy. I got out and ran down the alley...came out the other side and BAM—hit right in the shoulder. Another cop thought I was the guy."

"Jesus Christ," Nora said. "You got shot by another cop? He didn't recognize you?"

"All he saw was 'black dude running.' Good thing he's a shit shot, or I'd be a dead man."

"Fuck."

She didn't ask any stupid questions. Cyrus appreciated that. "Fuck" was the right response. At least she didn't ask *Did it hurt?* like a lot of people did. Yeah, it hurt. Of course it hurt.

"Two weeks laid up in the hospital. Nobody but family came to see me. I had my phone. I let every girl on my list know their poor baby Cy had taken a bullet in the line of duty. I was waiting for my medal, waiting on some sympathy."

"At least a sponge bath, right?"

"Not one of them showed up."

"Not one?"

"They had me figured out." Even as he said it, he

remembered one person had shown up at the hospital to check on him, one of the girls on his list. Detective Katherine Naylor. She'd made the mistake of coming when his mom was there. He'd pretended like they were nothing but coworkers, and that had been the last of Katherine.

"Not even Paulina?"

"I hadn't met her yet," he said. "I did a couple weeks after I got out. I was staying with Mom while I was recovering. Her rule—you stay in her house, you go to Mass with her every Sunday."

"Sounds like your mom and my mom went to the same Mom School."

"Mom introduced me to Paulina at church. Love at first sight. For me. She looked at me like she'd been reading my internet search history."

Nora laughed at that. She did have a good laugh. The kind of laugh that made a man stand up a little straighter in his seat.

"Took a long time to convince her to give me a chance. She'd heard enough horror stories from Mom in their prayer group to make me work for her. For three whole months I could only see Paulina at Mass. Lucky for me, she goes every day."

"So you started going every day?"

"Every God damn day," he said.

"Explains why your website says you only help out women and children. You're doing penance."

"Maybe so," he said. "Maybe that's what it is."

"I think you're more Catholic than I am."

"Bad Catholic. Paulina was this close to joining the Ursulines in town." He held up his hand, fingers a hair apart. "I stole her right out from under God's nose. Might be going to hell for that."

Nora said, "It's okay. We'll ride share."

He laughed, couldn't help it. The lady was fun. Fun enough to be a real friend? Time would tell maybe.

"You're all right, Nora."

She smiled. "Better reserve judgment there, buddy." Nora hit the gas.

Chapter Thirteen

They arrived at St. Valentine's, and Cyrus told her to park on the street near the back, close to the parish house.

When Nora turned off the car's engine, that's when Cyrus realized he didn't quite know how to introduce her to Sister Margaret.

"Ready?" Nora asked.

"Hold on. Trying to figure out how to lie to a nun," he said.

"Oh, that's my area," she said. "What are we lying about?"

"You. If I'm going to let you snoop around Father Ike's room, I better tell Sister Margaret something about you."

"Hmm...maybe tell her I'm a private eye in training?"

Cyrus stared at her.

"Okay, stupid lie," she said. "Tell her I'm a psychic you hired to read the vibrations of the room?"

"I could maybe tell that to anyone in this town but a nun."

"True. Catholics don't really trust psychics. You could

tell her I'm a therapist who knows a lot about the psycho-
logical issues Catholic priests deal with."

"Can you pull that off, though?"

"I think I can handle that one."

Cyrus escorted Nora to the front door of the parish
house. Sister Margaret greeted them at the door. She
looked Nora up and down a couple times but didn't object
to letting him and Nora into Father Ike's room.

"Can I help you with anything?" Sister Margaret asked
from the door.

"Did Father Ike have a laptop?" asked Cyrus.

"Not that I know of. We have a shared computer room
in the house," she said. She lowered her voice. "I already
checked the internet history."

"Nothing?"

"Nothing. Though I felt terrible for looking." She
shook her head.

"Don't feel bad, Sister," he said. "We all want to know
what was going on."

"Did you find out what that thing was we found?" she
asked, lowering her voice.

"Still looking into that," Cyrus said.

Sister Margaret nodded. Then she left them alone in
Father Ike's room without another word. Nora stood by
the picture window in the sitting room, staring down at
the courtyard below. He stood next to her and saw what
she was seeing—two elderly women in gray habits sitting
under the shade of an oak tree.

"She seemed really upset." Nora met his eyes.

"It's been hard for her," Cyrus said to Nora. "She's
known him for years. Thought she knew him."

"Can you ever really know anybody? Completely, I
mean? All the way down?"

"You been with your Viking for how long?"

"Known him twenty-three years," she said, throwing two fingers up, then three. "Kingsley's known him even longer. King once called Søren 'the infinite onion.' No matter how many layers we peel back, there always seems to be more to him..."

"The infinite onion?"

"We were really stoned at the time," she admitted. "But it's an apt description."

"You don't know him?" Cyrus couldn't imagine not knowing everything there was to know about Paulina after twenty-three years.

"I know his heart," she said. "But he can still shock me sometimes, still surprise me."

"Where'd you two meet?" Cyrus asked.

"Went to Starbucks one day," Nora said. "Ordered a tall blond with whip. They gave me Søren."

Cyrus glared at her. She winked at him but didn't pony up the real answer. Interesting. He'd figured her for an open book. Seemed like a few pages of that book were stapled shut.

"I guess we should get started," he said, glancing around the room. "But I only have one pair of gloves with me, so I better do the digging. You can tell me if I—"

"I got this." Nora rummaged through her handbag. She snapped on a pair of disposable, powder-free latex gloves. "I have my own."

"Do I want to—"

"No, you don't want to know."

"All right then. What room do you want? Sitting room or bedroom?"

"Bedroom," she said.

"Thank God," Cyrus said.

He thought Nora would smile or laugh. She didn't.

Cyrus started in on the sitting room, while Nora worked silently in the bedroom. He found nothing in the sofa but loose change and a pair of fingernail clippers. He had better luck with the coat closet. There was a shoebox on the top shelf full of old credit card bills.

He went through a few of them. The charges appeared benign. Gas, restaurants, Amazon. But Cyrus knew better —he'd seen it in the river in his mind. Father Ike had a secret, and keeping secrets costs money.

He carried the shoebox into the bedroom. Nora was sitting on the floor, her back to the bed, a Bible in her hands.

"Nora?"

She looked up at him, tears on her face. "Sorry," she said, hastily wiping them away.

Although he was wearing a suit, Cyrus sat down on the dusty floor across from her. "What's wrong?"

She closed her eyes, then took a breath before looking at him. "It just hit me what we're doing. A priest died, and these are all his private things. We're going through them like...like we can. Because he doesn't have any family here."

"This is the job."

"Father Ike keeps private notes in his Bible." She opened the Bible. It filled with scraps of paper. "Søren does, too. That's why I got Father Ike's Bible out when I saw it. Because I've found all kinds of secret stuff in Søren's Bible."

Cyrus waited. He could tell she had something to say to him. He'd been with enough women in his life to see that look in her eyes. He waited.

"I need to tell you something about Søren," she said. "If I can trust you. Can I?"

"I want you to," he said. "But I can't make you. All I can say is keeping secrets is part of my job. There's a whole lot that happens in this town, and I'm the only person who knows it or is ever gonna know it."

"You won't tell Paulina?"

"She understands I have to keep secrets in my line of work."

"Like a priest," Nora said.

"Right. Like a priest."

He waited. She waited. He looked at her. She looked away. Finally, she looked at him again.

"Søren...he's a priest."

Cyrus let that sink in. "You know what's crazy? I'm not surprised."

"You aren't?"

"Jesuit?"

She nodded.

"I went to Jesuit school," he said. "They're some scary motherfuckers, Jesuits. Scary smart. Scary-scary."

"They don't scare me."

"Guess they don't," Cyrus said, rubbing his chin. "You didn't want to tell me how you two met. I now know why."

"We met in church."

"Twenty-three years," he said. "How the hell did you two not get caught?"

She grinned. "Location, location, location. Tiny parish in a small town. And with the priest shortage, Søren didn't have to share the parish house with any other priests. Which is good. That place was tiny. But it was far back from the church, trees everywhere, and to get to it, you had to drive in from a side street. Very secluded. That helped. We also fucked at Kingsley's house a lot."

"You must have been young when you met him."

"I was," she said. "I don't like talking about it. People think things about us that aren't true. I was two weeks away from my sixteenth birthday when we met. But we didn't start sleeping together until I was a junior in college. Twenty years old. I'm not saying that makes us angels or anything but...you know."

"He's not a pedophile."

"Exactly."

Cyrus took a couple deep breaths. This was heavy, but he'd carried heavier secrets.

"Yeah, I'm definitely not telling Paulina that," Cyrus said. "She'd make some phone calls on him."

Nora laughed softly. "Too late. He's already been suspended. Forced leave of absence for a period of no less than one year."

"Cause of you?" Cyrus asked.

Nora ran her fingers gently over the binding of Ike's old Bible again.

"Søren has a son—Fionn. He's three now."

"He has a son? But you don't?"

"This would be so much easier to explain if you were a freak, too. You sure you aren't?"

He laughed. "Last I checked."

"I'll give you the short sweet vanilla version. First, it wasn't cheating," she said. "We're in an open relationship. Always have been. He didn't have sex with other people, but he did kink with them which can be much more intense and intimate than sex. Meanwhile...I actually had sex with other people."

"This is the sweet version of the story."

She took a deep breath. "Something...bad happened. I was nearly killed. Him, too. We were both staring death in the face. I'm not exaggerating. There were guns to our heads."

"Shit," Cyrus said. "How the hell did that happen?"

"Men like Kingsley, they have pasts. His, in particular, is filled with some very dangerous people. One of them caught up with him. Wanted to destroy us—King, Søren. Me. Thank God we got out alive."

"Jesus." Cyrus shook his head.

"You've been shot," Nora said. "You know what a near-death experience does to you. You see things you've never seen before. You feel like you better get your life together while you still have it."

"I hear you. If I hadn't gotten shot...I don't even want to think about it."

If he hadn't gotten shot, there'd be no Paulina in his life. Funny how the worst thing that happened to a man could turn out to be the best thing sometimes.

"There was always this secret part of Søren that wanted to have a child," Nora said. "And it was never going to be with me. I can't even have kids anymore—by choice, I promise. So...when given the chance, he took it. I don't blame him. I've taken my fair share of chances. Being in an open relationship, there's always more risk. Like someone getting pregnant, which...happens."

He sensed there was a story there, even more story than she was telling him.

"Anyway," she continued, "it's fine. I love Fionn. He was a surprise but a good one."

She took something out of her bag that looked like a passport wallet. She opened it and showed him a photograph of a little blond boy, about two years old.

"He's cute," Cyrus said.

She slid the photo carefully back into her bag, but only after glancing at it one more time and smiling.

"That 'ordeal,'" she said, putting "ordeal" in finger-quotes, "changed everything for us. I was seeing someone else at the time. Søren and I had been on and off for years. But after that, we were on and we've stayed on. And King and I had some bad blood between us. We cleaned the blood up finally. That was also right when King stopped fucking around with everyone on the planet. After Céleste was born, King decided to turn over a new leaf. That's why we all moved down here. We wanted to leave our pasts in New York."

"I think yours might have followed you down here."

"Seems to be the case," she said.

"Anything else you holding out on me?"

"Well...I told you I have two men in my life. My other lover, the twenty-seven-year-old...is Kingsley's son."

"God. Damn."

"Oh, it gets worse, my friend."

"I'm out."

She smiled, halfway giggled.

"About time you told me this," Cyrus said. "This matters to the case, you know. If Father Ike knew about you and your Viking—"

"I promise, Søren did not know Father Ike. He would have told me if he did. And Søren wouldn't have given Father Ike my business card. And if he had, for any reason at all, he would have told us both. Hand to God." Nora put her right hand on Father Ike's Bible and lifted her left hand. Cyrus had to admit it was compelling testimony.

"It's a motive, though, right? For a priest to call you? Say he found out this lady in town was sleeping with a priest. Maybe he's got a girlfriend, too, feels guilty as hell over it, wants to talk to someone who gets it."

"He had a chastity device in his nightstand. You really think he was calling me just to chat?"

"All right, good point." If they hadn't found the chastity whatever thing, Cyrus might be able to convince himself Father Ike was looking for some understanding in his final hours from a priest's mistress. But they had found it, and there was no pretending it didn't exist.

"You don't seem very shocked," Nora said.

"More priests than we want to admit got side pieces. I've had two cases with people cheating with clergy—one wife, church secretary. One husband, groundskeeper."

"Both Catholic priests?"

"Both," he said. "It happens."

"Yeah, it does."

They met eyes.

"You pissed at me?" she asked.

"Why? I stole Paulina from the Ursulines."

"She wasn't in the order yet. Søren's been an ordained priest for a long time."

Cyrus shrugged. "Done too much in my days to judge how you spend your nights."

She smiled. "I like you."

"We gonna be friends?" Cyrus asked.

"For the time being."

"It'll make our counselor happy. Check 'female friend' off the wedding checklist."

"Can I come to your wedding?" Nora asked, eyes wide.

"Hell no."

"Fair." She laughed again. Good to hear her laugh. He promised himself a long time ago he'd stop being the reason why good women cried in this town.

"Back to work," he said.

Cyrus stood up. His ass was falling asleep fast on that floor. He held out his hand and helped her to her feet.

"You all right?"

"Better. Still freaked out to be digging through a dead priest's things. Hard to not think about somebody doing this to Søren if something happened to him. Digging through his stuff, finding out his secrets." She glanced around the room, shuddered a little.

"Just remember, it's for a good cause. Nobody deserves to die because they're, you know—"

"A freak like me?"

"Right," he said. "Let's get back to work. You find anything in the Bible?"

"Nothing much," she said. "A few thank you notes from former parishioners. Birthday card from some Archbishop. Picture of him and his sister as kids. One poem. That was about all that stuck out."

"The poem?"

"Rumi," she said. "Heard of him?"

Cyrus shook his head.

"Legendary thirteenth century Persian Sufi mystic and poet."

"Oh yeah, him. You just know this off the top of your head?"

"My boyfriend is half-Persian. I mean, the other one."

"He a fan of this Rumi guy, or you just like bringing up all the time that you have two boyfriends?"

"Six of one, half a dozen of the other."

"Just tell me about the damn poem."

"Well, Rumi mostly wrote religious poetry and love poetry. I'd kind of expect a religious poem in his Bible, but not this one."

She opened the Bible and took out a folded sheet of paper. The poem was written in Father Ike's own hand on a sheet of linen paper, the kind people used when they were trying too hard to make their resumes look nice.

"'Poem of the Butterflies,'" Cyrus read aloud. He continued:

> *The people of this world are like the three*
> > *butterflies in front of a candle's flame.*
> *The first one went closer and said, "I know about*
> > *love."*
> *The second one touched the flame with his wings*
> > *and said, "I know how love's fire can burn."*
> *The third one threw himself into the heart of the*
> > *flame and was consumed.*
> *He alone knows what true love is.*

Cyrus folded the sheet of paper and pressed it back into the Bible.

"You think that means something?" Cyrus asked.

"It could," she said. "Could be romantic. Could be erotic. Could be masochistic, the thought that love equals being burned and consumed."

"Could be talking about God's love. Could be talking about his suicide, you know."

"Could be," Nora said. "Just caught my eye. What about you? You find anything?"

"Credit card bills," Cyrus said. "Might be something in here." He picked up the shoebox and pulled a chair to the bed so he could spread out the bills. "You find anything else?"

"What I didn't find is kind of interesting," she said.

"What's that?"

"That cock blocker you found...like I said, it uses a lock and key. That's how you keep the thing on you—with a padlock. I didn't find the key. That means someone else probably has it."

"What does that tell you?" Cyrus asked.

"It means Father Ike probably had a partner. Sex partner? Kink partner? A dominant maybe? Someone locked him into that thing and unlocked him from it. He wasn't doing it to himself."

"That's a big leap," Cyrus said. "He might have thrown the key away."

"Then why keep the chastity device?"

"Good question," Cyrus admitted. "Maybe he's got the key but not here..."

"The house he died in?"

"Cops already searched it looking for a note." He glanced around the room for secret hiding places. Nothing jumped out at him. He furrowed his brow as he looked at Nora. "Where do you keep all your gear?"

"My house. My dungeon," she said. "And I have a bag of gear in my car. Did Father Ike have his own car?"

Cyrus thought about that. "Let me find that out."

Chapter Fourteen

Nora listened as Cyrus sweet-talked and cajoled a detective he knew on the force into putting out an APB or whatever the hell they were called on Father Ike's car. So much work for no pay. He was either a very good guy or out of his mind. She gave it even odds.

"Well?" Nora asked when Cyrus got off the phone finally.

"They'll keep an eye out for it—unofficially," Cyrus said. "Until then, I'm going to walk around, see if I can find it myself."

"You're just going to walk around New Orleans and hope you find his car?"

They'd found out from Sister Margaret that Father Ike did own his own car, a 2005 Sentra in basic gray. Probably ten thousand gray Sentras in the city, at least.

"The neighborhood, not the whole city. Wanna join me?"

"In these shoes?" She held up her foot clad in those red high-heeled sandals.

"Maybe not. You can leave me here," Cyrus said. "I'll call Paulina to come pick me up."

"You sure? I hate to abandon you in the middle of a case."

"My case," he said. "Not your case."

"Fine. Your case. But is there anything I can do to help?"

"Figure out how Ike got your card," Cyrus told her. "Sooner the better."

"Right. Card. On it. Leaving."

She started to go but stopped at the door.

"Will you call me if and when you find his car?" she asked.

"You want me to?"

"You might need me to translate for you. I speak Kink and Vanilla."

"I noticed," he said. "I'll call you. I won't open the trunk until you get there. Just in case."

"Thank you."

"Don't thank me. If there's another one of those demonic cock rings in the trunk, I'm making you pick it up this time."

"I'll bring my gloves," she said.

"Bring lots of gloves," he said. "And a Hazmat suit."

She left Cyrus with his box of credit card bills, found her car, and drove straight home. She'd promised Søren she'd get back by five, and it was only a little after two when she walked through her backdoor.

Gmork jogged to her in happy greeting. A yellow Post-it was stuck to his back fur.

Muzzle me, it read.

"Søren," she growled. Gmork growled when she

growled. "Don't worry, boy. I'm not going to muzzle you. I might muzzle Blondie though." She went upstairs and found the door to her bedroom closed. She didn't remember closing it last night before leaving. Quietly, in case Søren was asleep, she opened the door.

No, not sleeping. He lay on her bed, head propped on her pillows, reading. What a sight—an excruciatingly handsome blond man in jeans and t-shirt in her bedroom, framed erotic pen-and-ink art on the red walls.

"Eleanor?" he said from behind his book.

"Give me a sec. I'm picturing you handcuffed to my headboard."

He looked over the top of her book at her, eyebrow arched. The look was *not* friendly.

"You aren't allowed to do that."

"A girl can dream."

He laid the book across his stomach. Nora stood in the doorway a moment longer just to appreciate the view of Søren on her bed. "Done sleuthing?"

"Done sleuthing for the day," she said. "We didn't find anything, but Cyrus is out looking for Father Ike's car. Might be something in there."

"Or not."

"Or not," she said. She didn't want to talk about Father Ike with Søren. Not yet. Too upsetting to talk to a priest about digging through the private life of another priest. She knew Søren would probably prefer she stayed far, far away from this case. But she couldn't.

"What are you reading?" she asked.

"*Where God Happens* by Rowan Williams," he said. "Book of sermons by the former Archbishop of Canterbury."

"I have porn, you know. The good stuff, too. Kinky. Hot. Well-written. I should know. I wrote it."

"This is Anglican porn," he said.

Nora shut the door, stranding Gmork in the hall.

"Anglican porn...you thinking of converting?" she asked, crawling to Søren on the bed and resting her chin on his chest. "Last I heard, Anglican priests were allowed to get laid."

"Not even Anglican priests are allowed to have mistresses. They're definitely not allowed to have mistresses and children with married women."

"You'd think the Church of England would be more understanding, founded by King Henry the Adulterer/Wife-murderer/Swan-eater."

"I believe the swan-eating was the least of his issues."

"We could, you know...do the thing, if you wanted."

"The thing? Could you be more specific?"

"Rhymes with 'carriage'?"

Søren laughed. "I suppose we could. If we were married, it would, as they say, cover a multitude of sins. What a husband and wife do behind closed doors is no one's business, not even if the husband is an Anglican priest."

"Or a husband and his former brother-in-law..." Nora said. Then rethought that. "I guess the Church of England wouldn't be keen on you and King doing your thing either."

"No. And even if they did, a priest or a pastor's wife lives in a fishbowl. It's more stressful in many ways than being in the clergy. Turning you into a pastor's wife would be sadism," he said, stroking her hair. "And not the kind either of us enjoy. No, becoming Anglican would cause as many problems as it would solve. And I can't imagine myself as anything but a Jesuit."

"Neither can I," Nora said. "A Jesuit or nothing."

Jesuits. The scary-smart priests. The scary-scary priests, as Cyrus had called them. The Jesuits were an army of Catholic intellectuals and so liberal, they were often accused of heresy.

Søren dropped his hand to his chest. His smile had disappeared.

"I was only eleven," he said, "when I was dropped on the doorstep at St. Ignatius. I had a letter with me, written by my father that I had to give to Father Henry, the head-master. I knew what it said. I was told what it said—that I was a violent delinquent and a deviant, and Father Henry and the other Jesuit priests and teachers should feel free to beat me daily as it was the only punishment I understood."

Nora closed her eyes, though she would rather have closed her ears.

Søren went on. "Father Henry took the letter, read it, and I knew I was going to spend the next seven years of my life in hell. Instead, he took me to the kitchen, sat me down, and gave me hot chocolate. He said, 'I think your father's full of shit, but don't tell him I said that.' Then he winked at me and put a dollop of whipped cream on top of the cocoa. 'We don't beat boys at this school,' he said. 'Except in chess.' Then we played chess for two hours."

"You used to give me hot cocoa, too," she said. "When I was upset."

"Forty years ago, and I can still remember how sweet the hot chocolate was and how good. I'd never had it before. My stepmother always said sweets were for 'poor people,' not 'our kind.'" A long pause. "I see him every time I look in the mirror."

"Father Henry?" Nora asked, assuming Søren meant when he wore his collar and clerical garb.

"My father."

Ah. So that explained the beard. Nora leaned over and kissed the back of Søren's hand. Then she took it and held it and said nothing. For years, Søren had kept his traumatic childhood mostly hidden behind a shroud of silence and shame. But since becoming a father, Søren's past had been slipping out in one little dark tale or another. Yes, King had heard a few stories, too, and asked Nora if she thought it was something they should worry about. She'd said "no," though she was worried.

Ever since Fionn came along, Søren's walls were coming down. But were they the walls that held Søren in? Or the walls that held Søren up? She didn't know, but she knew this...she could do nothing for him but listen, no matter how much it hurt to hear the suffering in his past. If anything in the world was truly a sin, it was letting one's own mild discomfort interfere with someone else's healing.

"I'm Catholic for a reason," Søren said, his eyes focusing again on her. The past was vanquished, temporarily at least. "The Church of England is fine, but it's not for me. I need all seven of my sacraments. King Henry threw out the baby with the baptismal water."

Nora knew this. They'd talked about it before, once or twice, when they had their serious "What happens if/when we get caught?" talks. Back then, however, those conversations had stayed in the realm of the theoretical, the maybe, the someday, the what if.

Now it was happening.

"Speaking of kings...you seeing King soon?"

"Tonight, at my new house that I do not know about yet."

"Remember to act surprised and also totally unimpressed."

"I'll remember."

"He'll see right through it."

"Without a doubt."

She picked up his book and read what he was reading out loud:

A hermit said, "Do not judge an adulterer if you are chaste or you will break the law of God just as much as he does. For he who said, 'Do not commit adultery' also said, 'Do not judge.'"

Nora put the book back on his stomach. "Nice. Loophole Theology is my favorite Theology."

"Not a loophole. Have you ever tried going a day without judging someone else?" he asked.

"Sounds impossible."

"Exactly."

"I prayed for you," she said softly.

"Did you?"

"A lot. Almost every night you were gone, I'd pray for you. Went to church, sat in a pew, prayed and prayed...last night, I even lit a prayer candle. *Voilà*. You're here."

"I was already back by the time you lit your candle. Very powerful prayer if it can time-travel."

She looked up at him. "I'm just that good."

He kissed her again. Not on her head this time, but on her lips. When he started to roll on top of her to deepen the kiss, the book on his stomach stopped him.

Nora laughed as Søren picked up the book of sermons and tossed it across her bedroom, where it landed in a pious heap on her rug. He slid on top of her and dragged her underneath him. Bliss, feeling his full weight and length and breadth on top of her again.

"You can't fuck me," she said as he kissed and bit her neck.

"I don't recall asking your permission."

"You're fucking Kingsley tonight. You need to save your strength."

By his strength, she meant, of course, his semen.

His eyebrow cocked skyward. "Are you implying I'm incapable of having you and Kingsley both in one night?"

"Well..." She shrugged. "You aren't as young as you used to be."

"You're trying to make me punish you."

"Is it working?"

He nodded.

"I'm in trouble?"

He nodded again.

"I'm in big trouble?"

"Enormous."

Her dungeon down the hall had gotten lonely while Søren was gone. Nothing sadder to Nora than the sight of a St. Andrew's Cross gathering dust.

Søren slid gracefully off the bed and to his feet. He crooked his finger at her. She smiled and followed him to her bedroom door. He opened the door and there was Gmork, in the hallway, growling deep and low in his throat. A solid black eighty-pound German Shepherd growling in a darkened hallway was almost as intimidating as Søren when you got him in the right mood.

"We can play in here," he said.

"Gmork, *aus*." She snapped her fingers, pointed, and Gmork obeyed, trotting down the stairs as if he hadn't just threatened brutal death upon Søren.

"Will that work for me?" Søren asked.

"Try it."

He snapped his fingers and pointed at the door to the dungeon.

Nora growled at Søren. But she obeyed.

Chapter Fifteen

✥

Nothing, Nora decided, was more fun than sitting in her pew at Mass, looking angelic and devout while recalling in vivid detail the erotic things the man sitting two seats down had done to her all afternoon...

It had begun with a flogging, of course. A good deep one that left her so sore that she winced every time her back touched the pew. And since Søren did have to save his "strength" for Kingsley that night, there'd been no sex. But Søren hadn't left her hanging. He'd tortured her for nearly thirty minutes with a vibrator that he used on her, bringing her almost to orgasm five times before finally letting her come.

And come she had, and so hard she was still seeing white spots dancing in the air in front of her eyes. They'd showered together after which was lovely but also necessary. As her mother said, *Always wear clean underwear to take communion.*

Since moving down to New Orleans, Juliette had insisted the "family" go to Mass together. Nora had found it strange, at first, sitting with Søren in a pew on Sunday evenings, but she'd gotten used to it. Since mornings were so hard on Juliette these days, that meant the Sunday evening service, and they sat in the next to last pew since they could never count on Céleste's attention span.

Søren took the far left seat, Céleste next to him and usually on his lap now that Juliette had no lap, Juliette next to Céleste and Nora next to Juliette.

Kingsley, of course, stayed home.

They attended Mass that night at Tulane's Catholic Center. Most of the parishioners were college students. Søren liked it since a couple of his former students attended there. One came up to him and shook his hand, said they couldn't wait until he was back at Loyola. Søren introduced them all to his student; Céleste as his niece—close enough—while Juliette was introduced as "Céleste's mother," and Nora was, of course, "Céleste's aunt."

"And this is my baby sister," Céleste said, patting her mother's stomach.

"Or brother," Juliette said quickly.

Søren's student didn't bat an eyelash at his former teacher's "family." It was kind of nice to feel like a member of Søren's family. Too nice. Nora had to wonder how it would feel to be his wife. Probably it would feel a lot like bondage did...sexy and exciting at first, but after a few hours, she would get bored and sore.

As Nora stood to walk to the front to receive communion, she felt her phone vibrating in the pocket of her jeans.

She veered out of the line and into the lobby. Søren gave her a curious look as she walked out.

"Cyrus," she mouthed. Søren slightly rolled his eyes. Just slightly.

Out in the lobby, Nora listened to Cyrus's voicemail.

"Hey Nor, it's Cy."

Oh, so they were on one-syllable terms now. She liked that.

"Found Father Ike's car two streets over from the house he killed himself in. Nobody can find the keys though, so I've got a locksmith coming by in about an hour to pop the trunk. If you want to come, the car's at—"

Nora didn't bother listening to the rest of the message. She immediately called Cyrus back.

"Cy, it's me," she said. "Cancel the locksmith. I'll come and pop the lock."

"You'll pop the lock?" he asked, laughing.

"You want to wait an hour, or do you want me to come pop the lock right now?"

"You a locksmith and didn't tell me?"

"I know locks. It's my job."

If there was something in that trunk worth seeing, she didn't want a locksmith seeing it.

"I'll see you in a few."

Nora snuck out the back and drove to Constance Street where she found Cyrus waiting on the hood of a silver Nissan Sentra.

"You sure it's his?" she asked as Cyrus hopped off the car and walked to her.

"It's his. We double-checked the plates. I don't want to get picked up for carjacking either."

"Yeah, been there," Nora said. "Not going back."

"You boosted cars?" Cyrus was watching her as she opened the trunk of her Mustang.

"My father owned a chop shop. I helped. Then I got arrested and Dad got whacked by people he owed money to."

"I guess you turned out pretty well," he said. "Considering."

"That's the nicest backhanded compliment anyone's ever given me."

Nora found the lockout kit she kept in her car for emergencies and pulled out the long thin rod which was nothing more than a fancy version of a bent wire coat hanger. But it did the trick.

Nora had the front door lock popped in seconds.

"Are you impressed?" she asked.

"Not really. I can pop locks, too."

"Then what the hell am I doing this for?" she asked.

"First, my kit's in my Honda back in the Quarter. Also, I don't know this neighborhood and this neighborhood does not know me. I don't want to get shot by some trigger-happy rookie because some old lady in the Irish Channel called the cops on a black guy popping the lock of a car that's been here two days."

"Oh, but you'll let me do it?"

"They won't you shoot you. Pretty white ladies make very good human shields."

"Nice to be needed. Ready?" she asked as she reached for the trunk latch by the steering wheel.

"I'll do it," Cyrus said. "You man the trunk."

"What if there's a monster in there?" she asked.

"You're scarier than I am," Cyrus said.

"This is probably true. Hit it."

Nora waited at the trunk as Cyrus pulled the lever. The latch released and the trunk opened.

"No monsters," Nora said. "I think."

"Uh-oh." Cyrus walked around to the trunk, kind of wincing as he went to stand by her. "What does 'I think' mean? Blanket."

"Yup, that's a blanket. And there's something under the blanket."

There was definitely something under that blanket. Nora stared long and hard at the bulge, which could have been anything from a flat tire kit to a dead animal in a garbage bag.

"I don't smell anything."

"Good sign," Cyrus said. "I'm gonna do it. Stand back."

She stood by and waited. Cyrus pulled the blanket back.

"That's not much better," Nora said.

"That's a suspicious-looking duffel bag."

She pointed at the bag in the trunk.

"Not big enough for a body," Cyrus said.

"Not a whole body, you mean."

"Don't do this to me." Cyrus shook his head.

"My turn," Nora said. "Stand back. I'm going in."

God bless Cyrus Tremont, the man actually stood back instead of doing any macho posturing. She took latex gloves out of her purse, pulled them on, and unzipped the duffle.

"Houston, we have a pervert," she said.

"What is it?" Cyrus stepped forward again.

"Let's see…" Nora started pulling items out of the bag. "We've got handcuffs. We've got ankle restraints. We've got rope, bondage tape, blindfolds, and three different gags."

She spilled the cuffs, rope, tape, and gags into the trunk to give Cyrus a look at them.

"Either he was kinky, or Father Ike was going to kidnap somebody."

"He was definitely stocking up on Aisle 15 in Home Depot." She picked up the two lengths of rope.

"You get this shit at the Depot? I've been shopping the wrong aisles."

"Not really," she said. "This is called love rope. It's much softer than real rope. Used for bondage. I mean, it can tie you the fuck up and you won't be able to get out, but it also won't tear your skin apart like hemp rope."

She pointed at a roll of something. "And that's bondage tape, not duct tape. It sticks to itself but not to the skin. Same thing. Ties you up but doesn't leave marks. You have to either go to a kink shop—and there aren't many of those in this town—or you order it online. Kidnappers don't usually care about not leaving bruises."

"So, he's kinky or the world's nicest kidnapper," Cyrus said. "I prefer kinky."

"You and me both, buddy."

Cyrus started to reply when an older white woman stepped out of the front door of a pale pink shotgun house.

"That your car?" the woman asked.

"Lord," Cyrus muttered before turning around and smiling at the woman. "No, ma'am. I'm a detective trying to find someone who might be missing. This is their car."

"Who are you?" the woman asked Nora. She didn't seem too satisfied with Cyrus's answer.

"I'm the cocksmith," Nora called back.

"What?"

"Locksmith," Cyrus said, giving Nora the look she deserved. "Did you happen to see someone park this car here a few nights ago?"

"No, but it's been there three days now. I was about to get it towed."

"We'll move it," Nora said.

"You allowed to do that?"

"Is it your car?" Nora asked.

"What? No, it's not mine." The woman sounded more irritated than ever.

"Then don't worry about it. We got this." Nora raised her hand and made a "shooing" gesture. It appeared the woman was about to say something, so Nora shooed her away again. With a disgusted shake of her head, the women retreated back into her home.

"I got to try that someday," he said. "You just..." He made the 'shooing' gesture. "And nosy old ladies go away."

"I'm not sure it would work for you. And she's probably calling the cops on us right now anyway."

Cyrus laughed and pointed at the car. "What do you think? Hotwire it?"

"Hotwire it," she said. "I need to dig through the bag a little more. Better not do it here if she is ratting us out. Where's your place?"

"Across town. Twenty minutes."

"I'm only a couple miles away. We'll take it to my house."

"Park it on the street. I'll have someone pick it up and tow it tomorrow."

"Can you follow me in my car?" she asked. "I can take you back to your car after."

"Yeah, I'll drive your car. But you'll be lucky to get it back." Cyrus took the keys to her Mustang.

It took three seconds for Nora to hotwire the car.

She pulled out into the street. Cyrus followed. She thought she lost him on the way to her house at one point, but a minute later, there he was behind her. The man knew how to tail.

They reached her house and she parked the Sentra in

front. When Cyrus got out of her Mustang, he was on his phone again.

"Half an hour," Cyrus was saying. "Home by eight." Pause. "Yeah, I know. I know. Love you, too, baby." A laugh. A smile. "Never again, I swear." He hung up.

"What's never again?" Nora asked. Cyrus pursed his lips at her. "I'm standing right here. Of course, I heard you."

"Never again am I doing a favor for the police department." Cyrus stashed his phone in his pocket. "Ready?"

Nora popped the trunk of the Sentra again and went back to it. Cyrus was staring hard at her house or something on it.

"What's up?" she asked.

"That is a lot of damn beads," he said, raising his hand to a clump of red and silver beads on a low-hanging branch. "You may be a little into Mardi Gras, lady."

"I didn't put them up here, I promise."

"Who did?"

She shrugged. "No idea. They weren't on the tree when I saw the house the first time. By the time I moved in a month later, there were a handful. Every few days, more show up."

"You never catch anyone doing it?"

"Søren thinks I have an 'admirer.' Maybe some teenage boy who lives on the street and is trying to be cute. I'd think Gmork would growl though if a boy were out here in the middle of the night beading my tree."

"So, a woman?"

"Who knows?" Nora asked. "They're pretty though. They don't seem to hurt the tree."

"It would freak me out if someone was beading my trees at night. Or Paulina's. I'd stand guard."

"Nico kind of felt the same way. He came to visit for a couple days and swore he felt like he was being watched while he was in my house. That's why he got me Gmork." She glanced up at her tree. She rarely gave it much thought, but Cyrus's questions had gotten her wondering about it again.

"He got you that dog because it's a man-eater, and if you'll tell me where he got him, I'll get one for Paulina."

"I'll tell you where we got him, if you invite me to the wedding."

"Just check Satan's duffel bag, please."

"It's just handcuffs and rope and blindfolds."

Cyrus gave her that look again.

"It's kink," Nora said. "These are toys." She pointed at the bag. "You are telling me you never tied a girlfriend to the bed or blindfolded her or anything?"

"I'm not telling you nothing, lady."

Nora drew on the latex gloves again. Seemed like overkill, "but better safe than accidentally exposed to Hep C," as her fellow dominatrixes say. She dug through the bag, finding nothing she hadn't found before.

"Maybe this is a dumb question, but if Ike had a, well, a *you*, wouldn't his lady keep all this stuff herself?" Cyrus waved his hand at the toy bag in the trunk.

"Depends." Nora shrugged. "Some people are germaphobes and keep their own private set of gear. Maybe he fetishized the stuff and wanted to keep it around. Maybe he was a switch, like me."

"Switch?"

"I do the beating, and also get beat. By different people, of course. I beat clients, but they don't beat me— only Søren does."

"You ever flip the tables on your Viking and tie him up? Wait. Don't answer that. I don't want to know."

"Never," she said. "He's all dominant. Unfortunately. He'd look so pretty in handcuffs."

"Stop."

Nora smiled as she kept digging, turning out pockets, checking linings. "Any luck on that key?"

"No luck there. But this is interesting." She held up an unopened box of K-Y lubricant.

"Okay, so, Ike *was* fucking someone," Cyrus said.

"Or someone was fucking Father Ike."

"Right. Yeah. Possible. Not gonna think about that, though." Cyrus turned his back to her, walked up and down her driveway. He hit the end of her street, turned on his heel, walked back.

"Who else might know about Ike?" Cyrus asked.

"What?"

"In this town, there's like ten guys who can hook you up if you want to sell drugs. Another ten guys for guns. Another ten guys for girls. There's gotta be a guy you go to if you want a...*you,* and you don't know where to start."

"Kingsley," Nora said. "And we already talked to him. He didn't have any interaction with Father Ike."

"But Edge is still new in this town. You gotta remember, this is New Orleans. We have bars in this city older than the country. Somebody was here before Edge."

Nora considered that as Cyrus paced another lap. What old-timers did she know around here? Someone deep in the community. Someone who knew everyone.

"I know a guy," Nora said. "He hosts a lot of events in town. I don't usually go to them, but he invites me to every single one."

"Who is he?"

"Retired art professor. I'm sure he'd talk to you if I were there. I'll get in touch. Although I doubt he'd know who Father Ike was seeing. Male subs don't, as a rule, talk to each other."

"Maybe. Maybe not. Worth asking."

"Fair warning, he's kind of weird."

"Weirder than you?" he asked. She nodded. "Damn. Now that's saying something."

Chapter Sixteen

"I know that look," John Breaux, the best tailor in New Orleans, said as he helped Cyrus on with his tuxedo jacket.

"You don't know a damned thing." Cyrus buttoned the jacket. He'd been caught grinning, but didn't try to hide it.

"How long until the big day?" Breaux asked.

"About two months."

The tailor raised an eyebrow.

"Fifty-three days," Cyrus said.

"That's better."

Cyrus stepped in front of the mirror and stared appraisingly at his reflection.

"What do you think? The blue look good?" Cyrus asked.

"Don't ask me. I'm not the one marrying you."

"You're the expert, man."

"I know what I like. I'm not in your wedding. Where your boys at?"

"No boys today," Cyrus said. "I like to do this stuff on

my own." Paulina took an entire crew of women with her when she went to her dress fittings. Her mother, her sister, her best friend, and three of her sorority sisters. At least. And just for the fittings.

But Paulina's girls took this stuff seriously. His friends, much as Cyrus loved them, would be doing nothing but cracking corny jokes through the whole thing, giving him hell for getting married, bringing up his wild past like they always did. He didn't want that today. He didn't want jokes. He didn't want his past. He just wanted to find a tux that would make Paulina, who never said a foul word in her life, look at him and say, "God damn."

His tailor only slapped him on the back and walked away to do busy work while Cyrus stared at his reflection. White tuxedo shirt, black tie, dark blue tuxedo with black lapels. He looked good. Damn good. At least he hoped he looked damn good. Did he, though? Did he look damn good to him but to Paulina he'd look a fool?

Maybe he should have brought his boys. Except none of them were married, so what the hell did they know about it?

Cyrus found his suit jacket and pulled his phone out. Before he thought better of it, he snapped a photo of himself in the mirror and texted it to Nora.

What do you think about the blue? he wrote.

Then he realized what he'd done.

He'd asked a white lady dominatrix for her opinion on his tuxedo.

For his wedding.

To Paulina.

What was next? Calling Lady Gaga and asking her to DJ the reception?

Cyrus started to write, *Disregard, meant to text someone else that* when Nora replied.

Wow.

Cyrus smiled. *Good wow?*

Hell good wow, she wrote. *The blue looks great. Damn.*

I'm looking for "God damn."

Can I show Juliette? she texted back.

Please do.

Cyrus paused, tensed, awaiting the verdict. *Well?*

She's purring. You can't get any better than that.

He made Juliette purr. Cyrus wasn't just renting the tux. He was going to buy the thing.

J says King needs that tux.

Ah, well, if this tuxedo was good enough for Juliette the Goddess, it was good enough for him.

Juliette wants to know if Paulina is traditional. Then she might want you in black.

She said she didn't care as long as I liked it and she didn't see it before the wedding.

She's a keeper, Nora wrote. *Juliette and I have spoken—go with the blue. Céleste agrees. She gives it two thumbs up.*

Thanks, ladies, he replied, intending to sign off but the little bubble dots warned him Nora had more to say.

The guy I told you about said he'd meet you. Can you come to my place tonight at six?

Your house?

My dungeon. She sent the address.

It's not normal for people to have dungeons, he wrote her. *You know that, right?*

Who wants to be normal?

Well. Cyrus had asked for this meeting. Might seem rude to cancel.

Conversation over, he replied. Then he swiped his finger and deleted that entire insane exchange.

"Well?" his tailor asked, glancing around the edge of the mirror.

"Measure me up," Cyrus said. "I'm taking the blue."

Chapter Seventeen

✦✦✦

After his fitting, Cyrus changed back into his brown suit and tie, stopped for an early dinner of shrimp and grits, and headed over to Piety Street and Nora's dungeon.

He was not sure about this dungeon thing.

When Cyrus arrived, he found the building looked pretty safe, pretty boring. A brick square place, like a small warehouse. He parked in the lot and went through the glass doors. In the lobby, he found an old-fashioned letter board with names and office numbers. Not too many.

She was the only one listed on the third floor. "M. Sutherlin," he read out loud. "By appointment only."

M? Not *N?*

Ah, he got it. *Mistress.*

According to the board, the first floor was occupied by a company called NOCS. The second floor was listed only as Warehouse.

Cyrus walked across the lobby to the door for the NOCS offices. He peeked through the glass. A handful of people were seated at desks in cubicles, working on computers, answering phones.

He bypassed the elevator and used the staircase. On the second floor, just out of curiosity, he decided to check out this "warehouse." There was a set of unlocked double-doors just off the foyer. He poked his head in.

Coffins. Nothing but coffins in a long, dim room. Black coffins and white coffins and wooden coffins. A single gold coffin. Then rows and rows of wooden crates, likely full of even more coffins.

NOCS. New Orleans Coffin Suppliers.

No wonder Nora got a good deal on her loft.

When he reached the third floor, he found Nora's door locked. Smart girl. She took her security seriously. He hit the buzzer next to the door, and immediately the door popped open for him.

Slowly, he pushed open the metal fire door.

He heard laughter inside.

Nora's laughter, definitely. Low, throaty, unmistakable. Then a man's bigger laugh. Cyrus followed the sounds down a short hall to an open door. He peered inside and saw what looked to him like a lobby from a turn-of-the-century hotel that was the respectful front for a brothel.

Sheer fabric the color of red wine hung from the ceiling to the floor. A fancy gold mirror hung on gold cords. A faded red and gold Turkish rug covered the stained cement floor. An older man, white, about sixty-five he guessed, sat on a dark red armchair while Nora lounged on a golden chaise looking like...well, she looked like something.

Cyrus could only stare as he took in the sight of Nora dressed for "work": black boots with red laces up to her knees. Fishnet stockings. Short black leather skirt. Black and red corset over sheer black top. Hair down and parted in the center, black waves all over the place. Cleavage for years...and the reddest God damn lips he'd ever seen in his life.

No wonder the old white dude next to her looked like he was in heaven. He was ten seconds away from a heart attack and a one-way ticket to the pearly gates.

"Damn, Nora," Cyrus said. "Warn a man."

"What do you think a dominatrix wears at work? A muumuu?"

"You would look exquisite in a muumuu, majesty," the old white dude in the suit said.

"Doc, behave yourself. We have company. Doc, this is Cyrus Tremont. Cyrus, Doctor Philip Danton, at your service."

"At your service, majesty," the man called Doc said. He reached for Nora's hand, took it, and kissed the back of it. Cyrus got the feeling this was one in a long line of hand kisses Nora had to put up with from that man. She took it a lot better than Cyrus would have.

"Mr. Tremont," Doc said, holding Nora's hand and looking up at him. "I owe you a debt of thanks. I've been trying to get a one-on-one with the Queen for years. And out of nowhere yesterday, she calls me. May I shake your hand?"

"You can shake it," Cyrus said, holding out his hand. "But don't kiss it."

Doc chuckled a crazy-old-man chuckle. Cyrus shook his hand and found his grip firm and sane. He'd give the old boy a chance. Maybe.

"Cyrus, have a seat." Nora had been lounging on the chaise, but she sat up then and crossed her legs, patted the seat next to her. Cyrus wasn't too sure about that.

"Maybe I'll stand," Cyrus said. "So what's with the Doc?"

"When I'm not making my art," Doc said, "I'm a bit of a card shark. You know the old Nelson Algren quote, his three rules for life. 'Never play cards with a man called Doc. Never eat at a place called Mama's.'"

"'Never sleep with a woman whose troubles are worse than your own,'" Nora said, finishing the quote. "You don't want to play cards with Doc, I hear. He can bluff like a mother."

"I'll keep that in mind."

"I would never bluff you, majesty," Doc said, kissing her hand again. Grossing Cyrus out again. "My heart is on my sleeve. Feel free to take it and put your high heel through it."

"Doc, you really do need to dial it down, please," Nora said. She swatted his knee which, from the expression that crossed Doc's face, gave the old man an orgasm, another heart attack, or both.

"For the Queen, anything." Doc picked up a cup and saucer and sipped at his tea. Cyrus didn't miss the glint in the man's eyes as he looked at Nora over the top of the cup. Cyrus couldn't remember the dude's name, but Doc looked a little like the bad guy from *The Hunger Games*. The president with the beard and the crazy eyes.

"Tea?" Nora asked.

Cyrus took tea and a scone, which was a weird thing to be doing in a dungeon. Or maybe not. This was his first time in one. "What's with the 'queen' stuff?" he asked as he sat next to Nora.

"Young man," Doc said, pointing at Nora, "this woman pouring your tea is none other than the Queen herself."

"Queen of...?" Cyrus took a bite of his scone. Nice.

Sweet. He wondered if Paulina could make him some of these.

"It was just my nickname in New York," Nora said as she topped-off her own cup of tea. "King was The King. I was his Queen. As nicknames goes, not very creative."

"Bah." Doc waved his hand. "Had nothing to do with Edge at all. You were and are the Queen, because you are the most beautiful, the most wicked, the most vicious...oh, I could go on forever. Mr. Tremont, this woman is a legend."

"A legend, huh?" Cyrus playfully elbowed Nora.

"Don't get too excited. Like Doc said, I was the most vicious. The most vicious can charge the most money. I did things other dommes wouldn't do. You know, because they didn't want to go to jail. Didn't have anything to do with being pretty. There are dommes who have me beat ten times over in the looks department."

Cyrus didn't know about that.

"The viciousness is true," Doc said. "God bless her dark heart, I have heard stories all the way down here."

"You into that?" Cyrus asked him. "Getting the shit kicked out of you?"

"By her? Who wouldn't be?" Doc chuckled again, and Nora only looked to the heavens. But she was smiling the way a woman does when paid a good hard compliment.

"You say you heard stories down here? Did you ever meet Queenie over here before she came down to Nola?"

"Never had the pleasure," he said. "But legend travels."

"You ever had one of Nora's red business cards in your possession?"

"If I did, I would wear it on a gold chain around my neck. Why do you ask?"

"Can you keep your mouth shut?" Cyrus doubted it.

"Let me handle this," Nora said. "Doc, you keep your fucking mouth shut about this or no dominatrix—in this town or any other—will ever strip you, whip you, and make you her bitch again. Ever."

"Yes, Mistress," Doc said.

Cyrus wiped his hands on a linen napkin before taking the photo of Father Ike out of his breast pocket.

"Could you tell me if you know this man?"

Doc gingerly took the photograph from Cyrus and gave it a long hard look. Cyrus tried not to get too excited, but he knew from experience that if somebody didn't know somebody, they knew it at once. If they kind of recognized somebody, it could take a long time to remember how and where and when they'd met them.

"Possibly," Doc said at last. "Though if I had to swear I'd seen or met him in a court of law, I couldn't."

"We're not in a court of law," Cyrus said. "But can you tell me maybe where you saw him? How you might know him?"

"Since I retired, I've started teaching classes on various kink and fetish topics," Doc said. He was still staring hard at the photograph. "I think this man came to one of my classes."

"Where are the classes held?" Cyrus asked.

"Adult bookstore in Metairie has a basement we use. I've been trying for two years to get the Queen to come teach a class," Doc said.

"Too busy being lazy," Nora said.

"When was this class?"

"This past summer. July." Doc said it firmly, no question mark at the end. He was more certain than he gave himself credit for.

"And this class you taught," Cyrus continued, "what was it about?"

"Again, I can't swear that was where I saw him," Doc said, "but if my old brain can be trusted, it was a class on medical fetishes."

He returned the photograph to Cyrus.

"All right, so, medical fetish?" That was a new one for Cyrus. Then again, they were all new ones.

"Oh, you know," Doc said, his voice airy, casual. "Latex gloves and naughty nurses, exam tables for very intimate examinations. Speculums. Forceps. Suturing. One of the Queen's specialties."

"Funny, I never could sew on a button," Nora said, "but give me a guy with a med-fet and some needle and thread, and suddenly I'm doing embroidery on his face."

Cyrus turned his head and eyed Nora.

"He thinks you're joking, Majesty," Doc said.

"Let him think that," Nora replied with a wink.

"I don't think you're joking. I think you're scary." Cyrus meant every word.

"Ah, now he's starting to see it," Doc whispered to Nora. "Why you're the Queen, and no one else is."

"Pfft," Nora said, batting the comment away with a wave of her hand. "Every domme I know does sutures."

"Yes, but you're the only one who left them in," Doc said.

"True."

Cyrus shifted a few inches away from Nora.

"Wise man," Doc said.

"So...all right. You think maybe the man in the photograph was at a medical fetish class. That stuff we found, though, it wasn't like forceps and needles."

"No." Nora pursed her lips. "True. That was all basic

bondage stuff in the bag."

"Will you ever tell me who we're talking about?" Doc asked.

"No," Nora said quickly. Doc took it well.

"Did that man possibly ask any questions in the class? Come up to you after?" Cyrus was not about to let this interview get off track, especially since it seemed they were finally onto something.

"He did not." He paused, brow furrowed. "He might have emailed me."

"What?" Cyrus's eyes widened. "You sure?"

"Not in the least. But after that class, I received an email from some anonymous account. The address was just gobbledygook, numbers and letters. Free Yahoo account or some such. I only think it might be him since he mentioned he'd been in my class and there were only three men in the class. One I knew. One who talked to me after the class. And then him."

"You still have that email?" Nora asked.

"I doubt it." Doc sounded unsure. "Even if I did, I don't know if I'd feel comfortable sharing it, however."

"If it's this man," Cyrus patted his breast pocket over the photo. "He's dead."

"What if it isn't him?" Doc asked.

"Then you know neither of us will say a word to anyone about it," Nora said. Cyrus nodded.

"I'll see if I can find it in my trash," Doc said. "But I tend to delete everything I can as permanently as I can. You have to be discreet in this line of work."

"What did the email say?" Cyrus continued. He really ought to be writing this stuff down in his notebook, but he'd do all that after Doc was gone. If he brought his notebook out now, Doc might clam up.

"A short email, the kind I get often. He said he was a man looking for a professional with medical expertise for work on male genitals, money no object."

"CBT?" Nora asked.

"What's that?" Cyrus said.

"Cock and ball torture," Nora said.

"I hate this job sometimes," Cyrus muttered. "Go on, Doc."

"I don't believe he specifically asked about CBT. Very short email. I replied that I didn't know any professionals who had medical degrees or medical training other than the sort for playing doctor in a dungeon. They call me 'Doc,' but that's just a nickname. Retired art professor. I replied to the email that I was sorry I couldn't help but mentioned a few contacts in other cities—San Fran, New York, L.A.—who might know pros. And that was that."

Nora said nothing. Neither did Cyrus. Something Doc had said earlier had struck him as strange though.

"Money no object," Cyrus repeated. "You said the email said, 'money no object,' yeah?"

"That's true," Doc said. "I do remember the writer clearly wrote that. He put it in all caps. Why?"

"The man we're investigating wasn't known for having a lot of money," Cyrus said. "That's all."

"He might have saved a lot. It happens. Or family money," Nora said. "I've known men in his position who had access to a lot of family money."

"We'll look into it." Yeah, Cyrus could believe Søren the Well-Groomed Viking came from money. Even the way he talked sounded like money.

"Anything else?" Doc asked. "Please, anything, my Queen. Order me to do anything, and I'm all yours."

"You gotta stop with the queen stuff," Cyrus said,

trying not to laugh. "The Queen is either Aretha Franklin or the old white lady in the big house in England."

"Oh, but in our kingdom, Mistress Nora is the Queen."

Cyrus couldn't believe it. That man kissed her damn hand again. He was about ready to suture the old boy's lips himself if he didn't stop mackin' on Nora. The girl had a man. *Two* men.

"Was that all you had for Doc, Cyrus?" Nora's hand was still clutched tightly in Doc's paw. "Any other questions?"

"I got one," Cyrus said. "What's the appeal?"

"Of what? Kink?" Nora asked. "You got all night?"

"For a man. Submitting to a woman." He nodded at Doc.

"I should think it was obvious," Doc said.

"Not to me," Cyrus said. "I mean, I get a woman submitting to a man. That makes sense."

"Sexist much?" Nora said.

"You know what I'm saying," Cyrus told her, suddenly sweating.

"No, what are you saying?" She smiled, batted her eyelashes. Cyrus tensed. He was about to get himself hard-core murdered by a tiny white woman wearing knee-high leather shit-kickers and truck-stop hooker lipstick.

Murdered. To. Death.

"You know, right?" Cyrus said to Doc. His voice had gone a few notes higher. "Don't you? You get me, right?"

"Correct me if I'm wrong," Doc began, "but I think what you're saying, young man, is that you understand why women desire—sometimes, not all the time, and certainly not all women—to submit to a powerful man as it's so hard to be a woman in a world so hostile to women. The fantasy of having a powerful protector is a potent one when it seems like the threats from dangerous men are everywhere all the time. And, of course, in an ideal world, a woman's first male love is her father, who was affectionate, adoring, and yet an authority figure. Why wouldn't a woman desire a man to be—as her father was—her protector, first and foremost, but also a source of unconditional affection as well as an authority figure and disciplinarian? Ergo, your statement that it's more understandable that women wish to submit to men was simply an acknowledgment of the sexist socialization that women experience in patriarchal cultures."

"Yeah. That's exactly what I'm saying. Took the words right outta my mouth, Doc."

"Good save, Doc," Nora said. "But can you explain male submission to women that succinctly?"

"Mr. Tremont, have you ever had a pretty girl in a short plaid skirt and white cotton panties stand over your head and piss through them onto your face?"

Cyrus's eyes went very wide. He couldn't find the words to even respond to that.

"Not even fantasized about it?" Doc sounded astonished.

"Hell no."

Doc threw his hands up in defeat. "Well, you can't say I didn't try, your majesty."

"Any other questions, Cy?" Nora asked.

"Not a God damn one?" Cyrus said. "I mean, thanks, Doc. That helps."

"I'll go, majesty, but just one order? Please? Before I go? Kiss your boots? Lick the floor? Take a bullet for you right through this old heart?"

He tapped his chest.

"My order is this," Nora began. "Go and do whatever sick, twisted, demented, perverted, deranged thing your old heart desires. Just don't hurt anybody in the process. Well, forget that. Just don't fuck anybody up in the process."

"Ah, *an it harm none, do what thou wilt.* You recite the Witch's Rede, majesty," Doc said, apparently more enchanted with Nora than ever. "I should have known you had a little magic up your sleeve. You've certainly cast a spell on me."

Cyrus waited for Nora to say something to Doc, tell him off, or send him packing. But she didn't. Her eyes narrowed, she glanced off to the side.

"Nora?" Cyrus said.

She seemed to suddenly come back to the present.

"Thank you, Doc," Nora said. "Now get your old ass out of here before I change my mind about putting you in the ER."

"One of these days, Mistress. I'll be your slave yet."

Cyrus shook Doc's hand again, and the old boy left them alone. Immediately Cyrus transferred from Nora's chaise to Doc's empty red armchair.

"That man is nuttier than a fruitcake," Cyrus said. "Makes you look almost normal, and God damn, that's saying something, isn't it?"

"I remembered something."

She sounded so serious that Cyrus sat up straighter. His heart pounded hard in his chest, the way it always did when he was about to make a break in a case.

"I remember who I gave my business card to down here," she continued. "That week I was house-hunting. Doc reminded me."

"Shit, who was it?"

Nora laughed a little.

"A witch."

Chapter Eighteen

Cyrus stared at her like she'd grown a second head. Then he shrugged.

"New Orleans," he said. "Shoulda guessed."

"I can't believe I'd forgotten it." Nora remembered it all now. "It was the day my real estate agent was negotiating for my house. I didn't know if I'd get it since I put in a low-ball bid. I was getting nutty waiting for the phone to ring, so I went for a walk. Stopped in some little stores to shop. One was some kind of witchy store."

"You remember the name?"

"No," she said. "I might know it if I saw it, though."

"Go on."

"Anyway, there was a woman in the shop, she worked there. She asked if I was there for a reading. I said I hadn't planned on it, but I had time to kill. The girl said the witch who did the readings—"

"She called her 'a witch'? Not a psychic?"

"Definitely called her a witch, like it was her job. 'Our witch is in today, and she does great readings if you want one.' Obviously, trying to sell me something, but I said okay.

Why not, right? Thought it would keep me from checking my phone every ten seconds to see if I had the house or not. I gave the girl at the counter my card. She said she'd call me when it was my turn. I left to walk around some more. I got the call. I went back, had my reading. The psychic, the witch, I mean, she had my card on her little table. I asked her if I'd get the house. She said I would. And I did."

Of course, there was more to it than that. Nora had received a half-hour tarot card reading. The topics had ranged from her writing career—"continued success"—to her love life—"about to get very complicated." Both turned out to be true, though Nora knew the statements were purposefully vague enough they could apply to nearly any situation.

When she told the witch about moving to New Orleans, that was when things got weird. The woman asked her, "Are you sure you want to do that? They call this town 'the Big Easy,' but it's not going to be easy for you."

Nora remembered that warning since it was the one part of the reading that had proved false. Apart from the heat, she and The Big Easy had greeted each other like old friends. She loved the history, the people, the beignets, the music, the laissez-faire attitude. Nothing not to love.

Cyrus held up his phone to show her red dots on Google maps. "Which shop was it?"

She read the names, the locations.

Voodoo Alley.

Gris-Gris's.

The Black Cat Corner Shop.

House of Voodoo.

"None of those ring a bell, but that doesn't mean it wasn't one of them."

Nora returned Cyrus's phone to him. That day had been almost three years ago. The shop could be closed down now.

"And you're sure the witch had your card?" Cyrus asked.

"I am one-hundred percent certain she had my card. I can still see her holding it." Nora put her palms flat together in a prayer position to mime how the witch had held her red business card.

"And she didn't give it back?" Cyrus asked.

"No. I don't remember her giving it back. I tipped her twenty dollars. I can see the twenty on top of the card." Nora pictured it now, the little room, not much bigger than a closet, the small round table with the paisley table-cloth, the tarot cards spread out like a fan before them. And the witch...yes, Nora remembered the witch. She'd been very beautiful. Strange serious eyes, like she really believed in what she was doing, like it was real to her even if she knew the dumb tourist across from her at the table didn't believe a word of it.

The witch had made Nora almost believe.

Cyrus stood up.

"All right, come on." He waved at her to follow him.

"Where are we going?"

"On a witch hunt."

"I should probably change first."

"For the French Quarter?" he asked.

"Ah, good point." She'd fit right into the French Quarter after dark. Then again, these particular boots of hers were not, in fact, made for walking.

Nora left Cyrus in her dungeon lobby and changed clothes in her bathroom, replacing her boots with black heels and switching her stockings and skirt for jeans. She kept the bustier top on.

"No other shirt?" Cyrus asked, glancing at her over his phone. No, not glancing at her. Glancing at her mounds of cleavage.

"Look, you want answers from strangers, my tits will get us answers."

"True," he said. "I'll drive."

"I don't mind driving."

"Can you see the road over your tits?"

Nora glanced down at her rather out-of-control cleavage.

"Okay," Nora said. "You drive."

Nora rode shotgun in Cyrus's Honda. It was getting late and were they in any other city, she might have worried that the shops would be closed by the time they arrived. But not in New Orleans. The Quarter woke up around noon and didn't go to bed again until dawn. With the bars on Bourbon Street open all night, most shops in the area stayed open late. Sure enough, when Cyrus parked on Barracks, the streets were alive with hundreds of people, soaking up the evening breeze off the water, already looking for good times and big trouble.

"Where to?" Nora asked when they reached the corner of Barracks and Chartres.

"You tell me. Where'd you go on your walk?"

"All right, well, let's start on Bourbon. First, I know I definitely walked down Bourbon that day. And second, let's get a drink. I'm buying."

"Yeah, you are."

Cyrus got a boring old beer, and Nora loaded up on rum and Coke, a double. They wandered down to Voodoo Alley, but nothing about the place seemed familiar. The turned a corner and found The Black Cat closing up for the night. Nora remembered going in there, but the man working the shop said they'd never offered psychic readings—no room. The man gave them a list of all the other witchcraft and voodoo shops in the neighborhood. Google didn't list them all, and a couple had changed names when they changed owners.

They walked down the other side of Bourbon Street when Nora looked up and saw her.

"What?" Cyrus asked.

"That's her." She pointed at a woman's face painted on a hanging shop sign.

Cyrus stood at her side and stared up.

"Marie Laveau," Cyrus said. "You sure?"

"Definitely."

"You're telling me that Marie Laveau, the Voodoo Queen of New Orleans, who has been dead for a hundred fifty years, gave you a tarot card reading."

"I'm not saying it was the real Marie Laveau. I don't believe in ghosts, okay? At least I've never met one. But she looked just like that and dressed just like that." She pointed up at the woman on the sign. "But younger. Maybe thirty."

"So, early thirties, light-skinned female in an old-timey dress and headscarf. You remember anything else about her? Name or anything?"

"She said her name was Marie. But if she led historical tours, she would, right?"

"Right." Cyrus nodded. "Anything else you remember about her?"

Nora stared up at the sign again.

"Earthquake eyes," Nora said.

"What?"

"I remember thinking the woman had earthquake eyes. You look in them and shake a little."

"Scary witch?"

"Not quite scary," Nora said. "I don't know. Powerful maybe. She made me a little nervous."

"Hell, if she made you nervous..." Cyrus said, then whistled. "Let's keep looking. If the voodoo store folk don't know her, maybe the other tour guides do. Come on."

"Where are we going now?"

"To interview a vampire." Cyrus headed into the crowd.

Nora didn't follow at first.

"You know vampires?" Nora called out. Cyrus only raised his hand and waved it, indicating she needed to get her ass in gear and follow him. Nora ran a little to catch up with him.

"If you know vampires and you've been holding out on me," she said, "I'm not going to be friends with you anymore."

"Vampire tours," Cyrus said. "Witch tours. Ghost tours. Gotta be a voodoo tour, right? There's one vampire guide who's been doing this forever. He'll know your witch if she even once ran a voodoo tour 'round here."

Cyrus started forward, but Nora was separated from him by a sudden crush of drunk frat boys leaving a bar *en masse*. One of them bumped into Nora, hard, and her foot slipped out of her shoe.

When she stumbled, the glassy-eyed frat kid grabbed her around the waist, not to steady her like a good guy, but just to grab her.

"Hey, there," he said, grinning. He smelled like an overpriced Hurricane (the drink, not the storm). "What's your hurry, baby?"

"I'm thirty-eight," Nora said. "I'm not a baby, baby. Let me go." She started to walk away, but the dumb drunk who didn't know what he was getting himself into, slid his arm around her waist and pulled her back against him.

"Don't leave me," he said. "We just met."

"Fuck, please don't make me kill you tonight," Nora said. "I'm busy."

Unfortunately, the kid was strong. And he had a whole lotta liquid courage in him. He pulled her back against him once more, and Nora decided she was ready to break a law or two—especially when two of the boy's "boys" noticed what was happening and started to cheer him on.

"Nice catch, man," one said.

"Dude, don't get us arrested," a slightly sober one said.

Arrest was the least of their troubles. Nora raised her foot, fully intending to bring her high heel down on the boy's toe.

And break it.

In many pieces.

She hoped he played football or soccer, that he was a prodigy, in fact...just so she could ruin his future.

Then one of the frat boys went flying.

Really, seriously, flying. One second, he was standing. The next second, he traveled through the air at a high velocity and landed a good ten feet away on the street. Bourbon Street. Which meant he was about to get a very nasty bacterial infection just from touching the concrete.

The frat boy let Nora go so fast, she stumbled again, this time against Cyrus who threw a protective arm around her.

"She fell, man," the frat boy said. "I was just helping her."

"Nora?"

"He grabbed me and wouldn't let me go even after I told him twice," Nora said.

Cyrus reached for the frat boy who tried to duck away but was just too drunk. Cyrus had him by the arms. "Where you from, jackass?" Cyrus demanded. He gave the boy a little shake.

"Back off, fuck. She fell."

"You fall, Nora?"

"He hit me by accident, grabbed me on purpose."

Cyrus shook the boy again.

"Where. You. From. Jack. Ass." Cyrus spoke in terrifyingly calm and deliberate tones. Even Nora was a little nervous at what he'd do. She wished she had popcorn. This was a good show. A small crowd had gathered to watch it. Luckily they seemed to be on her and Cyrus's side.

"California, man. Pasadena. Back the fuck off me!"

"Pasadena in the house!" Cyrus said. "Let me ask you something, Pasadena. You ever see me in California fucking with your California girls?"

"What?" The question didn't seem to penetrate the boy's brain.

"Did you? *Ever.* See me in California? Fucking with your California girls?"

"I never seen you," the boy said.

"Right. Cause I don't go to other towns and fuck with their ladies. So you don't come to my town and fuck with our ladies. You come to my town and fuck with our ladies, we fuck you up. We fuck you up New Orleans-style. We fuck you up until you can't get un-fucked. You got it?"

"Fuck off, bro."

Nora slapped the boy on his sweaty pink cheek.

"That's fuck off, *sir*, to you," she said. Cyrus cackled a little.

"I'll let you go," Cyrus said. "But I see you fuck with one more New Orleans lady, I will absolutely kill you. Kill you all the way gone. They gonna find you floating in the Mississippi, and when the cops ask me why I did it, I'll tell 'em you got rough with one of our ladies. And then they'll say, 'Sorry to bother you.' That's how we do it down here. You got it, son? You got it?"

"I got it, I got it."

Cyrus let the boy go.

Nora, however, did not. Before he could take one drunken step away, she brought her heel down on his toe.

And the jackass was wearing Birkenstocks. On Bourbon Street. Where public urination was nearly as common as public intoxication. Kid had it coming.

The boy screamed redrum, and there was no doubt in Nora's mind she had broken the holy living shit out of his toe.

Cyrus looked at her, his eyes wide as two shot glasses.

"I was just trying to scare him," Cyrus said.

"Yeah, well, I was just trying to break his fucking foot so he can never walk straight again."

"You fucking bitch," the boy keened in his delightful agony. His face was blood red and he was writhing in pain. "What's wrong with you, you psycho?"

"Do you have all night?" Nora asked him. "Five bucks says he calls me a cunt next," Nora said. "Wait for it."

She won the bet.

Cyrus oh-so graciously allowed Pasadena's two drunk friends to pick him up and cart him off.

"Bye, boys," Nora called after them.

Cyrus couldn't help himself. He'd been wanting to try it since yesterday. As the boys carted their limping comrade off, he made the "shooing" hand gesture.

"It does work," he said, nodding.

When they walked off, nobody got in their way.

Chapter Nineteen

The bartender told them the vampire in question was on a tour right now, but would be back in fifteen or twenty minutes. In the meantime, Cyrus bought them a second round. He had another beer, and Nora had another rum and Coke, hold the Coke.

Cyrus took a long deep draw on his beer.

"Can I say something?" He put his beer bottle on the bar.

"Say it," she said.

"You are one crazy bitch."

Nora laughed deep and low and hard. She took his statement in the spirit intended—as a compliment.

"Weren't you scared back there?" he asked.

"In the moment, you're more mad than scared. That's all adrenaline."

"You scared now?"

"I'm glad they're gone, I'll say that. I've been manhandled a lot in my life. You never get used to it. And it's never fun."

He picked up his beer again. "Fuck is wrong with kids these days."

"You were really good there." Nora rested her head on her fist, elbow on the bar. "They teach you that in cop school? How to scare the shit out of drunk frat boys?"

"We learn a few tricks. Not your tricks. That was a helluva trick."

"It was either his foot or his balls. Which would you rather have busted?"

"What if he's really hurt, though? Like for real. That bother you?"

"He could have hurt me for real. You think I should feel guilty?"

"Oh, fuck no."

"And this," she said, "is why we're friends."

They clinked glasses.

And that's when the vampire arrived.

No missing the man. He stood nearly seven feet tall in his leather platform boots and top hat. He wore gobs of black eyeliner, and when he grinned hungrily at her, she saw he'd filed his canine teeth into points. Leather jacket, of course. Long black hair, of course. Black fingernails filed into points as sharp as he teeth, of course. He was about as scary as a vampire in a kids' cartoon.

Nora liked him immediately.

Cyrus took a long deep drink of his beer, put the bottle down on the counter, and said, "Be right back."

The vampire tour guide stood near the doorway of the darkened bar with his arms crossed over his chest.

Cyrus turned and pointed to Nora. The vampire grinned. Then he lightly slapped Cyrus on the shoulder and walked over to her.

"Hello, little girl," the vampire said. He had mischief in his eyes and gravel in his voice. "Pleased to eat you."

"Hey, big man," she said. "What's your name?"

"Lord Chaz. To whom do I have the pleasure of eating? Meeting...I mean, of course."

"Nora," she said. "Mistress Nora."

Lord Chaz raised one dark eyebrow.

"*The* Mistress Nora?" he asked.

"Have you heard of me?"

"I have now."

"Jesus H. Christ," Cyrus said. Nora made herself settle down.

"Can you help me find someone I'm looking for?" she asked.

"Depends," he said. "Who are you and what are you gonna do to them when you find them?"

"Kill them and eat their hearts," Nora said.

That got a laugh from the goth giant.

"Are you sure you weren't my ex-wife in a past life?" he asked her.

"No, but I could be your ex-wife in this one."

"Excuse me," Cyrus said. "Dracula. Elvira. Can we focus?"

"Sorry." She put her drink down. They were working. Sort of.

"I'll help if you tell me what this is about," the vampire said.

Cyrus gave him the quick rundown, mostly lies but believable ones. Cyrus was a private detective. A college girl had run off, and Nora's business card had been found in her dorm room. Nora had only given her card to one person in New Orleans.

"A witch," Nora said.

"Which witch?" the vampire asked.

"I don't remember her name," Nora said. "Except that she dressed like Marie Laveau and worked at a witch shop somewhere around here. Closed down now, I think. None of the ones I saw on Google maps rang a bell. I know the shop was in the Quarter, but it wasn't on Bourbon Street. They did psychic readings there. The door was purple. That's it."

"Charm City," the vampire said.

"Charm City." Nora exhaled in relief. "That was the name of the place."

"Little place on Iberville. Owner was a witch from Baltimore," the vampire continued. "Older lady. Shut the shop last year and moved home to help with her grandkids."

"This witch wasn't very old," Nora said. "Thirty to thirty-five. Really pretty."

"Was your reading good? Or a bunch of bullshit?"

"How do you tell the difference?" Nora asked.

He smiled like Satan's cat. "Did she tell you only what you wanted to hear?"

Nora shook her head.

"Mercedes," the vampire said. "That's her name, not her ride."

Cyrus pulled out his notebook. "Mercedes. Spelled the same as the car, though?"

The vampire nodded. "The name comes from an old Creole family in town. One of her ancestors was a rich Irish banker who bankrolled half the city. Married a Creole lady and had thirteen children."

Nora's eyes went wide. "Thirteen?"

"Mercedes is in the bloodline of the thirteenth. That's the story she tells, and I believe her. She has a new shop now, all hers. The Good Witch on Tchoupitoulas and Alphonsus."

"Irish Channel," Cyrus said.

Nora glanced at him. They had just been over there yesterday with Father Ike's abandoned car.

"Mercedes at The Good Witch," Nora said. She slipped the man a fifty, to Cyrus's obvious chagrin. "Thank you so much."

The vampire held the bill between two needle-sharp fingernails. "She's the real thing," he said. "I hope you didn't lie to me."

"Are you scared of her?" Nora asked.

"No, but you should be, little girl."

"Bite me," Nora said.

"Nora," Cyrus said.

"I was being literal." She tilted her head to the side to bare her jugular vein. The vampire leaned in, teeth bared, as if to actually bite her. Cyrus threw up an arm between her and the man.

"Let's not do that," Cyrus said. The vampire only chuckled fiendishly, pocketed his fifty, and walked away to gather his next tour group.

"If that was my only chance to become a vampire, and you blew it for me, I'll never forgive you, Cyrus Tremont."

Cyrus was clearly not in the mood for it. He had his phone out again. "Closed right now," he said.

"The Good Witch?"

"Yeah. Opens at eleven tomorrow. Meet you there?"

"Meet you there," she said. "What do we do until then?"

"Go see my fiancée."

"Great. Can't wait to finally meet her." Nora slapped money down on the bar.

Cyrus stared at her.

"Oh, you mean alone."

"Come on," he said. "Let's get you and me both home."

They returned to Cyrus's car without incident. Although on their way to his Honda, she had to ask, "How the hell do you know a vampire?"

He laughed. "Uh...wish I had a good story. Cousin of mine visits from Atlanta every now and then. He loves vamps and ghosts and all that voodoo shit. We took Lord Chaz's tour last time. I remember him saying he'd been doing it for twenty years or more. And everybody in the Quarter seemed to know who he was. He's a nice guy." Cyrus paused. "You didn't have to tip him to answer one question, though. Remember, this is a *pro bono* case."

"I told him my real name. And you better believe he's going to talk about me to someone. When he speaks of me, he will now speak very fondly."

"I think he would've anyway. You two were kind of simpatico."

"I get along well with weirdos."

"I noticed that. After Doc and the Dark Lord of Bourbon Street, I'm done for the day. For the week."

"Oh, come on." She playfully shoved his shoulder. "We had a good day. So many clues. I feel like Scooby-Doo. Never solved a mystery before. Give me a Scooby Snack."

"We haven't solved it yet."

"The witch gave Father Ike my card. She'll tell us why tomorrow. Then we'll know what he wanted with me and that'll solve the case."

"Hope so," Cyrus said. He didn't sound certain of that and talked little on the way to her house. He pulled in front. Nora saw Father Ike's car had been towed while she was out.

"Anyway, thanks for the lift," she said.

"You really live here by yourself," Cyrus said. "Kind of big for one person. Or does it just look big?"

"Three bedrooms, two bath," she said. "Sounds like a lot for one but one room's my bedroom, one's my dungeon, and one's my guest room."

"Wait. You've got two dungeons?"

"One's business. One's personal."

Nora reached for the door handle.

"You'll be okay?" he asked.

"Yeah?" The question had caught her off-guard. "Oh, you mean because of the guy? I'm okay. Little shaky but I've survived worse, I promise. Comes with the territory."

"Bourbon can be pretty wild."

"No, I mean 'comes with the territory' of being a woman."

Cyrus pursed his lips, slowly nodded. "Yeah, I see that."

"But you know how it is. You got your own problems in your own territory."

"That is also very true."

"I really appreciate your help tonight. I think I could have gotten away from him on my own, but maybe not. It's that 'maybe not' that I'll be thinking about when I wake up at three a.m. Glad you were there. Søren is, too."

"Glad I'm in his good graces. Hope I stay there."

"You're fine. He's cool."

"Is he?" Cyrus asked. "We been spending a lot of time together. And he's already got to share you."

Nora almost said that she had to share Søren with someone, too, but she bit her tongue. What happened between Kingsley and Søren was nobody else's business.

"He's not jealous of you, I promise," she said.

"I guess if he doesn't trust you by now, he never will."

"Søren? Trust me?" She blurted out a single, sarcastic "Ha!"

"What? He doesn't trust you?"

"If by 'trust' you mean Søren has full faith in me and can sleep at night knowing that I will not do anything stupid or dangerous, then no, he doesn't trust me. He'd be insane to trust me."

"And that's okay with you?"

"He doesn't trust me, but he accepts me. And I'll take that over misplaced trust anyway."

"Paulina trusts me," Cyrus said. He said it simply but deliberately, and those three words said what a thousand words didn't have to say.

"I'm not going try to seduce you," she said. "Even if you are cute."

"Fuck, I am not cute."

"I'm keeping that tuxedo pic in my spank bank."

"Go away, Queenie."

"Night, Cy."

Nora appreciated that Cyrus didn't drive away until she was safely inside her house.

Paulina was a lucky lady.

Nora changed out of her insane tit-boosting bustier and into a comfortable black bra and tank. The skinny jeans she tossed aside for red lounge pants. She went out back in her slippers, through the off-street alley to collect Gmork from Kingsley's backyard. He followed her back home, wagging his bushy black tail behind him. She fed him, gave him fresh water, and found her dog brush to tackle his coat. She had him lie on a large towel in front of her on the living room floor.

"Good boy," she said as he lay still and let her run the brush through his wiry coat. "I wish all boys were as well-behaved as you are. Then again, we did cut your balls off. Maybe that's the secret to making men behave. You think?"

Gmork batted his tail against the floor, and she laughed.

He held still while she brushed him—it was his favorite thing. Just as she started in on his right side, however, Gmork tensed up. He leapt to his feet so fast that Nora had to scramble backward to get out of his way.

He didn't growl.

What he did do was trot over to the front door, sit down, and wag his tail. He only ever did that when Juliette stopped by with Céleste.

What would they be doing here at eleven on a Monday night? Nora jumped to her feet just as the bell rang. She hurried to the door and opened it.

A woman was standing on her front step, in the little sliver of streetlight that broke through Nora's oak tree.

Her hair was tied back up a red scarf, her lips full and lush, and her eyes...her eyes were dark. Nora shook a little when she saw them. Earthquake eyes.

The woman spoke in a warm and steady voice. "I heard you were looking for me."

Chapter Twenty

Cyrus found Paulina at her kitchen table, textbook open in front of her and a cappuccino in hand. She still had work clothes on—gray skirt, white blouse. And there it was, after eleven already.

"Oh, that's not good," he said from the kitchen doorway.

"You're telling me." She looked up from her book and grinned tiredly at him. He walked over to her, and she laid her head against his stomach, arms around his waist. Cyrus squinted at the small print in her book.

"'A theory of social cognitive development of the adolescent brain under stress...' Baby, you don't need coffee. You need cocaine to get through this."

Paulina swatted him on the ass, which Cyrus didn't mind one bit. She pushed a chair out for him with her foot for him to sit down on next to her.

"It's interesting," she said. "Sort of."

"You got a test?" he asked.

"Paper, due Friday. It's almost finished. And then only five more modules until master's degree *numero dos*." She raised her hands and waved them in praise-the-Lord fashion.

"Two master's degrees," Cyrus said. "I'm marrying a genius."

"You know it, Daddy." She leaned in and kissed him on the cheek. "I'm thinking of getting my hair done like Einstein. Get it dyed all white and gray, stick it up like I stuck my finger in a light socket. What do you think?"

"It's almost October," he said. "You could be Bride of Frankenstein with hair like that."

"And you'll be my Frankenstein?"

"I ain't going anywhere in public with you looking like that."

She swatted him again—his arm this time—then sat back in her chair, laughing. When she reached for her coffee on the table, Cyrus picked it up and held it out of her arm's reach. She reached for it anyway.

"Uh-uh. No more. It's past your bedtime."

"Give it...please...me..." she pleaded, begged, whimpered. Pitiful.

"No, ma'am." He sat the coffee cup behind him on the table where she couldn't get to it.

"Ah, so mean." She slumped in her chair like a grumpy ten-year-old who was about to get sent to bed without supper.

"You said you're almost done. Bedtime for beautiful girls."

"Fine, fine. But tell me about your night first. You kinda smell like you had a time of it." She sat up again, prim and proper, took his hand, met his eyes.

"I was on Bourbon Street. Remind me not to do that again."

"Don't do that again." She poked his nose.

"Thank you."

"What's going down on Bourbon Street tonight?"

"Trouble," he said. "Not my fault. Didn't start it. Might have finished it, though."

Her eyes widened. She blinked.

"Now I'm awake. Tell me."

He told her, starting with Doc who couldn't keep his lips off Nora's hands. Then Mister Pasadena who was, probably, right that minute, in the ER getting his foot put in a cast. And finally, the vampire and the witch.

"So," Paulina said, nodding, "typical night in Nola?"

"I wish you could have been there, baby. It was the craziest thing I've ever seen. That tiny little white girl broke the hell out of that boy's foot. Just STOMP and boom, kid's limping for life."

"I can't say I feel too sorry for him."

"Nah. If that's how he acts with a woman in public? Don't even want to think what he'd do in private."

That was one thing Cyrus never did and never had to do. He had never forced a woman in his life. Even at his worst, he had lines he didn't cross.

"You make sure your new friend got home okay?" Paulina asked.

"Nora? Yeah, she's home safe now. She keeps asking if she can come to our wedding." He snorted. "No way."

Paulina pretended to pout.

"You want a crazy white lady at our wedding?" he said.

"Your cousin Martin's wife is going to be there, remember."

"You want two crazy white ladies at our wedding?"

Paulina laughed so hard, she had to put her head on the table for a minute to recover.

"You're ornery," she said.

"I got nothing on Nora. That woman…my Lord."

Paulina looked up. "You like her."

"She's entertaining. Then again, so is playing *Mortal Kombat*."

She pushed his shoulder. "You like her."

"She's fun to get in trouble with, that's for sure. I'd let her throw my bachelor party, but we'd all be dead or in jail by morning."

"That's how you know it's a good party," Paulina said. "Maybe I'll let her throw my bachelorette party."

"No. No. No." Cyrus put his foot down with each and every "no."

"It's cute when you get all protective of me."

"Glad you think it's cute, because it's not going to stop anytime soon. Except when you get us rich with that big brain of yours and we can hire bodyguards. Then I'm off duty."

"I don't think I'm going to get us rich as a middle school principal."

"That's just the beginning," Cyrus said. "I got plans for you. You're gonna be in the governor's mansion in fifteen years."

"As what? A maid?"

Cyrus made a disgusted sound to go along with his disgusted expression. "Governor. Smart as you are, two master's degrees, working as a guidance counselor and then a principal. If anything can prepare someone for politics, it's working with middle school kids."

"That's probably true."

"I will make one fine first husband."

"That I can believe," she said, following it with a loud yawn.

"That's it," he said. "You have got to go to bed."

"I'm going. I'm going." She slapped her hands on the table dramatically and pushed herself up. Cyrus didn't mind a bit when she wrapped her arms around his shoulders and kissed the top of his head.

"You did that just to get to your coffee again, didn't you?" he asked. He could hear her drinking it.

"It's cappuccino," she said. "Technically."

Cyrus reached up and extracted the cup from her hand again. Without warning her, he picked her up off her feet and carried her to her bedroom.

"Oh, very nice," she said, settling into his arms. "This is almost better than coffee."

"Are we married yet?"

"Not yet," she said. "Almost."

"Not good enough." He tossed her onto her bed and she landed with a bounce. Half the bed was pillows. Big fluffy white comforter, lacy white blanket overtop, and then pillows, pillows, pillows. What the hell was it with women and pillows?

"Go to sleep," he said.

"You know me getting ready for bed is a ten-step process. And if you don't know it yet, you will the first night we're married."

"What? Ten steps? What do you do at night? Paint the house?"

Paulina scrambled to the head of the bed and lay back on her mountain of pillows. She held up both hands and started ticking off steps on her fingers.

"Step one—pajamas. Step two—wash my face. Step three—exfoliate."

"What happens if you skip step three?"

"You don't want to know. I don't want to know. Step four—moisturize. Step five—brush teeth. Step six—take my hair down. Step seven—put my hair up."

"I think I figured out where you can skip a step."

"Step eight—clean up the mess I just made in the bathroom."

"Another step I'd skip."

"Step nine—pee."

"That's fair. I take that step myself."

"Step ten—say my prayers. Then I go to sleep."

"You forgot step eleven."

"What's that?" she asked.

"Kiss your fiancé goodnight."

Paulina turned her head, looked at him, batted her eyelashes. Cyrus dove onto the bed and before she could wriggle away, he had Paulina pinned under him. He kissed her forehead, kissed her cheeks, kissed her neck and ears.

"You keep missing home plate," she said.

"I probably taste like beer."

"I won't mind your beer breath if you don't mind my coffee breath."

Cyrus didn't mind at all. He kissed her mouth, long and deep. He pressed his tongue gently into her mouth and she let him. Not only did she let him, she touched his tongue with hers and wrapped her arms around his shoulders to pull him closer and deepen the kiss.

It took more willpower than he had that night to stop himself from lying down on her. Mistake, he knew, because once she felt how hard he was, she would send him packing. But there was no hope for it. He rested his full weight on her, and she made a little happy murmuring sound.

"Aren't you supposed to kick me out?" he asked, between kisses.

"Give me a minute." She kissed him again and Cyrus let her. Another minute or two of deep kissing passed.

They kissed long enough and hard enough, Cyrus started to think she'd forgotten her job.

"Now?" he asked.

"I know I should," she said, "But I'm having too much fun." She wrapped her legs around his lower back and grinned up at him.

"I don't have to go," he said. "I could stay."

"I know you could."

"You know I won't."

"I know you won't," she said. "But I know you want to. And you know I want you to."

"You do?"

"You think you're the only one turned on in this room?"

"You want it?" he asked. "Really?"

She nodded slowly, her dark eyes hooded by her thick black lashes. She'd never looked sexier to him. His groin tightened. Cyrus would have happily spent the entire night tucked on top of Paulina, kissing her and digging his fingers into her curling soft hair, tasting coffee with every touch of his tongue against hers.

But.

He put each hand beside her shoulders and pushed himself up.

Paulina, however, would not let go. She whispered, playfully, but kept her feet firmly wrapped around his back.

"Ahem."

"Do I have to?" she asked.

"You don't have to. But you probably should. You got prayers to say. I need to say a few myself, I think."

With a put-upon sigh, Paulina—with obvious reluctance—removed her feet from his back and placed them on the bed.

"I knew we should have had a June wedding," she said.

Cyrus laughed as he dragged himself—with obvious reluctance—off the bed.

"One month," he said. "And a half."

"Fifty-three days," she said. "I'll survive."

"I better go before I change my mind about a few things."

"You better do that, Daddy."

Cyrus knew he should, but he couldn't quite leave yet. He sat down next to her on the bed, stroked his hand through her hair, stroked her cheek with one curl.

"You ever gonna tell me if you ever done this before?" Cyrus asked her.

"No, I am not."

"I'm not being nosy," he said. "I just don't want to hurt you."

"We been together over a year, Cyrus Tremont. You really think a woman can go a year without having sex and it won't hurt when she has it again? Whether I've done it before or not won't matter, and you know it."

"I just want you to enjoy it. I just...I want to get it right for you."

"Will you be there?"

"Planning on it."

"Then I'll enjoy it."

"I love you, baby."

"You better," she said.

He kissed her again, quick, on the cheek.

And though it hurt, he stood up and walked to the door. Before he left, he turned around and looked at her one more time. She lay on her side on the bed, looking pretty as Christmas in her gray skirt and white lacy blouse.

"Pray for me," he said.

"I do, every night."

"What do you pray for about me?"

She tucked the pillow under her head.

"Oh, the usual things. That you'll be safe, that you'll do good work, that you'll help the people who need helping. I always pray you'll remember God loves you. And I always pray you'll remember I love you."

"You ever pray that I behave myself?"

She shrugged. "I try not to," she said, "But sometimes I slip and one comes out. I don't want you to think deep down I don't trust you. I wouldn't be marrying you if I didn't trust you. Sometimes, though, I don't trust everybody else out there."

"I don't want you to worry. If hanging out with Nora's shown me anything, I'm done with that part of my life."

"She sexy?"

Cyrus laughed. "Baby, she is sex on two legs and both those legs are sexy legs. She is sex in a box wrapped in a bow with 'sex' written on the bow. If she were a song, she'd be 'Little Red Corvette.'"

"That's sexy right there," Paulina said.

"But when I'm with her...nothing."

"Nothing?"

He shook his head, almost apologetically. "Nothing. Hanging with her is like hanging with one of the guys. Except it's easier to talk to her sometimes. That make any sense?"

"Like she's maybe...a friend?"

"Now I wouldn't go that far. The woman is ten kinds of crazy."

Laughing, she said, "Maybe she is. You'd have to be crazy to help a man you barely know solve a case for no pay when she's got better things she could be doing."

"Guess I'm crazy, too."

"Maybe you should pray for her," Paulina said. "That'll help you both."

"Pray for what? That she doesn't get us both killed?"

Paulina pursed her lips, shook her head. Times like this, he remembered he was marrying an almost-nun.

"Pray for her the things I pray for you. That she's safe, that she's happy, that she knows God loves her."

"I'll do that," he said. "If anybody needs prayer, it's her. If she's having tea with the devil right now, I wouldn't be surprised."

"Selling her soul to him?"

"Nah. If anything, he's trying to buy his back from her."

Chapter Twenty-One

❧❦❧

Mercedes stepped in through Nora's front door and immediately slipped out of her shoes. With a graceful slide of her foot, she tucked the shoes—plain rope sandals—next to the door beside the brass umbrella stand. A large and slouchy crochet handbag was slung across her body.

She stepped away from the door and waited for Nora to lock up the house after her.

"I guess a certain vampire told you someone was looking for you," Nora said.

Mercedes nodded. "Don't be afraid."

"I'm not afraid," Nora replied. "A little surprised. Very confused. How did you know where I live?"

"If I said it was witchcraft, would you believe me?"

"Probably not," Nora said.

Mercedes held her hand out low, palm open. Gmork lifted his head and pressed it into her palm. She stroked his ears, tentatively at first, but when Gmork whimpered happily, she squatted down to his level and put her face near his face. She let him lick her cheek as she scratched and stroked Gmork's ears and head.

"Does she have a name?" Mercedes asked.

"He," Nora said. "Gmork. It's from *The Never-ending Story*."

"He's sweet."

"He's supposed to be a trained killer. Turns out, he's just a lady-killer."

"Loves the ladies?"

"And hates men."

Mercedes laughed softly. "I like you, Gmork." She patted Gmork one more time on the head before standing up straight again.

Gmork trotted back over to Nora, pressing his warm body to her legs. It comforted her. Nico had bought her the dog for protection, which she never thought she would need. Now she was grateful.

"I apologize for coming so late," she said. "If you were looking for me, I assumed it was important."

"My friend and I were going to stop by your shop tomorrow morning to see you."

"Your friend, the man you were with tonight?"

"Yes, he's a private detective."

"I would rather speak to you alone than with a man. If that's all right. I saw your porch light was on, but I'm happy to go, if you like. Would you like that?"

Her voice was low and soothing. Nora was too curious to turn the woman away, but she kept her guard up.

"No, you can stay. It's fine. Let's go into my office."

Nora had converted the house's formal dining room into her office. She led Mercedes there through the kitchen. Nora switched on the brass floor lamp. Six oak bookcases lined the walls. Nora's big boat of a desk sat in the middle of the room, facing the French doors that looked out onto her jungle of a patio garden.

"Can I get you anything?" Nora asked. "Water? Wine? Whiskey?"

"Wine would be nice."

Nora went into her kitchen and quickly poured two shallow glasses of Syrah. While alone in her kitchen, she thought about grabbing her phone to send Cyrus a quick text. But she had a feeling Cyrus would immediately come over, and Mercedes might not answer Nora's questions with a man present.

When Nora returned to her office, she found Mercedes standing at the bookshelves, eyeing the titles with interest.

"Your wine," Nora said. Mercedes took the glass with a nod of thanks.

"You have a very large library of books on Catholicism," Mercedes said. *"The Catholic Catechism. The History of the Catholic Church.* Pope John's *Journal of a Soul.* Thomas Merton. G.K. Chesterton. St. Augustine. St. Thomas Aquinas... Have you read all these books?"

"I like looking for the loopholes," Nora joked. Mercedes didn't smile.

"What do you mean?"

"Oh, nothing," Nora said. "I'm just a bad Catholic."

"Perhaps you aren't a bad Catholic," she said. "Perhaps you're just a very good pagan."

"Cradle Catholic."

"You're old enough to leave the cradle," Mercedes said. "Aren't you?"

"There's someone in my life who would be very put out if I did."

"If there's someone in your life trying to control your faith, you're the one who should be put out, Mistress Nora."

Nora tensed. Not often another woman put her on the defensive.

"You can just call me 'Nora.' The 'Mistress' is for those who want to serve."

"It's a title of respect, yes?"

"Well, yes."

"I respect your work, Mistress. But I'm happy to call you whatever you like. So Nora it is."

"Mercedes," Nora said. "Unusual name for an American."

She shrugged. "I'm impressed you say it right. Nobody ever says it right, even after I tell them."

"It's a French name," Nora said. "No accents. Not like we say the car brand."

Mare-SED-ess, not *Mur-SAY-deez*.

"You know French?" the woman asked.

"Some. My boyfriend is French. One of my boyfriends, I mean."

Mercedes raised her eyebrow but made no comment. No comment necessary.

"Sorry," Nora said. "I say that stuff all the time. I forget it makes some people uncomfortable."

"I'm a witch. Does that make you uncomfortable?" Mercedes asked.

"You know, I always thought if a witch showed up at my house in the middle of the night, it would be to tell me there was such a thing as a tesseract. That's from—"

"*A Wrinkle in Time*. I know. And there really is such a thing as a tesseract."

"Is there?"

She nodded. "A tesseract," Mercedes said, "is a cube cubed. A hypercube."

"I'm impressed," Nora said. "I didn't know witches knew advanced geometry."

"It's also known as 'sacred geometry.' Some believe geometry is God's native language and that by learning sacred geometry, one can access the mind of God."

"Do you believe that?"

"I don't recognize your god," Mercedes said. "I serve the Goddess."

"I thought everyone in this town was Catholic."

Mercedes smiled. "Not everyone."

She gestured toward her stomach. She was wearing a long red skirt that flared at her hips and a white top, cut off a few inches above her waist so that Nora could see the tattoos on her lower stomach. A sliver of moon on one side, a sliver of moon on the other, a full moon that surrounded her bellybutton.

Nora had seen that symbol before but couldn't say what it was. "What's your ink?"

"It's the symbol of the Triple Moon Goddess," Mercedes said. "Everyone in my coven gets marked with Her symbol. Not necessarily on the stomach, though. I just did that to cover a stretch mark. I made my daughter pay for it."

She smiled and Nora knew she was joking.

"It's pretty."

"Thank you." Mercedes nodded toward the armchairs set in front of Nora's desk. "Shall we talk about why you came to see me?"

"Sure. Let's do that."

Mercedes sat in one armchair. Nora took the other. Gmork sat at her feet, on her feet.

"I'm trying very hard not to demand you tell me how you know where I live," Nora said. "I'm not sure how much longer I can stop myself."

"Zillow," Mercedes said.

"What?"

She pulled her bag into her lap, covering the bare inches of her stomach, and crossed her legs at the ankle.

"Zillow. It's a real estate website."

"Yeah, I know what it is. You used it to find me?"

"When you came for your reading with me, you said you were waiting to hear about a house you wanted to buy. It was in the Garden District, a red house, and you'd put in a lowball offer. A week later, I checked the website. A red house in the Garden District was now under contract for twenty-thousand less than the original asking price. Didn't take sacred geometry to put two and two together."

"You told me I'd get the house. Were you checking to see if you were right?"

"I knew I was right."

"Then why—"

"My turn," Mercedes said, and Nora sat up, alert. It wasn't often another woman cut her off. Or anyone, really.

"Okay, go on," Nora said.

"Lord Chaz said you were looking for a missing girl. I don't think that's true, is it?"

A fair question, but not so easy to answer.

"It isn't. But I can't tell you the whole story."

"Please tell me what you can."

"A man was found dead recently. He'd shot himself."

"Accident? Or suicide?"

"Suicide. And I don't know this man from Adam, but for some reason, I was the last person he tried calling before pulling the trigger. The man was found with my business card in his pocket, so we know it wasn't just a wrong number —for some reason, he was trying to reach me. Unfortunately, that's no longer my number. It was an old card from when I worked in New York. He never reached me. For days, I've been beating my head against the wall trying to think who I might have given one of my cards to while I was down here. Earlier this evening someone mentioned witches. I finally remembered...you. I gave you a card."

"Only me?"

"Only you. As far as I can remember. Is it possible you gave my card to someone?"

"No."

"Are you sure? I know I told you what I did for a living."

"Writer. Dominatrix. I wouldn't forget that even if I'd wanted to."

"Did a friend of yours, a client, a stranger...did anybody mention they were trying to find a dominatrix?"

"No."

"Could one of your coworkers at the shop...did they maybe take it?"

"No."

"Did you throw it in the trash?"

"No."

"Recycling?"

"No."

"Come on," Nora said, exasperated. "It must have ended up in the trash at some point, right? If you know anything at all, please tell me. It's driving me crazy knowing a man reached out to me, wanted me for something, and when he couldn't reach me, he killed himself. You'd want to know why, right?"

"I suppose I would," she said. "But in this, I'm afraid I can't help you. You see…"

Mercedes paused and opened her bag and took out a large book—black, leather-bound, with two skulls embossed on the cover. Mercedes set it in her lap and opened it carefully. Carefully because the book was full of odds and ends—scraps of paper, recipe cards, photographs, pressed flowers and leaves. The pages themselves were thick, soft cotton, covered in black, red, blue, and green ink. Some of the pages bore elaborate drawings of triangles within circles, circles within squares, animals, trees, moons, and stars.

Other pages bore only writing, nearly as ornate as calligraphy. Back, back, back, Mercedes turned in the book, and Nora saw some dates written on top of the pages. Journal entries. Back she went through this year, then last year, before reaching the November she'd been in New Orleans house-hunting. Two years and ten months ago.

Mercedes stopped at last and took from the book a small slightly-crinkled envelope. An ordinary envelope. She slipped her fingers under the flap and from inside pulled out a red rectangle, no bigger than the palm of her hand.

She held it out toward Nora, who took it with the slightest quiver in her stomach.

"This is my business card," Nora breathed. "You kept it."

"I did."

"But…why?"

"I used it," she said. "To cast a spell of protection."

"Protection? I don't need protection." Søren, Nico,

Kingsley, Gmork...the last thing she needed was more people trying to protect her.

"You misunderstand me, Mistress Nora. I wasn't trying to protect you. The spell was for protection *from* you."

Chapter Twenty-Two

Nora's doubt about this woman turned to fear. She clutched her wine glass harder in her hand, holding it against her chest so Mercedes couldn't see it shaking.

"What the hell are you talking about?" Nora asked.

Mercedes clasped her hands together and rested them in her lap on the pages of the open book.

"We have a rule," Mercedes said. "*An it harm none, do as ye will.* It's our only commandment. It comes with a warning—whatever harm we do will be visited upon us threefold. So I have no wish to harm you, Mistress."

"Good. That makes two of us."

Mercedes gave her a gentle smile.

"If I thought you would believe a word I said," Mercedes continued, "I would explain what I mean. But you're Catholic. To you, our Old Ways are party games and cons. You came to me for a reading because it's what tourists do in the Quarter when it's too early to drink, and you've already eaten all the beignets you can handle for the day."

"I try to keep an open mind."

"You should. But will you, if I tell you my truth? Or will you call it a lie or a hoax or a con?"

"Would you blame me if I did?"

"Would you blame me if I called your faith a hoax? If I called Catholicism a sham? If I told you that you're enabling the patriarchal oppression of women every single time you walk through a Catholic church's doors? Would you blame me if I reminded you that only men are allowed to become priests in your faith because they do not deem women worthy of holding holy office?"

Nora let that sink in a moment.

"No," Nora said. "I might not appreciate the sentiment, but I wouldn't blame you."

"Then maybe this is a talk we can have. Woman to woman. Not enemies. Not rivals. If not friends, then allies."

"We can try," Nora said. "I think we're on the same side. You have your commandment, I have mine. Hurt, but don't harm."

"A good rule," she said, nodding. "If you will hear me, I'll tell you."

Nora couldn't recall a time when she'd been in the presence of a woman with enough presence to intimidate her. But as Mercedes sat in the armchair, hands on her books, eyes on Nora's eyes, she felt a chill run through her not unlike touching a live wire, like touching raw power.

Mercedes picked up her wine glass again and finished it off with a final swallow. She set it down and turned her attention back to her book.

"November ninth," Mercedes read aloud. "Difficult reading today. A woman came to me for a half-hour read. I should have made up an excuse to say 'no.' The second I saw her, I knew she was dangerous. So much male energy, so much violence in her blood. I did it anyway. Always a sucker for a beautiful woman."

Nora stared at Mercedes, eyes narrowed. Mercedes, however, wouldn't meet her eyes. She continued:

> She told me she was moving to New Orleans, here to buy a house. I used the Old Path deck, which I rarely use. I wasn't sure why until I turned over the card for the High Priest in present position and her green eyes went wide as two jade moons. In other decks, he's called the Hierophant. The card was in present position, reversed. Upright means conformity to the status quo. Reversed means departing from the status quo, the traditions and insinuations she's been bound to her in her life. And the next card was the Three of Staves. A journey ahead.

She laid her hand on the page over a paragraph of writing. Nora started to ask her what else she'd written when Mercedes turned the page and began to read aloud again.

> I told her the safe things I saw. That she would get her house. That she would have success in her twin careers.
>
> Other things I didn't tell her.
>
> A death coming that couldn't be prevented. Immediate family, I think.
>
> A new lover, too. The Knight of Cups—a quiet and gentle lover who carries a cup of wine in his sword hand. Though there was opposition to the match.
>
> I summed both up by saying there were challenges ahead, unavoidable, one good, one painful.
>
> Then I saw the fire. The Tower burning. I knew it was the city. I knew this woman started the fire. If she

makes the right choice, the fire will be a cleansing flame. If she makes the wrong choice, the innocent will burn.

I told her she would face a hard choice ahead. She asked me what it was. I couldn't tell her. It's too far down the line. Like trying to read words written in smoke. I don't think she believed me.

Knowledge is power, the old philosophers said. They were wrong. Knowledge is responsibility. I'll have to keep an eye on this woman and cast spells of protection. Hematite for protection. Beads for binding—purple for wisdom, silver for feminine power.

Mercedes closed her book, looked up, and waited in silence.

"I keep trying to figure out how you're trying to scam me," Nora said.

Mercedes held up her hands, palms up and empty.

"You see me asking for money? I'm not trying to sell you a thing."

"A month after that reading, I met my boyfriend. A Frenchman who acts like a knight-protector. He's calm and gentle and makes wine. My mother died of advanced lung cancer three months after that reading. Don't pretend you knew all that months before it happened."

"I didn't know. The cards did."

"If you really knew my mother was dying, why didn't you tell me that?"

"You wouldn't have believed me," she said. "And your mother would die anyway, and in addition to your sorrow, you would be saddled with guilt for ignoring what I told you."

"I might have believed you."

"You don't believe me now. Why would you then?"

"Okay, forget that," Nora said. "What about the fire? Burning innocent people? What the fuck is that supposed to mean?"

"The closer events are, the easier they are to see. The further out, the harder. I can see the titles of the books on the shelves near me. I can't read the titles on your books across the room. The future is the same. But I think it's getting closer."

"Could you be any vaguer?"

"You don't know. Why should I? It's your choice, not mine."

"I would never hurt innocent people."

"I don't think you would...not on purpose. But even if pain is unintentional, it still hurts, doesn't it?"

Nora had no answer to that. It was true. Couldn't argue with the truth.

Mercedes slipped her book into her bag and stood up.

"Are you leaving?" Nora asked.

"I have to be at the shop at ten for deliveries. Thank you for the wine."

Mercedes rose to her feet and Nora had no choice but to walk her to the door, like she was some normal houseguest.

Nora opened the door and Mercedes looked at it, didn't leave. Apparently, Mercedes still had something to say to her.

"This is between women," Mercedes said. "About women. For women. Men will only make it more complicated than it already is. Men will only make it worse."

"I trust the men in my life."

"You got to learn to trust the women, too. You've got to. Even the silence of a woman is wiser than the words of a man."

"Then let's be wise, shall we?"

Both of Mercedes's elegant eyebrows went up at that. But she playfully ran her fingers over her lips to zip them. She nodded, and Nora opened the door again.

Mercedes slipped on her shoes, turned to leave. She stepped onto the porch, but before Nora closed the door, she had to ask one more question.

"I saw you cover up a paragraph when you were reading to me. What was it?"

"You ask me that like you believe it's real."

"Pascal's Wager," Nora said. "Ever heard of it?"

Mercedes nodded. "We wager our souls when we choose to believe or not believe in God. Smart souls believe in God because if God does exist, God will reward them with eternal happiness. If God doesn't exist, the person has lost nothing. But if God exists and the person doesn't believe, he's lost eternity."

"So might as well believe," Nora said. "Just in case."

"You don't lose anything by asking me, you mean? And you might gain something?"

"Seems a safe bet." Nora paused. "Did you? See anything about me, I mean?"

"The Hierophant," she said. "The High Priest. He was in the present position reversed, but not the future."

"What does that mean? A priest I know is going to die?"

A priest did die.

"No," Mercedes said. "Three of Staves came next. I saw you taking a journey. A journey that will take you away from The High Priest."

"I went on that journey. I came back."

Mercedes shook her head.

"No. On this journey, you don't come back. You walk away and keep walking."

Nora stood up straighter. Her jaw clenched.

"This is why we don't tell people what they don't want to hear." Mercedes smiled apologetically.

"Now I know you're a fraud," Nora said.

"What is he to you? The High Priest?"

"That's none of your business."

"Whatever it is, it's not good for you."

Nora felt a jolt at those words. Her anger—dammed by her curiosity—finally broke through. She was done.

"Why don't you just go and cast a spell to make sure I do what you want me to do?" Nora demanded, her tone mocking.

"You're suggesting I go to a sacred temple by night, light a candle, and speak magic words?"

"That'll work."

"Like when you go to St. Mary's at night, light altar candles and pray?"

Nora narrowed her eyes at Mercedes.

"You have been following me."

"I walk the Garden District every night, as you do. I saw you out with only your dog, later than usual. I was curious."

"Stop following me."

Mercedes gave her a Mona Lisa smile. "Yes, Mistress."

Nora shut the door behind Mercedes, locked it and rested her forehead on the cool surface. She breathed, breathed again.

Stupid. So fucking stupid. She didn't believe in this garbage. It was all a hoax, a hustle, a con. A long con, at that. And Nora was done with it. She undid the lock. She was going to tell Mercedes that if she ever stepped foot on her property again, there would be a restraining order waiting with her name on it.

Nora threw the door open. Mercedes was long gone, but swinging from her doorknob was a string of silver Mardi Gras beads.

Chapter Twenty-Three

Cyrus got home to his apartment a few minutes after midnight. He had eyes for nothing or no one but his bed. He had his shirt unbuttoned and halfway off when he felt his phone buzzing in his pants.

A text from Nora. Soon as he read it, he called her.

"Cyrus," she breathed. "I'm so glad you're still awake."

"Just got home. She was at your house?"

"Yeah. She just knocked on my door."

"And you opened it?"

"Gmork didn't bark. He barks at men, not women. I just saw a woman and opened the door."

She sounded more scared now than she had when Pasadena had roughed her up on Bourbon Street.

"What did she say?"

"A lot. She said she's been keeping an eye on me for three years. I don't know why, but she's the one who's been putting the beads in my tree."

"Shit, shit, shit." Cyrus grimaced. "I never should have gotten you into this."

"It's not your fault, Cy."

"You need me to come over?" he asked. Where had that come from? Was that the old Cyrus talking or the new Cyrus? "I can sleep on your sofa. Paulina won't mind."

"I have to be honest, I'm kind of tempted to say 'yes.' But I don't want to be a coward."

"A woman came to your door in the middle of the night, told you she'd been watching you for three years. That she's been beading your trees. I think you're allowed to be scared shitless. Hell, I am."

That wasn't an exaggeration. Cyrus's heart was pounding like a bass drum.

"I don't want you alone," he said. "Can you stay at Edge's house tonight?"

Edge definitely seemed like the kind of man who could handle this kind of threat.

"King's probably not home yet. And I'm sure Juliette's already asleep. I'm not about to wake up a pregnant woman and scare the hell out of her."

Cyrus couldn't blame her for that. "Hotel? Søren's place?"

"Yeah, no. When he finds out what happened, I'll be off the case. I'll just go sleep at my dungeon," she said. "The building is alarmed and monitored."

"Fine, but I'll drive you," Cyrus said. "She might still be watching your front door, so I'll pick you up in front of Edge's. You can head out back, through the alley into his gated yard. I'll pull around front of his place and pick you up. Then we'll hang at your—" and Cyrus could not believe he was saying this, "—dungeon until morning."

"You don't have to do that."

"Gonna do it anyway. I got you into this. I'll change clothes and be right there. Don't leave your house until I text you I'm in front of Edge's place, okay?"

"Got it. See you soon." She paused. Then, "Cyrus?"

"Yeah?"

"Thank you."

"Hey, no problem."

Cyrus changed into jeans and a black t-shirt. He didn't want to wake—or scare—Paulina with a text or a call. She always kept her phone on and by her bed in case of emergencies. Instead, he sent her a short email telling her the basics—that Nora had been threatened by a possible witness, and he was going to keep an eye on her tonight.

That late, Cyrus encountered no traffic. He pulled up in front of Edge's house ten minutes after leaving his own. He texted Nora, and a minute later she came to the the front gate with her dog. She'd changed clothes, too. Jeans, white shirt, leather jacket, and boots.

Cyrus kept an eye on the street as the gate yawned opened and then closed behind her. He unlocked the car doors. Nora let her dog hop into the backseat, and then she slid into the front passenger seat next to Cyrus.

"Hi," she said.

"Ready?"

"Definitely."

He peeled away from the curb and headed in the direction of Nora's Piety Street place. They drove for a few minutes in silence until Cyrus felt calm enough to talk.

"You okay?" he asked.

"I can't tell if I'm over-reacting or under-reacting. Or in shock."

"Same." Cyrus glanced at her. "Town this size, you get a lot of kooks. Most are harmless. I'd say ninety-eight percent are harmless. The question is...is she in that ninety-eight?"

"Or the two," Nora said, then sighed.

"Come on. Tell me everything she said."

Cyrus listened to her story, then said, "She thinks you're the dangerous one."

Nora raised her hands, also baffled. "I admit, I'm no angel. I've broken laws and broken hearts."

"And feet."

"Broken feet. Noses. No, just one nose. Ribs. Two ribs, if I remember correctly. Busted my fair share of balls. Consensually and non. Though he was asking for it. And so was he. And him, too."

"I get it." Enough with the ball-busting talk already.

"But dangerous? And it wasn't just, 'You're scary, and I don't like you.' She got specific. She said I was going to hurt innocent people. Kids, maybe."

"I saw you with Edge's little girl. You're not dangerous to kids. This woman sounds nuts." Cyrus shook his head again. "And could she be a little more specific? Like, help us out here, Gwenda."

"Gwenda?"

"Wasn't that the witch in *Wizard of Oz*?"

"Glinda."

"Who the hell's Gwenda then?"

"Ex-girlfriend?" Nora asked.

He shrugged. "Good guess with me."

Nora laughed. Good to hear her laugh. Been a rough night for the lady.

"Can I ask you something weird?" Nora asked.

"Shoot."

"You don't believe in it, do you? Witchcraft and fortune-telling and stuff?"

Cyrus had to think about that, really think about it. "I don't want to believe in it, but it scares me. Why would it scare me if I didn't believe in it a little?"

"Good point."

"Plus, ah..." he began.

"What?"

"Don't laugh, but I meditate." Cyrus glanced at her to see what kind of face she made. She didn't make one. "The therapist Paulina sent me to suggested it, made me promise to try it. I did and it kind of surprised me how much it worked for me. It got me down into deep places in my head," he said, tapping his temple. "When I'm down there, I see things sometimes. I figure things out. It's hard to explain."

"Go on," she said. "What do you see?"

"A river," he said. "And there are things in the river. Answers to questions. Memories. Truths. I go there when I need to figure things out and sometimes I do and it's eerie. Almost spooky. Solved a lot of cases down in that place, my feet in the water. Husband who disappeared three months earlier, I figured out where to find him. Missing kid? Found her, too, while I was in the water."

"Our subconscious is a lot smarter than we are sometimes."

"I get that, but it's more than that. This is where it gets weird. The river feels real to me. Like it's really out there somewhere, and anybody who finds it can dip their hands in it, stick their feet in, and get something out of the water. My therapist says I'm a Jungian. That the river is the collective unconscious. You heard of that?"

"I have," she said. "Lot of writers believe in it."

"You?"

She shrugged. "Never thought about it really. But I will say, sometimes when I'm writing a story, it feels like it exists independently of me, not like I'm creating it. More like I'm finding it."

"That's it," he said. "That's it exactly."

She turned her head, smiled at him. "A Jungian private detective. I love it."

"Now I can't go around wading in imaginary rivers to solve cases and then get judgmental when a woman says she can cast spells and see the future. That'd be a little hypocritical, right?"

"Right." Nora nodded, crossed her arms over her chest.

"You?" he asked. "You believe in it? Witches? Witchcraft?"

Nora turned her head, stared out the passenger window. "When she was leaving, I told her if she thought I was really dangerous, she should just go and cast a spell to make me do whatever it was she wanted me to do. She said something about how she could go to an altar at midnight, light a candle, say some magic words. Does that sound like casting a spell to you?"

"Kind of."

"She was talking about me. I went to St. Mary's chapel the other night to pray for Søren to come home. Altar at midnight. I lit a candle. I said magic words."

"That's not casting a spell. That's praying."

"Is it really that different? Never occurred to me that it was all the same thing."

"It's different."

"How?"

Cyrus had to think about that, too. This was something he would have to meditate on.

"I don't know," he said finally. "Just feels different."

"You don't really think Catholics are the only people who get access to the spiritual forces in the universe, do you?"

"Well, no."

"Jews and Muslims and Baptists and Methodists and Sikhs and Hindus and Buddhists do, too, right?"

"I think so. Not that I advertise it around my grandmother."

Nora smiled. "Why not witches, then? If we think our prayers work, why don't we think theirs do, too, just because they call them 'spells'?"

"You ask a good question," he said. "You scared of her?"

"Not of her. Just...something she said."

"Something else?"

Nora slowly nodded. Then she turned his way again. "She said something about me and Søren."

"What did she say?"

"That I would leave him."

Cyrus rolled his eyes. "Real or not, you have free will," he said. "You don't want to leave him...you don't leave him. That's all you. Nobody can make you if you don't want to."

"True," she said. "I hope."

They arrived at Nora's dungeon. Cyrus made her stay in the car while he walked around the building. Then he nodded for her to get out of the car. She and Gmork—what kind of damn name for a dog was Gmork?—strode quickly over to the door. Nora punched in the security code and they went inside. Nora reset the door alarm.

"Guess we're safe for now," she said.

"Famous last words."

She glared at him.

"Just saying," he said. "Give me your keys. I'm going up first. Don't come up until I text you."

"You're being very chivalrous."

"I'm being a damn fool is what I'm being," he said as he went to the door to the stairs.

"You could take the elevator," she said.

"I've seen too many horror movies."

"People get killed on the stairs in horror movies, too."

Cyrus gave her the dirtiest look he could muster.

"That was payback," she said, "for the 'famous last words' comment."

"Just stay here with your stupid dog."

He went up the stairs, his pulse quickening. Nobody waiting around the bend. Thank God. He reached the third floor and unlocked her door. After a deep inhale and exhale, he gave it a small push. The lights were off inside, but he heard nothing, sensed nothing. He pulled the door shut. He'd wait for her to continue his sweep—he didn't want to leave her alone for too long downstairs. He texted her the all-clear.

Nora joined him on the third-floor foyer, and took Gmork off his leash. She gave a forceful command. The dog's ears perked up. His demeanor changed in an instant from that of a pet to a protector. He went straight to the closed door and sat, whimpering. Nora let him inside.

"What's he doing?" Cyrus asked, craning his neck to get a peek inside.

"Bomb-sniffing. Just in case."

"He's trained for that?"

"Trained for everything. If someone was hiding, he'd sniff them out, too. I think. That's what they told me anyway. He doesn't get much chance to practice his fancy tricks with me. Believe it or not, I don't get too many kooks following me around."

"You're a dominatrix dating a priest and a French farmer. You got a dog that worships you on command. You got a witch stalking you. You have your own dungeon on the third floor of a bank building. Lady, I hate to tell you this...but you are one of the kooks."

"That would hurt," Nora said as she shook off her black leather jacket, "except it's true."

Gmork returned to her, and she went inside and switched on the lights. She held the door open for Cyrus.

"Holy shit," he said.

"Welcome to my dungeon," Nora said, smiling. "Like it?"

Chapter Twenty-Four

C yrus blinked, blinked again, turned a slow circle. The walls of the room were blood-red. Hanging from what seemed like a thousand hooks was every kind of torture instrument he'd ever heard of and a few he now wished he'd never seen.

Floggers and whips, ropes and canes. But also lots of weird-looking metal objects and sitting in various spots on the floor like demonic gym equipment was a big metal cage, a medical table with leather straps hanging off it, and some kind of crazy-ass wooden throne with steel hooks in it.

"When you said this was a dungeon...you meant it."

Nora laughed as she put the tea things from their talk with Doc into a sink on the far wall. A sink? Yeah. A sink. Right next to a toilet. Not a bathroom. Just the toilet.

"I don't want to know," he said, pointing at the toilet.

"Puppy play," Nora said. "Dogs drink out of toilets. I make my puppies drink from the toilet. Nobody ever uses it as, you know, a toilet."

"Puppies?"

"Human puppies. Men who like being treated like dogs." Nora opened the cabinet door under the sink and took out a small bottle of Dawn.

"And the sink?"

"For washing up stuff," she said. "All this equipment touches human bodies. You don't want to spread infections or anything. This room used to be the company's break room. Sink, counter, coffee machine, half bath. I had everything taken out except for the sink and toilet."

"I just don't even know what to say," Cyrus said.

"You don't have to say anything. Promise. Make yourself at home. Watch what you touch, though. Some of the equipment is dangerous."

"You don't say."

While Nora washed her dishes, Cyrus roamed the room, trying to make himself as narrow as possible to avoid brushing up against something he didn't want to brush up against.

So many whips. So many floggers. Enough rope to build a bridge from here to his apartment. He came to a stop in front of a red curtain, the old-fashioned kind like what they hung in front of movie screens. It even had golden tassels, the sort you pulled to raise the curtain.

"Do I want to know what's behind the curtain?" Cyrus asked.

"My bed," she said.

"Just a bed? Like a normal bed?"

"Normal bed. I've been known to nap between sessions with clients."

"Oh," Cyrus said. "Makes sense."

"It's also for Sheridan."

"Who's that?"

"My little girl sub. She's not into dungeons. Prefers being beaten and fucked on beds. Spoiled little brat."

Cyrus glanced over at Nora, thinking she was yanking his chain. No. Not chain-yanking. She was, in fact, drying the dishes.

"I also keep the scary stuff in there under lock and key," she said.

"The scary stuff?" He glanced around the room again at the cages and whips. "You're saying this isn't the scary stuff? How much does this shit cost you?"

Nora turned her back to him, lifted the bottom of her t-shirt a few inches. Cyrus could just see the tail end of a red welt at the bottom of her ribcage.

"Damn."

"Belt," she said. "Basic black leather, fifty dollars. All he used on me. His own belt in a hotel room. No dungeon necessary."

"And you really, actually, swear-to-God liked that? If not, I may have to settle things with him."

"I really, actually, swear-to-God loved it. Don't beat up my dominant, please. But if you do, I'd appreciate it if you left his pretty face alone."

He studied a wall of canes but didn't touch any. This wasn't fuzzy handcuffs and silk blindfolds sort of stuff. This was the real deal.

"Tell me something," he said, glancing around, eyes wide, "how do you get into this? I mean...this is a lot."

"Everybody finds their way to kink by a different path. I know dominatrixes who learned the trade from their own mothers. I know male submissives who just got curious one day, Googled BDSM clubs, and fell down the rabbit-hole."

"What about you?"

She smiled. "Mine's a pretty common story. You fall in love with someone already kinky—Søren, in my case—and you discover you're as into it as they are. Kink is often sexually-transmitted."

"He just up and said, 'Hey, I know I'm your priest, but I'm also kinky as hell. Wanna play?'"

"He actually kept it a secret from me for a long time. He's...he's a little more kinky than your average kinky guy. Pain's his fetish. If there's no pain, there's no sex. That's a hard thing to tell the girl you're in love with."

"You mean it's kink 24/7/365?" he asked. "And he's always the one calling the shots?"

She nodded. "Always. No days off."

"But you're into calling the shots, too." He reached out and stroked the tails of one of the floggers on the wall. It was shockingly soft, suede probably. "Doesn't it get old? Him being in charge all the time?"

"It is what it is. If you fall in love with a foot fetishist, you have to accept a lifetime of high heels and weekly pedicures."

"So it does get old?" He knew when a witness wasn't telling him the whole truth and nothing but the truth. She took a seat on a big black throne-sort of contraption, a throne with D-rings screwed into it. She crossed her legs and sat back, looking almost like a real queen.

"I'll admit to having the occasional fantasy about topping him. But it's about the same as dreaming about what you'd do with the lottery money you're never going to win. I get all my topping out of my system in here. And there," she said, pointing at the curtained bedroom. "And in France."

"Yeah, yeah, with your 'other' lover."

"Now you're catching on." She smiled tiredly. He only

looked at her. Nothing got a suspect talking faster than silence. "It doesn't get old, being with him. It never gets old. Power is the ultimate aphrodisiac. Søren is the most powerful man I know. Therefore and ergo, Søren is the ultimate aphrodisiac. But...just once might be nice. There. You got me to confess. Now your turn."

"No."

"You acted very strange the day we met when I mentioned the word 'Daddy.' Why?"

"No," he said. "No way. I am not having this conversation with you."

"You're in my dungeon now. My dungeon. My rules. We're having this conversation. You brought it up."

He glared at her.

"Who called you 'Daddy'? Ex-girlfriend. Ex-wife? First lover? Tell me. The Mistress is listening..." She put her hand to her ear and leaned in.

He exhaled, hard and heavy, but he said it anyway. "Paulina."

Nora's eyebrow raised half an inch. "Really?"

Cyrus nodded.

"You like that?"

Cyrus nodded again.

"Nice," Nora said.

"You think she's kinky?" he asked.

"Because she calls you 'Daddy'? Maybe. Maybe just a pet name. Now if she calls you 'Dad'...that's definitely kinky."

"What happened to you as a child?"

"Nothing," Nora said with a shrug. "Totally normal childhood. I mean, other than getting arrested for grand-theft auto, my Catholic priest falling in love with me when

I was fifteen, and my father getting whacked by the mob. Why do you ask?"

Cyrus groaned and rubbed his forehead. There was a lot that needed unpacking in what Nora just said. He decided to leave it packed.

"Do you think she's kinky?" Nora asked, sounding suddenly—and eerily—like Cyrus's therapist.

He looked for a place to sit. Nothing except for the medical bed. Ah, hell. Why not?

"Her father is career Navy," he said, sitting on the edge of the bed and letting his feet dangle. He felt like a kid again about to get a tetanus shot. "He runs the house like he's captain of a ship. Everything on schedule. Everything in its place. Everybody behaves and does their job. No backtalk. No tears. Paulina never called him 'Dad' or 'Daddy.' She always called him 'Sir.' Still does. She says he's gotten more affectionate as he's gotten older, but he's still more 'Sir' to her than 'Dad.'"

"That's gotta be tough."

"She loves her father. Respects the hell out of him. But yeah, not a lot of hugging and kissing and laughing and goofing together. She says she calls me 'Daddy' because I make her feel safe and loved and, you know, we're goofs together. Always laughing. I don't know if I've ever even heard her father laugh. I think that's all it is. She just, you know, that word to her means 'the man who loves me, takes care of me, and we play together.'"

"Does she call you 'Daddy' in bed?"

Cyrus barked a laugh. He didn't mean to. It just came out.

"What?" Nora asked. "That was a weird reaction."

"Nothing."

"Something," she said. "Come on. Tell me. If it helps... I've called Søren 'Daddy' during sex before."

He should have said, *I don't need to hear this, Nora.* What he did say was, "Really?"

"One of those fantasies you think you want to try out, and then you do and it's so intense and awkward that you can barely handle it."

"You couldn't handle it?"

"I cried," she said. "It was..." she paused and exhaled. "Intense. Intense and humiliating. And sexy. That's where kink gets so complicated. That you hate it and love it at the same time."

"Sounds intense," Cyrus said. "Maybe too intense for me."

"It's okay. Paulina might not have any Daddy-kink in her at all. That's why I asked if she did it in bed or just whenever. 'Fuck me harder, Daddy' is a slightly different scenario than 'Pass the ketchup, Daddy.'"

Cyrus needed a few seconds to process all that. Finally, he said, "I don't know."

"Know what?"

"We, ah..." He took another few seconds, tried to figure out if he could say what he wanted to say. If he should say what he wanted to say. Then he just said it. "We've never had sex."

Nora's eyes nearly fell out of her head.

"Are you serious?"

"We're waiting until our wedding night."

"Holy...I knew she was Catholic but that's...that's too Catholic is what that is."

Cyrus dropped his chin to his chest and shook his head.

"You are telling me, Mistress."

"Oh God, poor you."

"No, no." He raised his head and exhaled. "It was my suggestion."

"Were you on drugs?"

"Love," he said. "Dumb stupid love."

"That was my other guess."

"I wanted her to know that I was in this for her, not using her for sex. You know, like I had with every other woman in my life since I was sixteen years old."

"So offering to wait until you were married was a romantic gesture?"

"Right."

"And you and Paulina have been dating how long?"

"Two years."

"So you haven't had sex in..."

"Over two years."

Nora put the fingers of both hands on her temples, like her head was about to explode and she needed to contain the blast.

"I've never wanted to slap a man so hard in my life. I mean, a man who wasn't Søren."

Cyrus tilted his head to the side, offering her his cheek.

"Do it," he said. "I deserve it."

Nora rose off her throne and walked over to him. There was a damn good chance the woman really was going to slap him. She raised her hand and patted his shoulder.

"My sympathies, my friend." She patted his shoulder again. "Been there."

"Thank you. I needed that."

Nora shook her head.

"Not even oral?"

"No."

"Oh my Jesus," Nora said.

Cyrus laughed hard enough he fell back on the bed. Then remembered this was a *medical bed* in a *dungeon*, and God only knew what went on there. He sat up very quickly.

Nora returned to her throne. She looked like a woman who wanted to smile but was trying very hard to keep it to herself.

"You think I'm a sucker, right?" he asked.

"You're a very good man, and Paulina is very lucky to have you."

"I appreciate that."

"But you should probably eat her pussy anyway."

"Nora, come on."

"I'm serious. You want to, right?"

"Is that a real question? Really? A real question? You're asking me that like it's a real question you don't know the answer to?"

"So do it."

"We said we'd wait."

"You made the rules. You can break the rules. Or bend them."

"We are not bending anything."

"Go to her house, pick her up, carry her to bed, put her down and say, 'I'm going to go down on you until you come on me and you're going to like it. That's an order.'"

"She would not go for that."

"Hmm...good point. We don't know if she's kinky yet or not. Better just ask nicely. 'May I please eat your pussy?' Try it. Dare you."

"Dare me? You just dared me? Are we in the seventh grade now?"

Who was this woman and, better question, why did he

like hanging out with her so much? Poor judgment. He owned that.

"Double-dare you."

"Why do I talk to you?"

"Bet you're good at it."

"Hell yes I am."

"Because if you aren't, you can ask Søren for tips. For a priest, he's surprisingly good at eating pussy."

"I hope that witch hexes you."

"You go to her and tell her you want to make her feel as good as she makes you feel...no way would she say 'no' to that. And if she does, I'll give you a hundred dollars. Cash. Today."

"I'm going out there." He pointed at the door to her fancy waiting room. "And you're staying in here. And I am never talking to you again."

"Does that mean I don't get to come to the wedding?"

Cyrus jumped off the med bed and onto the floor. He held out his hand, finger pointed at Nora's face.

"Yes?" she said.

"You're ten kinds of crazy."

She narrowed her eyes at him. "Only ten?"

Nora reached out and grabbed his finger.

"Thanks for keeping me company," she said. "I feel a lot less freaked out now."

"That makes one of us."

Laughing, she released his finger.

"Goodnight, Mistress. Please call your demon dog in here. I am not sleeping—"

Cyrus heard the sound of an organ playing terrifyingly eerie music.

"What the hell?" Cyrus glanced around looking for the Phantom of the Dungeon.

"Bach's Toccata and Fugue in D Minor," she said. "Søren calling."

"You gonna answer it?"

The strange, but oddly familiar organ music continued.

"I'm considering not answering it," she said.

"Nora."

"Fine."

The organ music stopped and the phone buzzed. "Text," she said. "Shit. He says he stopped by the house to check on me, wants to know why I'm not home."

"You have to tell him."

"Do I though? I mean...do I?" Her voice went up an octave on the last *do I?*

He stared at her, hard. "Do not get me on the bad side of a Viking. If he belts his own girlfriend, no telling what he'll do to me."

"That's a good point," she said. "And yet, I'm still not calling him." She stared at her phone like she wasn't sure what it was or where it had come from.

He cleared his throat pointedly. She got the message.

"Fine. I'm calling him." She called him. "Hello, Sir."

He waited, curious enough to eavesdrop.

"Ah...long story," Nora said. "I'm at my dungeon right now. I had something weird happen tonight. I didn't feel like staying at home." Pause. "No, Kingsley wasn't involved this time." Pause again. "Please. Cyrus would probably appreciate that." Pause. "Yeah, he's here. Keeping me company. Although I think he regrets it."

Cyrus nodded to make her smile. He was glad to see it worked.

"Okay, love you, too, Sir. See you soon."

Nora hung up the call.

"You're off the hook," Nora said. "He's coming over."

"Ah, that's good. I'll stay until he gets here."

"I appreciate that," she said and smiled. "But he's probably going to tell me I have to stop working on the case with you."

"It's all right. I'll miss your help, but I'll figure it out. When I know something, I'll let you know."

"Fun while it lasted. Pleasure working with you, Mr. Tremont." She held out her hand and they shook.

"Yeah, same, Mistress Nora."

He left her alone in her dungeon and sat in the armchair, waiting for the Viking to arrive. He closed his eyes, thinking of dozing off. While his body was bone tired, his mind wouldn't let him rest.

Instead of sleeping, he went to the river. He didn't mean to, but his mind took him there of its own will. Ever since he'd seen Father Ike with that gun, he'd stayed back, afraid of what he'd see if he went again. But now he couldn't stop the feet in his mind finding the path to his soul, and up and over the rise he found a night river flowing easy and sweet. Lightning bugs skimmed the surface, flashing their double lights—one true, one reflection. The full white moon rose over the tree tops, and he saw something moving under the water, something alive. He followed it with his eyes, waiting for it to surface. It dove deep and the water stilled.

From the opposite direction, he saw someone swimming toward where he stood on a flat stone that hung over the river's edge.

The swimmer rose up in the shallow end near the bank.

"Nora? What are you doing?"

She was fully dressed in the clothes she'd been wearing tonight—corset and jeans—but soaking wet.

"Water's nice tonight," she said. "Want to swim?"

"You better get out. Something's in the water."

"Only fish," she said. "I'm not afraid of—"

Something shot out of the water, grabbed her around the waist, and dragged her under. Fast, too fast for Cyrus to stop him. But not too fast to see who it was who'd taken her under.

Father Ike.

Cyrus jumped in the river but as soon as his feet hit the water, something shook him out of his meditative state.

His phone vibrated wildly in his jeans pocket. He took it out, breathing hard, pressed the phone against his chest and his pounding heart.

A text from Paulina.

Got your email. What's going on? Everybody okay?

Cyrus stared at her message, his eyes focused but his mind still in the river. He took a few deep breaths and slowly came back to himself. He knew exactly what he was seeing in his meditation, that this case was putting Nora in danger. He'd seen with his own eyes a drunk asshole holding her against her will. He'd heard the fear in her voice when she'd called to tell him one of their witnesses had shown up at her front door. Except why had it been Father Ike he'd seen grabbing Nora? Why him and not the drunk kid? Why him and not the witch?

He didn't have time to figure that out. Paulina was waiting.

What are you doing up? he texted back.

Woke up, went to the bathroom, checked my phone. How scared should I be right now?

Been a crazy night, but we're okay. I'll tell you tomorrow.

Call me if you want. We can talk. Wide awake now.

Cyrus thought about that. After seeing what he saw in

the river, he wanted to hear her voice so bad it hurt. Still, it was almost two in the morning. Paulina needed her sleep. So did he.

He was about to tell her "no," that it was okay, he'd tell her more about it tomorrow. But he didn't. The elevator thrummed. The Viking had arrived.

He texted back, *You mind if I come over?*

Cyrus could see the sleepy grin on her face as she replied.

Don't mind one bit, Daddy.

Chapter Twenty-Five

Nora was shocked by her own relief at seeing Søren stride into her dungeon. He didn't say a word, only pulled her into his arms and held her.

"I thought you'd be with Kingsley," she said. As soon as she was in his strong arms, she let herself relax. Exhaustion had finally caught up with her.

"You know he can't stay away from Juliette all night. He went home an hour ago. I wanted to check on you and when you weren't home..."

"You thought I was in jail, didn't you?"

"It did occur to me."

Nora laughed against his chest. He held her even tighter and she inhaled the scent of him—frost on frozen pine trees and the clean smell of soap from his recent shower.

"What happened?" he asked.

"It's a long story. Can it wait until morning?"

"No."

"Fine." She gave him the CliffsNotes version—the drunk dickhead, Cyrus interviewing a vampire, the witch they were looking for who found them first. She shook her head, sighed.

Søren seemed to mull that over for a moment.

"Were you planning on telling me any of this?"

"It crossed my mind," Nora said. A half-truth but still, a truth.

Søren narrowed his eyes at her.

"You were supposed to be with King," she reminded him. "I didn't want to interrupt."

"Tonight we were having dinner. Last night I might not have answered any calls." He smiled, but she knew it wasn't a real smile. "I am glad you had Cyrus to bring you here. Although I'm not happy with you helping him on this case. It's keeping me up at night for the wrong reasons."

"Yeah," she said. "Same here. But I don't want to stop either. We're getting closer."

He kissed her forehead. "We'll discuss it tomorrow."

As it was well after two now, they decided to sleep there in the dungeon. Nora had the bed. Might as well put it to use.

Søren went downstairs to reset the alarm. Nora went into her dungeon bedroom and switched on the lights. The bed was a Moroccan daybed with a canopy. She'd strung copper-wire LED lights all through the slats of the canopy, creating a low and gentle glow in the little room.

Nora undressed down to her panties and t-shirt and climbed into bed. Søren returned and undressed and slid in next to her.

"Very nice," he said, glancing up at her lights.

"Perfect light to do wicked things to Sheridan's body by," she said. "Speaking of...did you and King have fun last night?"

"Fun was had by all."

"How did the engraved handcuffs work out?"

"As well as non-engraved handcuffs."

"And what does King think of the beard?"

"He's coping."

"I guess you've decided to keep the house?"

"For now," he said. "Seems a shame to let it go to waste. Oh, housewarming party Sunday. Not my idea, but I can't seem to stop it."

Nora smiled and curled up on his chest, resting her head at the sturdy center under his collar bone. He wrapped his arms around her and held her close and tight. His strong arms were always her favorite sort of bondage.

"I'm never going to leave you," she said.

Søren cupped her chin in his hand and tilted her face up to him.

"Where did that come from?"

"I just wanted to tell you that."

Søren pushed her onto her back and he lay on his side, propped on one elbow and gazing down at her.

"Are you worried you're going to, Little One?"

Nora wasn't about to tell Søren about Mercedes and her insane prediction. No reason to upset him, too.

"Sometimes it doesn't feel like telling you I love you is enough. I was in love with you when I left you. And I was in love with you the whole time we were apart. Saying I'll never leave you means more than just 'I love you.' Besides," she said, lightly tracing his bottom lip, "you already know and believe I love you. But I'm not sure you believe I'll never leave you again."

Søren stroked her cheek, ran his fingers through her hair.

"Eleanor, you really should know better by now," he said. "Never flirt with a sadist in a well-stocked dungeon."

Chapter Twenty-Six

Cyrus arrived back at Paulina's and found she'd unlocked the door for him.

He went inside, into the darkened house, and locked the door behind him. He slipped out of his shoes and walked down the hallway toward the light coming from her bedroom.

Paulina had turned on her bedside lamp and lay there on her side, pillow clutched to her chest like a teddy bear.

"I thought I heard you," she said, blinking.

"You're half-asleep," he said, sitting down at her side. "I should let you sleep."

"No, no..." She shook her head. "Talk to me. I know when you need to talk."

He caught her up to speed—again—fast as he could. The whole time he talked, he rubbed her back. She was in her pajamas now, cute pink t-shirt and shorts. She didn't seem to mind the back rub one bit, not even when he slipped his hand under her t-shirt to rub the warm bare skin of her back.

"Cyrus..." Paulina said with a sigh. "This is getting a little crazy."

"You said it. But I've had crazy cases before."

"Now that's for sure. How's Nora?" Paulina asked. "She okay?"

"She seemed okay when I left her with her man."

"He mad that she called you instead of him?"

"Didn't seem mad. He thanked me, shook my hand. He's a good guy, I think. Good enough."

"Good enough?"

"Good enough for her, I mean."

Paulina rolled onto her back.

"Good enough for her?" she asked.

He shrugged. "She's, you know...different. She'd get bored with a normal kind of dude, I think. And smart as she is, she needs somebody smart. Her guy's really smart, you can tell. About as calm as she is crazy. I like him for her."

Paulina shook her head, laughing to herself.

"What?" he asked.

"I love you."

"Do you? Where'd that come from?"

"Listen to you—you sound like her big brother." Paulina dropped her voice an octave, mocking his deeper voice. "'He's good enough for her, I suppose. She needs a man like that. I suppose I approve of this match.'"

Paulina laughed again, laughed herself silly. Cyrus grabbed a pillow and dropped it on her laughing face.

From under the pillow, she kept laughing.

He took the pillow off her face.

"You're so cute," she said. "I like this side of you. Not sure I've seen it before."

"What side is that?"

"Cyrus Tremont, big brother," she said. "It's nice. Kind of sexy, too."

"Is it?"

"Oh, it is." She took his face in her hands and brought it down for a kiss.

If she wanted only a little kiss, he surprised her with a big one. A long kiss, long and deep. His tongue pressed into her mouth and she readily opened to the kiss. It nearly killed him to break it, but he had to. He had things to say to her.

"You're the most beautiful woman in the world," he said. "Did you know that?"

"The most?" she said. "I'd heard top ten but didn't know I'd hit the top spot."

"I'm not joking with you," he said. "To me, you are the most beautiful woman I've ever seen in my life. I'd rather look at you than anyone else out there."

She smiled up at him.

"You're in a mood tonight, aren't you?"

"And I'm just getting started." He slid his hand under her pajama top and rubbed it flat over her stomach. "Your skin is everything to me. Sometimes I'll touch it and I worry I won't be able to stop. You're so soft and warm and like silk. And you smell like roses all the time. Day or night. Even after a run. I don't know how you do it. You must be part rose."

He could see the pink roses blooming on her cheeks under her brown skin. He touched her face and found her burning.

"Cyrus Tremont, what has gotten into you?"

"You," he said. "You've gotten into me. You're in my head all the time. And you're in my blood. And I'm not going to be a happy man until you're in my bed, too, and I'm inside you."

"Cyrus, Lord."

"I want to make you come," he said.

Her eyes went wide as half dollars. He'd shocked her before, a time or two, but he could tell he'd never shocked her quite like that.

"I'm serious," he said. "I want to make you come. Now. Tonight. Will you let me?"

He heard Nora's voice in the back of his head—Since we don't know if she's kinky yet...better just ask nicely.

"Will I let you?" she asked. "Didn't we already make this decision?"

"We decided to wait until we were married because I wanted to prove to you that I wasn't after you for sex. And you wanted us to get to know each other, really know each other. Well, I think I've proven myself. And if we don't know each other yet..." He caught her hand in his and held it against his chest over his heart. "You know me, don't you? I know I know you. I know I do because I love you. Anybody who knows you loves you."

Paulina took a ragged breath.

"You are really getting to me," she said.

"I don't want to brag, but I have a few skills in this area. I can keep all my clothes on and still make you come so hard you have to call in sick to work tomorrow to recover."

"That so?" she said.

Cyrus caressed her ear, her neck. Caught a curl of her hair and lightly tugged it. He wasn't nervous, not a bit. In fact, he felt calm and steady and cool, like he'd slipped into his most comfortable clothes. He felt good. And this felt right.

"You can't even imagine how good you make me feel every day," he said softly. "I want to make you feel that good. Will you let me? Please?"

He almost didn't care if she said "yes" or "no." The whole thing had been worth it just to see her blushing and shivering and taking those shallows breaths.

Paulina had never looked so beautiful to him before— not in her sundresses, not in her church clothes, not even in that black bikini of hers that made him thank Jesus for allowing mankind to invent the two-piece. Just her, there, on her pillow, lips parted and breathing hard and blushing and burning and all for him. And he hadn't even laid a hand on her yet. His words had done it to her. And if she thought he was good with his words...she ain't seen nothing yet.

"What are you going to do to me, Daddy?" she asked.

"Nothing you don't love. Is that a 'yes'?"

Slowly, tentatively, looking scared as a child in front of her first roller coaster, and brave as a woman who wanted to show the man she loved how much she loved him...she nodded her head.

"Yes, Daddy."

Chapter Twenty-Seven

Nora watched Søren as he opened the drawers of her curio cabinet, hunting for something only he knew he was looking for.

"If you tell me what it is," she said, "I might be able to help you find it."

"I haven't decided what I'm looking for just yet. But not this." Søren pulled a massive twelve-inch dildo out of a drawer and held it up. "Really, Eleanor?"

"That's not mine, I swear," she said. "I only use it on Sheridan."

Søren raised his eyebrow. "She's tiny."

"She's bigger on the inside. That's a Doctor Who joke."

"I went to school in England as a child. I fully understood the reference," he said as he put the gigantic dildo back in the drawer. "My God, you have enough butt plugs to start a butt plug emporium."

"You can never have too many butt plugs. If you're looking for the scalpels and knives, they're in the bottom drawer on the left."

"I wasn't...or I thought I wasn't."

"I like that you can get an erection just by hearing the word 'scalpel.' It's like Pavlov's dog, except it's Pavlov's erection."

"Don't mention dogs if you want me to keep it."

Nora grinned sleepily. "You can slice me up if you want. I don't mind. You'll be hard until breakfast."

"Blood-play? On white sheets?"

"Hmm...good point. If they were cheap, I'd say go for it. But this is Millesimo Egyptian cotton. Sheridan got them for me."

"We'll avoid bloodstains then," he said. He took from a drawer a long thin carbon fiber rod—a misery stick—and set it on the bedside table by the lamp. Clearly, Søren was in a mood to bring the pain.

"Did you really not beat and fuck King tonight?"

"I did not. After last night, he'll be needing more than a day to recover," Søren said with a little sinister note of giddiness in his tone.

"Oh, great," Nora said. "Now I have an erection."

Søren lowered his head.

"What?" she asked.

He lifted his head. "Nothing. Except I'm glad you've decided you'll never leave me. Because even if I could live without you, I would never want to."

"You should kiss me after you say stuff like that."

"I will," he said. "But I'm going to torture you first. Adjustable spreader bar?"

"How short we talking?"

"Twelve to fourteen inches."

"There's a one-footer on the wall by the med table."

"Ankle cuffs?"

"In the cabinet over the sink."

Søren—magnificently naked—strode from the little

bedroom into her dungeon. Like she'd go anywhere with that view... He returned quickly with all his little wicked implements—the spreader bar and the ankle cuffs.

And one leather strip, about a foot long and a couple inches wide. He must have cut it off her flogger with the thick fat tails.

"What's that for?" she asked as Søren passed her the leather strip.

"You may need to bite down on something," he said. "Turn over."

Just like that...all the punch-drunk half-asleep joking stopped. It stopped like someone had flipped a switch, turned off the lights, turned on the pain. He could do that, Søren, with a glance and a subtle change of tone that came with the standard warning—*I am not playing anymore.*

She turned over as ordered and rested her cheek against the cool white sheets. Søren took each ankle in his hands and wrapped and buckled the cuffs around them. With small hooks, he secured the cuffs to the spreader bar.

Then he picked up the misery stick.

Then he grabbed the metal bar in the middle and pulled her into place as if she weighed nothing.

Then he lifted the bar, forcing her to bend her knees. Her feet were at his stomach on either side. Nora started breathing hard.

"I'd bite down on the strap now if I were you," Søren said.

"You're going to beat the soles of my feet, aren't you?"

"Yes."

"Fuck." Nora grabbed the leather strap and put it between her teeth.

She hated foot torture. Hated it. Not the good kind of hate. Not the playful kind of hate. Not "Oh no, not that,

Sir, anything but that, Sir." She would rather take a hundred cuts from a scalpel, an hour-long session with a single-tail whip, or even red-hot wax-play that left her covered in first degree burns. Foot torture was one of her limits. But it wasn't a hard limit, which meant she wouldn't safe out if Søren tried it.

No, she wouldn't safe out. But she wasn't going to enjoy it.

She couldn't even enjoy Søren's thumbs on her insoles, caressing them tenderly. She was too tense, too scared, already breaking out into a cold sweat.

"You broke someone's foot tonight," he said. Nora didn't say the kid deserved it. Søren knew that. "There is no one in the world that respects your sadistic impulses more than I, but I would be very disappointed if you got yourself arrested or sued. One of these days, Eleanor, you really are going to have to learn to control that temper of yours."

He caressed her ankles, all those delicate little bones. She wanted to cry. Instead, she grabbed a pillow and shoved it her under her breasts. It would help to have something to cling to during...

"Only five, I promise." He ran his fingertips gently over the tops of her feet.

Five.

She could take five. She could survive that.

"On each foot."

He picked up the misery stick.

The thing about misery sticks, Nora knew from experience, was that they were deceptive little toys. They didn't look like they could hurt much. Nothing but very long, very thin metal rods. That's it.

Except when you pulled the tip of the rod back and let

it go, flicking it against the bare skin, it hurt worse than being sliced open by a knife that had been sitting in a red-hot fire.

And she was about to take five strikes on each foot.

The metal spreader bar rested across Søren's stomach. She could flinch and twist, but there would be no getting away from him.

"Left foot or right first?" he asked. Nora shrugged. "I wasn't asking you. Only talking to myself. Flex your feet. No curling the toes or I'll make it ten."

Nora had to fight every instinct in her body to flex her feet. A hot tear ran from her eyes and down onto the Millesimo Egyptian cotton sheets.

Her entire body was tense as a violin bowstring. And Søren plucked it.

One.

He flicked the misery stick once and the strike landed at the back of her left heel.

Nora flinched. She couldn't help it. Flinched and whimpered again as her teeth dug deep into the leather strap in her mouth.

Two.

He flicked it again, half an inch down the heel, inching closer and closer to the sensitive arch.

Three.

The arch was next. She knew it. She braced herself and wasn't surprised when the next thing she felt was nearly the worst physical agony in her life.

She screamed into the pillow.

"I shouldn't enjoy it so much when you're in this kind of pain," he confessed. "But I do."

Four.

He struck her again, even higher, closer to the toes.

Nora's head swam. She thought she might actually pass out.

"Flex, Eleanor. Flex."

She couldn't. She was in so much pain, she couldn't make the muscles in her foot move.

"Oh, fine," he said. "I'll do it myself."

He took her toes in his hands and pushed, forcing her foot to flex.

"Now keep it there," he ordered.

She did.

Five.

He hit the ball of her foot.

"Five," he said. "Now that wasn't so bad, was it?"

He set the stick down on the table again and Nora shuddered. She shuddered because he'd started rubbing her foot, tenderly stroking all the burning places.

"I know you hate this," he said softly. "And deep down, a small part of me hates myself for how much I enjoy it. Sometimes I wish it didn't have to be like this. You understand?"

With the leather strap still clenched between her teeth, Nora could only nod, so she did.

"But," Søren said, "it is like this. And we have five more to go."

He picked up the misery stick again.

The last five hurt as badly as the first five, but she took them better, mostly because she was nearly out of her mind with pain. At five, she went limp, as limp as a rag doll or a corpse. She barely felt it when Søren cupped her between her legs, pushed his fingers inside her.

"And this is why I would never let you leave me," he said, rubbing the aching hollow of her g-spot with the tips of two fingers. "You hated that with every fiber of your being...and yet you're dripping wet." He pulled out and unhooked the spreader bar. She hardly noticed when he removed the leather strap from her mouth.

"You nearly bit through it," he said. He sounded impressed. Nora rolled into the fetal position, toes curled, feet aching. He pulled her to him and held her back against his chest.

"You can cry if you need to." He spoke softly into her ear as he ran his fingers through her sweat-damp hair.

"I hate that so much," she said, a small sob escaping her throat.

"I know, Little One. I know you do." He slid over her, on top of her and positioned her under him. He was so aroused, she felt the tip of his erection against her stomach, throbbing like it wanted to force its way into her, any way it could. He kneed her thighs open and she was too weak to stop him, even if she wanted to.

Søren braced himself over her and, through watering eyes, she saw him lick two fingertips and press them against her vulva. He pushed through her folds and into her vagina. She yielded to him easily, her body offering no resistance. He'd given her permission to cry and she took it, hot tears she couldn't stop rolling down her cheeks.

She was still crying when he entered her, splitting her. His thick cock went deep on the very first stroke. She cried out again, in pleasure this time, not pain.

Sometimes she hated herself, too. But not very much.

Søren found her mouth and kissed her, his cock slipping ever deeper into her as they kissed. Since her feet hurt so much every time they brushed the sheets, she wrapped her legs around his lower back as he thrust into her. They fucked in a frenzy, and the need was as much as hers as his. His hands dug into the tender flesh of her breasts as he held them, squeezing them as he rode her.

It wasn't enough to let him have her. She had to have him in return. Nora clung to his shoulders and, with her legs twined around him, she lifted her hips again and again, taking his cock as hard as he gave it to her. The pain wasn't the thing. She wasn't aroused by having her toes stepped on by a stranger in a crowd any more than she was aroused by the strike of a metal bar on her insoles. It was him, Søren, and who he turned into when he let himself free with her. The master. The monster. The beautiful sadist. That was the secret she never told anyone, not even herself, that she loved him more for his cruelties than his mercies. He was kind to everyone he met. He was only cruel like this to his lovers.

Since he hadn't bound her wrists, she was free to pass on a little cruelty of her own. She slid her hands down his long back, and every time his cock made her vagina spasm she dug her fingernails into his skin. He let her do it—but only twice.

Then he pulled out and turned her onto her hands and knees. He forced her legs wider from behind, so wide her belly touched the bed. He entered her with a rough thrust, impaling her hard enough she cried out. But his fingertips found her clitoris and stroked it as he used her from behind, stroked her until she was nearly blind with the need to come.

Søren gripped her by her shoulders, thumbs on the back of her neck, immobilizing her against the bed.

His thrusts seemed endless, as did her desire for them. Long moans escaped her lips, which she tried to stifle with the sheets. Søren's fingers knew her body too well. He had her trapped at the edge of orgasm. He held her there with his touch, with his organ that slid in and out of her slick hole. He might punish her if she went over the edge, if she came without permission.

She came anyway. She couldn't help it or stop it. She was too wet and the fingers stroking her were too wet and everything inside her quivered and tensed and there was no telling her body no when it was ready to scream "yes."

When she came, she buried her mouth against the bed to scream and only the last syllable of it hit the air as he lifted her back against him. She sank down on his cock as he held her on his knees. His hand came around and clasped her throat. His mouth was at her ear so she could hear his ragged breaths. He fucked up and into her until his own release. He inhaled and inhaled, his breath hitching and then he was coming inside her, filling her.

Only when he finished did he release his iron grip on her throat. He let her go and she collapsed onto the bed. Søren lay down on his back next to her, ran one hand through sweat-soaked hair and then used his hand as a pillow.

"You'll have to apologize to Sheridan about the sheets," he said.

"What? It's okay. Come comes out."

"Blood might not."

"Blood?"

Søren rolled onto his side away from her. He had eight bleeding claw marks on his back just under his shoulder blades.

"Fuck," she said, then laughed. "Oops?"

Søren only laughed and rolled onto his wounded back again. She rested against his chest, listening to his wild heartbeat.

"Broke a man's foot. Tore open my back. You are

bloodthirsty, Eleanor. It's no wonder you fell in love with me."

She made a little "humph" sound and Søren said, "What was that?"

"Nothing. Just...you're the second person tonight to tell me I'm violent."

What Søren said then said everything. "Only the second?"

She traced his collarbone with her fingertips. She'd nearly drifted off to sleep when Søren spoke.

"When did you start watching *Doctor Who*?" he asked.

"Oh, I don't really," Nora said. "Zach's favorite show when he was a kid. He's been showing the old episodes to Fionn. I've watched it with them a couple times. Just the ones with the guy with the long scarf. The new ones are too scary."

"Does Fionn like it?"

"He loves it. Last visit, I played Sarah Jane Smith and Zach was a Dalek. Fionn's always the Doctor." She raised her head and looked down at him. "Why do you ask?"

"It never would have occurred to me that he would like *Doctor Who*. He's only three." Silence again. Then, "Zachary's a good father to him."

"He is."

"I hate him."

Nora laughed. Søren did, too, a quiet self-deprecating laugh that turned into a soft groan. He rubbed his forehead.

"Being apart from him is harder than I ever dream. Why did I do this to myself? To you? To us?"

She reached across him and on the nightstand lay her keys. She grabbed them and held up a key.

"Here," she said. "Here's my TARDIS key. Take it. Hop

in. Go back in time and stop yourself from conceiving Fionn. Would you if you could?"

He took a long breath then reached out, not to take the keys but to stroke her face.

"I thought so."

Chapter Twenty-Eight

Cyrus lay down next to Paulina and pulled her to him. He kissed her. That was all. Nothing but kissing and more kissing for as long as he could stand it and as long as she could take it. Her small delicate hands moved over his shoulders and back, under his t-shirt to find bare skin to touch. As he kissed her, she made small soft murmurs of pleasure, beautiful sounds he wanted to record and put on his phone to play back tomorrow and the next day and every day until their wedding night.

They were both tangled in the covers and it was killing him not to feel her skin on his. He dug for the sheet and yanked it out of the way, found her long bare legs and stroked her thigh. She was a runner, like him, and had long strong thighs, and every time he stroked upward, toward her hip, he felt her muscle tense, and every time he stroked downward, to her knee, she relaxed.

He liked tense better. Cyrus slid his hand slowly up her leg, from knee to thigh to hip. He tickled the trim of her silky panties and the even silkier skin his fingers found everywhere he touched her. He slipped a finger under her panties, just to touch the smooth curve of her hipbone. Paulina tensed again, even took in a quick breath, but she didn't tell him to stop.

"Nervous?" he asked her.

"Yeah."

"It's all right. The second you want to stop, we'll stop. And we're not gonna go too far tonight."

"I'll go anywhere," she said, "as long as you go with me."

He heard nothing but love in her voice, love and trust, which sounded about the same to him.

"You'll tell me if you get scared?"

"I won't get scared."

"I know you won't." Of course she wouldn't. Whether she'd done this before or not, Paulina wasn't the type of woman to be scared by what she wanted, only scared of not getting it. So she had no reason to be afraid of anything because there was nothing in the world he wouldn't give her if she asked for it.

He slid his whole hand under the fabric of her panties and started to pull them down. Paulina went still in his arms, like she'd taken in a breath but wasn't ready to release it yet. Her eyes were closed, her thick dark lashes on her cheeks. Her face looked kissed by gold in the soft light of her bedside lamp. No make-up. Half-asleep. She'd never looked so sexy to him.

Cyrus was so hard it hurt and got harder as the palm of his hand cupped her soft round ass as he pulled her panties down and off of her. He'd patted her bottom of her clothes before, over her skirts and jeans and even her bikini bottoms, but there was nothing quite like his bare hand on her bare ass.

"Let's elope tomorrow," he said.

"Why wait?"

He laughed softly. Although they were alone in the house, they both were keeping their voices low, like what they were doing was a secret. And maybe it was, though who they were keeping the secret from, neither knew nor cared. It was just fun to have a secret to keep together.

Although it almost killed him to pull away from her warm soft body, he had to do it. He came up on his knees to finish taking her panties off, and threw them across the room out into the hall.

"You're crazy," she said, grinning. Despite the smile, he could tell she was nervous, at least a little. She'd clamped her legs tight together. He couldn't even fit a credit card between those knees, much less his body. But they'd work on that.

"You make me crazy." He rubbed his hands up and down her thighs again, the tops, the sides, the backs, trying to calm her, relax her. Her nightgown was long enough that it covered her. And though he was dying to see her, all of her, he wasn't going to rush it. They'd waited almost two years to be together like this. They'd survive waiting another five minutes.

Maybe.

"You are the sexiest man alive," Paulina said as she looked up at him.

"Damn."

"It's true."

"I wasn't arguing."

She giggled and shook her head. "I can't believe we're doing this."

Cyrus took his t-shirt off, threw it so it landed by her panties in the hall.

CHAPTER 28

She looked up at him again. "Now I can believe it."

"You're gonna give me a big ego," he said.

"You? I'm the one getting married to the sexiest man alive. My ego's big as this house and getting bigger all the time."

"I don't know what I did to deserve you, baby," he said, "but I'm glad I did it."

No more laughing. Paulina wasn't even smiling. She was dead serious when she met his eyes and said, "I love you."

"I love you, too. And you're gonna let me show you how much, right?"

She inhaled slow and exhaled even slower. He knew this was hard for her. Whether she'd ever done it before had nothing to do with it. She'd never done this with him. He slid his hands up and down her thighs again, and when he reached her knees, he pushed them apart.

Paulina didn't put up any resistance. If she had, even for a second, he might have put a stop to it all. But she didn't. He pushed and she spread her legs like she wanted to do it as much as he wanted it done.

Then it was done. He stared down at her beautiful body lying open for him in the lamplight. The soft dark curls, the slit just starting to open, the little bit of pink and red showing through.

"You better say something," Paulina said.

"I'm speechless."

"That'll do."

Cyrus slid down on top of her again, chest to her breasts, arms around her back, kissing her mouth with lips and tongue and love and need and twice of everything all over again. The way she kissed him now...he realized she'd been holding back with him. Before, her kisses had been sweet and tender, sometimes deep. But never like this. Never desperate.

Paulina lifted her hips and rubbed against him. Even through his jeans, he felt her heat. It wasn't enough. He had to touch her. He slid his hand slowly down and up her arm, over her breasts and down her belly. Finally, he pressed his hands between her thighs, cradling her in his palm.

She buried her head into the crook of his neck and shoulder as he held her there, soaking in the wet warmth against his skin. But she didn't close her legs. In fact, she opened up a little wider for him and lifted herself into his palm. He had to touch her and she had to be touched. With only one finger, he started to stroke her along the slit. She was wet and swollen. He'd almost forgotten how good it was to make a woman feel this way.

Almost.

As he stroked her, spreading the folds, he felt Paulina's fingernails digging lightly into his shoulders as she clung to him, breathing hard.

"It's all right, baby," he said. "I got you."

She nodded against his chest. It was happening again, that sense of complete and utter calm he'd felt earlier. He had one job and that job was to take care of Paulina. That he could do and would do for the rest of his life.

Cyrus stroked her a little harder, pushing in a little more until he felt the wet silk under his fingertips. He looked down at her, and at his own hand touching her. He'd never seen anything that turned him on so much as her beautiful thighs wide for him and his fingertips on her. He wanted to push in and push in deep, but he also wanted to save that for later. And he didn't want to push Paulina too far. They were just getting started, after all.

They had their whole lives to make love every which way they wanted to.

He turned his head and saw Paulina was watching the show, too, watching his hand touching her. Her eyes were wide, full of wonder. He knew how she felt. This woman, her love for him...what a wonder.

Cyrus kissed her once more on the forehead and she turned her mouth to his mouth for another kiss. He gave it to her. And when the kiss broke, he moved down the bed.

He started on her lower stomach, wanting to ease her into it. Not that it was any chore to kiss her stomach, that smooth dark skin and the muscles quivering underneath. Here she smelled like mint, clean and delicious, and he wondered if it was her soap or her lotion or just the natural scent of her skin. Whatever it was, he couldn't stop breathing her in and in, deep into his lungs.

Slowly, he kissed a path to her left hip and lingered there a while, kissing the curve of the hipbone where it met the top of her thigh. All the while, Paulina kept her hands on his shoulders, not to stop him or push him away, but just to touch him, he could tell. Just to keep the contact between them.

He dipped his head and kissed her inner thigh. New sensations here...even silkier, even warmer, with scents more delicious than Christmas. She was turned on and wet and he could smell it, almost taste it. And almost wasn't enough.

Cyrus turned his head and licked her. A little quick flick of the tongue, but it was enough to get a gasp out of Paulina.

She laughed at her own gasp. "Sorry," she said, breathless.

"Don't be sorry for anything," he said. "Not a thing, ever."

He really didn't know what he was talking about because he was out of his mind, more or less. Impossible to think straight lying between the two most beautiful thighs in all God's creation. He took those thighs in his hands and pushed them wide enough he could get down to work. Up on his elbows, he stroked the soft folds of her vagina again, opening her up like he'd dreamed about doing every day since the day she first let him kiss her.

Cyrus's self-control was starting to crack. He didn't want to go all in while Paulina was shaking like a leaf, but there was a good chance she was shaking from need, not fear. She had plenty of practice telling him to stop or slow down, but now she was saying nothing, only breathing short hard breaths. He told himself the second she said "back off," he would back off...but since she wasn't saying anything, he went in.

Gently as he could, he pushed back the tender flesh around her clitoris. There it was, like he'd dreamed of it, swollen and red. He pressed his tongue to it lightly, but it might as well have been lightning that struck it, judging how Paulina flinched.

"Sorry," she said again and clutched at the sheet by her hip.

Cyrus only laughed and licked her again. She flinched, but not so hard this time. And when he licked her a third time, she didn't flinch at all. She tasted perfect, tasted like a woman should, and her clitoris felt as right as anything ever did against his tongue. He went at it with the tip, carefully as he could, and it wasn't long before it started to have the desired effect on Paulina.

As much as he wanted to watch her enjoying it, Cyrus

forced himself to concentrate. Her pleasure mattered more than his. He'd have plenty of chances on their honeymoon to watch her come over and over again. Now he just needed to get her there and get her there hard.

He swirled his tongue all around her sensitive flesh and was rewarded with all sorts of dirty wicked sounds that came out of Paulina's lips. Little moans, little groans, tiny little gasps and grunts as he licked and sucked her, dropping his head every now and then to stroke the open folds of her with this tongue before focusing on her clitoris again.

All nervousness, his and hers, evaporated in that room. Cyrus knew he was going to get her there, and from the sound of it, get her there fast. If she had as much adrenaline pumping through her body as he had in his right now, she was going to come so hard he'd have to scrape her off the ceiling after. He'd never waited this long to be intimate with a woman before. The closest thing he'd ever felt was his very first time at age fifteen. But even that couldn't compare to this. There'd been no sweetness then, no affection, just anticipation, the frenzy, the climax, and the emptiness afterward of having won a game but no trophy.

But this was good and it was right. Anything that made Paulina feel loved and wanted and worshipped had to be right.

"Cyrus," she said. Just that. Just his name. She wasn't asking for anything. He doubted she even realized she'd said it. He'd never heard anything sweeter than his name on her lips while his lips were on her body.

She was so close. He knew it. He could feel it, feel the tension in her building to the breaking point. Nothing for him to do now but not stop, not break the rhythm. He ran his tongue over and over her clitoris again and again, kneading and teasing it, stroking and lapping it. Paulina was completely lost. She rocked her hips on the bed and dug her heels into the sheets, his back, and then back on the sheets. He dared to glance up once and saw her head back and her long lovely throat exposed. Her breasts rose and fell under the pink nightgown, and her nipples were hard and pushed against the fabric.

He made himself look away before he crawled up on top of her, stripped her naked, and made love to her until dawn of next year.

Paulina's voice rose, and her little moans and little groans turned into cries, erotic womanly cries of pleasure. He focused his entire attention onto her clitoris, on that throbbing knot between his lips and against his tongue, working until she couldn't take it anymore. Her back arched and she cried out again, and she came hard on his mouth, hard enough he felt the muscles contract and he could taste the rush of fluid pouring from her. He buried his mouth into her, lapping it all up, drinking her like wine, drinking until he was drunk on her and couldn't drink another drop.

She went still on the bed, and he crawled up her body. He pulled her limp body to him and held her against him in his arms. Though it seemed to take her extraordinary effort to open her eyes, her lashes fluttered and she looked at him.

"You're shaking, baby," he said. "You all right?"

She nodded but didn't speak. He had a feeling she couldn't speak. He mentally patted himself on the back for that.

Cyrus pulled her even closer and dragged the sheet and blanket over her. She'd started to shiver. That happened, of course, he remembered. Burning hot one second—orgasm —crash—cold.

"You want me to go so you can get some sleep?" he asked.

She shook her head. "Stay," she said. "All night. Just sleep with me. Will you?"

He kissed her forehead again and knew she'd be sound asleep in ten seconds, if that long. Nothing more would happen tonight. He didn't even want anything to. He just wanted to hold her while she slept.

"I thought you'd never ask."

Chapter Twenty-Nine

Nora woke alone in her dungeon bed. Søren hadn't left her, however. She rolled up, wrapped the sheet around her for warmth, and found him sitting in her waiting room, fully dressed with a cup of tea in his hand.

"About time you woke up," he said. "It's ten already."

"You are a monster."

"Am I?"

She padded across the floor to him, trying not to wince. She turned and bent her knee so he could see the bottom of her feet.

"Bruises," she said. "On the bottom of my feet. On the bottom of my feet...are bruises."

"This will happen when one's feet are subjected to foot torture."

"Did I mention the bruises that are on the bottom of my feet?"

"They'll heal quickly. The flesh on the bottom of the foot regenerates faster than any other part of the body. So says the tattoo artist that did my work," he said.

"You asked about tattooing the bottom of your feet?"

"No, I asked her what parts of the body healed the fastest. I thought such knowledge would come in handy." He grinned devilishly. "Or...footy."

"I hate you. I hate you. I hate you. I hate you more because you said 'footy.'"

He set his cup of tea on the table, reached for her and pulled her into his lap.

"And I love making you hate me." He kissed her and she let him. Begrudgingly. But soon she simply let herself enjoy the kiss and his arms around her. She settled in against him and he pulled her legs up over the arms of the chair and held her in his lap.

"We need to discuss Mr. Tremont," Søren said. "And this 'case.' I'm not happy with you playing detective."

"Are you going to order me to stop helping him?" Her heart sank at the thought. She really liked spending time with Cyrus, and she wasn't sure she would ever really be at peace until she knew why Father Ike had tried to call her.

"I don't want to, but I will if I have to. I'd like to talk to your new friend man to man."

"Like...have coffee with him?" Her voice went very high at the end of the question.

"Something like that. Would you call him for me?"

Nora stood up and walked to her dungeon to find her phone.

Just to annoy Søren, she said "ow" with every step she took. *Ow. Ow. Ow. Ow.* About fifty ow's in total by the time she returned with her phone. She settled again on his lap and sent Cyrus a text.

You up?

The reply came quickly.

Bright-eyed and bushy-tailed.

"Suspicious," Nora said under her breath before calling his number.

"Good morning," Nora said when he answered.

"Yes, it is," Cyrus replied. His voice sounded so chipper, it hurt her ears.

"Calm down," she ordered. "I have a bangover."

"A hangover? When did you drink?"

"Bangover," Nora corrected. "It's a hangover from sex. Everything hurts."

"And you decided to call me first thing? That's on you."

"Søren's making me. He wants to talk to you again. Oh, he just told me to tell you that you're not in trouble."

"That's good news. Put the man on."

Nora handed Søren her phone.

"Mr. Tremont?" Søren said. "Do you, by any chance, run?"

Nora's eyes went wide. She tried to grab for the phone.

"Say 'no,' Cyrus! It's a trap!"

Søren swatted her hand away.

"Good," he said. "Tomorrow morning? Let's say seven?"

"Don't do it!" Nora yelled as Søren named a park where they could meet.

"See you then," Søren said. He hung up.

"It's bad enough you torture me," she said. "But Cyrus, too? He doesn't deserve this. And he doesn't even have a safe word."

"We'll run and we'll talk. Afterwards, I'll tell you if you can continue working with him on the case. In the meantime, you're getting a security system installed on your house."

"Speaking of...where's Gmork?"

Søren whistled. Outside the door, Nora heard a bark.

"You locked him out? No wonder he hates you."

"I took him out when you were still sleeping. But then, yes, I did lock him out. With water and a blanket."

She scrambled to her feet, but when she tried to walk to the door to let Gmork back in, Søren tugged the sheet off of her. She turned around, naked, and glared at him.

"Was that necessary, Sir?"

"You can either let him in," Søren said, "Or we can go back into your dungeon, play, and make love before lunch."

Søren sat cooly in her big red armchair in his jeans and white tee, his beard with a touch of gray in it, his hair slicked back with water, a look of casual superiority on his face.

He wore casual superiority so well.

His steel-gray eyes gleamed with sinister intent as a self-satisfied smile played across his lips.

Gmork? Or Søren?

"He's a dog," she said. "He'll be fine."

Chapter Thirty

Cyrus had the pleasure of waking up in bed next to Paulina, a pleasure he thought he'd have to wait for until November. Even better, there was no morning-after awkwardness between them. That was a relief.

Still, she kicked him right out of her house.

"I gotta go?" he asked, still sleepy. It was just after six. They'd only spent a few minutes awake, enjoying the closeness.

"Right this second," she said. "I have to get ready for work and if you say one more thing to me, I'll call in and never forgive myself."

"Bu—"

That was as much backtalk as she allowed him. She pointed at her bedroom door, and he knew she meant business.

Cyrus dragged himself away from her warm soft bed and her warm soft body and yanked his jeans on. He found his shirt in the hallway and under it, her pink panties. He brought them back to her and when she tried to snatch them from his hand, he pulled them back and tucked them in his pocket.

"Cyrus!"

"Catch me if you can," he said, running out the door, waving her stolen underwear like a flag.

He'd been up for four hours by the time Nora called him. Good thing her Viking had been there or Cyrus might have let it slip that he'd had a very good night after leaving her. Paulina might not appreciate him spilling their business all over town.

But a man had a right to smile. Cyrus found himself grinning like a fool even as he drove back to his apartment, grinning like a fool as he walked up the stairs, grinning like a fool in the shower. He was still grinning like a fool when Nora's Viking got on the phone and asked him to go running the next morning.

Cyrus ran about three miles a morning five times a week. And he was thirty-five. Nora's Viking was fifty-one. Tall, though, with a longer stride than Cyrus...but fifty-one. He heard Nora's voice in the background, yelling, "It's a trap!"

Cyrus could handle himself with a fifty-one-year-old runner. He might be a Viking, but Usain Bolt he was not.

It sounded like Nora was off the case for today, however, bare minimum. And that was fine. Cyrus was happy to spend a day alone working on the case between having flashbacks from last night with Paulina. He'd taken care of a very insistent erection in the shower, but every time he thought about the way she looked and the way she smelled and the way she tasted and that sound she made when she came against his tongue, well, this was gonna be a two-shower day for sure.

In the meantime, he forced himself to focus on the case.

He had an entire shoebox full of Father Ike's credit card receipts and bank statements to go through, which he'd been putting off since Sunday. Nothing for it but to brew a pot of coffee, get out his yellow highlighter and his laptop, sit down at the kitchen table and get to digging.

First thing he found—Father Ike did have money. He wasn't a billionaire, but he'd died with ten thousand in his checking and eighty-eight thousand in savings. Not to mention a 401K with a little over a half a million in it. Of course, if he hadn't died, that half a million would've had to last him for his entire retirement. With people living longer these days, that could have been twenty years or more. Except instead of retiring to a condo in Boca, Father Ike had eaten a bullet. Personally, Cyrus would have taken Boca.

Very quickly, Cyrus figured out how a man making a priest's salary had that much money. Living expenses for a priest were pretty low. He owned his own car, but it was paid off. Insurance? Eighty bucks a month. His credit card bills showed charges for gas, for a few dinners at some mid-price restaurants, tickets to a Hornets game...nothing crazy, nothing wild, nothing out of place. Cyrus had most of the same charges on his card.

There was only one large charge.

From August, $4200 to something billed as "HAFH.-com." There was a ten-digit number next to it.

Cyrus opened his laptop, and searched "HAFH" in Google. No way was he going direct to some creepy kink website without checking it out first.

Praise the Lord. HAFH stood for "Home Away from Home." A house rental website, like Airbnb.

He clicked through to the website. It specialized in long-term rentals. Not for weekenders, but for people who rented secondary residences for months at a time. Vacation homes for people who could afford long vacations.

Cyrus entered the number from the card statement into the search box. It took him to a one-bedroom cottage on Grand Isle, Louisiana. Cyrus flipped through the photographs of the house. Not bad. He and Paulina might have rented a place like that for their honeymoon. A little yellow beach cottage on stilts with a white wraparound porch, white front door, small galley kitchen, and a great big bedroom with a king-sized bed that looked out onto the water.

Cyrus noted the bed frame was metal with vertical bars on the headboard and footboard. Nora had called it a "bondage bed."

All right. So Father Ike had rented a romantic one-bedroom vacation house on romantic Grand Isle. But when?

According to the website, the house was booked solid from September twenty-first to the end of the year. With rental rates of $5000 a month in the off-season, that $4200 had to be the deposit Father Ike paid on a long stay.

Cyrus sat back in his kitchen chair, sipped his coffee. It had cooled while he was working. Furthest thing from his mind right now, though.

Let's say Father Ike was about to spend a few months in a beautiful beach house. He would have told a few people, wouldn't he? Why not brag a little about getting laid in paradise? But that's what Cyrus would do. God knows that's what Nora would do. But is that what Father Ike would have done?

Priests were supposed to be humble. They weren't. Cyrus knew that for a fact. Father Ike never struck him as a show-off or a blowhard, however. Really, he seemed a quiet, responsible sort of man. Maybe a quiet, responsible sort of man wouldn't brag, but he'd request time off. At least warn Sister Margaret he was planning to be gone for such a lengthy time.

Cyrus called Sister Margaret. She answered on the third ring.

"Any news?" That was her hello. Poor lady, he didn't know what to tell her.

"Still looking, Sister."

"Well...I understand it might take some time. Isaac's sister is arriving tonight. I'm picking her up at the airport. Will you be at the funeral?"

"When is it?"

"Saturday at St. Valentine's."

"I'll try. Look, this is kind of a weird question, but did Father Ike mention anything to you about taking a long trip to Grand Isle?"

"Grand Isle? Oh yes, he went there a couple weeks every June. Soon as school was out."

"What about soon? Like before the end of the year?"

"He wouldn't take a trip in fall. He had to work. Why?"

"He paid a deposit on a house on Grand Isle. But I don't know when his reservation was."

"Maybe the owner of the house will tell you, if you let them know it's an emergency."

"That's a good idea. Thank you, Sister." Before he hung up, Cyrus decided to ask one more question. "Did Father Ike go to Grand Isle alone on his vacations?"

"As far as I know. He talked about how much he liked the peace and quiet of going down there."

"Do you know where he stayed?"

"I have the address somewhere. In case of emergency. I'll try to find it and get it to you."

"I appreciate that. Thank you, Sister. I'll call again when I know something."

"Mr. Tremont, you said Ike paid a deposit on a place on Grand Isle?"

"Yes, Sister. A big one."

"The place he stayed in the past, it's owned by a member of the parish. Ike paid for the place by check."

"You sure?"

"I'm certain. A very devout family owns the place and offers it to clergy at a decent rate. A sort of ministry of theirs."

"Yeah," Cyrus said, "I'll definitely need that info."

"I'll get it for you right away."

A few minutes later, Sister Margaret called back with the address. Cyrus jotted it down along with the name and phone number of the people who owned it.

As soon as he got done speaking with Sister Margaret, he called the owners of the house. Since nobody answered their phones anymore, he had to leave a voicemail message. Not wanting to tip his hand, Cyrus lied and said he had heard from a friend at St. Valentine's that their Grand Isle vacation home might be available for rent.

Since he'd posed as a potential customer, the owner called him back immediately. A man, a Robert Hill, said the house was available for most of October and all of November. December was booked, however. Cyrus pretended to take the dates and prices down and promised to call Hill back.

So. What did that tell Cyrus? He could only guess at Father Ike's motivations, but, as a detective, half of his job was guesswork. Father Ike had a place he could've rented pretty cheap, cheap compared to the Honeymoon Cottage he did rent. So why rent that place instead of his usual place? Maybe Father Ike wanted to go back to Grand Isle, but for some reason, he didn't want anyone to know exactly where he was on Grand Isle. But if he didn't want anyone to know where he was...why go back to a place he'd visited before?

Because there was something there he wanted to see again?

Something? Or someone?

Someone...yeah, maybe someone was there. Maybe someone he'd met in June when he'd gone there for his vacation.

Cyrus turned that over in his mind.

June. Father Ike heads down to Grand Isle for a three-week vacation. He's been there before. Only wants some R and R. But. Maybe. He meets somebody there. A woman, let's say, on vacation herself. She and Father Ike hit it off. He's on vacation, right? No priest collar, no black jacket, no clerical shirt. He's wearing khakis. He's wearing flip-flops. He's a good-looking sixty. She's forty, fifty. And maybe she's kinky. And maybe she's from New York City. And maybe she knows the "legendary" Mistress Nora.

People from New York came down to Nola all the time on vacation. Why not Grand Isle? Beautiful place.

All right. So Ike meets a lady. Maybe a man, but Nora got a straight sort of vibe from Ike. So did Sister Margaret. Maybe this kinky New Yorker lady and Ike have an affair. Happened a billion times before, right? Solo vacations were made for getting laid by strangers you never meant to see again.

So Father Ike went for it. Had a grand old time on

Grand Isle. The lady's heading back to New York at the end of her trip. Bad news. Sad news. She tells Ike, "Hey, don't worry. I know a local gal who might give you want you want and need, just like I could. You don't even have to go all the way to New York to get it. Mistress Nora. Here's her card. We used to party together before she moved down here. It's a cell phone, so that's probably still her number."

Father Ike takes the card and keeps it.

And later on in June, maybe he starts getting notes or threatening phone calls...

Okay, so somebody knows about his lady. Somebody knows Ike got wild with a kinky lady at his vacation home. Only two hours from Nola. Anybody could go there on a day trip.

Or maybe the lady herself figures out she'd been sleeping with a Catholic priest and she gets mad he lied to her—it could happen—and she threatens to tell on him. He's got over half a mill in a retirement account. A lot of money. Very tempting to blackmail a priest for that money, trip to hell be damned.

What's Ike's first instinct? Well, everybody's first instinct is fight or flight. Flight? Put in for a transfer. Get out of Nola before the shit hits the fan.

Fight? Fight might mean he kills his blackmailer. Priests had committed murder before. Maybe it was an accident during a confrontation with the blackmailer? Either way, somebody or something ends up on Ike's conscience. He can't live with himself after what he did.

He kills himself.

But first he calls Mistress Nora. Why though? Why her? Why right before he eats a bullet? It's all over by then, right? Not like he was going to make an appointment with a dominatrix he never planned to keep.

To confess his sins? He sinned with a kinky lady, so he wants to confess to a kinky lady?

That didn't sound right.

Except Nora was sleeping with a priest herself. And if Ike was being blackmailed for sleeping with somebody, maybe he'd want to talk to Nora about it.

Or warn her.

Imagine there was a blackmailer out there going after sexually active priests. Wouldn't it stand to reason that Father Ike might try to warn other possible victims before taking his own life, as a last act of compassion?

Farfetched? Yes. Impossible? No.

Only one way to find out if it had any legs to it.

He had to go down to Grand Isle, find some locals who lived near that vacation home Father Ike had rented. Ask if they remembered seeing Ike with anyone.

He shot Nora a quick text.

Long story but I'm heading to Grand Isle. Can you come with?

Nora replied a minute later. *Can't. Tied up.*

Too busy?

No, literally tied up.

I thought you had a bangover, lady.

Only cure for a bangover, she wrote back, *is hair of the Dom that bit you.*

Chapter Thirty-One

Søren's piano was being delivered to his new house that day. He offered to reschedule the movers, but Nora wouldn't let him. And it wasn't as if Gmork could fit on the back of Søren's bike anyway.

Once she sent Søren on his way home, Nora called Kingsley to come and pick her up at her dungeon. That was a mistake. He spent the entire ride lecturing her about letting strange women into her house in the middle of the night. He wasn't very happy when Nora reminded him that he'd spent his entire thirties letting strange women—and men—into his house in the middle of the night and therefore he had, as they say, no room to talk.

"That's an entirely different situation. I was fucking them," he said.

"One of them stole your Rolex, remember?" Nora said.

"Ah, but she was good enough in bed I didn't mind."

Clearly, they had very different recollections of that incident.

Kingsley stood guard while Nora packed a bag at her house. She would be living with him, Juliette, and Céleste until she could get a security system installed on her house. Actually, she wasn't allowed to handle the security system installation. Kingsley decided he would handle it since she couldn't be trusted to make good decisions where her own safety was concerned.

"You're being a little sexist here, King," Nora said when he was scrolling through his phone, looking for the number of the company that installed his. "I can take care of my own house."

"You have a thousand strings of cursed Mardi Gras beads hanging from your tree left by a witch over the course of three years trying to put a spell on you," he said as he put the phone to his ear. "Tell me again why I should let you handle this?"

Nora opened her mouth to give him five good reasons he should back off and let her handle it.

Then he said, "I'll pay for it."

"All right," Nora said. "It's all yours."

Kingsley ordered her to his house while he stayed at hers and waited for the installers to arrive. She was halfway out the door when she heard him on the phone with a new person now, requesting a tree trimmer come and trim her front tree and remove all the beads.

"No," Nora said to him.

"What?" He told the person on the other end of the line to hold.

"My house. My tree. My beads. You can handle the security system, fine, but leave my tree alone."

"A witch put them on your tree."

"You don't actually believe in witchcraft, do you?"

That got him. "Of course not."

"Then no reason to have them removed, right?"

Kingsley hung up on the tree trimmer.

"Thank you," she said although she didn't mean it. The men in her life were getting a little overprotective for her taste. "Do I need to remind you that I am not a child? This is my house. I own it. You get an opinion," she said, "but you do not get a vote."

"I'm sorry," he said.

"It's okay. I know you're on edge, Edge."

He smiled a little, but just a little.

"If anything happened you to," he began, glancing away like he was wont to do when admitting feelings he didn't like having. "We're all knitted together so tightly...one thread unravels, we all fall apart."

"I know you're scared. You always turn into a control freak when you get scared."

"Why aren't you scared?" It was a good question. Why wasn't she?

"I don't know," she admitted with a shrug. "I met her. You didn't. What she did scares me. What she said scares me. But she doesn't scare me."

"She scares me enough for the both of us. Now go." He opened the door and pointed in the direction of his house.

"I have to run an errand first."

"It can wait."

"I'll take Gmork."

"It can wait."

"Until when?"

"Until I stop being terrified," he said. He met her eyes again and she saw his fear. Kingsley was right about all of them being interlaced, but wrong about how. They weren't knitted together like a blanket or sweater. If those unraveled, they could be fixed. They were more like a spider-web, all of them, made of filaments so fragile and fine nothing could put them back together if one of them was torn away.

Which is why she had to do what she had to do.

She kissed his cheek. "It can't wait that long."

Nora whistled and Gmork followed her to her car and jumped into the backseat and lay down on his blanket. "Don't tell on me, boy," she said as she started her car and pulled out onto the street, "But we're going to go have a little talk with our witch."

Chapter Thirty-Two

Cyrus was lucky with traffic and made it to Grand Isle in an hour and fifty minutes. He plugged in the address of Father Ike's vacation home into Google maps first. It led him to a picturesque street a couple of blocks from the nearest beach. The houses were all painted in bright colors—sky blue and sunny yellow, pink and green—and stood on stilts to avoid the inevitable flooding from tropical storms and hurricanes. They had names like *Slow M'Ocean* and *Shore Beats Work*. The beach house was smack dab in the center of the street, a white A-frame with red shutters.

As he was canvassing that day and knew he'd have to talk to strangers, he'd put on his best suit before driving down. Cyrus had his story ready, too. Black or white, male or female, old or young—fact was, people were nosy as hell. If he gave up a little gossip, he was sure to get some in return. He climbed the stairs to the first house on the street and rang the bell. Nobody seemed to be home, and the people in the next house over were on Grand Isle for the first time. No help there.

He got a little luckier with the third house, the pink house. Pink, in Cyrus's opinion, was an old lady color and sure enough, an older white woman opened the door.

"Sorry to bother you, ma'am," he said, passing her his business card. "I'm a detective. Do you live here on Grand Isle?"

"Since my husband retired in 2008. Why do you ask? Should I call my husband?"

"I'm just looking for some information about someone who stayed next door to you this summer. This man," Cyrus said and held up the photograph of Father Ike. She took it from and peered at it, nodding.

"Oh yes, I remember him. He stayed next door for a long time. Very nice man. Isaac, I think he said. Is that right?"

"That's right."

"We get so many tourists, they tend to be a blur after a while. But he was around a lot. I must have talked to him every day. But just to say hello and chat a little. Why? Did he do something?"

Cyrus decided now was the time to start answering her questions. He let her hold onto the photograph. Might help jog her memory.

"I'm afraid he's dead," Cyrus said. "His family hired me to look into it."

"Dead? Was he killed?"

Cyrus nodded. He was killed. That was true. He didn't mention that Ike himself pulled the trigger. The woman gasped and covered her mouth with her fingertips in shock.

"I just...he was so nice. I can't imagine...was he mixed up in something?"

That was movie talk right there. *Mixed up in something.*

Cyrus liked playing the part of the TV detective since that was what people expected of him.

"That's what I'm trying to find out, ma'am. Did you see him with anyone at the house while he was here? A visitor? Someone who might have stayed with him? Overnight possibly?"

"You mean like a girlfriend? No, he didn't have a girlfriend. Or, you know..." She lowered her voice. "A *man* friend."

"I see," Cyrus said, disappointed. There goes that theory. "Do you remember if he stayed at that house every night? Or maybe he stayed with someone else around here? Or somewhere else?"

"Oh, I think he was there every night," she said. "Liked to walk every morning on the beach. By the time he got back, I was making breakfast. I could see him from the kitchen window climbing his steps."

All right. So he didn't have company at the house and Ike didn't go to anyone else's house at night.

"Did he...do you think he had a girlfriend," the woman asked, "and she killed him?"

"It's a theory I'm working on," he said. Cyrus decided to shake up the woman a little, shake her and see what he could shake out. "Ma'am, were you aware that Isaac was a Catholic priest?"

Her eyes widened, big as the sand dollars painted on her mailbox.

"He was?" she said. "He never told us that. Why wouldn't he tell us that? We've had several priests stay at that house. We're not Catholic, but we don't have any problem with priests."

"Oh, a lot of reasons. Priests can make people feel uncomfortable. Or people immediately want to tell priests everything they did wrong or get into theological discussions. He may have just wanted his privacy while he was here."

"A priest...that just doesn't make any sense at all."

"Louisiana is a very Catholic state," he reminded her.

"I guess you're right. He asked me about my grandchildren, and I think...well, I thought he had grandchildren, too, since he seemed to know a lot about children."

"He worked in a school."

"Ah," she said, nodding. "Well, that explains that. I said something about it being paradise down here but that my grandson hated visiting, nothing to do. I remember him saying a lot of kids hate being away from their things and their friends. Not even a big beautiful beach makes up for it. It just sounded to me like he knew kids. But if you say he worked at a school, that makes sense. Although...I could have sworn—"

"What could you swear?"

"Oh, he asked what there was for kids to do around here. I thought for sure he had kids or grandkids of his own. Grandkids, at his age. I told him a few things and he wrote them down."

"Maybe he was thinking about field trips or something."

"Maybe so."

She shook her head. "Murdered...I can't even imagine... he was just so nice."

"Yes, he was," Cyrus said.

"You find out who did it to him, you hear," the woman said.

"I plan on it, ma'am."

She nodded, managed a smile. "I need to get lunch started. Is there anything else?"

Cyrus took her name and number in case he had follow-up questions, and thanked the woman profusely for her time. He turned to leave but then thought of a question. He knocked and she answered the door with a real smile this time.

"Forget something?" she asked.

"Just real quick," Cyrus said, "what did you tell him when he asked what there was around here for kids to do?"

"Oh, the usual." She lifted her hands. "Swim at the beach. We got a park, too. And the butterfly dome."

"Butterfly dome?"

"Just a nature park, all butterflies. Schools visit it all the time."

"Got it. Thank you. Have a nice day, ma'am."

Cyrus tried a few more houses on the street. If anyone was home, they weren't answering. He did catch a couple people walking back from the beach, but they were tourists and had nothing to add.

Nothing more he could do on that street. Cyrus got in his car and punched in the address for the house Ike had secretly rented for a two-month stay from Home Away From Home.

Grand Isle might have been grand, but it wasn't very big. Cyrus arrived at the new address in only ten minutes. The neighborhood was almost identical to the one he'd left. Brightly painted houses on stilts, all in a row. These looked a little nicer, a little newer. And they were closer to the water and would have a good view of the sunset. Romantic as it got.

Cyrus had trouble finding the house Ike had rented. He walked up and down the block twice looking for the number. His phone's GPS was no use. New development. A lot of places still weren't precisely mapped, and there was nothing to do but gumshoe it until he found the place.

The street was called Atlantic Way and the house number was 15. He found 10, 12, 14, and 16, but no 15. Odd numbers had to be somewhere.

Cyrus reached the end of the block and kept going. Turned out the street curved like a *U*. The odd numbers were on a ridge a little higher up.

He found the house he was looking for at the very end of the street.

Number fifteen was just as quaint as the Home Away from Home pictures had painted it, but the photographs hadn't done justice to how secluded it was. There were three undeveloped lots between it and the next house— three empty lots full of trees, trees that had survived a hundred years of hurricanes. The property was fenced in. A passcode was required to access the staircase leading to the house.

No need to jump the fence or anything. Not yet, at least. Cyrus walked the perimeter of the lot to get a feel for the place.

Good thing this beach house was so secluded, he thought. Somebody might have called the cops on him, the way he was nosing around it...

Wait. Why *this* beach house? The answer was staring him in the face. Number fifteen rented at a premium for a reason, and it wasn't the view—every beach house had a view. All were spectacular. None were this isolated. The privacy number fifteen afforded renters seemed like overkill, if all they planned to do was go for morning walks on the beach and sit on the back porch and read. But it wasn't overkill if your livelihood was on the line.

Location, location, location.

That's what Nora had said when Cyrus had asked her how she and her Viking had never got caught fooling around.

Tiny parish in a small town. And with the priest shortage, Søren didn't have to share the parish house with any other priests. Which is good. That place was tiny. But it was way back in the woods, trees everywhere, and to get to it, you had to drive in from a side street. Very secluded.

But if Father Ike was having an affair with somebody... who the hell was it?

Cyrus was going to have to meditate on that. But not until he got home and was feeling safe in his own place.

On the drive back, he tried instead to think about Paulina, her long legs around his shoulders, the taste of her, the sound of her coming.

But even that didn't work.

All the way back to Nola, Cyrus could only think of one thing:

What the hell was Father Ike planning to do in that secluded beach house for two months?

Chapter Thirty-Three

The Good Witch, Mercedes's occult shop, was located in the Irish Channel, on the corner of Tchoupitoulas and 7th. Even after three years, Nora was still struggling to pronounce the city's street names like a local. Tchoupitoulas, though, she had in the bag: "Chop-a-Two-Liss." Just as long as no one asked her to spell it.

Nora drove a block past the shop and parked on a sidestreet. On the off-chance dogs were allowed in The Good Witch, she leashed Gmork and took him with her. Otherwise, she'd have to leave him tied outside the store. Not a problem, really. Wasn't like anyone was going to try to steal a huge black German Shepherd wearing a spiked dog collar.

The storefront of The Good Witch was painted lavender with a creamy white trim. The display window was brightly-colored with stained-glass hangings of harvest scenes, owls and ravens and deer, triple-phase moons, and the strange faces of men grinning through green foliage. On the door, a sign declared the shop OPEN. A brass plaque next to the door was engraved with the words FAMILIARS WELCOME.

"I guess that's you, boy," Nora said to Gmork.

She pushed open the door and heard a gentle tinkling of bells. A string of silver bells on a golden cord hung on the back of the doorknob. Nora spotted Mercedes behind a counter, on the opposite side of the store. A customer—a well-heeled white woman of about fifty—was chatting to her. Nora only caught a few words, something about arthritis inflammation. Mercedes was recommending spearmint tea in addition to whatever compound she was preparing for the woman.

Mercedes glanced Nora's way, and nodded her head in recognition and greeting. She didn't seem too surprised to see Nora. Maybe a little pleased? Or was Nora imagining that?

As she waited for Mercedes to wrap things up with her customer, Nora wandered the store, Gmork at her side on a very short leash. "You break it," she whispered to Gmork, "you buy it."

The shop was a good size, about twice Nora's living room. A converted cottage, she decided. The main front room had been a living room at one point. The back room, hidden behind a curtain, had likely been a bedroom. A sign beside the curtain said it was now the READING ROOM. That was where the private tarot and palm readings happened.

Nora found the store welcoming. Nothing strange or scary here. No eyes of newt or voodoo dolls. She found a wall of scented candles that had apparently been "charged" with magical properties. A green candle worked a money spell. A yellow candle stoked creativity. A pale blue candle promised to help with anxiety. A red candle promised love.

Another wall was replete with books of magic and spells. Journals, too, with embossed leather covers and thick with heavy cotton paper. From the ceiling of the shop hung Mardi Gras beads, mostly silver, and draped in elegant loops. The sunlight through the stained-glass panels in the shop window reflected off the beads and tossed rainbows throughout the entire store. And the whole place smelled of blooming flowers, potent but not over-powering. Nora felt better just inhaling the air in there.

While Mercedes rang up her customer's purchase at another counter, Nora examined the decks of tarot cards. There were dozens of different decks, dozens of different sets of artwork. Some she recognized. Everyone had seen the Rider-Waite decks. Others were stranger, lovelier, sillier. She found tarot decks for cat-lovers, for witches, for medievalists. There were vampire decks, angel decks, African decks, and Italian Renaissance decks. Nora fell in love at first sight with the Aquarian deck and its eerie Art Deco illustrations.

Nora moved away from the decks before she bought all of them simply to stare at the artwork for hours on end. She wandered to a table of jewelry, but it wasn't the gems and beads that caught her eye.

A newspaper article had been cut out, framed, and hung on the wall in a back corner. Time had yellowed the paper, which was dated November 1984. Nora skimmed the article about a woman named Doreen Goode, a local New Orleans witch, who had helped the police recover a missing child. Though the image was grainy, Nora could spot the resemblance to Mercedes in Ms. Goode's face.

"My mother," Mercedes said.

Nora glanced over her shoulder and found Mercedes standing behind her at a respectable distance.

"She rescued a little girl?" Nora asked.

"She helped the police whenever they asked her." Mercedes held out her hand and Gmork strained against his leash to reach those extended fingers. Nora loosened her grip so Gmork could reach Mercedes and get petted.

"Do you?" Nora asked.

"I would if they asked me. City's not what it once was. But nowhere is." Mercedes had gone down into a squat to meet Gmork eye to eye. She stroked his head, his long ears. If Gmork had been a cat, he would have purred.

"What do you mean 'nowhere is'?"

"Ah, cities are self-aware now. New Orleans used to be a little strange and wild because it was strange and wild. Now it's strange and wild because tourists expect it of us. Internet makes it hard, too. In '84, a missing child in New Orleans wasn't national news. No Facebook or Twitter to make it national news. Nobody around here batted an eye at the police asking a witch for help. Now you don't want to be the police chief that's made a laughingstock on the world's stage by admitting you believe in the occult."

"Guess not," Nora said. "How did your mother find the girl? Did she, ah, 'see' where she was?"

"She would chew moonflower to put herself into a trance," Mercedes said. "She said it took her 'into the deep.' Where the 'deep' really was, I don't know, but she never went into the deep without bringing something or someone out with her. She went in and saw the girl through a little window lying on a bed of bare wood, sunlight streaming in, beams like a church roof."

"An attic," Nora said. The girl had been found in her

own home, the newspaper article had said. Found half-dead from hitting her head while hiding.

"She'd thought she was in trouble," Mercedes said, rising up from her squat but still keeping her fingertips on Gmork's dark head. "She'd broken the grandfather clock in the house by playing with it. So she'd hid. Tripped over a box or a beam, knocked herself out. Couldn't hear everyone screaming her name. She was up there over twenty-four hours in the attic heat, passed out and dying of thirst. If Mama hadn't found her, she would have died in a couple hours. Now she's thirty years old. Two kids. One girl named Doreen for my mother."

"You have a daughter, right?"

"Just the one girl," she said. "Got it right the first time. Had her at eighteen. She's a freshman in college now."

Nora did quick math. Eighteen plus eighteen meant Mercedes was thirty-six years old. Maybe thirty-seven. About Nora's age.

"Around here?" Nora asked.

Mercedes shook her head. "In Boston."

"Boston? She's at Harvard?"

"We're not supposed to brag about that," Mercedes said. "So Rosemary tells me. But we do. My mother used to wear peasant blouses every day. Now she wears Harvard t-shirts."

"So your mom's still alive?"

"Oh yes, the Goode women are long-lived. But she's in Savannah, taking care of my grandmother."

"How did you know my mother was dying?" Nora asked.

Mercedes lifted her hands. "I just saw it."

"Did you see me coming to see you today?"

"I can't see my own future," Mercedes said. "It's like

trying to read a book pressed to your face. Too close to make anything out."

"Well, that's a bitch, isn't it?"

They laughed companionably. Hard to believe she'd been terrified of this woman only last night.

"My grandmother always said that our gifts came from the Goddess, but the Goddess was far off. We shouldn't be surprised when our gifts arrived banged up and battered. Like getting a package from Siberia, it'll be a little worse for the wear. But better than nothing."

Mercedes beckoned Nora to follow her with a wave of her hand. She pushed the curtain to the reading room aside and switched on an antique lamp with a green shade.

The floral scent in the shop had been coming from this room. Instead of Mardi Gras beads dangling from the ceiling, bundles of herbs were tied to crossbeams to dry.

Gmork seemed unusually alert in the reading room. He didn't want to sit or lay down. He stood, sniffing, his ears straight up.

"Gmork? What's wrong?"

"He smells Hestia."

"Is that some kind of herb?"

Mercedes smiled. "She's my cat. She's supposed to stay upstairs, but somehow she always manages to come down here and sleep on my reading table."

Nora noticed little black hairs on the lacy white table-cloth, where a dozen tarot decks lay in a neat row.

"You aren't in the market for a black cat, are you?" Mercedes asked. "I have a spare. People dump them on my doorstep. Either a joke or they really think all witches have black cats as familiars." She shook her head and clicked her tongue, tut-tutting the ways of fools.

"I'm not sure I could handle a weird dog *and* a weird

cat. But if I change my mind, I'll let you know."

"Please. Hestia is much happier as an only child."

Mercedes pulled a chair out for Nora. She sat, still studying the reading room. Shelves were stacked with books stuffed with loose papers. Impressionistic paintings of hares and harts hung on the walls.

"I like it here," Nora said, not meaning to. The words just came out. Mercedes nodded like she wasn't at all surprised to hear that. She took a seat opposite Nora.

"Every four days I charge the whole place, stem to stern, with good energy. I just did it yesterday, focusing on welcoming. The Goddess must have known I'd have a special guest."

"How do you do that?"

"How does your pope bless rosaries?" Mercedes said. "Same way I imagine. You hold it, you speak words of power over it, sometimes you sprinkle it with water. I don't know if your pope puts magical herbs in the water, but the Church used to sprinkle holy water with bunches of rue."

Nora couldn't deny it. She'd seen Søren himself using flowers to sprinkle holy water.

"My priest used basil," Nora said.

"Basil's good," Mercedes said. "I use it in love spells. Maybe your priest wanted his people to love God more."

"I think he just liked the scent of it."

"Would your priest approve of you being here?" Mercedes sat back in the chair and crossed her legs. She wore an ankle-length floral-print skirt, sandals, and a white blouse embroidered with flowers at the low neckline.

"No," Nora said. "He definitely wouldn't. But maybe not for the reason you think. None of the men in my life would approve of me being here right now."

"Is that why you're here?"

"Probably."

Mercedes said nothing. Nora folded her hands in her lap, crossed her legs and patted her thigh. Gmork rested his head against her leg. Nora took comfort in his presence.

"They're all scared of you," Nora said.

"I believe I would be, too, if I were them. It's not often I get this involved in a situation that's out of my control. I just...I didn't know what else to do. When something's boiling, you can't but watch the pot."

"They think you're a crazy stalker," Nora continued.

"Stalker? No. Crazy? Ah. Who's to say?'

Nora smiled. "You've been putting cursed Mardi Gras beads on my house for three years. Hard to explain that away as harmless."

"*Blessed,*" Mercedes said, her voice sharp. "Blessed beads. Not cursed. Charged with power, good power. Nothing evil. I don't curse anyone. Unless you cut me off in traffic. And those are just the usual curses."

"Charged Mardi Gras beads?"

"Something my mother used to do," Mercedes said. "A lot of women got hurt around here during Mardi Gras. It's a prime hunting time for male predators. She would charge beads with protection spells every year on Fat Tuesday, hoping to protect some of those girls from rapists. That's all I was doing with those beads in your tree. Trying to protect you from bad influences."

"Bad influences? Like what? R-rated movies? Violent video games?"

"Men who don't know what they're talking about," Mercedes said. "Men who don't know anything about anything. In other words...men."

Mercedes pointed at the silver bracelet she wore around her wrist.

"Silver," she explained, "is feminine. Female energy. Female wisdom and intuition. That's why I put up the silver beads. The black beads are straight-up wards against evil. Red for courage and blue for opening your mind. No curses in there at all."

Nora stroked Gmork's long back as she considered how much to tell Mercedes, how much to keep to herself.

"One of the men in my life tried to call a tree-trimmer this morning to cut all the beads down. I wouldn't let him."

"Good."

"He's scared."

"Of me?"

"Of everything. His girlfriend's about to have a baby. He's seeing danger everywhere."

"Potent days, right before a baby is born. The veil thins between the other world and this one. Has to thin so the soul can break through. Tell him to burn some sage incense and sleep with an agate under his pillow."

"Got anything that'll just knock him out until the baby's born? He's turning into a control freak."

"Fear will do that to a man, make him into a tyrant. You can't let him rule you."

Nora smiled to herself.

"What is it?" Mercedes asked, her head tilted like a curious cat.

"His name is King," Nora said. "Just funny, you called him a tyrant, said he shouldn't rule me."

"Is he family?"

"Sort of. Like common law family. I've known him

since I was sixteen. His oldest son is one of my two lovers."

Mercedes picked up one of her tarot decks and found a card with quick fingers. The Knight of Cups.

"Yes, that's him," Nora said. "Nico. He owns a winery in the south of France."

"He's good," Mercedes said. "Good for you. Protects you. Respects you. Serves you. A wine-maker...he'll believe in earth magic, whether he's ever said it aloud or not. His love for you is simple and powerful, like a sword. But not a sword for battle. He uses it to cut through the thorny vines in your heart. He's where you go when you want to be safe."

"All that's true."

"That one I don't worry about," Mercedes said as she flipped through the deck. "If it was just him, you'd never have to lose a wink of sleep in your life. It's this one that worries me."

She flipped through the deck again and pulled out another card, The Hierophant, otherwise known as The High Priest, and set it on the table between them.

Nora stared at the card and said nothing.

"What is this card to you?" Mercedes asked.

"You tell me."

"The cards aren't books full of answers," Mercedes said. "They're doors. They tell us what doors we need to open in our lives. But only you can open that door and walk through. All I can say is that this card, it's male. Male power. Male energy. Male power and men in power. I would guess you have a male authority in your life who has great power over you. Too much power. Power that influences you and leads you astray."

"I can't believe that. Not of him."

"Him?"

"Him," Nora said. "*My* him."

"Might not be a *him*. Might be an *it*. The cards have people on them but they don't always represent actual people. This could be a force in your life, not necessarily a person."

"The High Priest," Nora said, "is a person to me."

"Who is he then?"

"Someone I will never leave." Nora met Mercedes's eyes.

"Someone you love."

"Yes."

"Tell me, Mistress Nora. I can't help you if you don't let me."

"I don't believe in any of this." Nora waved her hand, as if to knock it all aside.

"You believe in all of it," Mercedes said sharply. "You're Catholic. You believe in prayers, which we call spells. You believe in blessing, which we call charging. You believe in God. We call that force the Goddess. You believe in magic, except you don't call it that. But it is magic, all the same. Magic words, magic songs, magic spells. Light a candle, whisper a name, summon him home to your bed. That's a love spell. You cast one and it came to pass."

"I decorate for Christmas, too. I don't believe in Santa Claus."

"But you believe in Jesus."

Nora couldn't look at Mercedes and her dark waiting eyes anymore. She glanced away, stared at a painting on the wall, a painting of a white stag in a field of snow.

"What is it? What are you afraid of?"

Nora swallowed a lump in her throat.

"I'm not leaving the man I love. I'm not. I won't."

"I would never tell you to."

"You already did." She reached out, picked up the card of The High Priest.

"Your lover is a priest, isn't he?" Mercedes asked. Nora nodded slowly. "You're the mistress of a warlock. No wonder there's so much power around you. You're sleeping with a warlock."

Nora laughed out loud. Rude? Yes. Unbelievably rude. But she couldn't stop herself. It was all too ridiculous. Søren. A warlock.

"Laugh all you want," Mercedes said. "Laugh all you can. I know you think I'm crazy. It's all right. I'm not the one sleeping with a priest. Even I know better than that."

"What's wrong with sleeping with a priest? Other than I'm not supposed to do that and neither is he."

"Priests have power. Too much of it. You can't go around sticking your fingers into light sockets and not expecting to get shocked. But be the Fool if you like. There's a place for them in this world, too." She held up another card—The Fool.

"You're not going to make me leave the man I've loved my entire life. The only reason I came here was to make sure I didn't need to be afraid of you. I can tell I don't have to be, so I won't be. Although if I were you, I'd stay away from my house from now on. We're installing a security system."

"I'll stay away."

Nora stood up though she didn't want to. The shop felt as comfortable as a soft warm bed and leaving it just as hard. Mercedes stayed at her table, staring at the cards before her.

"Nora," Mercedes said. Nora turned back. "Just so you know, I'm more scared of you than you are of me."

Chapter Thirty-Four

Okay, so Nora had been right. Going for a run with Søren? It was a trap.

The first mile was okay. Cyrus could do an eight-minute mile, no problem. He could do an eight-minute mile for a mile. Mile two got a little tougher. For Cyrus, that is. Søren kept on running, feet pounding the pavement like clockwork, breaths pumping steady and hard as a locomotive. But that couldn't last, right? Not running eight-minute miles.

Mile three? Holy shit.

Cyrus actually said, "Holy shit!" out loud when the run stretched into mile four.

"You need to stop?" Søren asked.

"Two minutes."

They jogged to a stop and stepped off the trail. It had been Søren's suggestion they run the Mississippi River trail, something he'd been meaning to do. Cyrus had assumed they'd run a couple miles of it, maybe make a loop.

Seemed to him like Søren was intent on running all 60.8 miles of it. That morning.

"Are you all right?" Søren asked.

Cyrus glared at the man. They'd both shown up at the start of the trail wearing t-shirts. Cyrus paired his with his favorite Nike shorts, while Søren wore black running pants. Cyrus had stripped out of his t-shirt by the end of mile one. Søren was still wearing his. Cyrus was breathing hard, eyes burning from sweat. Søren wasn't even winded.

"What did I ever do to you?" Cyrus asked.

Søren grinned. He pushed his black wraparound sunglasses up on his head. "It's not personal." A red-headed woman of about twenty, twenty-two jogged past them and glanced back over her shoulder to smile seductively at Søren.

"I hate you." Here he was, doubled over trying not to puke from running four miles in thirty-two minutes, and this big blond Viking son of a bitch was over here getting eye-fucked by an Emma Stone clone.

"I'm fifty-one. Let me enjoy it. Shall we go again?"

"Hell no."

"We can walk back."

"Thank God."

Cyrus stood up straight, took as much air into his lungs as he could manage, and set off back toward the parking lot.

"I have a long stride," Søren said. "That's why I can run a little faster than most men my age."

"Yeah, tell me I'm short. That helps."

"You aren't short. I'm tall. There's a difference."

"Fuck off with all that. We're done. I'm getting a new running buddy, and he's gonna be short and fat, and I'm gonna pull him behind me in a wagon."

"I can tell why Eleanor likes you so much. She approves of anyone who is comfortable telling me where to go."

"Eight-minute mile for four miles? And you don't even get a free t-shirt at the end? Nora's right. You are a sadist."

"Guilty as charged," he said. "Though I promise, I'm getting no sexual pleasure from this run. Or...stroll."

Cyrus shook his head. He swore to himself he would never—ever—go running with Søren again. He was also definitely not getting a wedding invite.

"What's this about then? You trying to see if I'm tough enough to hang with Nora?"

"You've survived four whole days in her company and don't seem any worse for the wear."

"She does wear me out though. How do you sleep at night knowing your woman is that wild?"

"Helps to tie her ankle to the bedpost," Søren said.

"No offense, but you're kind of a weird priest. Ex-priest. Whatever."

"There is no such thing as a normal priest. I would know."

The morning was warming up fast. When they started running, it hadn't quite been seventy yet. Now it was on its way to eighty, fast.

"I have to ask. You grounding Nora after last night? Keep her from playing detective with me?"

"I've tried grounding. Doesn't work." He shook his head, exasperated as the father of a rebellious teenager. "Honestly, I wanted to thank you for helping Eleanor on Bourbon Street last night."

"Guess it was my fault she was there to start with."

"Eleanor is wholly responsible for her own decisions. If

she didn't want to go with you, she wouldn't have been there. I'm only glad you were there when she was being harassed."

"No problem. I don't let that shit happen around me if I can help it. That it?"

"I was also hoping you'd fill me in the case. It's consuming Eleanor. That worries me."

"I think she thinks because Ike called her, she's responsible for figuring out why he killed himself. It's more than just curiosity, I can tell you that much. She's taking it as seriously as I am."

"If Father Murran were still alive, I might kill him for dragging her into this. I can't say I blame her. If someone had called me right before committing suicide, I would have trouble sleeping until I knew why."

"It's more than that. She keeps seeing you in this case. Like when we found Ike's Bible full of private notes, she said you do that, too. She thinks he was kinky on the side and that somebody drove him to kill himself. I can tell she's thinking that could happen to you, too, someday. That girl loves you, man. In case you didn't know."

"I know. But it never hurts to hear it again." He smiled to himself. "Any breaks in the case?"

"Right now, I'm running on the theory Ike was being blackmailed, only because it makes sense, not because it fits the evidence. Nothing fits the evidence except he had a secret something weighing on him, and he died keeping it." Cyrus rubbed fresh sweat off his forehead again. "I'm thinking of going to Dunn and talking to him. He seems pretty convinced Ike was depressed. And they're old friends."

"I wouldn't if I were you. Archbishop Dunn is more a

politician than a pastor these days. He'll simply hint that he knows more than he can say about Father Murran's mental state, and he'll pat you on the head and send you home."

"You don't trust him?"

"I don't know trust most members of the clergy. Not because they're clergy. Because they're people."

"We're on the same page there." Cyrus exhaled. "You got any other ideas?"

"I'm intrigued by the Rumi poem you found in his Bible."

"The butterfly poem? Why is that?" Cyrus had wondered about that himself.

"I keep very personal notes in my Bible. Old notes from my high school love. Letters Eleanor sent me while I was in Rome working on my Ph.D. Photographs of my son. The sort of irreplaceable things I would save first in a fire. If Father Isaac and I have anything in common, the poem might be meaningful. You can pick up a copy of Rumi's poetry in any used bookstore. Why write the poem out by hand on fine paper and slip it in your Bible like some sort of *billet-doux*?"

"A what?"

"A love letter."

Cyrus wasn't too sure about that, but he filed it away as a "maybe."

"Well, you know priests and their shit better than I do."

"True. And we have a lot of shit," Søren said. Cyrus laughed to himself.

"You do. Seriously. You sure you want to be a priest? Don't take this the wrong way," Cyrus said, glancing around to make sure they were alone. "But you got Nora. Now she's not my type, but she's your type. Why don't you marry that girl? Hit it for the rest of your life without having to look over your shoulder to see if the archbishop's watching."

"The girl in question has little to no interest in marrying me. I ordered her to marry me once and didn't see her again for a full year."

"Damn. Most girls just say 'No, thank you, let's be friends.'"

Søren laughed, though Cyrus had a feeling the man had not been laughing at the time.

"So you going back?" he asked. "Nora says you got until Friday to decide."

"I have to decide by Friday if I want to go back to teach when the new school year starts. There are hoops galore I have to jump through before they'll put me back in a classroom."

"That long stride will help you jump those hoops."

Now Søren glared at him. Cyrus cackled to himself.

"You could be a professor without being a priest," Cyrus said. "Right?"

"I wouldn't be teaching pastoral studies at Loyola."

"Then teach running at LSU. They got profs for that. Don't know why, but they do."

"I'm trying to picture myself as a Track & Field coach. It's not working."

"Just saying, you got options. It's not 'marry Nora' or 'be a Jesuit priest.' There's a range..." Cyrus held out both hands three feet apart. "Right hand, marry Nora. Left hand, be a priest. You see all that space in-between? That's other shit you could be doing."

"I'm well-aware of my options," he said. "I just don't like any of them. Professors, piano teachers, and track & field coaches don't get to perform weddings and baptize babies, celebrate Mass, and perform Last Rites on the dying and bring a sense of comfort and peace to the family."

"I get that. I do. I was a cop, then I was shot, now I'm a private detective. Even when I'm not a cop...I'm still a damn cop."

"We are called to what we are called to," he said, sounding just like a priest when he said it.

"I'm going to tell you something," Cyrus said, "and it might come off as me getting back at you for running me ragged back there, but it's not, okay?"

"Go on."

"It's what I tell the married men I talk to when I catch them cheating. You can't keep your vows, you don't get to keep your wife. It's just that simple."

"Simple," he agreed. "Not easy."

"Nobody's saying it's easy. I won't even say it's fair. I think you priests should be allowed to get married. Not easy. Not fair. But it is what it is and you knew that when you signed up for it. And that's exactly what you're allowed to tell me if I ever cheat on Paulina, God help me."

"You are a wise man," he said. "And I don't like you very much right now."

Cyrus had to laugh at that. "Truth hurts."

A middle-aged woman jogged toward and then past them, giving him and Søren a knowing look. Cyrus could guess what she was thinking—*definitely a weird gay hook-up.*

"Here's a thing you don't know about me," Cyrus said. "I'm in therapy. Paulina's idea, but now I'm a convert. My therapist, she's a Jungian. Now Jung was a little woo-woo but he's helped me solve a lot of cases."

"Very impressive for a man who's been dead over fifty years."

"Right. Anyway, he had this idea that people needed to have secrets. A secret is the thing that separates you from the masses. That secret is what makes you an individual."

"And your point?"

"Dunno. Just seems kind of interesting that your whole life is a secret—by choice. Why do you think that is? You think maybe you like being separated from other people? Other priests, maybe?"

The Viking laughed a little—a very little—at that. "Worth considering."

"Why would you want to be a priest if you don't, you know, like them? Or want to be like them?"

"I promise you, Cyrus, you do not want to go anywhere near my psyche. You'd be better off walking blindfolded through an active minefield."

"That bad, huh?"

"Worse."

"Good. I don't feel bad now about asking you a creepy question."

"You have me intrigued. If you can creep me out, I'll be very impressed."

Priest. Sadist. Sleeping with a dominatrix. Yeah, probably took a lot to creep this old boy out.

"Speaking of priests and death—what makes a priest want to kill himself? It's not just a sin. It's *the* sin. The biggest sin. The sin that gets you kicked out of the cemetery. You can shoot up a 7-11 and still get in the cemetery. But you shoot yourself? That's it. You're evicted. Even the dead don't want you in their neighborhood."

"The usual, I imagine. Depression. Mental illness. Traumatic event. All those can be exacerbated by the loneliness of being a Catholic priest. No spouse to confide in, very few intimate friends. Also, there's the fishbowl effect. We're watched. We're seen. We're put on pedestals we don't belong on. Most men feel the pressure to bottle up their emotions and priests experience that as well. But whereas other men are at least allowed to express anger, priests are expected to be godly and perfect at all times. We're denied even the outlets other men are allowed."

Cyrus nodded. He couldn't imagine how hard it would be to go through life without Paulina in it. "What about you? Can you think of anything that would make you want to do it?"

"Ah, now that is a creepy question, isn't it?"

"Creepy as hell," Cyrus said. "Don't answer it if you don't want to."

Søren took a long breath. "The two people in my life I love the most, I've hurt them both and hurt them deeply. Betrayed them, their trust, their love for me. And even then, I always had faith that the wounds would heal. And they've both done their fair share of damage as well." He paused again. "I'd say the only thing that would make me tempted to take my own life would be if I hurt my son or found myself tempted to hurt my son. My father...he hurt my sister. And me when I tried to stop it. Yes, if I were tempted to hurt a child, my child especially, I would be very tempted to do myself in."

"You wouldn't have to kill yourself," Cyrus said. "You hurt a kid? I'd do it for you."

"And I would thank you for saving me the trouble."

"You think it means anything he did it at that little house on Annunciation Street?" Cyrus asked.

"He would have wanted privacy, of course."

"He had a car. He could have driven out to the middle of nowhere and done it."

"True. Perhaps the house holds some special meaning for him?"

"Not that I know of," Cyrus said. "But I haven't looked at that angle yet either. The house has been locked up for cleaning. I'll see if I can get in, nose around."

They were nearing the parking lot. Cyrus couldn't wait to get into his air-conditioned car, get home and get in the shower. And then he might take a nap. A long God damn nap.

He whistled softly when he saw Søren's ride. A black Ducati motorcycle.

"Who'd you have to sleep with to get one of those?"

"This was a bribe," Søren said as he took his helmet out of the saddlebag. "My father—who was vile in every way imaginable—tried everything in his power to stop me from joining the Jesuits and becoming a priest. Threats of violence. Threats of public humiliation. Threats of harming the few people in my life I loved. In the end, he resorted to simple bribery. Jesuits aren't allowed to own personal property and everything is owned in common. If I wanted to keep the bike for myself—which I did, of course—I would have to leave the Jesuits."

"But you got it."

"My father didn't know about the loophole—a Jesuit can ask permission to keep gifts. Sometimes it's granted, usually for small personal things, rarely anything large or expensive. My advisor and confessor, however, gave me permission to keep it. I believe his exact words were, 'You keep the Ducati. Your father can go to hell.' And when he died, he did."

"Damn," Cyrus said. "You're pretty cold for a priest."

"You don't know much about priests if you think we're better people than everyone else. I am living proof of that. In fact, if I had one piece of advice to give you as you investigate your case—"

"I'll take it," Cyrus said.

"Assume the worst."

Chapter Thirty-Five

The verdict was in. The color was Return to Paradise—a pale blue-green. Kingsley approved, begrudgingly, and Céleste approved wholeheartedly. As always, what Céleste wanted, Céleste got, God bless that girl.

Juliette preferred oil-based paint for its finish, but it stunk to high heaven. Juliette, Céleste, and Kingsley decamped to the Ritz-Carlton for a few days, leaving Nora alone with the fumes. With the windows open and a paint mask on, Nora was fine, more or less. Except for when she hallucinated a young Christopher Plummer, riding on the back of a white horse, coming to carry her away. She'd taken a break after that.

With the family gone, Nora could have simply hired someone to paint the nursery. Though tempted, she'd decided against it. Better to stay busy than sit around obsessing over everything Mercedes had said to her. So she cranked the music—Madonna and Prince were good company for manual labor—and got to work.

Music helped for an hour or two, but once Nora

settled into the rhythm of the work, the swish and whoosh of the roller brush on the wall, her mind wandered again to the warnings Mercedes had given her.

She would face a difficult choice. She would make the wrong choice. Innocent people would be hurt. And it was a man who would lead her astray.

It was that last part that turned Nora into a skeptic. Deep down, she knew she was perfectly capable of fucking up royally and hurting people without even realizing what she'd done. She'd been that person more times than she wanted to think about. But the men in her life? Søren. Nico. Kingsley. Cyrus. Gmork?

Nico was in France and wasn't even aware of what was happening right now. Nora would tell him, but only when she had more answers than questions.

Kingsley? True, he was a reformed rake, minus the reformed part, but he was protective of the women in life —especially Juliette and Céleste but her, too.

Cyrus? Cyrus was up to his eyeballs in love, lust, and adoration of his fiancée. He wouldn't do anything to mess things up with Paulina, much less lead Nora "astray."

And Søren? He would die for her, plain and simple. He would never talk her out of doing the right thing or into doing the wrong thing.

Would he? Not on purpose anyway.

She was fairly sure she was hallucinating again when she received a text message from Cyrus that read, *Emma Stone wants to fuck your Viking.*

Nora left the nursery and went out to the backyard to breathe some fresh air and make sure she'd read that right.

She had.

Therefore she replied, *Do I get to watch?*

You're as crazy as he is.

I warned you about the running thing. But no, you didn't want to listen to me.

Yeah, you warned me. That's on me. Call me.

Nora called him.

"What's up?" she asked him. "Wait. How sure are you this phone call is actually happening?"

"Ninety percent. Why do you ask?"

"I've been inhaling a lot of paint fumes. Oil paint. I'm not sure about reality at the moment. Not that I'm complaining."

"You're not even gonna ask me about Emma Stone?"

"Sexy young redhead with good tits flirted with Søren while you two were running this morning?"

"How'd you guess?"

"Either Søren has a thing for redheads or redheads have a thing for Søren, I swear. You should have seen it when he and Kingsley played on the same team in church league soccer. Women would slide off the bleachers."

"I don't need that image in my head."

"Sorry. Blame the paint fumes for that. Trying to get the nursery done. Wanna come help?" she asked, her voice bright and obnoxious as a fluorescent light.

"Yeah, no. Just calling to tell you your Viking says we can keep working together."

"So the fellowship of the cock rings isn't breaking up?"

"You are not right, woman. Not right at all. And don't even try to blame the paint fumes for that."

She couldn't, so she didn't.

"What's our next move then, partner?" she asked.

"The police finally released the house where Father Ike died. My next move is checking that house, seeing if they missed anything."

"Like what? Suicide note?"

"Most people don't leave a note," he said. "And cops looked for one. Closest we got was that voicemail he left for Sister Margaret."

"What did it say exactly?" Nora asked. He'd never told her.

"Give me a sec. I'll get my notebook."

Nora heard Cyrus put his phone down. When he picked it up again, she heard the rustle of pages flipping.

"According to Detective Katherine Naylor," Cyrus said, "Father Ike said, 'I'm sorry for what I'm about to do but I'd be sorrier if I didn't do it. I can't do this anymore. Forgive me. Pray for me, Margaret.' And that was it."

"Pretty vague. I guess 'I'm sorry for what I'm about to do' means he's sorry for committing suicide. But why would he be sorrier if he didn't commit suicide?"

"No God damn idea."

"Did you listen to it yourself?" she asked.

"The voicemail? No, didn't want to."

"Maybe we should," Nora said. "Maybe he said something else. You got that from the detective, not Sister Margaret."

"You're gonna make me listen to that message, aren't you?"

"I'll do it if you don't want to."

"Fine. I'll call Sister Margaret, see if we can hear the message. Although I'm already thinking that's a dead-end. Detective Naylor would have told me if there was anything in that voicemail worth listening to."

"You never know," Nora said. "So if not a note, what are you looking for in the house?"

"Maybe that key?" he said.

"Good thinking. I should come, too, and help you look for it."

"You want to go to the scene of a bloody suicide?"

"It's not still bloody, is it?"

"No. It's cleaned up now."

"Then, yes, I want to go with you."

"All right. Meet me there at six," he said. "Yellow house on the corner of Annunciation and Rose."

"I'll be there. See you later. If I don't pass out from paint fumes first."

Nora hung up, took in a few more lungfuls of fresh air, then returned to the nursery where Christopher Plummer was waiting for her.

Naked.

"Captain Von Trapp," she said. "We really should stop meeting this way."

Maybe when she was done with the nursery, she'd repaint her bedroom. Or the whole house...

Chapter Thirty-Six

Cyrus paced the sidewalk while he waited for Nora to turn up. It was almost six, the sun still up, and he wanted to search the outside of the house for Father Ike's missing car keys. He had a feeling if they found the car keys, they'd also find the missing padlock key. Nora seemed to like her theory that Father Ike had a lady somewhere who was wearing that key around her neck on a chain, but Cyrus doubted it. Things weren't that mysterious and sexy in real life. Violent deaths were ugly and brutal and stupid, and beautiful corpses were only on TV.

Although the sun was up, Cyrus used his flashlight to scan the little front yard. He didn't find anything in the weedy grass. Before he could check the backyard, Nora pulled up in her Mustang and parked in front of the house on the street. Thank God, she was dressed normal. Jeans, white tank, sneakers. Duffle bag, which probably had that cock-ring chastity thing in it.

"Over here," he said and waved her to the front door.

"You heard back from Sister Margaret yet about the message?" Nora asked.

"Not yet."

Using the key Katherine had given him, Cyrus opened the front door and let them both in the house.

They paused at the entryway as if afraid to go in further. The house didn't look like the scene of a crime. The clean-up was over. No red left on the old oak floors. It just looked like a little guest house—bookshelves filled with mismatched knickknacks and old books that either came from Goodwill or ought to go there, ugly plaid sofa, coffee table from the '70s, wallpaper from the '60s, brick fireplace plugged up since the '50s. Why do it here? Of all the places to kill yourself...

"It's clean," Cyrus said, glancing around. "Nothing to worry about."

"Why do you look so worried then?" Nora asked. She didn't look too relaxed herself.

"We're not supposed to be here, technically. So look hard and fast and try not to mess anything up."

Nora nodded. Cyrus said, "Good luck."

He left her in the living room while he walked through to the kitchen and out the backdoor. With his flashlight he made a circuit of the yard. Didn't find anything. Not until he went all the way around the side of the house again and noticed paper sticking out of the mailbox.

He knew he shouldn't be digging through the mail—federal crime and all that—but it wouldn't kill him to look. Turned out the box was stuffed solid with several days of mail. Junk mostly. Flyers and notices. But there was something else, a big pink envelope, the kind that went with a big greeting card. Except this envelope had no address or name written on it, no return address or stamp. And it didn't hold a card. It held something hard, something solid, something that jingled.

Shaking, Cyrus pulled a handkerchief out of his pocket and grasped the envelope by the corner before he got his fingerprints all over it. Cyrus stepped into the front door and found Nora had taken all the couch cushions off and was digging through the seats.

"Come here. I got something."

She stood up fast and Cyrus nodded toward the kitchen where there was good bright light.

At the kitchen counter, Cyrus laid the envelope down.

"Feels like keys," he explained to Nora as he dug latex gloves out of his pocket. "Sounds like them, too."

He turned the envelope over. Holding the flap down was a sticker.

"A butterfly," Nora said.

That's what it was, all right. A round sticker about the size of a half dollar with an illustration of a monarch butterfly.

Carefully, Cyrus peeled back the flap. A set of car keys fell out on the counter.

"Hot damn," Cyrus said.

"That looks like a padlock key." Nora pointed at the littlest key on the ring.

"Get the thing," he said.

Nora ran into the other room, came back with the duffel bag. Cyrus passed her another set of gloves. She pulled the chastity device out of the bag and set it on a few paper towels that Cyrus had set out.

Cyrus tried the key. The lock popped open.

"Okay, so there goes my theory," Nora said.

Cyrus didn't answer, too busy thinking.

"Keys in the mailbox. No stamp. Somebody found the keys? No."

"If they just found them on the street, they wouldn't know who they belonged to."

"Right." Cyrus nodded. "So somebody had the keys already, found out Ike was dead, and wanted to return them quietly."

"Somebody who likes butterflies. Who likes butterflies?"

"Father Ike did. He had that poem in his Bible."

"He was in love with someone who likes butterflies? Maybe? Or sleeping with someone who likes butterflies?"

"We don't know that. It's a guess, but we can't say that for sure." Cyrus turned the envelope over and looked inside but found nothing other than that one butterfly sticker.

"Doesn't seem possible it's just a coincidence though, does it?"

No, it didn't.

And something else...

"Grand Isle," Cyrus said. "It has a butterfly dome. Some kind of park, all butterflies. Ike went on vacation there in June. In July, he booked a two-month stay on Grand Isle at a different place, a real secluded place. Lady who met him said Father Ike asked what there was to do around there. She said 'beach, nature hikes, biking, and the butterfly dome.'"

"So he wanted to go back because he likes butterflies," Nora said. "Or because he knew someone who did."

Cyrus needed to think and think hard and think deep.

"I'm going for a walk," he said.

"You want me to come?"

"No, you stay here. Keep looking. I'm gonna walk from here to where we found the car again."

"Why? We already found the keys."

Cyrus turned so that he was facing the street. "You have any trouble getting a parking spot on this street?"

"No. I parked right in front of the house."

"You see lots of spots?"

"Half the street was empty."

"Right. Exactly." Cyrus wagged his finger at her. "Ike didn't park his car three blocks away because there was no parking here. He parked it there for a reason."

"What reason?"

"Ike had his own apartment at St. Valentine's, but he came here to the church's guest house a mile away, supposedly for 'peace and quiet.' Sister Margaret said he likes the neighborhood. What's so special about this neighborhood?"

"What are you thinking?"

"Maybe the man or woman he gave his keys to lives around here. Maybe that's why he came here. I just want to see what I can see."

"Good luck," Nora said. "I'll call you if I find anything."

Cyrus left her in the house and headed out on foot. He walked slowly, carefully eying every house he passed. What was he looking for? Something told him he'd know it when he saw it. And something else told him he'd already seen it.

But what was it?

Butterflies. Butterfly poem. Butterfly dome. Butterfly sticker.

Maybe the woman Cyrus was doing kink with had a butterfly tattoo. He knew a whole lotta girls who had butterflies inked on their backs or ankles. He'd even picked one girl up at an Usher concert who had a butterfly tattoo on her upper chest so that the little butterfly's head was at her throat, the wings on her cleavage.

Of course while he was remembering fucking the butterfly girl, Sister Margaret called him back.

"Sister," he said. "Thanks for calling me. I know this is terrible to talk about, but I'd like to hear the recording of Father Ike's message to you. Would you let me do that?"

She took a deep breath. "If you think it'll help. Let me call you back on our landline, and I'll play it over the phone. Would that work?"

"That would work fine. I'm out on the street, though. I'll text you in a couple minutes and you can call me then."

Cyrus jogged back to the house on Annunciation Street. This time he found Nora in the bedroom going through the dresser drawers.

"No luck," she said. "And I turned this place upside-down. You?"

"Sister Margaret's gonna let us listen to the message. You ready?"

"As I'll ever be."

Cyrus sent the Sister a text. A few seconds later, his phone rang. Cyrus put it on speaker and set it on top of the dresser.

"Ready," he told Sister Margaret.

"All right," she said. Her voice was hollow. "I'll push play and hold it up. Here we go."

A beep, and then a male voice: "Maggie."

Nora reached out and grabbed Cyrus by the forearm. He knew how she felt.

"I'm sorry for what I'm about to do," the voice said, "but I'd be sorrier if I didn't do it. I can't do this. Anyway. Forgive me. Pray for me, Margaret."

It was one thing to hear the words repeated by Katherine, another thing to hear the words from Father Ike's own mouth. His voice was surprisingly strong and steady, a man who had made a decision and there was no going back from it.

"That's it," Sister Margaret said. "Did you need to hear it again?"

"No," Cyrus said. Nora still had him by the forearm. She looked paler than usual. "I got it. Thank you. I'm sorry to upset you."

"You didn't upset me. I was already upset. Goodnight." She hung up.

"Well?" Nora said. "That's it then."

Was it? Cyrus pulled his reporters' notebook from his pocket and flipped back.

"I can't do this anymore," Cyrus read out loud. He looked up. "That's what Katherine told me. But that's not what Ike said. He said, 'I can't do this.' Pause. 'Anyway...'"

There was a world of difference between "I can't do this" and "I can't do this *anymore*." A simple mistake. One word. But it reframed everything.

"I can't do this—period," Nora repeated. "What's 'this'? He can't mean his suicide because he just said he was going to do it."

"He was talking about doing something else," Cyrus said. *"I'm going to kill myself because I can't do...what?"*

Nora only shook her head. Maybe when they figured that out, this fucking case would finally be over.

Chapter Thirty-Seven

Cyrus returned to his apartment. Paulina had asked him over for dinner, and though he'd been tempted to say "yes," he told her he had to work on the case. He knew they were close. He didn't want to stop. Not now.

Paulina was a born detective's spouse. She said, "You do what you have to do. I'll save you the leftovers for tomorrow."

God damn, he loved that woman.

Back in his apartment, Cyrus spread out a plain white towel on his kitchen table and placed everything on it in a line.

Pink envelope with the butterfly sticker.

Car keys.

Rumi poem about the butterflies.

The chastity device.

Then Cyrus typed and printed out a timeline of events, beginning with the trip to Grand Isle in June, the engagement party in July, and coming up on today, finding the keys in the mailbox.

He sat at the kitchen chair and looked one by one by one by one at the items on the table. Then he closed his eyes and began to breathe deliberately. Breathe in for four —one, two, three, four—hold it for three at the top—one, two, three—breathe out for four and hold it for three at the bottom.

One.

Two.

Three.

Cyrus did this again and again, until he'd breathed himself so deep into his mind that he couldn't see or feel his own body anymore.

But he didn't need his body, just his brain. His brain and the river that ran wild through it.

When he opened his inner eye, he was already in the river.

This had never happened before. Always he'd come to the river, waded in, found what he needed to find there. Now he was knee-deep in the river.

And the water was rising.

Already it had risen from his knees to his waist. He had to get out before it was up to his neck. He started forward and found he couldn't get out. Something had him around the ankle. He lifted his foot. A chain was wrapped around his leg, a chain padlocked shut.

Okay, so he needed the key. They had a key. They'd found the key.

He patted around his pockets. There, in the breast pocket of his suit.

He took the key out of his pocket again and opened his hand. The key turned into a butterfly and flew away.

Cyrus opened his eyes.

He collapsed back in his kitchen chair, breathing hard.

Didn't take a psychologist to tell him what he'd seen deep in his own mind—fear. Fear this case was going to kill him if he didn't unlock the secret like they'd unlocked the padlock.

Unlocked the padlock.

They had unlocked it. They found the key and unlocked it. Cyrus stared at the chastity device. The padlock, open, was still on it. Why? Because Nora had said the lock held the two pieces together.

Cyrus removed the lock and let the two pieces of the device fall apart. Curious, he studied the two parts in his hand—the cage, as Nora called it, and the ring.

He saw something.

At first, Cyrus thought it might just be some kind of maker's mark, like the kind he'd seen on the bottom of old silver plates and other antiques. But it wasn't that. He narrowed his eyes. Two letters were engraved inside the device, followed by three numbers.

MT 529

And underneath...there was a tiny butterfly.

Cyrus wasn't nearly as religious as Paulina, but he knew a Bible verse when he saw it.

Matthew 5:29.

His heart raced with excitement. Something told him this was the thing. This was it. This would break the case.

Cyrus called Nora. She picked up on the first ring.

"It's engraved," Cyrus said before she could even get out a quick "hello."

"What? What is?"

"The cock thing. The chastity thing. It's got a butterfly and a Bible verse engraved on the inside. Couldn't see it when the lock was on but it fell apart and I saw it. Matthew 5:29. I haven't looked it up yet but—"

"Søren," Nora said. He must have been with her. "Matthew 5:29."

Cyrus held his breath. His lungs nearly burst while he waited.

"Okay," Nora said. She repeated after Søren: "If your right eye causes you to sin, tear it out and throw it away. It is better for you to lose one of your members than for your whole body to be thrown into hell."

"Søren's got that memorized?"

"Are you surprised?"

He wasn't. "What do you think it means?"

"That you should do anything you can to avoid sinning, including amputation."

"Not the verse," Cyrus said. "That he's got it engraved inside his chastity thing. Why would he do that?"

"It was actually engraved in there? Like how?"

"I don't know. Like you engrave anything."

"Not written in Sharpie or scratched in with a knife?"

"No, I said engraved, and I mean engraved. Fancy letters made by a pro. Why?"

She went silent. Then, "Give me one minute."

Silence again. Cyrus pressed the phone to his ear as hard as he could. He held his breath and heard the low, low murmur of voices. Sounded like Nora was asking Søren something else.

Then the phone crackled.

"We need to go to the Ritz-Carlton."

"What's there?"

"Kingsley's there. He's not answering his phone, which probably means he's eating dinner. He hates it when people talk on phones during meals. But if he's there, he'll tell us. I'm sure he knows."

"Knows what?" Cyrus was so excited he was almost shouting at her.

"He'll know who engraved Father Ike's chastity device."

Chapter Thirty-Eight

Nora ended her call. She looked at Søren, who was standing with his back to the kitchen counter, a glass of white wine in hand. Casually, he sipped at it, but she noticed his grip was a little tighter than it needed to be.

"Cyrus is coming to pick me up," she said. "Break in the case. Maybe."

"So I gathered." He sipped his wine while she sat at the table and slipped on her shoes.

"Not sure when I'll be home."

"You could just call the hotel," Søren said. "Ask them if Kingsley's in. He'll take an emergency call from you, even if they are having dinner."

"If he has a name for us, we'll probably go and see them right away."

"Of course. I suppose we'll have to reschedule our evening plans."

Nora winced. In her excitement over Cyrus's phone call, she'd forgotten she and Søren were supposed to be having a date night. Nothing special. Nothing fancy. Indian for dinner —it was on its way now. A movie—*The Third Man*, Criterion Collection. Kink and sex afterward most likely, though maybe not. Maybe they'd just drink wine until they were sleepy, go to bed, fall asleep together like a normal couple. That's what normal couples did, right? Like she would know.

"I'll be back. If not, tomorrow night," she said. "I'm sorry."

He set his wine glass on the counter.

"You're already used to it."

"What?"

"Having time together." he said. "In the past, every evening together between us was guarded, special. Now, if we don't do it tonight, there's always tomorrow night."

She laughed a little, at herself. He was so good at seeing the why behind her what.

"Maybe so," she said. "Kind of nice. Are you mad?"

"Not even remotely." He picked up his wine glass again but didn't drink. The way he said it, she knew he was telling the truth, but not necessarily the whole truth. "Maybe I'm getting used to it, too."

She heard a car horn discreetly honk. Cyrus.

She rose up on her toes to kiss him. "I love you, Sir," she said. "If you eat my korma, I'll kill you in your sleep. Don't watch the movie without me."

"I wouldn't dream of it."

She left him in her kitchen, grabbed her bag, and ran out to Cyrus's car.

"Sorry," she said as she hopped in and yanked on her seatbelt. "Had to kiss Blondie goodnight."

"Did I interrupt something?" Cyrus asked.

"Nothing that can't be rescheduled."

"You could have told me. We could have done this tomorrow." But he was already pulling away from the curb.

"Let's get it over with," she said. "I have to know."

"Yes, ma'am," he said, and they headed to the Ritz-Carlton, Cyrus's foot heavy on the gas.

Even exceeding the speed limit by a healthy margin, it was a good twenty minutes to the Ritz. They were both tense, Nora could tell, and it made the quiet in the car heavy. Cyrus broke it with an inane question, the kind people ask when they're nervous but don't want to show it.

"You get your security alarm installed?" he said.

Nora smiled to herself. Such a man question. He'll be asking if she'd gotten her car's oiled changed recently.

"King's taking care of it."

"Good. Hope it's witchproof."

"I didn't ask. Don't get mad, but I went to talk to her."

"What?" Cyrus said it loudly and dared to take his eyes off the road just to give her a furious look.

"Don't be like that. She's a person, not some kind of monster."

"She's been stalking you, Nora. Stalking. I gotta explain what that is to you?"

"I know what it is. But I just... I just couldn't believe she was dangerous. I went to her shop to talk it out with her. She's not going to hurt me. I don't think she has it in her."

"Everybody has it in them. Everybody. And if I didn't believe that before, I sure as hell believe it after spending a week with you."

She took that as a compliment. It wasn't one but she took it as one anyway.

"I don't want you to be my next case," Cyrus said softly. "Okay?"

Nora smiled to soothe him, the way women did when humoring men. "Okay."

At the Ritz, she told Cyrus to drop his car with the valet. They went straight to the concierge desk. Cyrus seemed to know the way.

"You been here before?" Nora asked.

"Some men like to cheat in high style," he said. "Grab that guy, Manny. I always see him here. He knows everything."

Nora saw a handsome twenty-something Hispanic man in a black suit walk away from an older woman who'd stopped him in the lobby. Nora put on her best smile and oh-so-sweetly asked him if he'd mind checking around for a guest of theirs, a Kingsley Boissonneault. Family emergency, Nora explained, giving her name.

Manny, concierge extraordinaire, told her to leave it to him. Less than a minute later, Kingsley walked into the storied marbled lobby. He held both hands out in a question and gave her a look that said, *This better be good.*

"What's he doing here?" he asked Nora.

"Hey, Pierre Capretz," Cyrus said, "I'm standing right here."

"This is important," Nora said. Kingsley rolled his eyes. "Cyrus, cover your ears."

"What?"

"Trust me, you don't want to hear this."

"Weird sex stuff?"

"Gay stuff," Nora said.

"I'll just go stand by the fountain."

As soon as Cyrus was out of earshot, Kingsley said, "Gay stuff?"

"Okay, bi stuff. Whatever. You gave Søren engraved handcuffs. Where did you get them engraved?"

"What? Why do you ask?"

"Long story. Do you remember?"

"Of course I remember. I bought them two weeks ago."

"I need a name, number, address, whatever you have."

Kingsley turned his phone on, waited for it to power up. "I'll be glad when you're done playing Watson and Sherlock. You interrupt me in the pool, at dinner with Jules—"

"I babysit for free. All the time."

"Ah," he said with a pained smile. "A little interruption never hurt anyone. Here we go." He was scrolling through the contacts in his phone. "His name is Philip Danton but everyone calls him—"

"Shit."

"You know him?" Kingsley raised his eyebrow at her.

"Yeah, I know him. And I'm going to fucking kill him."

She kissed Kingsley on the cheek, grabbed Cyrus by the arm, and marched him toward the door.

"Bad news," Nora said. "We have to commit a murder."

"Save it for the car," he said, glancing around. "Too many witnesses."

They walked quickly to the parking lot.

"Pierre Capretz? Really?" she asked when they reached his car.

Cyrus opened the car door. "Only French guy I could think of. Now who we killing?"

Chapter Thirty-Nine

G od damn motherfucking Doc.

Cyrus should have known. He should have. Nobody was that squirrelly just 'cuz. Doc had been putting on a show for them, a song and dance routine, but Cyrus had fallen prey to his prejudices against the man and ignored his gut that warned him Doc was something other than a nut.

Never play cards with a man called Doc.

And Cyrus had done just that.

"We could be jumping to conclusions here," Nora said. "It's possible—maybe—that Doc wasn't the man who engraved Father Ike's cage."

"I know it's him," he said. "I knew then he wasn't telling us everything."

"You did?"

"You know your own face when you see it in a mirror, even when you don't like what you see," Cyrus said. "The way he was all over you, that's how I used to be with women. I mean, not that crazy, but, you know, I'd play like that, go over the top like that. Make them think I was playing a game *with* them when the whole time I was just playing a game *on* them."

"He played us. Both of us."

"Yes, he did."

"Why would he lie to me? If Father Ike bought something from him, got it engraved even, why wouldn't he just tell us? I mean, he told us about seeing him in a class."

"I don't know," Cyrus said. "But he better have a damn good, excuse or I'm gonna be the one tying him up and working him over with a whip."

"He'll probably still like it."

"Yeah, but so will I and that's all I care about."

Doc worked from home, according to Kingsley Edge. Big garage out back of his house. His made custom kink pieces, did engraving, repairs, that sort of thing, but it was a cash-only business, completely unlicensed and unregulated. Nora wondered out loud if that was why Doc had kept his trap shut when they asked him about Father Ike or if he had a more sinister reason for lying.

His house was exactly what Cyrus expected. A Victorian, of course. One of those sorts called "painted ladies"—blue, pink, and white with gingerbread trim and a wraparound porch, rocking chair included. Perfect for a retired art professor. Nora rang the bell and knocked on the door. The porch light was on, but there was no answer.

Cyrus nodded toward the driveway. "Light's on out back," he said.

The backyard was hidden behind an eight-foot high privacy fence at the end of the drive. The gate was half-opened, and they went through.

Everywhere they looked, they saw metal sculptures. Naked women cavorting, naked men cowering. A high-pitched whine was coming from a free-standing shed. The Doc's shop.

Nora stared at one sculpture of a woman in a robe holding an arrow and ramming it into the balls of a male angel who was either really into it or really, really not into it. Hard to tell if the face was moaning or screaming.

"A reverse St. Theresa and the Angel," Nora explained. "I think I want it."

"Nora."

"Sorry."

They went to the shop doop. Cyrus was half-worried they'd scare Doc into setting himself on fire if he pounded on the door.

He did it anyway.

BAM BAM BAM.

He had to do it a few more times, but eventually it got the man's attention. The machine sound ceased and a clattering came from within, then a muffled swearing sound. Finally, the door opened.

Doc stood before them in stained canvas trousers and a t-shirt that appeared to have burn holes in it.

"Oh, Doc," Nora said. "You are in so much trouble."

"Mistress Nora," he said with a grin. "I was hoping we'd meet again."

"You better let us in," Cyrus said.

"With pleasure." Doc stepped back from the door and held out his arm to usher them in. "Watch your step."

There was shit everywhere. Boxes and buckets full of sand and water, equipment, tools, the whole insane nine yards. As the smoke cleared, Cyrus saw various workstations in the shop. One for welding, one for polishing, one for engraving.

"I'd ask you to sit," Doc said, "but—"

"We'll stand." Nora crossed her arms over her chest. "You don't seem very surprised to see us."

"Surprised? No. Pleased, most definitely." He reached for her hand, and Nora swatted it away, rather viciously Cyrus thought, pleased.

"Give it up," Cyrus said. "I'm done watching your stupid act. You lied to us."

"I didn't lie." Doc held up both hands. "I would never lie to the Queen."

"Doc, seriously," Nora said. "It's getting old."

He lowered his hands. "You're really not as much fun as they say you are, you know."

"Ah, you're one of those," Nora said, nodding. "You only like the *idea* of women. You don't like actual women."

"You wound me."

"You wish," Nora said.

"The man whose picture we showed you—that's Isaac Murran," Cyrus said. "You know him. You either made or engraved a chastity device for him. Or both."

"I don't reveal the names of my customers," Doc said.

"You already ratted him out as being in one of your classes," Cyrus said.

"That was before he was a customer. After trading a few emails with the man, then he became a customer. After that, you get nothing else from me."

"He's dead, Doc. He killed himself. Shot himself in the head. Right before he did that, he called me." Nora pointed at herself. "He had my business card. You gave it to him, right?"

"The seal of the confessional doesn't break simply because the sinner dies," Doc reminded her. "You, of all dommes, should know that. Yes?" He grinned a mean, nasty grin.

Nora narrowed her eyes at him. So Doc knew she was sleeping with a priest. And he didn't mind taunting her about it.

Cyrus minded, however.

"That's it. I'm going to punch him. You don't mind?" Cyrus was speaking to Nora while looking at Doc.

"Go for it," Nora said.

Cyrus reached for Doc's shirt, but the old man stepped back and into a table. A small butane torch rolled off the table and onto the floor.

"Fine. Fine. But this can't get out," Doc said. "Not a word of it. I do private commissions and those private commissions pay my mortgage. The business isn't licensed. It's all cash. I don't want to spend the rest of my golden years in jail for tax fraud, all right?"

"Come on," Nora said. "You really think I report my tips to the IRS. We're on the same page. We're supposed to be on the same side."

"Can we go into the house, at least?" Doc asked as he picked up the torch. "Before we burn the place down?"

"Lead the way," Cyrus said. "You do anything squirrelly though, and I'm calling Uncle Sam on you *today*."

They let Doc turn off all his equipment. He seemed to be working on some sort of human-sized cage. An ornate iron locking mechanism was in the middle of being assembled on his worktable. The man had talent, that was for sure. Not that Cyrus was going to tell Doc that.

They followed him from his shop and into his house through the backdoor. He led them into the living room, books on every surface. He offered them seats. Nora took the large leather armchair. Cyrus declined to sit, instead standing behind her, the power behind the throne.

"So…" Nora began as Doc took a seat opposite her in a club chair. "What's up, Doc?"

"Did you really have to go there?" Cyrus muttered.

"I really had to," she said. Doc laughed but he didn't seem very happy, not as happy as he'd been the last time they spoke.

"It's not flattery, you know," Doc began as he eased back in his seat. "You really are a legend, Mistress. A friend of mine had a session with you in New York at your old club, the 8th Circle. Said it was the best kink he'd ever had in his life. Told me I had to get my old ass up to New York and beg for an hour with you."

"Did this friend of yours give you one of my cards?" Nora asked.

Slowly, Doc nodded.

Fucking finally. Cyrus wanted to pump his fist, but he refrained. For now.

"When a man asks you for the name of a dominatrix who would do anything for the right price, there's only one name—Mistress Nora."

"Fair," Nora said. "What did he want me for?"

"I'm getting to that."

Cyrus could tell the man didn't really want to be having this conversation. He could respect that. A little.

"So you had one of Nora's New York cards and you gave that card to Isaac Murran?" Cyrus asked.

"Yes. Yes, I did. I had mentioned in that class on medical play, that I made custom chastity devices. He ordered one from me, and I made it for him."

"When was this?" Cyrus had left his notebook in his pocket, afraid the presence of it would scare Doc into silence. But Cyrus made a mental note of everything Doc said.

"Two months ago," Doc said. "Late July."

"What did he ask for?" Nora said. "When he made the order, what did he say?"

"He wanted something that would punish erections. A trainer of sorts so that every time he got hard, it would be agony. Then a month ago he was back, and said it wasn't enough."

"Wasn't enough?" Cyrus repeated. "What the hell did he want? A dude standing over him kicking him in the balls 24/7?"

"As he said, he wanted a more 'permanent solution,'" Doc said.

"Permanent?" Nora narrowed her eyes at the man.

Doc said nothing for a moment, a long moment, and then an even longer moment. Cyrus was about ready to choke the answer out when he finally spoke.

"He wanted someone to castrate him."

"Shit," Cyrus said while Nora let loose a long whistle. Even she was impressed by that request.

"Castrate?" Cyrus said. "Like...literally castrate him. Cut his balls off."

"Cut them right off," Doc said. "And he was willing to pay through the nose for it."

"How much we talking?" Nora said.

"Nora."

"What?" she asked. "It's a fair question."

"He said price was no object. I threw out 50K as a number, and he didn't blink."

"Fuck," Nora said. "That would be tempting."

"Forget the money," Cyrus said. "Why? Why would any man want that?"

"He didn't say explicitly," Doc said. "But I got the

distinct impression he was having trouble controlling himself."

"Excessive masturbation?" Nora asked. "Spontaneous erections? Flashing?"

"I don't believe so. I think..." Doc said, pausing again. "I think he..."

"Doc, spit it out," Cyrus ordered. "He's dead. I saw the body."

"Yes, he's dead," Doc said, "so it shouldn't matter. Let him rest in peace."

"It does matter. It matters a lot to me." Nora pointed at herself. "Answer me right now. Why did Ike Murran want to be castrated?"

"Like I said, he didn't come right out and say it," Doc said at last. "But when I said that castration seemed a bit extreme, even for a masochist, he agreed. He said it was a 'last resort' solution but that it was..." Doc swallowed. "He said something to the effect of, 'Better than spending the rest of my life in prison.'"

"Prison?" Nora said.

Doc nodded.

Nora and Cyrus exchanged worried looks. "He was afraid he was going to rape someone," she said.

Assume the worst, Søren had told Cyrus. What was the worst?

Cyrus felt his jaw tighten. "He was afraid he was going to...or he already did and thought he'd do it again."

Chapter Forty

Doc refused to talk to them anymore. He looked old when they were done with him, old and tired and rung out. Cyrus knew how he felt.

"Guess Doc didn't want to face that maybe he was helping out a rapist," Cyrus said when he and Nora were back in his car. "One thing to not ask questions when someone comes knocking on your door. Another thing to know the answers and not tell anyone."

Nora said nothing. She seemed lost in her own thoughts.

Cyrus hated to leave her there, lost and alone. "Nora? You okay?"

"Just wondering," she said. "What I would have done?"

"If he'd gotten through to you?"

She nodded.

"You wouldn't have really castrated the man, would you?" Cyrus asked. "Please say 'no.'"

"No," she said. "I don't know how. I could find out how. I know someone who did it—don't ask."

She must have seen his mouth starting to open to ask that very question.

"I've left permanent scars on male clients. I've done branding, scarification. I once nailed a guy's testicles—"

"Stop right there."

"Sorry," she said. "But actual castration? That's major surgery. I could have killed him. But if he'd called me, I would have talked to him," Nora said. "Tried to get him to talk to me. But it wouldn't have worked, would it?"

"Why not?"

"This whole time, I thought he was one of us," she said. "Kinky. But he wasn't calling me for kink. He wanted surgery no doctor would perform—without a good reason anyway. What surgeon would castrate a healthy man for no medical reason whatsoever?"

"None in this country," Cyrus said. "Not if they want to keep their license. Doctors are mandatory reporters, too. If a patient says, 'Cut my balls off or I'm going to rape my neighbor tomorrow,' somebody's gonna make a phone call about that."

"Right," Nora said. She took a long deep breath, a long slow exhale. "Right."

The car was silent except for Christian Scott playing through the speakers, low and sad and slow.

"Wait," Nora said, turning to look at him. "You said rape his neighbor. Do you think that's what he was planning?"

"Just a guess," Cyrus said. "He was at that house on Annunciation, right? And the car was parked a few blocks away, like, I don't know, like he was planning a getaway? And remember what was in the bag?"

"Rope," Nora said. "Handcuffs and lube."

"Rape supplies," Cyrus said. "Kidnapping supplies.

Somebody was supposed to get into his car. That's why they had his keys. That's why it was parked a few blocks away."

"The Butterfly?" Nora asked.

"Gotta be her, whoever she is."

The Butterfly. Not his mistress...his victim.

Father Ike had given her his keys. She must have thought they were going on a trip somewhere. Then he doesn't show up at the car when he was supposed to..."

She pressed her hands to her face, breathed hard. "Are you thinking what I'm thinking?"

He knew what she was thinking. "I'm trying not to think it. He and Paulina were friends." It was unbearable to imagine his Paulina alone with a man who would—

No. Cyrus wouldn't go there until he had to.

"I think I'm going to be sick," she said.

Cyrus didn't know what to do. He wanted to take her hand, squeeze it, tell her he was sorry. But he didn't know quite how to do that yet, with any woman who wasn't Paulina.

"I did what you dared me to do," Cyrus said. Nora turned her head, looked at him, eyes wide.

"You did?"

He nodded. "Worked, too. I shouldn't tell you that."

"You should always tell me things like that. Did she enjoy herself?"

"Yeah. Loudly."

"Good woman. Good man." She held out her fist. He bumped it if only to make her smile again.

"Back before Paulina, when I was with a girl and we'd had a good date and we were back at her place...if we were fooling around and she said 'no' to going any further, I'd say that was fine and then I'd immediately get up to leave.

354 THE PRIEST

I wasn't mean about it. I played it cool like, 'I get it. You're tired. I'll let you sleep.' She'd be upset I was leaving so she'd give in so I'd stay. I thought I had game," Cyrus said. "Now I know I was manipulating them. I've never told anyone that."

He went on. "With Paulina, it was nothing like that. It was good. Good for her. I was just honest, and if she'd said 'no' I would have stayed and held her all night and been happy to do it. I just wish I knew it could be like that twenty years ago."

"If I told you all the shitty things I've done to people," Nora said, "we'd be here all night."

"You've been putting it on the line all week to help me figure this case out," he said. "Maybe you've done some shitty stuff in your life, but you've done some good stuff, too."

"Maybe this is my penance, too." She gave him a tired smile.

"I guess I ought to take you home."

She sat up straight and looked at him again. "No, I want to go back to the house. Someone had to have seen someone near his car, right?"

"You sure about that?" Cyrus asked.

"What if the Butterfly needs our help?"

There they were, Cyrus thought, two fuck-ups with so many sins in their past, they'd need an army of priests and a five-gallon bucket of holy water to absolve them both. Since they didn't have any priests or holy water, they would find the Butterfly and make sure she was safe. They couldn't do a God damn thing about their pasts anyway tonight. But they could do this.

Chapter Forty-One

They didn't talk on the way to the house. Cyrus's mind ran with the possibilities. The Butterfly, whoever she was, had stuffed the pink envelope into the mailbox. Someone might have seen her. Cyrus pictured a beautiful young woman, probably in her twenties, someone with a shitty boyfriend or an abusive husband. The kind of troubled young woman who'd had a bad relationship with her father and would latch onto a kind older man, a kind older priest. She'd pour out her heart to him and he'd comfort her and tell her how beautiful she was and how she didn't deserve to be treated the way she was...and all the time Father Ike was falling for her, falling hard, so hard he couldn't stop thinking about her, how much he wanted her, how much she tempted him. But he was a good man and he refused to give into temptation.

Until he did.

Assume the worst, Cyrus thought again.

Was she pregnant? Possibly. A priest finding out he got a young woman pregnant would be a good motive for a suicide. Or a murder. Men killed their pregnant partners all the time. Or maybe she wanted an abortion, and he offered to take her to get one when really he was going to keep her captive until it was too late for that. The thought turned Cyrus's stomach.

Assume the worst.

There was something worse than even that. *Don't be a kid. Don't be a kid. Dear Lord Jesus in heaven, don't let it be a kid,* Cyrus prayed silently.

They parked in front of the house on Annunciation Street.

"Ready?" Cyrus asked.

"Ready."

They headed in the general direction of the street where Father Ike had left his car the day of the suicide. When they saw someone was home, they knocked on the door. Nora flashed her smile. Cyrus flashed his P.I. credentials. Nobody had seen a priest around, but they hadn't been paying attention either. Lots of Catholic schools in the area. Priests and nuns didn't make a big impression.

"I'm glad you're with me," Nora said as they turned the corner onto Rose. "Knocking on stranger's doors is a little dicey."

"I was thinking the same thing," Cyrus said. "Glad you're with me."

She felt safer walking around at night with a man. He felt safer walking around at night with a white woman.

"What now?" she asked as they stopped at the place where Cyrus had found Father Ike's car.

"I guess we come back tomorrow," he said. "And do it again."

Nora exhaled heavily, nodded. As they walked back to

the car, back to Annunciation Street, Cyrus tried to meditate, to reach the river and the answers he hoped were waiting there for him. But he couldn't find his way there. Instead, his mind kept taking him back to that morning he was called to the house and had seen Father Ike's body on the floor.

Maybe that meant something.

"If you were planning to meet someone somewhere," Cyrus said, "and they didn't show up, what would you do?"

"Call them."

"If they didn't answer?"

"I'd call again. If they still didn't answer...I'd get very scared."

"So what would you do?"

"Probably try to find them," she said. "Go to their house, knock on the door, make sure they're okay."

Cyrus spun on his heel.

"Cy?"

"Come on," he said, waving his hand and Nora jogged after him.

They ran all the way back to the street where Father Ike had parked his car that morning.

"What are we doing?" Nora asked, panting, out of breath.

Cyrus wasn't sure. He only had a hunch. A strong hunch, but still just a hunch.

"Remember that nosy lady who asked us about the car? Where'd she live?"

Nora pointed to a pink house. Cyrus went up to the door and knocked.

A woman answered. It was the same woman who'd given them the third degree about the car.

"Yes?" she asked. "Wait. You two were here before."

"Sorry, ma'am," Cyrus said. "I'm a detective, I think I told you. You said something about kids messing with the car that was left on the street. Did you recognize those kids?"

The woman wore an embarrassed expression.

"Well, it was only one kid," she said. "And she was mostly just standing by the car."

"She? A little girl?" Nora asked. "Do you know her?"

"She lives over there in that little gray brick house. That's her."

He and Nora turned at the same time toward the house. A girl was sitting on the concrete porch steps, drawing or coloring. Cyrus looked at Nora. As casually as they could, they crossed the street. They stopped on the sidewalk in front of her house.

"Hi there," Nora said. Her voice was painfully bright and cheerful. "Is your mom or dad home?"

The girl shrugged. "Soon."

"That's the girl," Cyrus said under his breath. "I saw her walking by the house the morning after."

Nora gave him a worried look. "Are you coloring?" she asked the girl.

The girl held up her book. It was a coloring book but not one for kids. This was the sort of coloring book adults used for personal therapy, with intricate patterns that took hours to complete—all butterflies. Those books weren't cheap. Had someone given it to her?

Cyrus felt something inside him shatter and the pieces cut into his gut. She couldn't have been more than twelve years old.

"I know you," Cyrus said, smiling at the girl, the fakest smile he'd ever smile. "Where's your fairy wings at?"

"Fairy wings?" The girl looked at him, wide-eyed.

"I saw you on Saturday walking on Annunciation. You had on fairy wings."

"Those aren't fairy wings," she said. "That's my backpack. It's a butterfly backpack."

Assume the worst, Søren had said. This was the worst.

"I'm Cyrus," he said. "This is Nora. We knew Father Ike. Did you know him?"

Cyrus walked slowly to the porch, Nora at his side, still smiling. They both were, smiling like it would kill them not to smile.

"He was chaplain at my school last year," she said, closing her coloring book. "He died, right?"

Nora stepped up onto the front porch first. Cyrus kept a little more distance.

"Yes, sweetheart," Nora said. "He died. I'm sorry."

Her bottom lip quivered. Nora reached out and lightly touched the girls' shoulder.

"What's your name?" Nora asked her.

"Melody." Her voice was choked, hoarse.

"Pretty name, Melody," Nora said. "You and Father Ike were friends?"

She nodded, unable to speak. Tears welled in her eyes.

Cyrus pulled his white handkerchief from his pocket and handed it to Nora. She held it out to Melody, who cautiously took it.

"Were you going somewhere with Father Ike?" Cyrus asked. He kept his voice soft and gentle. He'd had to ask kids tough questions before. It never got easier.

Melody wiped at her face. "I came by... He was late."

"Late?" Nora asked. "Late for what?"

Melody glanced around like she was looking for a way to run, to get away from them before they made her break a promise Father Ike had surely told her she had to keep.

Then Nora said something to make the girl stay. "When I was fifteen, my best friend in the world was my priest. He helped me with my homework because I was terrible at math. And he gave me hot cocoa in winter. And he gave me a beautiful saint's medal, Saint Louise. That's my middle name. Eleanor Louise Schreiber."

"They're not supposed to," Melody whispered.

"I know they're not," Nora whispered back. "But sometimes they do. And sometimes it's kind of nice. I wore my saint's medal all the time. But just because they break the rules sometimes, that's not... It's never your fault if they do that. And you'd never be in trouble for telling someone about it. Was Father Ike going to take you somewhere last Saturday?"

"Dad promised," Melody said. "But we haven't seen him in months. And Mama works all weekend. I never see her either. So Father Ike, he said he'd take me to the Butterfly Dome."

Some prayers don't get answered. Jesus Christ, it was a kid. Cyrus didn't want to hear anymore. He wanted to cover his ears.

"The Butterfly Dome sounds fun," Nora said, her bottom lip quivering.

"They say the butterflies will land right on you," Melody went on. "And they have all kinds. *Papilio nireus*— that's the blue-banded swallowtail. And *Caligo memnon* —the owl butterfly. It has big eyes on its wings. And *Papilio palinurus*—the emerald-banded peacock. It's the prettiest butterfly in the world."

"You had your butterfly backpack on Saturday?" Nora said. "You were going to be gone for the whole day?"

"Father Ike said I might want to swim. I should bring other clothes. It's on an island. And Mom doesn't get off work until ten," she said. "We could spend all day at the Dome."

"You like butterflies a lot, then?" Nora said. Cyrus couldn't even stand to hear her voice, she was trying so hard not to fall apart. He wanted to scream, to weep, to howl, to pull Ike out of the ground and then put him back in it.

"Yeah, I love butterflies."

"So do I," Nora said. "I love them, too. Butterflies are beautiful."

Cyrus walked away, down to the sidewalk, and quietly called Katherine. He asked her to come down, no lights, no sirens, and to bring a female detective from the special victims' unit. One who was very good with children.

Chapter Forty-Two

❧❧❧

Nora sat in the rocking chair in the finished nursery, one leg curled up to her chest, one leg on the floor, foot pushing to keep the rocker rocking. They would be home soon—Juliette and Céleste and Kingsley—to see the nursery for the first time.

Céleste would squeal, as she did when she saw anything pretty. Kingsley would nod approval though deep down, he would have preferred pink or yellow walls to the blue-green they'd settled on. Juliette would gasp in delight. Nora made sure the nursery was gasp-worthy. She would wander the room, hand on her swollen belly, and touch the ivory changing table, the ivory cradle and crib, the antique rocking chair Nora had scoured the city to find. Céleste had been a New York City baby and her nursery had been in Kingsley's old Manhattan townhouse in a room with red wallpaper and gilt-framed mirrors. The mirror on the ceiling had been removed before Céleste's birth, of course. They'd made it as pretty as they could, but the entire house had been an Adult-with-a-capital-*A* oasis and there was no more turning a sow's ear into a silk purse than a dungeon into a daycare center.

So they'd moved to New Orleans. A fresh start for all of them. For Kingsley, who'd made enemies in New York. For Juliette, who wanted to raise her daughter in a warmer, more welcoming city. For Søren, who was ready to teach again after years pastoring in a small Connecticut church. And for Nora, who could use some space between her and the heartbreaks of her past, which were too many to count (but rounding out the top three were Kyrie, Lance, and Wes). Of course, she was up for anything, as long as she could be with Søren. New Orleans? Why not? An old, beautiful, strange, arcane city bursting with sex and sin and jazz. What was not to like about it?

And it didn't hurt either that the cost of living was so much lower than New York City. Twice the house for the same price? Sign her up.

They called New Orleans The Big Easy. Her dream city. But that evening, it didn't feel so easy anymore.

It felt hard. And cold. And sad.

Nora heard the floor creak with footsteps. She turned her head and saw Søren come into the room.

She didn't smile at him though she wished she could. He said nothing, but walked over to her, then sat across from her on the window bench right next to the big stuffed ducky she'd put there for Céleste.

Nora pushed off the floor again, set the rocker rocking.

"How are you?" he asked. His tone was careful, like a single word might break her.

"Not good."

He nodded. Waited. Then said, "Father Murran?"

"Turns out he was sexually obsessed with an eleven-year-old girl named Melody," Nora said. "He was chaplain at her middle school. He gave her butterfly stuff as gifts and promised to take her to the Butterfly Dome on Grand Isle last Saturday. Her mother works two jobs and is gone from 5 a.m. to 11 p.m. on Saturdays. He had a kidnap kit in the trunk of his car. He'd been looking for someone willing to castrate him—the chastity device wasn't doing the trick —that's why Doc pointed him to me."

The room was silent for a minute or two, silent but for the squeak of the rocking chair on the floor.

"Not as bad as I'd feared," Søren said at last.

"What did you think it was?"

"That he wanted you to kill him," Søren said. "Or be with him while he did it. I have never been so glad in my life you changed your phone number."

"You and me both," she said. She pushed her foot against the floor, rocked once, then stopped. "There's no way he was calling me to castrate him. Maybe if he'd called before he... I think he thought about it but changed his mind. I think he knew about you and me—Doc definitely knew all about us, that you're a priest, I mean. Doc knew Isaac Murran was a priest. He told him about us, and that's why he lied to me and Cyrus. Murran had already decided to kill himself when he called me. He had the gun, locked the doors. The only reason I can think of that he'd call me, of all people, right before committing suicide, is he wanted—"

"Absolution," Søren said.

"I'm the grownup version of Melody Flores, aren't I? We were just the same. A lonely girl with a mom working two jobs and a useless father who comes and goes and never keeps his promises. Then a priest comes along who might as well be God to her, and she trusted him with her life. Just like me. So who could absolve him but her? Or me who was just like her?" She met his eyes. "I would have told him to stop wasting my time and pull the trigger."

"So it comes at last," Søren said, nodding. "I've been waiting for you to get angry with me. I thought it would be over Fionn. But it's not. It's because of us."

"He was going to destroy her. He had ropes in the car, handcuffs. God, he had lube." Sickened, she bent over and put her face in hands, breathed deep and long. She sensed Søren kneeling in front of her, close to her, not touching her.

"I never wanted to destroy you. And I didn't. I couldn't."

She raised her face, looked at him. "But you could have. If I'd been any other fifteen-year-old girl..."

"What can I say?" he said, his voice soft. "Do you want me to defend myself? Or do you want me to say what I did to you was wrong and apologize? Tell me anything you want from me. I'll give it to you if I can."

"Can you defend yourself? Is there a defense?"

"Several. None adequate on their own. Taken together, possibly. One," he said, holding up one finger. "You were fifteen, almost sixteen, not eleven. Two: when I offered to help you when you were arrested at fifteen, you wouldn't agree to accepting my help unless I agreed to have sex with you. I agreed for the sole purpose of your cooperation, in order to save you from years wasted in juvenile detention."

This was all true. No denying it.

"Then I waited over four years, until you were twenty years old, to keep my end of the bargain. I waited, hoping you would grow out of your crush on me, grow up, forget me, and move on with your life. You didn't. So I didn't."

No, she didn't. She was more in love with him at twenty than she'd been at fifteen.

"Three requires me to quote Ignatius Loyola—the ends *sanctify* the means. The means were unholy, yes, but for a holy purpose and a holy end—keeping you out of trouble and saving your life. Do you doubt for one minute if you'd gone to live with your father you would like what your life looks like right now?"

No, she didn't doubt it. But that wasn't the only choice, was it?

Søren went on when she didn't say anything. "Was what I did wrong? Yes. Was it akin to grooming behavior?" He paused, then said, "Yes."

The "yes" hung in the air like the incense of a holy day —cloying, choking.

"I admit it, Eleanor. But I ask you this—would you be here now, alive and healthy and thriving in your art and your work and your life if I hadn't done what I did? You tell me. For my own part, I look back on what I did when you were a teenager with genuine shame. But I also can't think of anything else that would have worked with you. You were hardly a typical teenager. You didn't want money and you didn't want exotic vacations or gold stickers on your report card. You wanted me. Nothing and no one else. Only someone evil and cruel would put a choke collar on a poodle puppy but on an untrained Rottweiler? Simply good sense."

"I did growl at you all the time, didn't I?"

"All the time."

"There is one little difference though," Nora said. "As evil as the means were...you enjoyed it. You got off on it. You weren't putting a choke collar on a Rottweiler because you were afraid of getting bitten. You were putting it on because it turned you on. Yeah, your method worked, but don't get all Father Flanagan with me, Søren. You loved what you did to me. The jokes about tying me up with rope to make me behave, making me water the stick every day for six months, withholding answers to my questions until I jumped through all your hoops, whistling at me like I was a dog you had to make come to heel. It made you hard. You didn't just do it for me. You did it for you, because you liked it."

"No," Søren said. "I didn't like it. I loved it. Hence the shame. At the time, I didn't see any other way to help you, none that would work. Certainly, no other way that you would willingly go along with. You weren't the sort of teenager who'd respond well to Outward Bound, were you?"

She almost laughed. He almost had her there. But she didn't laugh and he didn't either.

"You didn't see any other way to help me," Nora said. "But did you really look?"

He glanced away, not meeting her eyes. "I didn't look. I was afraid I'd find another way, one that meant walking away from you." He stood and turned. She saw him staring out the window onto the street, one hand on the windowsill, the picture of deepest contemplation.

"I wanted to be like Father Henry to you, the way he was to me. I wanted to be the kindly caring father figure you were missing in your life," he said. "But I was more like Father Murran than Father Henry. Father Henry's love for his students was pure. I can't say that about my feelings for you. I wish I could."

"I wish I could, too."

"Let me ask you this." He turned from the window, faced her. "Now, twenty-three years after we met—what would you go back and change? Here. This is my key to the TARDIS. Take it."

She knew he expected her to not take the key, to change nothing about their shared past.

She took the key.

"I remember something King told me once a few years ago," she began, feeling the bite of the teeth of the keys against her palms. "You all had a Plan B if King couldn't help me stay out of juvenile detention for helping my dad steal all those cars. You remember Plan B?"

"Of course. It was my plan. Kingsley would smuggle you out of the country and take you to live with my mother in Denmark. He knew people who could forge all the necessary documents. Do you wish we'd gone with Plan B?"

"Sometimes, yeah," she admitted, nodding. "My own mom could barely stand me when I was that age. I think... I think I needed a mother then a lot more than I needed a sexy priest flirting with me. As much as I liked it—fuck it, I admit it, I loved it—I have to wonder if Plan B wasn't the better plan. For me, anyway. Your mom always took such good care of me. A kid needs that. It probably wouldn't have worked. Someone would have noticed I'd gone missing and started asking questions. Maybe even my own mom. Still, I've wondered..."

"Would we still be together if it had been Plan B?"

"I have no doubt in my mind we'd still be together."

"What's different then?"

She looked away, afraid to tell him the truth knowing it would hurt him. Then again, she wanted to hurt him.

Meeting his eyes, she said, "No Nico on the B timeline. I wouldn't need him. I wouldn't need someone in my life who...who never hurt me."

He lowered his chin to his chest. He raised his chin, didn't meet her eyes.

"I'll await your verdict and accept whatever sentence you impose on me."

"I can't," she said. "Can't judge you without judging myself. I'm no saint either."

She'd had more than her fair share of underage lovers, after all. For some reason it didn't seem so bad with a teenaged boy dying to lose his cherry to a sexy, experienced older woman. But now she had to wonder...if she could give the keys for the time machine to Wes or Noah or Michael, would they take them? Would they take them and go back and turn left when they would have turned right and met her?

She had to wonder.

Her phone buzzed with a message. She glanced at it.

"Cyrus," she said. "He's on his way over."

"I'll let him in." He started to leave. "I remember rocking you, after we'd saved you and you were too scared to sleep. Do you remember that night?"

"Of course I remember. I remember you offering to die for me, too. And you would have."

"I would have. I would again. Now."

"Is that what Father Ike did? He died to save Melody? Was it really suicide or was he killing the man who was going to hurt her? Is he a hero? Is he a monster? Was killing himself heroic? Or was it cowardly?"

"I don't know," Søren said.

"You're supposed to know. You're a fucking priest."

"A priest, not God," he said. "I don't know, Eleanor. I wish to God I did. But this I believe—God was in that room with him when Father Murran died. And wherever he is right now—heaven, hell, or purgatory—he can't hurt anyone anymore."

She looked up at him. "Then why does it hurt?"

Søren reached out to touch her face.

"Please don't," Nora whispered, moving her head away from his hand. "Not yet."

She'd said "Not yet," but what she meant was "Not *you*." She didn't want him touching her. Not him. Not any man. And the one person she did want wasn't there...and would never be there again.

He pulled back his hand. "Of course."

"Sorry."

The doorbell rang.

Chapter Forty-Three

"Drink?" Nora asked Cyrus. They were in the sitting room, the same one they'd sat in together a week ago when he'd first come here asking about Father Ike. Only a week ago. Felt like ten years.

"Please," he said. "A big one."

She poured him a double whiskey, poured one for herself.

Last time they had talked in that room, Cyrus had taken the chair, as far from Nora on the sofa as possible. Now they sat together on the sofa, facing each other.

"Tell me the bad news first," she said, clutching her highball glass in both hands, scared she'd drop it.

"No, good news first. Detective Naylor says he never touched her," Cyrus said. "Pretty clear he was planning to, but he hadn't yet. Except for a couple long hugs, he never raped or molested the girl."

Nora exhaled so hard she almost fainted. All the air just whooshed right out of her. Her whole body sagged with relief. And for no reason she could name, she started to cry.

"Keep talking," she said to Cyrus. "Please."

"That's the good news. Best news," Cyrus said. "Detective Naylor said Melody's mother had no clue at all that her daughter had formed a 'friendship' with Father Ike. She'd only met him a couple times at school. They think Ike started hanging out at the house on Annunciation just because it was two blocks from Melody's house. He'd given her the keys to wait in his car parked by her house. When he didn't show up by six in the morning to take her to Grand Isle, she walked to the house to see where he was."

"Dead."

"Dead for over six hours by then. They're trying to keep as much as they can from Melody. She doesn't know about the stuff in the trunk, or the house he rented for two months where he was going to keep her."

Nora took a long shuddering breath.

"Go on."

"So there was no crime committed," Cyrus said. "Nothing really for the cops to do but have a good long talk with Melody's mother. They may let Melody get some counseling, maybe find an aunt or somebody to spend more time with her. Lonely kids with busy parents got targets on their backs."

"I know," Nora said. "I was one of those kids, too. Go on."

"Like I said, no crime committed. Nothing to do now. That's the bad news. We know what happened. We know why he killed himself. It's over."

Nora put her drink down.

"Over? It can't be over."

"The cops can't arrest a dead man, Nora. What do you want them to do?"

"I don't know," she said. "But not nothing."

They sat in silence and drank their drinks.

"I'm sorry," Cyrus said.

"I thought it would fun, you know, solving a case."

"It's not the Sunday crossword."

"I know. I know. I *didn't* know," she said. "*Now* I know."

Nora looked up when she heard the sound of doors opening and closing, hushed voices whispering. Kingsley walked past the sitting room, and when he saw them in there, came inside. Nora had to smile. Céleste was passed out on Kingsley's shoulder. She had a habit of falling asleep on any drive that lasted longer than five minutes.

"What's going on?" Kingsley asked, his voice half a whisper.

"Just talking about the case," Nora said, wiping her face.

Juliette followed him into the room, with Søren close behind. Nora saw Cyrus sit up a little straighter when Juliette made her entrance.

"Evening, ma'am," Cyrus said to her, with a wide smile. Nora lightly punched him in the shoulder. Juliette pretended not to see Nora's reprimand, though there was a twinkle in her eyes.

"I can take our daughter to her room," Juliette said to Kingsley. Kingsley had sunk into the big armchair. Céleste, still on his shoulder, hadn't stirred a muscle.

"She's out, she's fine," he said to Juliette. "What's the news?" Kingsley asked Cyrus and Nora.

Nora looked at Cyrus, who nodded. She told everyone everything.

Søren sat on the edge of the love seat, elbows on knees, hands clasped between, and head down as if praying. Juliette sat next to him, arm over her stomach like it was a shelf, head on her hand, elbow on the back of the seat. Kingsley listened intently and made no comment and showed no emotion. But Nora saw him drop a kiss onto his daughter's sleeping head while they quietly recounted the events of the week.

"So it's over," Nora said at the end. "We figured it out but the police can't do anything with it."

"Would you want them to?" Kingsley asked.

"Maybe," Nora said. "Like Cyrus said, Archbishop Dunn had told the police not to bother with an investigation. That's why they asked Cyrus to look into it. What if they knew something?"

Søren raised his head. "Even if Father Isaac had confessed his plan to the archbishop, he wouldn't be allowed to tell anyone or act on that knowledge."

"That's crazy, you know," Cyrus said. "No offense, but doctors, shrinks, teachers, they're all mandatory reporters. Why not priests?"

"Seal of the confessional," Søren said. "You have to have someone in this world you can trust with your secrets."

"Not when the secret is that you're planning to—" Cyrus didn't finish that sentence. He shook his head. "Unfortunately, it doesn't matter if Dunn knew or didn't know. The police aren't going to look into it. As far as they're concerned, this was a lone priest planning a bad act. He killed himself before he could do it. The end. They sure as hell don't have the resources, the manpower, or even the desire to go up against the Church in this town, not without any proof there's some bigger conspiracy involved."

Juliette said something softly in French.

"No," Kingsley replied.

"What was that?" Cyrus said.

"Juliette said, 'Call the press.'"

"The press?" Cyrus repeated that like he was thinking it over. "Could work. I know a couple investigative reporters in this town been looking for any excuse to go after the Church. I could leak the story to them."

"Why?" Søren sat up straight and held up his hands. "A man is dead and the child is safe. No crime was committed. You'd only be leaking salacious gossip, not actual news. You can't possibly want that little girl's story in the papers."

"Or your name," Kingsley said to Nora. "You're part of this. It gets out that priest called you before he shot himself... Ah, this isn't the old days, Elle. I can't protect you like I used to in New York."

"As far as that little girl knows," Søren said, "a priest from her school broke a rule and offered to take her to a park she wanted to visit. If the story gets in the news, and she finds out what Father Isaac was planning to do to her? Or what he did to himself because of that... Do you have any idea how much that could traumatize her?"

"A lot," Cyrus said, nodding.

Kingsley said, "I vote 'no' to getting the press in on the story. If I get a vote."

"If I get a vote," Søren said, "I also vote 'no.' Twice. This could blow up and I don't want you getting hit by shrapnel, Eleanor."

Juliette stood up and went to Kingsley. Without a

word, she took Céleste from his arms and carried her out of the room. Nora heard her footsteps on the stairs.

"Excuse me," Nora said and left the three men in the sitting room. She followed Juliette up the stairs, and found her standing in the nursery, Céleste still in her arms, the ivory crib before her.

"You left?" Nora said from the doorway.

Juliette nodded. She kissed Céleste's sleeping forehead.

"You left before you could vote," Nora said. "What's your vote?"

Juliette said nothing. Nora went into the nursery and stood at Juliette's side in front of the crib.

"I hope you like it," Nora said.

"It's perfect. Everything's perfect. Especially the color."

"King will get used to it. Having a boy, if it's a boy."

"He's afraid to have a boy," Juliette said. "Because Céleste is so dark, he's afraid our son will be dark. And if our son is dark, he'll be... Well, you read the news."

"Yeah," Nora said. "I read the news." She didn't mention Cyrus downstairs, a black man, a former police officer who'd been shot by a white police officer.

"And I'm afraid to have another girl," she said, "because of men like Father Murran. But boys aren't safe either."

Juliette blinked back tears. "I will never forget the blessing Søren said when he christened her. Do you remember it?" she asked Nora. "'Here is the world. Beautiful and terrible things will happen. Don't be afraid.'" Juliette dropped a kiss on the top of Céleste's head. "But I am afraid."

"Let me take her," Nora said. Juliette passed Céleste to her carefully, and Nora felt the familiar weight of the little girl in her arms. "I'll put her in bed."

"Thank you."

Nora turned to leave. Before she stepped out of the nursery, Juliette said, "Nora?"

She looked at Juliette, who was standing by the crib, her hand on her stomach. Juliette said nothing. She didn't have to. She'd cast her vote.

Nora went to Céleste's little pink bedroom, holding the girl with one arm, while she pulled the covers down on the bed. She lay Céleste down on her pillow and pulled off the girls' shoes. She put the covers back over her and turned off the lamp and turned on the pink ballerina nightlight.

On the door, Nora noticed Céleste had gone wild with her stickers again. Stars and moons, flowers and trees, birds and bees and butterflies. Nora went back downstairs to the sitting room.

Nora said, "Juliette and I vote to call the press."

"Bad idea," Kingsley said, though he sounded resigned. "And the vote is still three against two."

"No, it isn't," Nora said. "You don't get a vote." She looked at Søren. "And neither do you."

Søren stood up and looked at her, stared at her.

"Eleanor," he said. "Cyrus works with the police. Do you have any idea how much this could damage his working relationship with them?"

"You take care of your business," Cyrus said to Søren. "I'll take care of mine."

Nora had liked Cyrus up to that point in their acquaintance. At that instant and forever after, she loved him. Cyrus stood up and walked over to her, looked her square in the eyes.

"If this is what you want, I'll do it," Cyrus said. "You sure?"

Nora looked past him and at Søren. "I'm sure."

Chapter Forty-Four

Sunday.

The housewarming party at Søren's new place was canceled. Nora skipped Mass.

* * *

Monday.

Another article about Father Isaac Murran. Closer to the front. The papers weren't dropping the story yet. That meant they knew there was more to it.

She didn't sleep very well that night.

* * *

Tuesday.

Nora got an email from Grace in London asking if she was okay. That was all. Just *Nora, Are you all right?*

Nora replied, *We'll survive. Kiss Fionn for me. And your husband.*

Later that day, Nora got a text from Cyrus. *Hey, is your Viking okay?*

She replied, *I doubt it. Why do you ask?*

I shouldn't tell you this but I'm paranoid now, he wrote. *He asked me for the name of my therapist.*

Nora stared at the text a long time, certain she knew what it meant. She closed her eyes, saw her and Søren together again in her mind's eye. They were standing side by side in front of a church. He broke away from her, and approached the double red doors alone. One opened and he walked inside. He looked back, and instead of following him inside, she turned and walked away.

When she opened her eyes, she knew what her cards meant—leaving the High Priest.

Don't worry. He's not going to kill himself, Nora replied. *He's decided to go back to the Jesuits.*

* * *

Wednesday.

Nothing in the news. Nora texted Cyrus about that. He told her to sit tight, the tea was brewing.

She waited though the wait was hard and lonely. They'd all seen little of each other since last Thursday when Nora had made her choice. Kingsley, Juliette, and Céleste were holed up in their white palace behind the black iron gates. Nora stayed in her office mostly, trying to work or trying to read, but really doing nothing much but stroking Gmork's head and staring out the French doors to her wild backyard garden. And Søren? She wasn't ready to talk to him yet. Even Cyrus disappeared on her, spending his free time with Paulina doing their wedding errands. It made Nora smile to think of him taste-testing wedding cakes, his eyes glazing over when the florist tried discussing bouquets and boutonnieres with him. He needed that time with Paulina doing sweet easy things.

They all needed that time. They were like injured animals, isolating themselves from the pack to lick their wounds and privately heal.

Gmork nudged Nora's hand, his signal she needed to get back to petting him. And she did. It was a sweet and easy thing to do, and while it didn't make her feel too much better, it didn't make her feel any worse.

* * *

Thursday.

Nora hated waiting. She told Cyrus that in a text message. He replied with a message asking her to come have dinner with him and Paulina.

She wants to meet you, Cyrus wrote her.

I'm not fit for company.

Get fit. You do not tell my fiancée "no."

Nora didn't want to leave her house but knew she couldn't hide forever. She took a shower, dressed in her most conservative outfit—red slacks, white boatneck blouse, and matching red ballet flats. When she arrived at the little white cottage, a pretty brown-skinned woman in a yellow dress and white lace cardigan opened the door. This was Paulina. Cyrus stood behind her, watching the show.

"Hi," Nora said. "I'm Nora. Thank you for—"

She didn't get to finish her sentence. Paulina stepped forward and took Nora in her arms for a long hug. Cyrus said, gloating, "I knew you two would get along."

Chapter Forty-Five

Friday.

Cyrus had been right with his prediction. On Friday, the front page of the paper revealed damning evidence of a coverup in the Archdiocese of New Orleans. Archbishop Dunn's secretary had served as a source. At age thirty-seven, while working as a school chaplain at a New Orleans parochial school, Father Isaac Murran had kissed a student and rubbed her thighs. That girl's family made a complaint. Another girl came forward and said he'd done the same to her. Father Isaac was transferred to a post working as a chaplain in a men's prison, then at a nursing home, then back at a middle school. Archbishop Dunn was aware of the complaint in the file, the prior bad acts, but still chose to transfer Father Isaac to a new position at a different school. It seemed the archbishop was well-aware of many prior bad acts of *several* priests in the diocese. Instead of defrocking the priests or calling the police to report the crimes, the men had simply been transferred, then transferred, then transferred again.

Nora took a copy of the paper to Mercedes at The Good Witch. She found her in the reading room, already pasting a cut-out of the article into her big black leather magic book.

She stood in the doorway of the room, watching Mercedes work.

"I made the scrapbook," Nora said. Mercedes looked up from her cutting and pasting.

"It's called a book of shadows, not a scrapbook," she said, though Nora could tell she was trying not to smile. "If your name had been in the article, I would have framed it and put it on the wall with the others."

"I'm glad my name's not in the article."

"I've been working spells to protect you all week."

"I think they're working. They haven't said a word about me. Not even a hint. Cyrus's name is everywhere though."

"I didn't cast any spell of protection for him."

"That's not very nice." Nora tried to scowl.

"Your friend is a detective. Getting his name in the paper for solving a case is good for him, bad for you."

Mercedes motioned at the chair across from her currently occupied by a small black cat that didn't look much older than a kitten.

"Is this Hestia?" Nora said.

"No, this is one of the stray 'familiars' someone dropped off at my doorstep. I need to change the sign to say, ALL FAMILIARS MUST BE ACCOMPANIED BY THEIR HUMAN."

She smiled. Mercedes said, "How are you?"

Nora picked up the half-sleeping cat and took the

chair. The cat merely stretched and yawned and fell back asleep on her lap.

"Everyone keeps asking me that. Angry. But I'm okay. Just worried about that little girl."

"Even a cleansing fire can burn you, if you stand too close. Churches are burning in this town. I see the fires on the altars. But better careers burning than children."

"They're saying Archbishop Dunn may have to resign. There might even be criminal charges."

"Hope so," Mercedes said. "If he does go to jail, it'll be thanks to you."

"Thanks to you," Nora said. "I wouldn't have done it if you hadn't warned me I was going to make the wrong choice. The men in my life made very persuasive arguments."

"So easy to choose between good and evil. So hard to choose between good and good. Hardest of all is choosing between what you want to do and what you ought to do."

"It was all on me," Nora said. "My choice. Just me. I was the one vote and if I'd voted the other way, how many kids would... I guess we all thought it was over." The big clergy abuse scandals of the '90s had been all over the papers. Then they just stopped. Out of sight, out of mind.

"You know how many supposed 'witches' and 'psychics' are just con artists?" Mercedes said. "How many of those 'mediums' take the hope and the money of grieving parents, claiming they can communicate with their dead children? My own house needs cleaned, too. Nothing new about people abusing their power. Your Church doesn't own the copyright on that."

Mercedes gave her a little smile, a littler wink.

Nora had to ask. She just had to.

"Is it real? Did you really see what you say you saw in my cards?"

"Does it matter?" Mercedes shrugged. "Maybe I saw it in the cards. Maybe I had a vision. Maybe I just used my brain and two eyes when I saw a handsome man in black drive up to your house one night, Bible in his saddlebag, inscribed, 'To Father Stearns with deepest love and gratitude.'" The Bible was a gift from parishioners at Sacred Heart when he left to come to New Orleans.

"So you knew I was sleeping with a priest. That still doesn't explain—"

Mercedes held out her hand. "You Catholics have your mysteries of faith. We have ours."

You Catholics.

"You already know what I'm going to do, don't you?" Nora asked.

"I think I know," she said and took The Hierophant card out of her desk and laid it before Nora. Dressed as the pope with two priests at his feet as if in worship, Nora found herself repelled by him, by his throne, his staff of power, his cold, uncaring eyes "Scared?"

"I don't want to hurt him. He'll think I'm doing it to get back at him."

"Give the man some credit," Mercedes said. "He's loved you all your life. Would he think that little of you?"

"You're defending him? The Catholic warlock I'm sleeping with?"

"You're no fool. If you love him, there must be a reason. Isn't there?"

There were. Many. Too many to count. But one in particular.

"I was fifteen when I fell in love with him," Nora said. "Or whatever feels like love to a fifteen-year-old girl. There was nothing I wouldn't let him do to me, and he knew that, too." Nora swallowed hard. "I hated him when he pushed me away. Now I'm so grateful it hurts. I didn't realize how much power he had over me until now. The only reason I'm not more fucked up than I already am is because he...protected me. From himself. As best he could anyway." Nora wiped the tears off her face. "You know how we met? He was never supposed to be a parish priest. They'd trained him for a career in Academia. He'd be president of a Jesuit university by now if things had gone differently. But he found out about a coverup of an abusive priest, and he contacted the victim's attorney. They punished him with the last assignment he ever wanted—pastoring a little church in a small town. And there I was. Why was it so easy for him to turn in a priest then and not this time?"

"No one he knew or loved was at risk back then. Only his own career. This time...you know how ugly this could have been for you if the media knew about you two."

"I know. It'll keep me up at night for a few weeks."

"I won't give your man any medals," Mercedes said. "But I'll tell you this: when I look for him in your cards, I don't find this one." She held up the Hierophant card, the High Priest. "He's this one." She held up the Emperor. "Authority. Wisdom. Experience. The strong father. The good father. And I see you with him." She placed the Empress card next to the Emperor. "And I see this, too." She laid down a card, a naked man and woman cavorting. The Lovers.

"Not for a while," she said. "This case has killed my sex drive."

"I give that about five minutes."

"Hey."

She held up the Lovers tarot card. "Don't blame me. It's in the cards."

Laughing, Nora reached for the Emperor card.

"Can I tell you something crazy? My mom and I never —I mean never *ever* in my life—got along. Oil and water from birth. Anyway." Nora swallowed, steadied herself with a breath. "After we found out about Father Murran and Melody, I wanted—" Nora slapped a hand over her mouth hard, silencing a sob that seemed to come from nowhere but in fact came from deep, deep in her heart. "I wanted my mom." She laughed at herself, laughed at her crying, laughed at her stupid, useless wanting. Mercedes didn't laugh. She waited. "My mom. Søren's mom. Any mom. Why the fuck do mothers have to go and die five minutes before you figure out how much you need them?"

Mercedes reached out and put her hand over Nora's.

"I'm a mom," she said softly. "And it's going to be all right."

Chapter Forty-Six

Good Saturday. Cyrus and Paulina on his boat in Lake Pontchartrain. He wore khaki shorts, no shirt, enjoying the lake breeze in the late summer heat. Paulina had on her black bikini and lay on the deck on a yellow-striped beach towel.

He must have been quiet too long because Paulina stretched out her arm and wrapped her small, delicate hand over the top of his big bare foot.

"What's on your mind, Daddy?"

"You. Always."

"Oh, come on." She smiled as he pushed her sunglasses up off her eyes.

"They knew the cop that shot me was dirty," he said. "Had a file thick as a brick. Racial profiling. Police brutality. Harassment. They knew he was dangerous, and they let him keep his badge until he shot me. And they knew Ike was dangerous, and they let him keep his collar, let him around little girls even. This ever gonna end?"

"If it does end in this town, it'll be thanks to men like you."

"I wish I could believe that."

The boat rocked gently under them, easy and steady. A breeze blew by, and it smelled like the ocean on a clear, cool day. He'd always loved it out here on the lake. He'd even taken Katherine out here on one of their only real dates. The other "dates" had been in her bedroom.

"You mind if a make a call, baby?"

"Of course not. Nora?"

"Katherine." He paused, steeled himself. Honesty was getting easier for him, but it wasn't easy yet. "You know she and I had a little thing right before I got shot." She sat up and looked at him. He went on, "I want to make sure she's okay."

"I think you should," Paulina said. She squeezed his foot, let it go.

He walked to the bow where his phone was stashed in his duffel. She picked up on the first ring. She didn't even say hello when she answered. Her first words were, "Please don't tell me there's more."

"No more," he said. "I think."

"Good. Great." She exhaled. "I'm almost sorry I got you into this."

"It was my choice."

"True. I guess what I mean is…I'm sorry I got *me* into this." He heard her soft, sad laugh, then a sigh.

"You doing all right?" he asked.

"Okay, I guess. You?"

"I might not be going back to Mass for a while."

"Paulina'll let you get away with that?"

"She understands."

"She's been really good for you, hasn't she?"

"Yeah, yeah she has."

"Glad you're okay. Look, I'm about to go. Did you—"

"I'm sorry," he said.

"What?"

"I'm sorry, Katherine. I'm sorry for treating you the way I did. Especially when you came by the hospital, and I acted like—"

"Like you didn't know me?"

"Mom was there, but that's no excuse. I could have told her we were friends, at least. She thought I was seeing someone else and it—never mind. Like I said, no excuse. I treated you like shit, and you didn't deserve that. I'm sorry. Genuinely."

A long silence followed. Then, "Wow. This case really did get to you."

"It did, yeah," he said. "You don't have to forgive me or anything. I'm not asking for that. I just—"

"I forgive you."

He didn't know how much he needed to hear that until she said it, didn't realize he was carrying that weight until she lifted it off and tossed it in the lake.

"I really do need to run," she said.

"Yeah, of course. Thank you."

"Bye, Cyrus. Hope you and Paulina are very happy together. I mean that."

"Katherine?" he said fast, before she could hang up.

"Yes?"

"If you ever call me again with a case," he said, "I'll answer."

Chapter Forty-Seven

W hen Nora checked her mail that afternoon and found another blank postcard, her stomach plummeted through the floor. Did Søren leave her again? Then she saw the postmark—New Orleans. She flipped the card over. It was just a vintage postcard of the French Quarter, the sort you could pick up for a dollar from any old bookstore in town. The night he'd returned from his trip, he'd told her what his blank postcards meant. *I love you. I miss you. This is where you can find me.* The card was an invitation, asking her to come back into his life. He wouldn't force his presence on her. He was waiting, just waiting for her to decide what came next for them.

Later that evening, Nora sent Søren a text message to accept the invitation.

Warning, I have a housewarming gift for you, Nora told him. *Three gifts actually.*

Søren answered, *Gold, frankincense, and myrrh?*

Even better. See you soon.

Nora stopped by The Good Witch one more time to

pick up Søren's first housewarming gift, then drove over to his house. She found him in his music room at his piano, playing a song she vaguely knew but couldn't name.

She came in and sat next to him on the piano bench. His hands stilled at the keys, but when she didn't say anything, he began to play again. The sun was setting outside, the room growing darker. When he reached the end, he lifted his fingers from the keys and set his hands in his lap.

"Pretty," she said. "What was that?"

"An old Welsh lullaby—'All Through the Night.'" He sung the lines to her, softly:

> *Sleep my child and peace attend thee*
> *All through the night*
> *Guardian angels God will send thee*
> *All through the night*

He faced her the first time. "Grace used to sing it to Fionn to put him to sleep. She let me listen on the phone one night." His brow furrowed. "Does that hurt you?"

"That you listened to the mother of your son sing to him? Of course it hurts. It breaks my heart because you only got to hear it over the phone and only once. Why do you ask?"

"I think I hurt you more in more ways than I know. No, I hurt you in more ways than I want to know."

"I can take it." She smiled—a wicked smile, but a brief one. It was all for show anyway. "Sometimes. And sometimes I can't take it."

"*Miserere mei, Deus—secundum magnam misericordiam tuam. Et secundum multitudinem miserationum tuarum, dele iniquitatem meam.*"

She laughed softly. "Are you trying to turn me on by speaking in Latin? If so, it's working."

He smiled, almost. "It's known as the 'neck verse,'" he said. "The first verses of Psalm 51 in Latin. In old Britain, clergy received less sentences for their crimes. Anyone accused of a crime could claim 'benefit of the clergy.' You would save your neck from a noose if you could recite to the courts that verse in Latin and thus prove you were in the clergy. Of course, many non-clergy members used it. Who wouldn't?"

"Seems a little unfair. I doubt they'd believe a woman accused of murder was a member of the clergy even if she recited the whole Bible in Latin."

In fact, they would have probably accused her of witchcraft.

"Massively unfair, but I'll take any help I can get right now."

"I'm not going to hang you. Or shoot you."

"Or leave me?"

She kissed him. A gentle kiss at first, then deeper as Søren took her face in his hands and kissed the breath from her body. Who needed air anyway? The kiss stilled like a storm and they sat there, foreheads resting together. Søren found her hands and held them.

"I love you," she said.

"Still?"

"Always. You are a wicked priest, but I'm a wicked woman. Let's just accept we deserve each other."

"I'm more than happy to accept that," he said. She smiled up at him.

"Now, you tell me what you want first—your house-warming gifts or the bad news."

"I'll take the bad news."

"Nope, you're getting a gift first. I'll go get her."

"Then why even ask me?" he said as she went into the other room. "Wait, her? Eleanor? *Her?*"

Nora cackled softly as she went to fetch the carrier from the guest bedroom. She took the cat, gone limp with the terror of new surroundings, out of the carrier and brought her to Søren at his piano bench.

"She's a stray, but a sweet stray, Mercedes said," Nora told him as she piled the soft furry bundle into Søren's arms. "And she doesn't have a name yet. But I think you two will get along."

"A cat? You're giving me a cat?" Søren seemed dazed by the gift, though he was already settling the terrified cat onto his lap, stroking the glossy black coat with the back of his hand.

"She's got food and water in the kitchen. Litter box in the downstairs bathroom. You can make Kingsley clean it." He looked at her, a little dazed. Very rare day when she managed to surprise him. "You only have about a year on the outside. Might as well enjoy it as much as you can, do all the things you can't do when you're back in the order. And when you do go back, Céleste can take her. She's been dying for a cat."

"Why are you so certain I'm going back?"

"Grace emailed and asked if I was all right. That's all the email said. I guessed you had contacted her, asking for the letter absolving you of parental responsibility toward Fionn, and she wanted to check in with me. Then Cyrus said you'd asked for the name of his therapist. You have to go to therapy before they'll let you back in the Jesuits, right?"

"A good guess, but the wrong one. Don't give up your day job yet, Miss Marple."

He didn't look at her, only his new cat who'd started to purr in his hands. He always did have a way with cats.

"So...are you not going back?" she asked.

"I don't know yet," he said. "I called Grace to reassure her that I had no intention of seeking joint custody—or any form of custody from Fionn—whether I went back or not."

"Why? If you're not going back, if you're not sure, why make that decision now?"

"Hard to explain," he said, glanced away, breathed.

The cat bumped her head against his hand, and he obligingly scratched the top of her head.

"You would be a wonderful father," she said. "I know you're worried you'd be like your father, but you wouldn't be. I know you wouldn't."

"I took advantage of a teenaged girl in my church, Eleanor. I am already like my father." He looked at her as if daring her to contradict him. She opened her mouth, but nothing came out. "If I truly believed, down to the bottom of my soul, that I was better for Fionn than Zachary and Grace, nothing would keep me from my son." He ran his hands over the cat's sleek back as if seeking comfort. "I...I wouldn't be very good at playing Doctor Who with him."

"Søren," she said, wishing she'd never mentioned Zach and Fionn and Doctor-fucking-Who. He took a long breath, then met her eyes, and from the look he wore on his face, she knew the subject was closed. For now.

She swallowed a lump in her throat. "So why the therapist then, if you're not going back?"

"As much as I loathe the very thought of seeing a therapist, I thought it might help. Us."

"Us?"

"Me," he said with finality.

"I think we should both go. Can Catholic priests go into couples counseling?"

At least that got a smile out of him.

"So...dare I ask what the bad news is?" he said. "Or are you giving me my other two gifts first?"

The cat jumped off his lap and started exploring her new surroundings. She hopped onto the camelback love seat and started grooming, already at home.

"Bad news. Then more gifts. Fair?"

"Fair enough."

"Before I tell you, you need to know I didn't make this decision lightly."

"What decision?"

"Whether or not you go back to the Jesuits, I'm not going back," Nora said, "to the Church."

"What?" He looked at her sharply.

"I'm leaving the Church. The Catholic Church. For good."

"Eleanor—"

"Just listen. I can't be around men playing God anymore. I can't give an organization that won't ordain women as priests any more of my time or money while they play shuffleboard with sexual predators. The punishment for a raped woman having an abortion is more severe than for a priest who molests a child."

"Is this because I tried to talk you out of calling the papers? I was wrong, I admit it. That was fear talking, fear of you getting named in a scandal like this. And I couldn't take my own advice. I told Cyrus to assume the worst, and then I couldn't bring myself to do it."

"It's not that," she said. "You made very good points. Under other circumstances, you might have been right.

That's not why I'm leaving. I'm leaving because I want to."

Søren rose from the piano bench and walked to the window. He rested his hand on the sill, one hand on his hip, the very picture of deepest contemplation.

"Don't do this to me," he said softly.

"I'm not doing it to you. I'm doing it for me."

"How is leaving our church good for you? The Catholic Church is its people, its sacraments, not its priests."

"I'll miss the sacraments, too. But sacredness is everywhere. I'm going to look for it, and I'm going to find it."

"Is this because you're angry at me? Or angry at God?"

"Neither. It has nothing to do with you." Nora had to make him understand. "I love her, you know."

"Who? Your new witch friend?"

"God."

He turned, met her eyes.

"Even you, the most liberal Catholic priest I know," she said, "can't wrap your mind around God being a 'her.'"

"That is incredibly unfair, Eleanor."

"Tell it to all the women throughout history who have been treated like second-class citizens in the Church, all because it was 'Our *Father.*' All because Jesus had a dick. The Church only likes Mary because she was a virgin." Nora braced herself, then delivered her knock-out blow. "How many Catholic women we know would have made a better priest than Father Murran? Most of them?"

The blow landed. Søren lowered his head. He raised it again, a man defeated by a worthy adversary.

"If you turn into a witch," he said, "I'm not going to be pleased."

"Oh, shove it, warlock," she said. "You turn wine into God's blood. You have no room to talk."

"Do you know what 'warlock' means?"

"Evil wizard?"

"Oath-breaker," he said. "*Vow* breaker."

She waited. He had his own news to share.

"If I do go back," he began. Then, "Cyrus said something to me about the married men he catches cheating. How if they can't keep their vows, they don't get to keep their wife."

"The Church's rules are antiquated and wrong," she said.

"But they are the rules. And if I do go back…"

He didn't have to finish the sentence. She knew. If he went back, he would keep his vows.

She reached out, stroked his face again, and the beard that protected him from seeing his father's face in the mirror.

"I hope the next present is very good," he said.

"I think you'll like it." She reached into her bag and pulled out a pair of handcuffs and presented them to him as if they were a priceless jewel.

"Handcuffs? I have my own."

"These are new handcuffs, unmarked, straight from my own dungeon. I know King gave you the engraved ones, but I thought you might want to get rid of those. Considering."

"Considering they're a reminder of a very unpleasant chapter in our life?"

"Boner-killer, right?"

"Precisely."

He held the handcuffs in his hand, studying them almost as if he'd never seen handcuffs before.

"Søren?"

"A cat and handcuffs. Two very good gifts. I should give you something in return."

"Like what?"

"Like this." He held out the handcuffs to her, and she took them back. Then he did the last thing she ever expected him to do. He held out his hands for her to cuff.

"You are shitting me."

"You said you dream about it."

"Everyone who's seen you has dreamed about it. But you know I can't top you. It won't work." They'd tried sex without him hurting her one night when he'd woken up hard. They'd managed it for about a minute before he'd lost his erection. Vanilla sex wasn't for them, but he wasn't talking about vanilla sex. He was giving her permission to top him.

"It might. We've never tried."

"Just when I think I have you figured out..."

"You will never have me figured out."

"This is crazy. Absolutely crazy. I can't—"

"Nervous? Scared?"

"You think?" Even as she protested, she clutched the handcuffs in her grip, holding them like a child with a favorite toy that might get taken away any second.

"When I was in your dungeon, it occurred to me, there's an entire side of you I've never truly experienced. A very important side of you."

She exhaled heavily, suddenly shaky, nervous as a virgin. "It's incredibly...generous? Let's go with that. Incredibly generous—and brave—of you to offer. But I really don't think it's gonna work."

"What's the worst that could happen? Neither of us enjoy it, so we stop and do something else? Céleste gave me a housewarming gift. We could play that instead."

"What was it?"

"Candy-Land."

Nora laughed. She had to, it was all so ridiculous.

"I know what you're doing," she said.

"Making you an offer you can't refuse?"

"Will you ever stop manipulating me? Ever?" She hadn't gone near him in a week, staying home, all alone, hiding from him, hiding from her pain. Only this offer would tempt her back into bed with him after all she'd been through. Truly, only this and nothing else. And he knew it.

"I'll stop the day you stop enjoying it, Little One."

She snapped her fingers in his face as he'd done to her a thousand times.

"That's Mistress Little One to you."

Chapter Forty-Eight

T hey retreated to the downstairs guest room. Inside it was quiet, still. Nora imagined she could hear her own heartbeat, but it was only the pounding of nervous blood in her ears.

The last of the evening's sunlight streamed through the sheer white curtains over the large mullioned windows above the bed. The room was filled with golden light and silver shadows.

As soon as they entered the room, Nora shut the door to keep the new roommate out for the next hour. Something about the lock clicking made it all real to her and she closed her eyes, hand still on the knob.

"Eleanor?"

"Tell me this is real."

He took her in his arms and held her to his heart. She rested her ear against his chest, his heart beating steady and ready and slow. He wasn't scared. Of course not. Just a game, she told herself. Just another mind game.

"It's not real," he said. "It's only a dream. And we never have to be afraid in our dreams." Was he talking to her? Or himself? Either way it helped. The pressure lifted. Only a dream. Just a dream. Just her most deliciously decadent impossible dream.

Slowly, she pulled herself from his arms, faced him.

"Stand there." She pointed at a spot on the floor at the foot of the bed next to the steamer trunk. He raised an eyebrow but obeyed.

"Here?" His bare feet were placed precisely where she'd pointed. "Or here?" He moved one centimeter to the right.

"Submitting for five seconds and you're already a brat." This was a very good dream. "There is fine. Stay."

She found the matches and lit the candles arrayed on the fireplace mantel. The room was dark and growing darker. Soon the candlelight would be the only light they would dream by.

"Tell me again you want this?" She turned to face him.

"I want you," he said. "All of you. For once."

All of her. If that was what he wanted...

"Take your clothes off."

She waited for the refusal, for him to remember who and what he was—dominant, master, owner—and who and what she was—submissive, slave, possession. Instead, he pulled his t-shirt off, folded it in half and lay it neatly over the back of the leather armchair. Jeans next, then his black —of course—boxer briefs, both folded and left on the chair, just so.

A clock gently chimed from somewhere in the house, telling them the hour was nine. The sun was almost gone.

"Lay on the bed, on your back, hands behind your head."

His only act of rebellion was to wait a full three seconds before obeying. But obey he did. He went to the bed, lay down on the thick white antique lace counterpane and rested his head on the pillow.

"Safe word?"

"Yours will do," he said. Hers was Jabberwocky.

"Hard limits?"

"Decapitation."

"Søren."

He looked at her, his eyes saying "silly girl" and his expression patted her on the head.

"Do you really think I have any limits when it comes to pain?"

No, of course she didn't.

She placed a candle on the bedside table, picked up the handcuffs and took out the key, which she set next to the candle. She wanted to have it in case Søren changed his mind about being restrained.

Carefully, as if he were a wild animal easily startled into attack, she moved onto the bed, kneeling at the head. She took his wrists into her hands, pulled them into place, feeling his pulse under her thumbs. Steady pulse, cool skin. She cuffed his right wrist, and wrapped the links around the center iron bar. Then she snapped the other bracelet on the left wrist, where Søren had his son's name tattooed over his pulse point. Fionn's name. Nora's handwriting. Now she knew what she was going to do to him.

Only when the cuffs were on did she let herself enjoy the moment. She touched his side, touched that shivery spot between his ribs. His skin was cool and supple but at the first trembling contact between his body and hers, gooseflesh rose up all over his chest. Smiling, she lowered her head, kissed the spot she touched. Søren breathed once, hard, but held still. When she raised her head, she saw him watching her every move, like a captured wolf watches its captor from the back of the cage.

Nora left him on the bed and went to the steamer trunk. She took a deep breath and opened the lid of the trunk. Kingsley did not disappoint. One whip. Two sets of floggers. Spreader bar. X-bar. Rope. Rope cuffs. Lube. Bamboo cane. Misery stick. And a tiny brown leather bag full of scalpels. And under the scalpels, a first-aid kit.

While he was looking at the ceiling—no doubt ruing whatever idiotic romance impulse that had led him to make this offer—she looked at him, all six-feet-four long lean strong perfectly proportioned body of a man half his age inches of him. He was probably hating every minute of this. She was in unholy heaven.

Nora took the scalpels out of the trunk and tossed the case on the bed. He wasn't aroused, not yet, but she could tell he was intrigued. He knew perfectly well what was inside that leather case.

While he watched her, she undressed, laying her clothes on the armchair next to his. She could have tormented him, tossing his clothes on the floor, walking on them, bossing him around and about like he did with her for the sheer heathen pleasure of it all. But she didn't, couldn't. This meant too much to her to make light of it. And she knew he'd meant it when he said this was it. She only had this one chance, and she wasn't going to waste it.

The sun was gone now. The only light came from the candles on the mantel, the candle by the bed. She returned to the bed and crawled next to him. Because she could, she touched his face, his lips, traced the perfect lines of his perfect ears. He wasn't aroused, but Nora was, wet and shaking like a sapling in a storm inside. Her training went too deep, however, so she feigned calm on the outside, collected and in control.

She straddled him at the waist, pushing her vulva against his still soft cock. She bent to kiss him, because she had to, because she had never wanted him more than she did right then. She kissed him hard and deep, forcing his lips to part and pressing her tongue inside his mouth. When he returned the kiss, it was tentatively at first, letting her have her way with him, humoring her, she knew. Then something changed. The room darkened, the darkness deepened. He kissed her back harder. He pressed his tongue to hers. As she moaned in response, he caught her bottom lip between his teeth and bit it.

Nora gasped, sat up, and pressed her fingertips to her lip, saw he'd drawn blood. He licked the blood from his lips. Her blood. Then he lifted his hips and she felt him growing hard against her. With her hands on his chest for support, she pushed down and back onto his cock, rigid now and thick. It slid along the slick seam of her vulva. She spread her knees, pushed down again, and he entered her. With each slow roll of her hips, he filled her more and more. Slowly she rose and sank down again, taking more of him into her, letting him fill her, spread her, pierce her until he was so deep inside her body she felt the tip of his penis nudge her cervix.

She clenched her inner muscles around him, squeezing him. His head fell back and his throat was bared. And there she was with a set of knives in a case on the bed. With one little flick of her wrist, she could kill him and he couldn't stop her, couldn't fight back. As strong as he was, the iron bed was stronger, the steel cuffs were stronger. For the first time in their twenty-three years together, he'd put himself entirely at her mercy.

Maybe, possibly for the first time since he was a child, he'd made himself this physically vulnerable to another person.

"Why did you do this?" she asked him softly.

He opened his eyes, met hers.

"If the day comes when I can't give you anything, at least here, now, I can give you everything."

"I will never leave you," she said.

He nodded solemnly. "Now that's all I wanted to hear."

With their bodies locked together, Nora reached for the leather case. She took out the smallest, thinnest, sharpest scalpel and used the flame of the candle to clean it. His watching wolf eyes followed her every move.

Carefully she set the candle on the center of his chest. A short, wide candle, it would stay in place as long as he didn't flinch. She didn't have to tell him that. She'd spent many a terrifying hour with a votive candle balanced between her breasts while he worked some sort of erotic havoc on another part of her body.

With the slightest, lightest touch, she carved a quick shallow *N* over his heart. His eyes closed as bright red blood welled to the surface of his skin. Now an *O* made from two parentheses, made to kiss. She let the blade do all the work as she cut the *R* into him, even as his hips moved slightly under her, his cock pulsing inside of her. Her concentration was unbreakable. She would cut him, carve him, slice him open, but she wouldn't harm the man to save her life. With a last little flourish, she finished off the *A*.

She lifted the candle off him, put it on the table. The key gleamed gold in the firelight.

"Can you come?" she asked.

"I want to," he said. "I don't know if I can."

The vulnerable honesty in his answer broke something in her that needed breaking.

"Let me help." She picked up the key and released his right wrist, but left his other cuffed to the bedpost. She offered him the scalpel. "One for you."

Again, he waited a full three seconds before obeying her—she counted. But he did take the blade from her at last. Nora sat up, arched her back, offered her body to him, offered all of her.

The blade grazed her lower stomach. She dug her fingers into his thighs to steady herself. As aroused as she was, she barely felt the cut. Only when she opened her eyes did she see what he'd done—with one practiced cut, he'd carved an *S* under her bellybutton over that aching place where the tip of his cock met her cervix. She'd claimed his heart. He'd claimed her cunt.

She could only smile. The smile evaporated instantly when Søren used his free hand to grab the key off the bedside table and release his left hand. Free, he pushed her onto her back, mounting her like the whore who'd taken his last penny. He dragged her against him, holding her hard in place under him. She lay trapped beneath him, her head half off the bed as he speared her.

Trapped, she didn't put up a fight. She simply let him have her. Her one act of revenge was to bite his chest where she'd cut him, causing him to let out one small cry even as her blood stained his belly.

He pounded her hard and slow and the harder he pounded her, the harder she wanted it. Split and speared, her surrender was complete. She gave him her breasts and he sucked her nipples sore. She gave him her neck which he bit to the point of bruising. She gave him her heart and he swallowed it whole. A thousand heady nights ached in her memory, a thousand heavy hours under him, keeping her screams silent and careful with her cries. But those were the old nights, long gone, spent in the bed of a man who would turn back into a priest in the morning. She wasn't sure who this man inside her was, only that she wanted him there, beautiful stranger that he was.

Nora moaned because she could. Her cunt hurt from needing to come. Every thrust was a punishment until she came. Once more, twice more, three times more he rammed her and with that third thrust she came writhing and crying out his name. As her stomach spasmed, he poured into her, filling her until his scalding semen slicked her thighs.

After, they lay entwined, cock and pussy, arms and legs, blood and sweat and come. Her vagina pulsed around him even as the organ inside her softened. Søren released her wrists and stroked her hair. He held her to his chest.

"I'm sorry. I tried."

"Don't be sorry," she said, meaning for that, for them, for everything. "I'm not."

Slowly they pulled themselves apart and tenderly tended to each other's wounds. Nora cleaned Søren's cuts with alcohol and gauze. The *S* on her stomach had stopped bleeding. A little antiseptic ointment, and she was good as new. She started to ask him if he wanted some water when a small squeak sounded through the door.

Søren turned his head.

Nora said, "Was that your pussy or mine?"

"Mine, I think."

He rose up off her, opened the door, and the little black cat sashayed into the bedroom like the guest of honor. She hopped onto the bed with one nimble leap, sauntered over to Nora and let out a meow.

"Guess she's made herself at home," Nora said.

Søren sat on the bed, scratching the cat under her chin.

"Are you all right?" Nora asked him.

"I am. You?"

"Still in shock."

He smiled, almost shyly. "It went better than I thought it might. But if you tell Kingsley, it'll be foot torture for a month."

The cat, still unnamed, sat between them. Nora reached across her and touched Søren's hand.

"Eleanor?"

"You're cold."

"I'm fine."

"You were cold from the second I put the handcuffs on you. Cold sweat. Cold skin. Symptoms of panic."

He said nothing. The cat shook herself, seemingly for no reason, then leapt onto the pillow. She turned in circles to soften a place for herself, and laid down again, making herself into a soft black donut.

"You were scared the entire time," she went on, "but you didn't stop me." He stroked the cat, long gentle strokes from between her ears to her happy twitching tail. "Things happened to you as a child so awful you begged me once to never even think about it. And I've never even asked you what this has done to you." It seemed fitting they would have this conversation, both of them naked.

She waited. Still, he stroked the cat. Still, he said nothing.

"Søren?"

"Should I have taken you to my mother?" He looked at her once, then returned to petting the cat.

"Maybe," she said. "And maybe I would have loved

being with her. But, knowing me, I would have run away eventually and come back to you."

That got him to smile. A little. A very, very little.

"I got your postcard," she said. "That split-second I thought you had left again, I think my heart stopped." She laughed at herself. "Then I saw the postmark and it started again."

"I won't leave without telling you again. There was something I wanted to say to you, but it wouldn't fit on a postcard. I only wanted to say it to you when you were ready to hear it."

"What is it?"

"What I wanted to say was this. If you ever asked me to choose between you and the Church..."

"I would never—"

"I know you wouldn't. But if you did, I would choose you. When I was trying to stop you from calling the media, it was only because I was afraid it could come to that. If the Church turned on you, accused you of something, made you the into their scapegoat—"

"I know you'd leave them if they did that to me."

"I wouldn't leave them. I would destroy them."

He met her eyes so she could see he meant it. The threat hung in the air, sweet as perfume, and she fell in love with him again, like she had a thousand times before, like she would a thousand times again before their story was over.

The cat rolled over again, leaving a hundred black hairs on the bed. The spell was broken.

"Blood, come, and cat hair on the antique white counterpane," Søren said with a sigh. "I'll have to ask for black sheets as a housewarming gift."

"It's fine. It'll all come out in the wash."

The cat began licking her own stomach. It was not a graceful procedure.

"Cats are very strange," Søren said.

"You like your housewarming gift?"

"I do. Both of them." He picked up the handcuffs, twirled them once, just to show her who was boss. He was. Of course he was. Now. Always.

"Wait. I forgot the last present. Stay here." Nora grabbed her panties off the floor and her tank top, pulled them on. "Hope it's still warm."

"*Warm*? Eleanor, what's warm?" he called after her.

She ignored him, went into his kitchen, returned with two mugs. He'd put on his clothes again and sat in the armchair, the cat still on the bed, cat-napping. She sat on the floor at his feet and offered him one of the mugs.

"Drink," she said. He stared at her. "Please?"

He drank. At the first sip, his eyes widened. Though he was fifty-one years old, it was a wounded eleven-year-old boy's eyes that met hers.

"Sometimes you need hot cocoa, even in New Orleans in September."

He held the cup in his hands, cradling it as tenderly and carefully as he'd ever carried a communion chalice.

"You're nothing like your father," she said, "and you're full of shit if you think that."

He smiled behind his mug and said softly, "Thank you."

She held out her mug. "To Father Henry," she said, "a very good priest."

They clinked glasses and drank.

Chapter Forty-Nine

Cyrus drove by Nora's house that morning to check on her. He found her standing in her front yard, looking up at her beaded oak tree. He parked, got out and leaned on her fence. She wore a long swishy witchy black skirt and white tank top. She looked pretty, if a little tired. But they were both tired. It would pass.

"You," Nora said, acknowledging him without taking her eyes off her tree. "What are you doing here? You should be at honeymoon practice, right?"

"Is that a thing?"

"I just invented it, but it's a thing now."

Crazy like a fox.

"What are you doing to that poor tree?"

"You don't want to know."

"I asked, didn't I?"

"Mercedes took a set of my rosary beads, and she took all the sad and bad energy out of me and put them in the beads. Now I'm supposed to find a tree to give the beads to. Trees, she says, breathe out what we breathe in—

oxygen, and trees breathe in what we breathe out—nitrogen. So she figures that if we exude bad energy, trees take it and absorb and then release it as good energy. I realize how insane that sounds, but it's worth a shot, right?"

"That kind of makes sense. You and the Good Witch are getting kinda tight? Something going on there I need to know about?"

"I have two men in my life already."

"So that's a maybe?"

Nora only smiled. Good to see her smiling again.

"If all your bad jujus are in your beads," he said, "maybe you ought to take them far away from your house."

"I was thinking that, too. Know a good tree that could take some pain?"

"I know the best tree in town. You wanna see it?"

"Definitely."

"Come with me."

They drove to the house on the corner of Annunciation and Rose. They didn't go into the house and they never would again. Time to move on. St. Valentine's must have thought so, too. There was a FOR SALE sign in front.

"This way," he said and pointed down the street. They set out walking.

"How are you handling this?" she asked. "Better than me, I hope."

"I'm remembering why I swore I'd only work for women and children." He laughed softly at himself. "But I'm okay. Paulina's feeling really hurt. Bad."

"I'm sure she is. Is there any new news coming?"

"Archbishop's releasing more names of abusers tomorrow. It's starting to steamroll," he said. "But no more case talk. What's goin' on with you? How's things with you and the Viking?"

"We're all right," she said. "A little shaky, but we'll make it."

"That's good. I like him for you. I'd like him more for you if he wasn't a priest."

"Well, you might get your wish. Or not. Still figuring that one out."

"I need to meet the other one though. Gotta give him my stamp of approval," he said, punching his fist into his palm.

"I get to see him Tuesday," she said as they passed houses that were growing bigger and fancier as they got away from Rose Street. "But I'm going to France. He's not coming here."

"You're leaving?" It surprised him how much that bothered him.

"Just to be on the safe side," she said. "In case my name shows up in the news."

"How long you gonna be gone?" he asked.

"As long as I have to be. A couple weeks. A month or two. If the shit hits the fan, I'll see you in a few years."

He couldn't blame her for being worried. The story had already gone national—CNN, Fox News, *New York Times*. He'd had to turn off his phone Friday because of all the calls coming in from the media. In the next few weeks, things were only going to get hotter as more victims came forward, more names were named. Probably a good thing for Nora to get out of Dodge.

"You might miss the baby coming."

"I hope I'll be back in time. If not, Juliette says she understands."

"All right, you can go, but you gotta at least come back for the wedding."

"Your wedding? I'm invited?"

"Yeah, you're invited."

"That's very sweet, Cy," she said, "but you don't really want a dominatrix in a leather catsuit at your *very* Catholic wedding, do you?"

"Can you do the electric slide?"

"Is that a kink thing?"

"Nora."

"I went to high school in the '90s. Of course I can do the electric slide."

She smiled again. This time the smile stuck around a little longer.

"Almost there," Cyrus said. "Come on." He tugged her arm and pulled her past a white SUV blocking their view. And there it was.

"Oh my God," Nora said, eyes wide, mouth open.

Before them stood a tree, a great gorgeous monster of a tree with a million branches and a billion leaves.

"I give you the Tree of Life."

"It's so beautiful." She wandered around the tree, staring up at it. Cyrus had done the same the first time he saw it as a kid. "I had no idea this was here."

Cyrus and Paulina had taken their engagement photos here. It was a massive ancient live oak tree with low branches made for climbing. Follow Annunciation Street to the very end and BAM, a little bit of Eden right before your eyes.

"This tree is amazing," she said.

"It gets better. Ready to climb?"

"What? Climb the tree? I'm wearing a skirt."

"It's a long skirt. Trust me, you want to climb this tree."

"Fine. Fine. Let's do this."

The branches of the tree were thick and low to the

ground, easy for climbing. Nora clambered up first and Cyrus followed. It wasn't hard, but it wasn't easy. About fifteen feet up, he stopped and pointed.

"Oh my God!" Nora burst into startled laughter.

"That's the zoo," he said. "Wave at the giraffes."

Nora waved at the two giraffes hanging out in their pen at the zoo next door. Cyrus waved, too.

"We're standing in a tree," Nora said, "waving at giraffes. I think the paint fumes did permanent damage."

Cyrus laughed. "Paulina showed it to me on our first real date. I knew about the tree, but I didn't know you could see the giraffes until she dared me to climb it." He couldn't wait to bring their kids here.

"You and Paulina are a great couple," Nora said. "You two have my blessing."

"Good. I was thinking about not marrying her until you said that."

She glared at him. "Smartass." One giraffe stuck its tongue out at another. She laughed gently. "Céleste has to see this."

"What about Søren's son? Fionn? When's he coming to visit?"

She blinked. He saw her do it and he wished he hadn't asked. "He's not."

They were quiet together a moment, watching the giraffes.

"You ready to get down?" he asked.

"Almost." She reached into the pocket of her skirt and pulled out a set of beads—rosary beads.

Nora clutched them in her hand for one second more, then reached up and draped them over a low branch. They carefully climbed down, leaving the silver rosary beads glinting solemnly on a high branch.

"Feel better?" he asked once they were on the ground again.

"A little," she said. Then, "Do you really want me at your wedding?"

"Yeah, I do. Paulina does, too."

"What the hell are you going to tell people when they ask who I am? Just your friendly neighborhood dominatrix?"

"I'll tell them the truth. I'll tell them you're my friend."

"Okay," she said. "I'll be there. It'll be my honor."

They both stood back to get a good long view of the tree.

"Pretty tree," Nora said.

"Yeah," Cyrus had to agree. "It's not too bad."

He took her hand in his and squeezed it. She squeezed back.

"You were kidding about wearing a leather catsuit to my wedding, right?"

"Guess you'll find out."

The End.

About the Author

 Tiffany Reisz is the *USA Today* bestselling author of the Romance Writers of America RITA®-winning Original Sinners series from Harlequin's Mira Books.

Her erotic fantasy *The Red*—self-published under the banner 8th Circle Press—was named an NPR Best Book of the Year and a Goodreads Best Romance of the Month. It also received a coveted starred review from *Library Journal*.

Tiffany lives in Kentucky with her husband, author Andrew Shaffer, and two cats. The cats are not writers.

Subscribe to the Tiffany Reisz email newsletter and receive a free copy of Something Nice, *a standalone ebook novella set in Reisz's Original Sinners universe:*

www.tiffanyreisz.com/mailing-list

facebook.com/littleredridingcrop

instagram.com/tiffany_reisz

Also Available from Tiffany Reisz

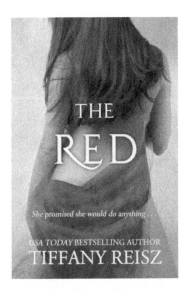

Mona Lisa St. James made a deathbed promise that she would do anything to save her mother's art gallery. Just as she realizes she has no choice but to sell it, a mysterious man comes in after closing time and makes her an offer: He will save The Red…but only if she agrees to submit to him for the period of one year.

"Deliciously deviant…. Akin to Anne Rice's 'Beauty' series." — *Library Journal* (Starred Review)

eBook, Paperback, Library Hardcover, and Audio
8th Circle Press and Tantor Audio

Also Available from Tiffany Reisz

Lieutenant Kingsley Boissonneault has done it all—spied, lied, and killed under orders. Now his commanding officer's nephew has disappeared inside a sex cult, and Kingsley has been tasked with bringing him home to safety. Will he be able to resist the enigmatic Madame, a woman of wisdom, power, and beauty?

"Masterly and rich.... Highly recommended." — *Library Journal* **(Starred Review)**

eBook, Paperback, Signed & Numbered Hardcover, Library Hardcover, and Audio
8th Circle Press and Tantor Audio

Also Available from Tiffany Reisz

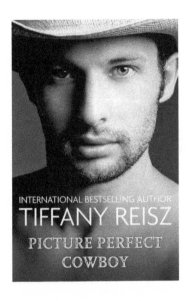

Jason "Still" Waters' life looks perfect from the outside—money, fame, and the words "World Champion Bull-Rider" after his name. But Jason has a secret, one he never planned on telling anybody...until he meets Simone. She's the kinky girl of his dreams...and his conservative family's worst nightmare.

***Picture Perfect Cowboy* is a standalone erotic romance from Tiffany Reisz, set in her bestselling Original Sinners series.**

eBook, Paperback, Library Hardcover, and Audio
8th Circle Press and Tantor Audio

Also Available from Tiffany Reisz

INTERNATIONAL BESTSELLING AUTHOR
TIFFANY REISZ
THE CONFESSIONS

Father Stuart Ballard has been Marcus Stearns' confessor since the young Jesuit was only eighteen years old. He thought he'd heard every sin the boy had to confess until Marcus uttered those three fateful words: "I met Eleanor." So begins *The Confessions,* a moving coda to the award-winning Original Sinners series.

"This is the reward for the tempestuous journey of all those who have read the series…" — Heroes & Heartbreakers

eBook, Paperback, Library Hardcover, and Audio
8th Circle Press and Blunderwoman Productions